A BONE OF CONTENTION

Also by Susanna Gregory

AN UNHOLY ALLIANCE

A BONE OF CONTENTION

Susanna Gregory

St. Martin's Press New York

Library of Congress Cataloging-in-Publication Data

Gregory, Susanna.
    A bone of contention : the second chronicle of Matthew
Bartholomew
    / Susanna Gregory.
        p.   cm.
    ISBN 0-312-16792-X
    1. Great Britain—History—Edward III, 1327–1377—
Fiction.   2. Civilization, Medieval—14th century—Fiction.
3. University of Cambridge—History—Fiction.   I. Title.
PR6057.R3873B66   1997
823'.914—dc21   97-23032
                                                        CIP

First published in Great Britain by Little, Brown and
Company

First U.S. Edition: November 1997

10   9   8   7   6   5   4   3   2   1

To Bob and Phyl

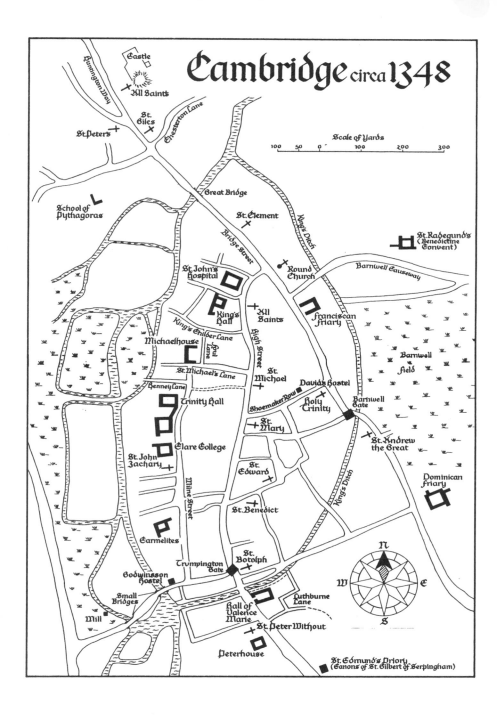

PROLOGUE

Cambridge, 1327

REATH COMING IN PAINFUL GASPS, D'AMBREY RAN
even harder. His lungs felt as though they would
explode, and his legs burned with the agony of running. He reached an oak tree, and clutched at its thick trunk as
he fought to catch his breath. A yell, not too far away, indicated
that the soldiers had found his trail, and were chasing him once
again. Weariness gave way to panic, and he forced himself to
move on.

But how long could he continue to run before he dropped?
And where could he go? He pushed such questions from his
mind, and plunged on into the growing shadows of dusk. His
cloak caught on a branch, and, for a few terrifying seconds, he
could not untangle it. But the cloak tore, and he continued his
mindless running.

He burst out from the line of trees and came on to the
High Street, skidding to a halt. At sunset the road was busy
with people returning home after a day of trading in the
Market Square. People stopped as they saw him. His green
cloak with the gold crusader's cross emblazoned on the back
was distinctive, and everyone knew him.

He elbowed his way through them towards the town gate, but
saw soldiers there. He could not go back the way he had come,
so the only option was to make his way along the raised banks
of the King's Ditch. The King's Ditch was part fortification
and part sewer. It swung in a great arc around the eastern
side of the town, a foul, slow-moving strip of water, crammed
with the town's waste and a thick, sucking mud washed from
the Fens. There had been heavy rains with the onset of autumn,
and the Ditch was a swirling torrent of brown water that lapped
dangerously close to its levied banks.

D'Ambrey scrambled up the bank, mud clinging to his hands and knees and spoiling his fine cloak. He saw the soldiers break through the trees on to the road, pushing through the people towards him, and turned to race away from them along the top of the bank. But it was slippery, and moving quickly was difficult. The soldiers spotted him, and were coming across the strip of grass below, beginning to overtake him.

It was hopeless. He stopped running, and stood still. His cloak billowed around him in the evening breeze, blowing his copper-coloured hair around his face. The soldiers, grinning now that their quarry was run to a halt, began to climb up the bank towards him. Knowing he was going to die, he drew his short dagger in a final, desperate attempt to protect himself.

He heard a singing noise, and something hit him hard in the throat. He dropped the dagger and raised his hands to his neck. He felt no pain, but could not breathe. His fingers grasped at the arrow shaft that was lodged at the base of his throat. The world began to darken, and he felt himself begin to fall backwards. The last thing he knew was the cold waters of the Ditch closing over him as he died.

chapter 1

September 1352

HAT, AGAIN?' ASKED MATTHEW BARTHOLOMEW incredulously, watching Brother Michael for some sign of a practical joke.

Michael rubbed his fat, white hands together with a cheery grin. 'I am afraid so, Doctor. The Chancellor requests that you come to examine the bones that were found in the King's Ditch by the Hall of Valence Marie this morning. He wants you to make an official statement that they do not belong to Simon d'Ambrey.'

Bartholomew sighed heavily, picked up his medical bag from the table and followed Michael into the bright September sunshine. It was mid-morning and term was due to start in three days. Students were pouring into the small town of Cambridge, trying to secure lodgings that were not too expensive or shabby, and conducting noisy reunions in the streets. Although Bartholomew did not yet have classes to teach, there was much to be done by way of preparation, and he did not relish being dragged from his cool room at Michaelhouse, into the sweltering heat, on some wild goosechase for the third time that week.

As he and Brother Michael emerged from the College, Bartholomew wrinkled his nose in disgust at the powerful aroma wafted on the breeze from the direction of the river. Cambridge was near the Fens, and lay on flat, low land that was criss-crossed by a myriad of waterways. To the people who lived there these were convenient places to dispose of rubbish, and many of the smaller ditches were continually blocked because of it.

The summer had been long, hot and dry, and the waterways had been reduced to trickles. People had made no attempt to find other places to rid themselves of their rubbish, and huge blockages had occurred, growing worse as summer had progressed. The first autumn rains had seen the choked water-ways bursting their banks, flooding houses and farms with filthy, evil-smelling water. The situation could not continue, and, for once, the town and the University had joined forces, and a major ditch-clearing operation was underway. The University was responsible for dredging the part of the King's Ditch that ran alongside the recently founded Hall of Valence Marie.

Michael headed for the shady side of the road, and began to walk slowly towards Valence Marie. The High Street was busy that Saturday, with traders hurrying to and from the Market Square with their wares. A ponderous brewery cart was stuck in one of the deep ruts that was gouged into the bone-dry street, and chaos ensued when other carts tried to squeeze past it. A juggler sat in the stocks outside St Mary's Church, and entertained a crowd of children with tricks involving three wizened apples and a hard, green turnip. His display came to an abrupt end when a one-eyed, yellow dog made off with the turnip between its drooling jaws.

'Have you seen these bones that have been dredged up?' Bartholomew asked, striding next to the Benedictine monk.

Michael nodded, plucking at Bartholomew's tabard to make him slow down. Bartholomew glanced at him. Already there were small beads of perspiration on the large monk's pallid face, and he pulled uncomfortably at his heavy habit.

'Yes. I am no physician, Matt, but I am certain they are not human.'

Bartholomew slowed his pace to match Michael's ambling shuffle. 'So why bother me?' he asked, a little testily. 'I am trying to finish a treatise on fevers before the beginning of term, and there is a constant stream of students wanting me to teach them.'

Michael patted his arm consolingly. 'We are all busy, Matt – myself included with these new duties as Senior Proctor. But you know how the townspeople are. The Chancellor insisted that you come and pronounce that these wretched bones are from an ani-mal to quell any rumours that they belong to Simon d'Ambrey.'

'Those rumours are already abroad, Brother,' said Bar-tholomew, impatiently. 'If the townspeople are to be believed, d'Ambrey's bones have been uncovered in at least six differ-ent locations.' He laughed suddenly, his ill-temper at being disturbed evaporating as he considered the ludicrous nature of their mission. 'As a physician, I can tell you that d'Ambrey had about twenty legs, variously shaped like those of sheep and cows; four heads, one of which sprouted horns; and a ribcage that would put Goliath to shame!'

Michael laughed with him. 'Well, his leg-count is likely to go up again today,' he said. 'You may even find he had a tail!'

They walked in companionable silence until Michael stopped to buy a pastry from a baker who balanced a tray of wares on his head. Bartholomew was dissuaded by the sight of the dead flies that formed a dark crust around the edge of the tray, trapped in the little rivers of syrup that had leaked from the cakes. Voices raised in anger and indignation attracted their attention away from the baker to a group of young men standing outside St Bene't's Church. The youths wore brightly coloured clothes under their dark students' tabards, and in the midst of them were two black-garbed friars who were being pushed and jostled.

'Stop that!'

Before Bartholomew could advise caution, or at least the summoning of the University beadles – the law-keepers who were under the orders of Brother Michael as Proctor – the monk had surged forward, and seized one of the young men by the scruff of his neck. Michael gave him a shake, as a terrier would a rat.

Immediately, there was a collective scraping sound as daggers were drawn and waved menacingly. Passers-by stopped to watch, and, with a groan, Bartholomew went to the aid of his friend, rummaging surreptitiously in his medicine bag for the sharp surgical knife he always kept there. Two scholars had already been killed in street brawls over the last month, and it would take very little to spark off a similar incident. Bartholomew, although he abhorred violence, had no intention of being summarily dispatched by unruly students over some silly dispute, the cause of which was probably already forgotten. His fingers closed over the knife, and he drew it out, careful to keep it concealed in the long sleeve of his scholar's gown.

'Put those away!' Michael ordered imperiously, looking in disdain at the students' arsenal of naked steel. He gestured at the growing crowd. 'It would be most unwise to attack the University's Senior Proctor within sight of half the town. What hostel are you from?'

The young men, realising that while student friars might be

an easy target for their boisterous teasing, a proctor was not, shuffled their feet uneasily, favouring each other with covert glances. Michael gave the man he held another shake, and Bartholomew heard him mutter that they were from David's Hostel.

'And what were you doing?' Michael demanded, still gripping the young man's collar.

The student glowered venomously at the two friars and said nothing. One of his friends, a burly youth with skin that bore recent scars from adolescent spots, spoke up.

'They called us cattle thieves!' he said, blood rising to his face at the mere thought of that injustice. Bartholomew suppressed a smile, hearing the thick accent which told that its owner was a Scot. He glanced at the friars, standing together, and looking smug at their timely rescue.

'Cattle thieves?' queried Michael, nonplussed. 'Why? Have you been stealing cows?'

The burly student bristled, incensed further by an unpleasant snigger from one of the friars. Michael silenced the friar with a glare, but although his laughter stopped, Michael's admonition did little to quell the superior arrogance that oozed from the man.

'It is a term the English use to describe the Scots,' muttered the student that Michael held. 'It is intended to be offensive and spoken to provoke.'

Bartholomew watched the friars. The arrogant one stared back at him through hooded lids, although his companion blushed and began to contemplate his sandalled feet so he would not have to meet Bartholomew's eyes.

Michael sighed, and released the Scot. 'Give your names to my colleague,' he said peremptorily, waving a meaty hand towards Bartholomew. He scowled at the friars. 'You two, come with me.'

Bartholomew narrowed his eyes at Michael's retreating back. Being Fellows of the same college did not give Michael the right to commandeer him into service as some kind of deputy proctor. He had no wish to interfere in the petty quarrels that broke out daily among University members between northerners and southerners; friars and secular scholars; Welsh, Scots, Irish and English; and innumerable other combinations.

The Scots gathered around him, subdued but clearly resentful. Bartholomew gestured for them to put away their daggers, although he kept his own to hand, still concealed in his sleeve. He waited until all signs of glittering steel had gone, and raised his eyebrows at the burly student to give his name.

'Stuart Grahame,' said the student in a low voice. He gestured to a smaller youth next to him. 'This is my cousin, Davy Grahame.'

'My name is Malcolm Fyvie,' said the student Michael had grabbed, a dark-haired man with a scar running in a thin, white line down one cheek. 'And these two are Alistair Ruthven and James Kenzie. We are all from David's Hostel. That is on Shoemaker Row, one of the poorer sections of the town. You would not want Scotsmen in Cambridge's more affluent areas, would you?'

Ruthven shot Fyvie an agonised glance, and hastened to make amends for his friend's rudeness.

'He means no offence,' he said, his eyes still fixed on the resentful Fyvie. 'David's is a very comfortable house compared to many. We are very pleased to be there.'

He looked hard at Fyvie, compelling him not to speak again. Bartholomew regarded the students more closely. Their clothes and tabards were made of cheap cloth, and had been darned and patched. Ruthven knew that antagonising the Proctor and his colleagues would only serve to increase the fine they would doubtless have to pay for their rowdy behaviour that afternoon. They were probably already being charged a greatly inflated price for their lodgings, and did not look as though they would be able to afford to have the fine doubled for being offensive to the University's law-keepers. Ruthven's desire to be conciliatory was clearly pragmatic, as well as an attempt to present himself and his fellows as scholars grateful for the opportunity to study.

'Is David's a new hostel?' asked Bartholomew, choosing to ignore Fyvie's outburst. There were many hostels in Cambridge, and, because the renting of a house suitable for use as a hall of residence was largely dependent on the goodwill of a landlord, they tended to come and go with bewildering rapidity. New ones sprung up like mushrooms as townspeople saw an opportunity to make money out of the University – a bitterly resented presence in the small Fen-edge town. Many of the hostels did not survive for more than a term – some buildings were reclaimed by landlords who found they were unable to control their tenants, while others were so decrepit that they, quite literally, tumbled down around their occupants' ears.

'It was founded last year,' said Ruthven helpfully, seizing on the opening in the conversation to try to curry favour. 'There are ten students, all from Scotland. The five of us came last September to study, and we hope to stay another year.'

'Then you should avoid street brawls, or you will not stay another week,' said Bartholomew tartly.

'We will,' said young Davy Grahame with feeling. His cousin gave him a shove one way and James Kenzie the other, and Bartholomew immediately saw which of the five were in Cambridge to study and which were hoping to enjoy the other attractions the town had to offer: brawling, for instance.

'Have you arranged masters and lectures?' asked Bartholomew. Ruthven and Davy Grahame nodded vigorously, while the others looked away.

'Is there anything you wish me to tell the Proctor?' Bartholomew asked, knowing who would answer.

Ruthven nodded, his freckled face serious. 'Please tell him that it was not us who started the brawl. It was those friars. They think that their habits will protect them from any insults they care to hurl.'

'But it takes two parties to create a brawl,' said Bartholomew reasonably. 'If you had not responded, there would have been no incident.'

Ruthven opened his mouth to answer, but none came.

'We don't have to listen to such insults from those half-men!' said Kenzie with quiet intensity.

'You do if you want to remain in Cambridge,' said Bartholomew. 'Look, if you have complaints about other students, take them to your hostel principal; if he cannot help, see the proctors; if they cannot assist you, there are the Chancellor and the Bishop. But if you fight in the streets, no matter who started it, you will be sent home.'

'No!' exclaimed Kenzie loudly. The others regarded him uncomfortably. He glanced round at them before continuing in more moderate tones. 'It would not be fair. We did not start it – they did.'

'People in this town do not like the Scots,' agreed Fyvie vigorously. 'Is it our fault that they choose to fight us?'

'Oh, come now,' said Bartholomew wearily. 'The Scots are not singled out for any special ill-treatment. That honour probably falls to the French at the moment, with the Irish not far behind. Go back to David's and study. After all, that is the reason you are here.'

Before Fyvie could respond, Ruthven gave Bartholomew a hasty bow, and bundled his friends away towards Shoemaker Row. Bartholomew watched them walk back along the High Street, hearing Ruthven's calming tones over Kenzie's protestations of innocence, and Fyvie's angry voice. Ruthven would have his work cut out to keep those fiery lads out of trouble, Bartholomew reflected. He rubbed a hand across his forehead, and felt trickles of sweat course down his back. The sun was fierce, and he felt as though he were being cooked under his dark scholar's gown.

On the opposite side of the street, Michael dismissed the student friars with a contemptuous flick of his fingers, and sauntered over to join Bartholomew. The friars, apparently subdued by whatever Michael had said to them, slunk off towards St Bene't's Church. The plague, four years before, had claimed many friars and monks among its tens of thousands of victims in England, and the University was working hard to train new clerics to replace them. The would-be brawlers were merely two of many such priests passing through Cambridge for their education before going about their vocations in the community.

The large number of clerics – especially friars – at the University was a continuing source of antagonism between scholars and townspeople. Much of the antipathy stemmed from the fact that clerics – whether monks and friars in major orders like Brother Michael, or those in minor orders like Bartholomew – came under canon law, which was notably more lenient than secular law. Only a month before, two apprentices had been hanged by the Sheriff for killing a student in a brawl; less than a day later three scholars had been fined ten marks each by the Bishop for murdering a baker. Such disparity in justice did not go unremarked in a community already seething with resentment at the arrogant, superior attitudes of many scholars towards the people of the town.

'I suppose the friars said the Scots started it,' said Bartholomew with a grin at Michael, as they resumed their walk up the High Street.

Michael nodded and smiled back. 'Of course. Unruly savages trying to start a fight, while our poor Dominicans were simply trying to go to mass.' He pointed a finger at the friars as they disappeared into the church. 'Remember their names, Matt. Brothers Werbergh and Edred. An unholy pair if ever I saw one, especially Edred. I am surprised the Dominican Order supports such blatant displays of condescension and aggression.'

'Well, perhaps they will make fine bishops one day,' remarked Bartholomew dryly.

Michael chuckled. 'I will go to David's Hostel later today,' he said, 'and see their Principal about those rowdy Scots. Then I will complain to the Principal of Godwinsson Hostel about those inflammatory friars.'

Bartholomew nodded absently, walking briskly so that Michael had to slow him down again, so that they – or rather the overweight Michael – would not arrive too sweat-soaked at the Hall of Valence Marie.

As they approached the forbidding walls of the new College, Michael turned to Bartholomew and grimaced at the sudden stench from where the King's Ditch was being dredged. Years of silt, sewage, kitchen compost, offal, and an unwholesome range of other items hauled from the dank depths of the Ditch lay in steaming grey-black piles along the banks. The smell had attracted a host of cats and dogs, which rifled through the parts not already claimed by farmers to enrich their soil. Among them, spiteful-eyed gulls squabbled and cawed over blackened strips of decaying offal and the small fish that flapped helplessly in the dredged mud.

Bartholomew and Michael turned left off the High Street, and made their way along an uneven path that wound between the towering banks of the King's Ditch and the high wall that surrounded Valence Marie. Because Cambridge lay at the edge of the low-lying Fens, the level of the water in the Ditch was occasionally higher than the surrounding land; to prevent flooding, the Ditch's banks were levied, and rose above the ground to the height of a man's head.

Away from the High Street, the noise of the town faded, and, were it not for the stench and the incessant buzz of flies around his head, Bartholomew would have enjoyed walking across the strip of scrubby pasture-land, pleasantly shaded by a line of mature oak trees.

'You have been a long time, Brother,' said Robert Thorpe, Master of the Hall of Valence Marie, as he stood up from where he had been sitting under a tree. There was a hint of censure in his tone, and Bartholomew sensed Thorpe was a man whose authority as head of a powerful young college was too recently acquired for it to sit easily on his shoulders. 'I expected you sooner than this.'

'The beginnings of a street brawl claimed my attention,' said Michael, making no attempt to apologise. 'Scots versus the friars this time.'

Thorpe raised dark grey eyebrows. 'The friars again? I do not understand what is happening, Brother. We have always had problems with warring factions and nationalities in the University, but seldom so frequent and with such intensity as over the last two or three weeks.'

'Perhaps it is the heat,' suggested Bartholomew. 'It is known that tempers are higher and more frayed when the weather is hot. The Sheriff told me that there has been more fighting among the townspeople this last month, too.'

'Perhaps so,' said Thorpe, looking coolly at Bartholomew in his threadbare gown and dusty shoes. As a physician, Bartholomew could have made a rich living from attending wealthy patients. Instead, he chose to teach at the University, and to treat an ever-growing number of the town's poor, preferring to invest his energies in combating genuine diseases rather than in dispensing placebos and calculating astrological charts for the healthy. His superiors at the University tolerated this peculiar behaviour, because having a scholar prepared to provide such a service to the poor made for good relations between the town and its scholars. Bartholomew was popular with his patients, especially when his absent-mindedness led him to forget to charge them.

But tolerance by the University did not mean acceptance by its members, and Bartholomew was regarded as something of an oddity by his colleagues. Many scholars disapproved of his dealings with the townspeople, and some of the friars and monks believed that his teaching verged on heresy because it was unorthodox. Bartholomew had been taught medicine by an Arab physician at the University of Paris, but even his higher success rate with many illnesses and injuries did not protect him from accusations that his methods were anathema.

Thorpe turned to the obese Benedictine. 'What word is there from the Chancellor about our discovery?' he asked.

'Master de Wetherset wants Doctor Bartholomew to inspect

the bones you have found to ensure their authenticity,' said
Michael carefully. What the Chancellor had actually said was
that he wanted Bartholomew to use his medical expertise to
crush, once and for all, the rumours that the bones of a local
martyr had been discovered. He did not want the University
to become a venue for relic-sellers and idle gawpers, especially
since term was about to start and the students were restless.
Gatherings of townspeople near University property might
well lead to a fight. The Sheriff, for once, was in complete
agreement: relics that might prove contentious must not be
found. Both, however, suspected that this might be easier said
than done.

The Hall of Valence Marie had been founded five years
previously – by Marie de Valence, the Countess of Pembroke
– and the Chancellor and Sheriff were only too aware of the
desire of its Master to make the young Hall famous. The bones
of a local martyr would be perfect for such a purpose: pilgrims
would flock to pray at the shrine Thorpe would build, and
would not only spread word of the miraculous find at Valence
Marie across the country, but also shower the College with
gifts. The Chancellor had charged Michael to handle Thorpe
with care.

Thorpe inclined his silver head to Bartholomew, to acknowledge the role foisted on him by the Chancellor, and walked
to where a piece of rough sacking lay on the ground. With a
flourish, Thorpe removed it to reveal a pile of muddy bones
that had been laid reverently on the grass.

Bartholomew knelt next to them, inspecting each one carefully, although he knew from a glance what they were. Michael,
too, had devoured enough roasts at high table in Michaelhouse
to know sheep bones when he saw them. But Bartholomew did
not want to give the appearance of being flippant, and was
meticulous in his examination.

'I believe these to be the leg bones of a sheep,' he said,
standing again and addressing Thorpe. 'They are too short to
be human.'

'But the martyr Simon d'Ambrey is said to have been short,'
countered Thorpe.

Michael intervened smoothly. 'D'Ambrey was not that small,
Master Thorpe,' he said. He turned to Bartholomew. 'Am I
right? You must remember him since you lived in Cambridge
when he was active.'

'You?' asked Thorpe, looking Bartholomew up and down dubiously. 'You are not old enough. He died a quarter of a century ago.'

'I am old enough to remember him quite vividly, actually,' said Bartholomew. He smiled apologetically at Thorpe. 'He was of average height – and certainly not short. These bones cannot be his.'

'We have found more of him!' came a breathless exclamation from Bartholomew's elbow. The physician glanced down, and saw a scruffy college servant standing there, his clothes and hands deeply grimed with mud from the Ditch. He smelt like the Ditch too, thought Bartholomew, moving away. The servant's beady eyes glittered fanatically, and Bartholomew saw that Master Thorpe was not the only person at Valence Marie desperate to provide it with a relic.

'Tell us, Will,' said Thorpe, hope lighting up his face before he mastered himself and made his expression impassive. 'What have you found this time?'

They followed Will across the swathe of poorly kept pasture to the Ditch beyond. A swarm of flies hovered around its mud-encrusted sides, and even Bartholomew, used to unpleasant smells, was forced to cover his mouth and nose with the sleeve of his gown. The servant slithered down the bank to the trickle of water at the bottom, and prodded about.

'Here!' he called out triumphantly.

'Bring it out, Will,' commanded Thorpe, putting a huge pomander over his lower face.

Will hauled at something, which yielded itself reluctantly from the mud with a slurping plop. Holding it carefully in his arms, he carried it back up the bank and laid it at Thorpe's feet. His somewhat unpleasant, fawning manner reminded Bartholomew of a dog he had once owned, which had persisted in presenting him with partially eaten rats as a means to ingratiate itself.

Holding his sleeve over his nose, Bartholomew knelt and peered closely at Will's bundle.

'Still too small?' asked Michael hopefully.

'Too small to belong to a man,' said Bartholomew, stretching out a hand to turn the bones over. He glanced up at Thorpe and Michael, squinting up into the bright sun. 'But it *is* human.'

*   *   *

Bartholomew and Michael sat side by side on the ancient trunk of an apple tree that had fallen against the orchard wall behind Michaelhouse. The intense heat of the day had faded, and the evening shade, away from the failing sunlight, was almost chilly. Bats flitted silently through the gnarled branches of the fruit trees, feasting on the vast number of insects that always inhabited Cambridge in the summer, attracted by the dank and smelly waters of the river. That night, however, the sulphurous odours of the river were masked by the sweeter smell of rotting apples, many of which lay in the long, damp grass to be plundered by wasps.

Bartholomew rubbed tiredly at his eyes, feeling them gritty and sore under his fingers. Michael watched him.

'Have you not been sleeping well?' he asked, noting the dark smudges under the physician's eyes.

'My room is hot at night,' Bartholomew answered. 'Even with the shutters open, it is like an oven.'

'Then you should try sleeping on the upper floor,' said Michael unsympathetically. 'The heat is stifling, and my room-mates sincerely believe that night air will give them summer ague. Our shutters remain firmly closed, regardless of how hot it is outside. At least you have a flagstone floor on which to lie. We have a wooden floor, which is no use for cooling us down at all.'

He stretched his long, fat legs out in front of him, and settled more comfortably on the tree trunk. 'It will soon be too cold to sit here,' he added hastily, seeing Bartholomew's interest quicken at the prospect of a discussion about the relationship between summer ague and night air. Fresh air and cleanliness were subjects dear to his friend's heart, and Michael did not want to spend the remainder of the evening listening to his latest theories on contagion. 'The nights are drawing in now that the leaves are beginning to turn.'

Bartholomew flapped at an insistent insect that buzzed around his head. 'We could try an experiment with your room-mates' notion about night air,' he said, oblivious to Michael's uninterest. 'You keep your shutters closed, and I will keep mine open—'

'Strange business today,' Michael interrupted. He laughed softly. 'I felt almost sorry for that greedy dog Thorpe when you told him his precious bones could not belong to that martyr he seems so intent on finding. He looked like a child who had been cheated of a visit to the fair: disappointed, angry, bitter and resentful, all at the same time.'

Bartholomew sighed, regretful, but not surprised, that Michael was declining the opportunity to engage in what promised to be an intriguing medical debate. 'I suppose Thorpe wants to make money from d'Ambrey's bones as saintly relics,' he said.

Michael nodded. 'There is money aplenty to be made from pilgrims these days. People are so afraid that the Death will return and claim everyone who escaped the first time, that they cling to anything that offers hope of deliverance. The pardoners' and relic-sellers' businesses are blossoming, and shrines and holy places all over Europe have never been so busy.'

Bartholomew made an impatient sound. 'People are fools! Relics and shrines did not save them the last time. Why should they save them in the future?'

Michael eyed his friend in monkish disapproval. 'No wonder you are said to be a heretic, Matt!' he admonished, half-joking, half-serious. 'You should be careful to whom you make such wild assertions. Our beloved colleague Father William, for example, would have you hauled away to be burned as a warlock in an instant if he thought you harboured such irreligious notions.'

Bartholomew rubbed a hand through his hair, stood abruptly, and began to pace. 'I have reviewed my notes again and again,' he said, experiencing the familiar feeling of frustration each time he thought of the plague. 'Until the pestilence, I believed there were patterns to when and whom a disease struck. But now I am uncertain. The plague took rich and poor, priests and criminals, good and bad. Sometimes it killed the young and healthy, but left the weak and old. Some people say it burst from ancient graves during an earthquake in the Orient, and was carried westwards on the wind. But even if that is true, it does not explain why some were taken and some were spared. The more I think about it, the less it makes sense.'

'Then do not think about it, Matt,' said Michael complacently, squinting to where the last rays of the sun glinted red and gold through the trees. 'There are some things to which we will never know the answers. Perhaps this is one of them.'

Bartholomew raised his eyebrows. 'It is encouraging to see that Michaelhouse supports a tradition of enquiring minds,' he remarked dryly. 'Just because an answer is not immediately obvious does not mean to say that we should not look for it.'

'And sometimes, looking too hard hides the very truth that you seek,' said Michael, equally firmly. 'I can even cite you an example. My Junior Proctor, Guy Heppel, lost the keys to our prison cells yesterday. I spent the entire period between prime and terce helping him search for them – a task rendered somewhat more urgent by the fact that Heppel, rather rashly, had arrested the Master of Maud's Hostel for being drunk and disorderly.'

'You mean Thomas Bigod?' asked Bartholomew, between shock and amusement. 'I am not surprised you were so keen to find the keys! I cannot see that a man like Bigod would take kindly to being locked up with a crowd of recalcitrant students.'

'You are right – he was almost beside himself with fury once he awoke and discovered where he was. But we digress. I searched high and low for these wretched keys, and even went down on my hands and knees to look for them in the rushes – no mean feat for a man of my girth – and do you know where they were?'

'Round his neck, I should imagine,' said Bartholomew. 'That is where he usually keeps them, tied on a thong of catgut or some such thing.'

Michael gazed at him in surprise. 'How did you know that?'

Bartholomew smiled. 'He had me going through the same process last week when he came to see me about his cough.'

'Is it genuine, then, this cough of his? I thought he was malingering. The man seems to have a different ache or pain almost every day – some of them in places I would have imagined impossible.'

'The cough is real enough, although the other ailments he lists – and, as you say, it is quite a list – are more imagined than real. Anyway, when I told him he must have lost his keys in the High Street, and not in my room, he almost fainted away from shock. He had to lie down to calm himself, and when I loosened his clothes, there were the keys around his neck. I was surprised when he was appointed your junior. He is not the kind of man the University usually employs as a proctor.'

'All brawn and no brain you mean?' asked Michael archly, knowing very well how most scholars regarded those men who undertook the arduous and unpopular duties as keepers of law and order in the University. 'Present company excepted, of course. But poor Guy Heppel has neither brawn nor brain as far as I can see.'

'Why was he appointed then?' asked Bartholomew. 'I cannot see how he could defend himself in a tavern fight, let alone prevent scholars from killing each other.'

'I agree,' said Michael, picking idly at a spot of spilled food on his habit. 'He was a strange choice, especially given that our Michaelhouse colleague, Father William, wanted the appointment – he has more brawn than most of the University put together, although I remain silent on the issue of brain.'

'That cough of Heppel's,' said Bartholomew, frowning as he changed the conversation to matters medical. 'It reminds me of the chest infection some of the plague victims con- tracted. It—'

Michael leapt to his feet in sudden horror, startling a black- bird that had been exploring the long grass under a nearby plum tree. It flapped away quickly, wings slapping at the under- growth. 'Not the Death, Matt! Not again! Not so soon!'

Bartholomew shook his head quickly, motioning for his friend to relax. 'Of course not! Do you think I would be sitting here chatting with you if I thought the plague had returned? No, Brother, I was just remarking that Heppel's chest complaint is similar to one of the symptoms some plague victims suffered – a hacking, dry cough that resists all attempts to soothe it. I suppose I could try an infusion of angelica . . .'

As Bartholomew pondered the herbs that he might use to ease his patient's complaint, Michael flopped back down on the tree trunk clutching at his chest.

'Even after four years the memory of those evil days haunts me. God forbid we should ever see the like of that again.'

Bartholomew regarded him sombrely. 'And if it does, we physicians will be no better prepared to deal with it than we were the first time. We discovered early on that incising the buboes only worked in certain cases, and we never learned how to cure victims who contracted the disease in the lungs.'

'What was he like, this martyr, Simon d'Ambrey?' interrupted Michael abruptly, not wanting to engage in a lengthy discussion about the plague so close to bedtime. Firmly, he forced from his mind the harrowing recollections of himself and Bartholomew trailing around the town to watch people die, knowing that if he dwelt on it too long, he would dream about it. Bartholomew was not the only one who had been shocked and frustrated by his inability to do anything to combat the wave of death that had rolled slowly through the town. The monk flexed his fingers, cracking his knuckles with nasty popping sounds, and settled himself back on the tree trunk. 'I have heard a lot about Simon d'Ambrey, but I cannot tell what is truth and what is legend.'

Bartholomew considered for a moment, reluctantly forcing medical thoughts from his mind, and heartily wishing that there was another physician in Cambridge with whom he could discuss his cases – the unsavoury Robin of Grantchester was more butcher than surgeon, while the other two University physicians regarded Bartholomew's practices and opinions with as much distrust and scepticism with which he viewed theirs.

'Simon d'Ambrey was a kindly man, and helped the poor by providing food and fuel,' he said. 'The stories that he was able to cure disease by his touch are not true – as far as I can remember these stories surfaced after his death. He was not a rich man himself, but he was possessed of a remarkable talent for persuading the wealthy to part with money to finance his good works.'

Michael nodded in the gathering dusk. 'I heard that members of his household were seen wearing jewellery that had been donated to use for the poor. Personally, I cannot see the harm in rewarding his helpers. Working with the poor is often most unpalatable.'

Bartholomew laughed. 'Spoken like a true Benedictine! Collect from the rich to help the poor, but keep the best for the abbey.'

'Now, now,' said Michael, unruffled. 'My point was merely that d'Ambrey's fall from grace seems to have been an over-reaction on the part of the town. He made one mistake, and years of charity were instantly forgotten. No wonder the townspeople believe him to be a saint! It is to ease their guilty consciences!'

'There may be something in that,' said Bartholomew. He paused, trying to recall events that had occurred twenty-five years before. 'On the day that he died, rumours had been circulating that he had stolen from the poor fund, and then, at sunset, he came tearing into town chased by soldiers. He always wore a green cloak with a gold cross on the back and he had bright copper-coloured hair, so everyone knew him at once. As the soldiers gained on him, he drew a dagger and turned to face them. I saw an archer shoot an arrow, and d'Ambrey fell backwards into the Ditch.'

'It is very convenient for Thorpe that his body was never found,' observed Michael.

Bartholomew nodded. 'A search was made, of course, but the Ditch was in full flood and was flowing dangerously fast. There were stories that he did not die, and that he was later seen around the town. But I have seen similar throat wounds since then on battlefields in France, and every one proved fatal.'

'I still feel the town treated d'Ambrey shamefully,' mused Michael. 'Even if he were less than honest, the poor still received a lot more than they would have done without him.'

'I agree,' said Bartholomew, with a shrug. 'And, as far as I know, it was never proven that he was responsible for the thefts. Just because his relatives and servants stole from the poor fund did not mean that d'Ambrey condoned it, or even that he knew. After his death, his whole household fled – brother, sister, servants and all – although not before they had stripped the house of everything moveable.'

'Well, there you are then!' said Michael triumphantly. 'His family and servants fled taking everything saleable with them. Surely that is a sign of their guilt? Perhaps d'Ambrey was innocent after all. Who can say?'

Bartholomew shrugged again, poking at a rotten apple with a twig. 'The mood of the townspeople that night was ugly. D'Ambrey's family would have been foolish to have stayed to face them. Even if they had managed to avoid being torn apart by a mob, the merchants and landowners who had parted with money to finance d'Ambrey's good works were demanding vengeance. D'Ambrey's household would have been forced to compensate them for the thefts regardless of whether they were guilty or not.'

'So d'Ambrey paid the ultimate price, but his partners in crime went free,' said Michael. 'A most unfair, but not in the least surprising, conclusion to this miserable tale. Poor d'Ambrey!'

'No one went free,' said Bartholomew, sitting and leaning backwards against the wall. 'The town nominated three of its most respected burgesses to pursue d'Ambrey's family and bring them back for trial. Although the d'Ambreys had gone to some trouble to conceal the route they had taken, they were forced to sell pieces of jewellery to pay their way. These were identified by the burgesses, who traced the family to a house in Dover. But the evening before the burgesses planned their confrontation with the fugitives, there was a fire in that part of the town, and everyone died in it.'

'Really?' asked Michael, fascinated. 'What a remarkable coincidence! And none of the fugitives survived, I am sure?'

Bartholomew shook his head. 'The town erupted into an inferno by all accounts, and dozens of people died in the blaze.'

'And I suppose the bodies were too badly charred for identification,' said Michael with heavy sarcasm. 'But the requisite number were found in the d'Ambrey lodgings, and the burgesses simply assumed that the culprits were all dead. D'Ambrey's family must have laughed for years about how they tricked these "most respected burgesses"!'

'Oh no, Brother,' said Bartholomew earnestly. 'On the contrary. D'Ambrey's household died of asphyxiation and not burning. None of the bodies were burned at all as I recall. D'Ambrey's brother and sister had wounds consistent with crushing as the house collapsed from the heat, but none of their faces were damaged. The bodies were brought back to Cambridge, and displayed in the Market Square. No member of d'Ambrey's household escaped the fire, and there was no question regarding the identities of any of them.'

'I see,' said Michael, puzzled. 'This body-displaying is an addendum to the tale that is not usually forthcoming from the worthy citizens of Cambridge. Do you not consider these deaths something of a coincidence? All die most conveniently in a fire, thus achieving the twofold objective of punishing the guilty parties most horribly, and of sparing the town the bother and cost of a trial.'

Bartholomew flapped impatiently at the insects that sang their high-pitched hum in his ears. 'That was a question raised at the time,' he said, 'although certainly not openly. I eavesdropped on meetings held at my brother-in-law's house, and it seemed that none of the burgesses had unshakeable alibis on the night of the fire.'

'What a dreadful story,' said Michael in disgust. 'Did any of these burgesses ever admit to starting the fire?'

'Not that I know of,' said Bartholomew, standing abruptly in a futile attempt to try to rid himself of the insects. 'They all died years ago – none were young men when they became burgesses – but I have never heard that any of them claimed responsibility for the fire.'

'So, dozens of Dover's citizens died just to repay a few light-fingered philanthropists for making fools of the town's rich,' said Michael, shaking his head. 'How unpleasant people can be on occasions.'

'We do not know the burgesses started the fire,' said Bartholomew reasonably. 'Nothing was ever proven. It might have been exactly what they claimed – a fortuitous accident, or an act of God against wrongdoers.'

'You do not believe that, Matt!' snorted Michael in amused disbelief. 'I know you better than that! You suspect the burgesses were to blame.'

'Perhaps they were,' said Bartholomew. 'But it hardly matters now. It was a long time ago, and everyone who played any role in the affair died years ago.' He sat again, fiddling restlessly with the laces on his shirt. 'But all this is not helping with our skeleton. Did you have any luck with the Sheriff this afternoon, regarding to whom these bones might belong?'

'Do bones belong to someone, or are they someone?' mused Michael, rubbing at his flabby chins. 'We should debate that question sometime, Matt. The answer to your question is no, unfortunately. There are no missing persons that fit with your findings. Are you sure about the identification you made? The age of the skeleton?'

Bartholomew nodded slowly. 'After you had gone to the Chancellor, I helped Will dredge up the rest of the bones and the skull. I am certain, from the development of the teeth and the size and shape of other bones, that the skeleton is that of a child of perhaps twelve or fourteen years. I cannot say whether it was a boy or a girl – I do not have that sort of expertise. There were no clothes left, but tendrils of cloth suggest that the child was clothed when it was put, or fell, into the Ditch.'

'Could you tell how long it had been there?' said Michael. 'How long dead?'

Bartholomew spread his hands. 'I told you, I do not have the expertise to judge such things. At least five years, although, between ourselves, I would guess a good deal longer. But you should not tell anyone else, because the evidence is doubtful.'

'Then why do you suggest it?' asked Michael. He leaned

forward to select an apple on the ground that was not infested with wasps, and began to chew on it, grimacing at its sourness.

The blackbird he had startled earlier swooped across the grass in front of them, twittering furiously. Bartholomew reflected for a moment, trying to remember what his Arab master had taught him about the decomposition of bodies. He had not been particularly interested in the lesson, preferring to concentrate his energies on the living than learning about cases far beyond any help he could give.

'All bones do not degenerate in the same way once they are in the ground, or in the case of this child, in mud. Much depends on the type of material that surrounds them, and the amount of water present. These bones had been immersed in the thick, clay-like mud at the bottom of the Ditch, and so are in a better condition than if they had been in peat, which tends to preserve skin, but rot bone. But despite this, the bones are fragile and crumbly, and deeply stained. I would not be surprised if they had been lying in the Ditch for twenty or thirty years.'

'So, we might be looking for a child of fourteen who died thirty years ago?' asked Michael in astonishment. 'Lord, Matt! Had he lived, that would make him older than us!'

'I could be wrong,' said Bartholomew. He stood and stretched, giving such a huge yawn that Michael was compelled to join him.

Michael tossed his apple core into the grass. 'Simon d'Ambrey died twenty-five years ago,' he said thoughtfully. 'Perhaps even at the same time as this child. Can you tell how this child met its death?'

'Again, I cannot be certain,' said Bartholomew, rubbing his eyes tiredly. 'But there is a deep dent on the back of the skull that would have compressed the brain underneath. Had the child been alive when that wound was delivered, it would have killed him – or her – without doubt. However, if the body has lain in the King's Ditch for thirty years, the damage may have been done at any time since by something falling on it. So, this child may have been knocked on the head and disposed of in the Ditch; he may have fallen and hit his head; or he may have died of some disease and his body disposed of in the Ditch and the skull damaged later.'

Michael disagreed. 'Not the latter. Why would anyone need

to hide a corpse of someone who had died in a legitimate manner? And surely someone would miss a child if it had had an accident and fallen in the river? The only likely solution, I am sorry to say, is the first one. That the poor thing was killed and the body hidden in the Ditch.'

Bartholomew shook his head, smiling, and slapped his friend on the shoulders. 'You have become far too involved in murder these last few years,' he said. 'Now you look for it where there may be none. How do you know the child was not an orphan, or that his parents simply did not report him missing? You know very well that a death in a large, poor family is sometimes seen as more of a relief than a cause for grief, in that it is one less mouth to feed – especially with girls. Or perhaps he was one of a group of travellers, who had passed out of Cambridge before he was missed? Or perhaps he was a runaway from—'

'All right, all right,' grumbled Michael good-humouredly. 'Point taken. But you were in Cambridge as a child. Did any of your playmates go missing with no explanation?'

Bartholomew leaned down to pick up his medicine bag. 'Not that I recall. It was a long time ago.'

'Oh, come now, Matt!' exclaimed Michael. 'You are not an old man yet! If you are right in your hunch about the time of this child's death, he may well have been a playmate of yours. Older than you, perhaps, but you would have been children together.'

Bartholomew yawned again. 'I can think of none, and I did not play with girls, anyway, which means I only have knowledge of half of the juvenile population. You should ask someone else. And now it is late, and so I will wish you good night.'

He turned to walk back through the orchard to the College, leaving Michael to his musing. He cut through the kitchens, his leather-soled shoes skidding on the grease that formed an ever-present film over the stone-flagged floor. The great cooking fires were banked for the night, and the kitchens were deserted. A door, concealed behind a painted wooden screen, led from the kitchen to the porch where Michaelhouse's guests were received before being ushered to the hall and conclave above. Bartholomew walked through the porch, and across the beaten earth of the courtyard to his room in the north wing.

The last rays of the sun were fading, and the honey-coloured stone of Michaelhouse's walls was a dark amber. Bartholomew paused, and glanced around at the College, admiring, as he always did, the delicate tracery on the windows of the north and south wings where the scholars slept. The dying sunlight still caught the bright colours of the College founder's coat of arms over the porch, a cacophony of reds, blues and golds. He yawned yet again, and gave up the notion of reading for an hour by the light of a candle before he slept – all that would happen would be that he would fall asleep at the table and candles were far too expensive a commodity to waste, not to mention the possibility that an unattended candle might fall and set the whole College alight.

His mind wandered back to the grisly display of asphyxiated corpses in the Market Square some twenty-five years ago, the result of another careless candle if the burgesses were to be believed. Then, he pushed thoughts of murder and mayhem to the back of his mind, opening the door to his small, neat room. He lay on the bed, intending to rest for a few moments before rising again to wash and fold his clothes, but he was almost immediately asleep, oblivious even to the sharp squeal of a mouse that the College cat killed under his bed.

Alone in the orchard, Michael chewed his lip thoughtfully. Bartholomew had a sister who lived nearby, whose husband was one of the richest and most influential merchants in the town. Edith was some years older than her brother. She had married young, and Bartholomew had lived with her and her new husband until he went to the school at the Benedictine Abbey in the city of Peterborough to the north. Perhaps Edith, or her husband, Sir Oswald Stanmore, might remember something about a missing child.

Michael saw the Stanmores the following day on his way back from church. It was a fine Sunday afternoon, and the streets thronged with people. Gangs of black-gowned students sang and shouted, eyed disapprovingly by the merchants and tradesmen dressed in their Sunday finery. Edith and her husband looked happy and prosperous, walking arm-in-arm down Milne Street to the large house where Stanmore had his business premises. Although Stanmore worked in Cambridge, he preferred to live at his manor in Trumpington, a tiny village two miles south of the town. It was unusual to see him and his wife in Cambridge on a Sunday, and Michael strongly suspected that the merchant had been conducting some covert business arrangement when he should have been paying attention to the words of the priest at mass. Edith, a lively soul who enjoyed the occasional excursion into the town from the village, would not have noticed what her husband was doing, and would have been more interested in catching up with the local gossip from the other merchants' wives.

Edith had the same distinctive black hair and pale complexion of her brother, a stark contrast to Stanmore's slate-grey hair and beard. She wore a dress of deep crimson, and she carried a blue cloak over one arm, one corner of it trailing unheeded along the dusty road. With a smile, the monk recognised that she apparently had the same careless disregard for clothes as her brother, whose shirts and hose were always patched and frayed. He headed towards her, dodging past a procession of Carmelite friars heading towards St Mary's Church, and jostling aside a pardoner with unnecessary force. Michael did not like pardoners.

Edith hugged Michael affectionately, making the usually sardonic, and occasionally lecherous, monk blush. Oswald Stanmore admonished her for her undignified behaviour in the street, but his words lacked conviction, and they all knew she would do exactly the same when she next met Brother Michael.

Stanmore, ever aware of the latest happenings in the town from his extensive network of informants, asked Michael about the skeleton that had been found. Michael told them briefly, and asked whether they were aware of any missing children during the last twenty or thirty years.

'Thirty years!' exclaimed Edith. 'Has this body lain in the Ditch so long?'

Michael shrugged indifferently. 'No, no. I am just keen to ensure we do not confine ourselves to looking recently, when the child may have died much earlier.'

Stanmore scratched his chin as he wracked his brains. 'There was old Mistress Wilkins' daughter,' he said uncertainly.

Edith shook her head. 'Reliable witnesses saw her alive and married to a farm lad over in Haslingfield village a few weeks after she disappeared. What about the tinker's boy? The one who was said to have drowned near the King's Mill?'

Now Stanmore shook his head. 'His body was found a year later. And anyway, he was too young – four or five years old. There was that dirty lad whom Matt befriended, who told us he was a travelling musician, and led the local boys astray for a few weeks.' He turned to Edith. 'It may well be him; he would have been about twelve. He set the tithe barn alight and then ran away. What was his name?'

'Norbert,' said Edith, promptly and rather primly, her mouth turning down at the corners in disapproval. 'I remember him well. We had only just arrived in Trumpington, and Matt immediately struck up a friendship with that horrible boy. It hardly created a good impression with my new neighbours.'

Stanmore gave her hand an affectionate squeeze, and spoke to Michael. 'After the barn fire, we locked this Norbert in our house, so that the Sheriff could talk to him about it the next day. But somehow he escaped during the night.'

'Poor Norbert!' said Bartholomew, coming up silently behind them, making them all jump. 'Still blamed for burning the tithe barn, even though he had nothing to do with it.'

'So you insisted at the time. But he fled the scene of the crime, and that was tantamount to admitting his guilt,' said Stanmore, recovering his composure quickly.

'He fled because he knew that no one would believe his innocence,' said Bartholomew. 'And because I let him go.'

There was a short silence as his words sank in. Michael smothered a grin, and folded his arms to watch what promised to be an entertaining scene.

'Matt!' exclaimed Edith, shocked. 'What dreadful secrets have you been harbouring all this time?'

Bartholomew did not reply immediately, frowning slightly as he tried to recall events from years before. 'I had all but forgotten Norbert's alleged crime.'

'Alleged?' spluttered Stanmore. 'The boy was as guilty as sin!'

'That was what everyone was quick to assume,' said Bartholomew. 'No one bothered to ask his side of the story and then make a balanced judgement. That was why I helped him to escape.'

'But we locked the priest with him in the solar!' said Stanmore, regarding Bartholomew with patent disbelief. He turned to Michael, who quickly assumed an air of gravity to hide his amusement. 'Norbert was only a child, and even though he had committed a grave crime, we did not want to frighten him out of his wits. We also thought the priest might wring a confession from him.' He swung back to Bartholomew, still uncertain whether to believe his brother-in-law's claim. 'How could you let him out without the priest seeing you?'

'The priest was drunk,' said Bartholomew, smiling. 'So much so, that the cracked bells of Trumpington Church and their unholy din could not have roused him. I waited until everyone was asleep, took the solar key from the shelf outside, and let Norbert out. After, I relocked the door, and Norbert disappeared into the night to go to his sister, who was a kitchen maid at Dover Castle.'

'But this is outrageous!' said Stanmore, aghast. 'How could you do such a thing? You abused my trust in you! And those bells are not cracked, I can assure you. They just need tuning.'

Edith suddenly roared with laughter, and some of the outrage went out of her husband. 'All these years and you kept your secret!' she said. She reached up and ruffled her brother's hair as she had done when he was young. 'Whatever possessed you to risk making my husband look foolish in front of his neighbours?'

Bartholomew looked at Stanmore thoughtfully for a moment before answering. 'I am not the only one who knows Norbert was innocent. I suppose I still should not tell, but it was such a long time ago that it cannot matter any more. It was not Norbert who fired the tithe barn: it was Thomas Lydgate.'

'Thomas Lydgate? The Principal of Godwinsson Hostel?' said Michael, halfway between merriment and horror.

Bartholomew nodded, smiling at the monk's reaction. 'I suspect he did not set the building alight deliberately, but you know how fast dry wood burns. I suppose he had no wish to own up to a crime that might make him a marked man for the rest of his life, and Norbert was an ideal candidate to take the blame, since he was an outsider, and had no one to speak for him.'

'But how do you know this?' asked Stanmore, still indignant about the wrong that had been perpetrated against him in his own house. 'Why are you so certain that Norbert did not commit the crime and Lydgate did?'

'Because Norbert and I saw Lydgate enter the barn when we were swimming nearby; we saw smoke billowing from it a few moments later and someone came tearing out. Naturally curious, we crept through the trees to see who it was. We came across Lydgate, complete with singed shirt, breathing heavily after his run, and looking as though he had seen the Devil himself. If you recall, it was Lydgate who raised the alarm, and Lydgate who first blamed Norbert.'

'But what if Lydgate followed Norbert and killed him to ensure he would never tell what he had seen?' mused Michael, suddenly serious. 'It is perfectly possible that the bones in the Ditch belong to your Norbert. From what you say, he was the right age, and all this appears to have happened about twenty-five years ago.'

'Impossible!' said Bartholomew. 'I received letters from Norbert in Dover a few weeks later to tell me that he had joined his sister, and he wrote to me several times after that, until I went to study in Paris. He has made a success of his life, which is more than could be said had the Trumpington witch-hunters laid their vindictive hands on him.'

'And how could you receive letters without my knowledge?' demanded Stanmore imperiously. 'This is nonsense! How could you have paid whoever brought these messages, and how is it that my steward never mentioned mysterious missives from Dover? Not much slips past his eagle eyes!'

Edith shuffled her feet, and looked uncomfortable. 'Letters from Dover, you say?' she asked. 'From someone called Celinia?'

Stanmore rounded on her. 'Edith! Do not tell me you were a party to all this trickery, too!'

'Not exactly,' said Edith guiltily, looking from her husband to her brother.

'Not at all,' said Bartholomew firmly. 'Norbert's sister was called Celinia. I imagine she wrote the letters, since Norbert was illiterate, and she signed her own name so that no one would know the letters were from him. Celinia is an unusual name, and Norbert knew I would guess that the letters were from him if she signed them. Edith simply assumed I had found myself a young lady. She did not ask me about it, so I did not tell her.'

'Extraordinary!' said Michael gleefully. 'All this subterfuge in such a respectable household!'

'Really!' said Stanmore, still annoyed. 'And in my own house! The villagers were not pleased that Norbert had evaded justice while in my safekeeping, and neither was the Sheriff when he found he had made the journey for nothing. Thank God Norbert was not caught later to reveal your part in his escape, Matt!'

'Well I never!' drawled Michael facetiously, nudging Bartholomew in the ribs. 'You interfering with the course of justice, and Lydgate an arsonist! Did you confront him with what you had seen?'

'Are you serious?' queried Bartholomew. 'Since Lydgate was not above allowing a child to take the blame for his crime – for which Norbert might well have been hanged – it would have been extremely foolish for me to have let him know that I had witnessed his guilty act. No, Brother. I have carried Lydgate's secret for twenty-five years and none have known it until now except Norbert.'

'I still cannot believe you took the law into your own hands in my house in such a way,' said Stanmore, eyeing his brother-in-law dubiously. 'What else have you done that will shock me?'

Bartholomew laughed. 'Nothing, Oswald. It was the only serious misdemeanour I committed while under your roof . . . that I can remember.'

Stanmore regarded Bartholomew with such rank suspicion that the physician laughed again. He was about to tease Stanmore further, when he saw the Junior Proctor, Guy Heppel, hurrying along the street towards them, his weasel-like face creased with concern.

When Heppel reached them, he was breathless, and there was an unhealthy sheen of sweat on his face. He rubbed his hands down the sides of his gown nervously.

'There is another,' he gasped. 'Another body has been found in the King's Ditch next to Valence Marie!'

chapter 2

BARTHOLOMEW AND MICHAEL HURRIED TOWARDS Valence Marie, while Guy Heppel panted along behind them. Bartholomew glanced round at the Junior Proctor, noting his white face and unsteady steps.

'Another skeleton?' he asked.

Heppel shook his head, but was unable to answer, and clutched at his heaving chest pathetically. Bartholomew wondered anew why the Chancellor had chosen such an unhealthy specimen to serve as a proctor, especially since he might be required to control some of the more unruly elements in the University with physical force. Bartholomew doubted if Heppel could control a child, let alone some of the aggressive, self-confident young scholars who roamed around the town looking for trouble. Not only was Heppel's appointment a poor choice for the University and the town, it was a poor choice for Heppel himself. Bartholomew studied him hard.

Heppel was a small man, with a peculiarly oblong head. His face was dominated by a long, thin nose that always appeared to be on the verge of dripping, and underneath it rested a pair of unnaturally red lips. He had no chin at all, and his upper teeth pointed backwards in his mouth in a way that reminded Bartholomew of a rodent. Bartholomew supposed Heppel's hair was dark, but the Junior Proctor always wore a woollen cap or a hood, even in church, so that his head was never exposed to the elements.

'Does that physic I gave you help your cough?' Bartholomew asked, concerned by Heppel's pallor.

'This is no time for a medical consultation,' said Michael briskly, pulling on his friend's arm. 'You can do that when no more bodies claim your attention.'

'I am a physician, not an undertaker,' said Bartholomew,

pulling his arm away irritably. 'My first duties are to my patients.'

'Nonsense, Matt,' said Michael. 'Your first duties are to your University and to me as Senior Proctor. Your second duties are to your patients – one of whom may well be waiting for you to unravel the mystery of his death.'

Bartholomew stopped dead in his tracks and gazed at Michael. 'I can assure you, Brother, that the University, with all its treachery and plotting, is not more important than my patients. If I thought that were ever the case, I would resign my Fellowship and abandon teaching completely.'

'No, you would not,' said Michael with total assurance. 'You like teaching, and you believe you play a vital role in training new physicians to replace those that died during the plague. You will never leave the University – unless you decide to marry, of course. Then you will have no choice. We cannot have married masters in the University. Although, I suspect there is no danger of that: you have been betrothed to Philippa for more than three years now, and you have done virtually nothing about it. Of course, there is always that whore of yours.'

'What?' asked Bartholomew, bewildered by the sudden turn in the conversation. 'What are you talking about?'

Michael poked him playfully in the ribs with his elbow. 'Do not play the innocent with me, Matt! I have seen the way you look at that Matilde, the prostitute. You should watch yourself. If Father William sees you ogling like a moonstruck calf, you will not need to worry about where your loyalties lie, because you will be dismissed from your Fellowship faster than you can lance a boil.'

'But I have not . . . he cannot . . .'

Michael laughed. 'If being tongue-tied is not a sign of your guilt, I do not know what is! Come on, Guy. We cannot be standing around all day listening to Dr Bartholomew describe his secret lust for the town's most attractive harlot.'

Bartholomew grabbed Heppel's sleeve as he made to follow Michael. 'Ignore him,' he ordered, scowling after the monk's retreating back. 'Did you take that physic I gave you?'

Heppel nodded vehemently, coughing into a strip of linen. 'Every drop. I was going to ask you for more because it was beginning to have an effect. Of course, when the pains in my chest had eased, the ones in my stomach and head started.'

'In your stomach and head,' echoed Bartholomew thoughtfully, wondering which of the herbs in his medicine had adversely affected his patient.

'And then there are my legs,' continued Heppel, lifting his gown to reveal a skinny limb swathed in thick black hose. 'They burn and ache and give me no rest.' He rubbed his hands vigorously down the side of his gown in a peculiar nervous habit Bartholomew had noticed before. 'And my ears ached last night. I think Saturn must have been ascendant. And I have an ulcer on my tongue, and my little finger is swollen.'

'Anything else?' asked Bartholomew dryly, now certain his medicine could not be to blame for Heppel's impressive list of maladies.

Heppel gave the matter some serious thought. 'No, I think that is all.'

'Right,' said Bartholomew, thinking that patients like Heppel were exactly the reason why he had no desire to treat the wealthy. The cure, he was sure, would be for Michael to allocate the Junior Proctor extra duties, so that he would not have time to dwell on every twinge in his body and imagine it to be something serious. Perhaps exercise and fresh air might help, too, although Bartholomew's attempts to suggest that bizarre remedy to patients in the past had met with a gamut of reactions ranging from patent disbelief to accusations that he was in league with the Devil.

'As I said, I think Saturn was ascendant last night,' said Heppel helpfully. 'I was born when Jupiter was dominant, you see, and there was a full moon.'

'Good,' said Bartholomew, unimpressed. 'I shall tell Jonas the Poisoner . . . I mean the Apothecary, to make you an infusion of angelica mixed with some wine and heartsease. I think when your cough eases, these other symptoms will disappear, too.'

'But angelica is a herb of the sun,' protested Heppel. 'I need a herb of the moon to match the time when I was born. And I must have something to counteract the evil effects of Saturn.'

Like most physicians, Bartholomew did not particularly like patients who claimed a knowledge greater than his own – especially when that knowledge was flawed. He bit back his impatience, recalling his Arab master's insistence on listening to every patient with sympathy and tolerance, regardless of how much nonsense they spoke.

'Angelica is gathered in the hour of Jupiter,' he said reluctantly, not particularly wanting to engage in what might be a lengthy discussion of herb-lore with Heppel when Michael was waiting. 'You say you were born when Jupiter was dominant, and angelica is very effective against the diseases of Saturn. Heartsease, of course, is a saturnine herb.'

Considering the conversation over, he made to walk on. Heppel scurried after him, and tugged at his tabard to make him stop.

'I think I shall require a complete astrological consultation,' said the Junior Proctor. 'Herbs of Saturn and Jupiter will not help my ears.'

Bartholomew sighed. In his experience, the planet that governed a particular herb made little difference to whether it healed a patient or not, and, over the years, he had gradually abandoned astrological consultations as a tool to determine the causes of a person's malaise. It was a decision that made him unpopular with his fellow physicians, and often resulted in accusations of heresy. But there was no denying that he lost fewer patients than his colleagues, a remarkable achievement given that most of his clients were less well-nourished and more prone to infections than the wealthier citizens the other physicians doctored.

'Just take the medicine,' he said to Heppel impatiently. 'And Saturn most certainly does control diseases of the ears, so the heartsease will work.' He did not add that if, as he believed, Heppel's ears ached only in his imagination, then Saturn could quite happily explode with no ill-effects to the organs under discussion.

'All right, then,' said Heppel dubiously. 'But I will have my astrological consultation next week if your concoction does not work.'

Not from me, thought Bartholomew. Complete astrological consultations were time-consuming affairs, and while Bartholomew conducted the occasional one to ensure he still remembered how, he was certainly not prepared to do one at the beginning of term with corpses appearing in the King's Ditch every few hours. Thoughts of the King's Ditch made him look away from Heppel for Michael. The fat monk was puffing towards him.

'What happened to you?' Michael demanded. 'There I was, regaling you with a list of the prostitute Matilde's physical virtues, when I saw Father William staring at me. Then I saw that you were nowhere to be seen, and I had been strolling up the High Street talking loudly to myself about a whore!

Really, Matt! You might have more regard for my vocation. I am a monk, chaste and celibate!'

'You might have more regard for it yourself,' said Bartholomew, smiling at the image of Michael being caught in the act of airing some of his less monkish thoughts by the austere Father William. 'You should not be filling your chaste and celibate mind with thoughts of prostitutes – especially on a Sunday.'

'I was trying to help you,' retorted Michael pompously, eyeing him with his baggy green eyes. He smoothed down the lank brown hair that grew around his perfectly circular tonsure. 'Now, Matthew, if you can spare a few moments away from your unseemly, lustful imaginings, a dead man awaits us at Valence Marie – assuming the poor fellow has not turned into the dust from whence he came in the interim.'

He turned abruptly, and stalked away, glancing around to ensure that Bartholomew and Heppel followed him. The dark grey stone of St Botolph's Church came into view, and Valence Marie stood a few steps away, on the far side of the King's Ditch. They walked quickly along the small path that ran between the College and the Ditch to where Robert Thorpe stood, wringing thin hands.

'This way, gentlemen,' he said, clearly relieved at their eventual arrival. Without further ado, he ushered them over to the patch of scrubby grass near where the small skeleton had been retrieved the day before.

'More bones?' asked Bartholomew, curious at the man's obvious agitation.

Thorpe flung him a desperate glance and gestured that he should look over the raised rim of the Ditch and into the water that trickled along the bottom. Puzzled, Bartholomew scrambled up the bank, while Michael followed more warily. Heppel declined to climb, and went to stand in the shade of one of the old oak trees, scrubbing his hands against his tabard. Bartholomew watched him, intrigued. The garment was shiny where the material had been rubbed so often, and Bartholomew wondered whether Heppel might have some itchy skin complaint that caused him to move them so.

Turning his attention back to the Ditch, he was greeted by the sight of a body floating face down in the shallow water, its arms raised above its head, almost as if it were swimming. Blood from a wound in its head stained the water in a pink halo around it.

Bartholomew turned questioningly to Thorpe, who had remained where he was, and obviously had no intention of scaling the bank.

'He was found about an hour ago by one of the servants,' Thorpe called. 'I immediately sent word to the Chancellor, and he, presumably, sent the Junior Proctor to fetch you.'

Bartholomew slipped and skidded down the inside of the muddy bank and tried to haul the body over on to its back. It was so stiff that the task proved difficult, and Michael was obliged to clamber down into the smelly water to help. Their eyes met as Bartholomew wiped away some of the thick, black mud to reveal the face.

'Which one is it?' asked Michael, holding his sleeve over his nose against the smell rising from the Ditch.

'James Kenzie, I think,' replied Bartholomew, wracking his brains to try to recall the names of the five young Scots from David's Hostel he had encountered the day before.

'I saw the Principal of David's yesterday, and he agreed to be responsible for the good behaviour of those five unruly undergraduates for the rest of the term,' said Michael, shaking his head as he looked down at the student. 'It looks as though he did not keep them out of trouble for long.'

He helped Bartholomew to pull the corpse out of the water and up on to the rim of the Ditch, away from the clinging mud that sucked at their feet and stained the hems on their gowns with an oily blackness. Bartholomew began a preliminary investigation.

'He has been dead a good while,' he said, pulling at one of Kenzie's arms. 'See how stiff he is? Of course, the heat will accelerate such stiffness; it would not be so if it were winter now.'

'I am not one of your students, Matt,' said Michael tartly. 'Just tell me what I need to know and keep the lectures for the ghouls that enjoy them.'

Bartholomew grinned at him, but completed his examination in silence. Eventually, he sat back on his heels and looked thoughtfully at the body.

'I think it likely that he died last night,' he said, 'nearer dusk than dawn. He was killed by the wound to the top of his head, which has stoved in his skull. You can see that splinters of the skull have penetrated the brain. He must have been put in the water after his death because his mouth is empty. Had he drowned, he probably would have inhaled mud and water from the Ditch as he tried to breathe air. I will make a more thorough examination later, if you wish.'

'I do,' said Michael. 'So, are you saying he was murdered? He did not just die from a fall?'

Bartholomew just managed to stop himself from running his mud-coated hand through his hair as he surveyed the Ditch and its surroundings.

On one side of the Ditch were the high walls of Valence Marie, meeting the narrow stretch of poorly tended pasture on which Thorpe and Heppel now waited. Although this strip of land belonged to Valence Marie, it was not fenced off, and access to it was possible from the High Street at one end, and Luthburne Lane at the other. On the opposite side of the Ditch was an untidy line of houses, most wattle and daub, and all frail, dilapidated and mainly abandoned. The plague had struck hard at those people who had lived in cramped, crowded conditions, and Bartholomew knew that only a handful from these hovels had survived.

'Yes, he was murdered,' he said, having considered the possibilities. 'I would say it was not possible to sustain a wound like this, on the top of his head, from a fall. I suspect Kenzie was hit with a heavy instrument, and his body was brought here or left where it fell – the current in the Ditch is not strong enough to move something as heavy as a corpse at the moment. Either way, I am certain he was dead when he entered the water.'

'Was he drunk? Are there signs of a struggle?'

Bartholomew inspected the young man's hands, but his finger-nails were surprisingly well-kept, and there was no sign that he had clawed or attacked his assailant. His clothes, too, were intact, and Bartholomew saw only the mended tears he had noted the previous day.

'I would say he had no idea his attacker was behind him. Or that he knew someone was behind him, but felt no need to fear. As to drink, I can smell only this revolting Ditch on him. Perhaps he was drunk, but if so, the water has leached all signs of it away.'

He looked suddenly at Michael as if to speak, but then thought better of it and turned his attention back to the body.

'What is it?' asked Michael, catching his indecision.

Bartholomew frowned down at the body. 'Remember I told you that the skeleton we found also had an indentation on the back of its skull? Possibly hit on the head and dumped in the Ditch?'

'Of course,' said Michael. 'But you said there was not enough evidence to prove that the child was murdered, and you seem sure that Kenzie has been. What are the differences?'

Bartholomew rubbed his chin absently, leaving a black smudge there from the mud on his hand. 'The child lay dead in the Ditch for many years, providing ample time for damage to occur to the skull after death; Kenzie has been dead only a few hours. Also, Kenzie's wound bled copiously as you can see from his stained clothes. Wounds do not bleed so if inflicted after death, but we do not have such evidence for the skeleton. I did not say the child was not murdered, only that I cannot prove it.'

'But let us assume he was,' said Michael thoughtfully. 'It is surely something of a coincidence that the body of a murdered child is discovered one day, and the very next, a man is killed in the same manner. You think there might be a connection?'

Bartholomew grimaced. 'Yes, I do. But that is the essence of why I was reluctant to speak. If I am right about the length of time the skeleton has been in the Ditch, Kenzie would not even have been born when the child died.'

'But you could be wrong, and the skeleton is only a few years dead. That would mean that there might be some connection between the two victims.'

'Not even then, Brother,' said Bartholomew. 'Kenzie is a Scot and not local. He has only been here for twelve months at the very most. How could there be a connection?'

'Can you not tell more from this child's bones?' asked Michael.

Bartholomew looked at him for a moment, and then laughed. 'Despite the fanciful teachings of an Oxford astrologer who maintained in a lecture I once attended that the Scots are a "cruel, proud, excitable, bestial, false and underhand race who must therefore be ruled by Scorpio", it is not possible to tell one of them from an Englishman from bones alone, Scorpio or otherwise!'

'Oxford University supports that?' said Michael, astonished. 'No wonder their Scots are always rioting and looting its halls and colleges.'

'It is only the claim of a single scholar,' said Bartholomew. 'And doubtless Scottish astrologers have cast an equally unflattering national horoscope for the English. But we are digressing from our task.'

'So the child might have been born a Scot,' mused Michael, looking back at Kenzie's body, 'but there is no way to prise that information from his bones?' Bartholomew nodded, and Michael gave a sigh of resignation. 'I have a feeling this might be more difficult to resolve than I first thought. If the link between these two bodies spans many years, we might never know the truth.'

'There are some things to which we will never know the answers,' said Bartholomew in an exaggerated imitation of Michael's pompous words to him in the orchard the night before. 'Perhaps this is one of them.'

Michael shot him an unpleasant look. 'If you value peaceful relations between town and gown, Matt, you had better hope not,' he said primly. 'The students might riot if they believe one of their number has been murdered – especially if we cannot provide evidence that the culprit was not a townsman.'

Bartholomew shook his head impatiently. 'That would be an unreasonable assumption on their part. Kenzie's killer might just as easily be one of his four friends from David's Hostel.'

'And since when has reason ever prevented a riot?' demanded Michael in a superior tone. 'You know as well as I that the mood of scholars and townsfolk alike is ugly at the moment. It seems to me that Kenzie's death might provide the perfect excuse for them to begin fighting each other as they so clearly wish to do.'

Bartholomew regarded him soberly. The fat monk was right. Over the last month or so, he had noticed a distinctly uneasy atmosphere in the town: it had been the subject of discussion at high table at Michaelhouse on several occasions. Optimistically – overly so in Bartholomew's opinion – the Master and Fellows hoped that the tension would ease once term began, and most students would be forced to concentrate on their studies.

Michael climbed to his feet clumsily, wincing at his stiff knees, and called down to Thorpe. 'Why did you take so long to discover the body, Master Thorpe? Doctor Bartholomew says this man might have died as early as yesterday evening.'

Thorpe shrugged elegantly. 'It is Sunday,' he replied. 'No

one is dredging the Ditch today, and the body might well have remained undiscovered until tomorrow, but, by chance, our scullion, Henry, noticed the body when he came to dispose of some kitchen scraps.'

Bartholomew sighed. There was little point in dredging the Ditch if scullions were not prepared to dump their kitchen waste elsewhere. In a year or two, the town would be facing the same problems all over again.

'I heard that their other servant – that little fellow, Will – claims to have seen more bones in the Ditch on the other side of the High Street,' said Michael in an undertone to Bartholomew, drawing the physician's mind away from the litany of diseases he believed owed their origins to dirty water. 'Master Thorpe will doubtless move the workmen to look for martyr relics in more fertile ground tomorrow.'

'What are you two muttering about?' said Thorpe uneasily, taking a few steps up the bank towards them.

'We are wondering whether you know this man who died on your property last night,' Michael called back pleasantly. 'Will you come to see?'

Very reluctantly, Thorpe scrambled towards them, and looked down at Kenzie's body. He gave it the most superficial of glances, and then looked a second time for longer.

'It is not a student of Valence Marie,' he said, his voice halfway between surprise and relief. 'I do not believe I have met him before. He is a student, though. He is wearing an undergraduate's tabard.'

'Thank you, Master Thorpe,' said Michael, regarding the scholar with a blank expression. 'I might have overlooked that, had you not pointed it out.'

Thorpe nodded, oblivious to the irony in Michael's voice, and turned to make his way back down the bank, swearing when he slipped and fell on one knee. Heppel hurried to help him, and Bartholomew heard him regaling the Master of Valence Marie with an infallible remedy for unsteadiness in the limbs that could be procured from powdered earthworms and raw sparrows' brains.

'If Thorpe is foolish enough to take that concoction, then he deserves all the stomach cramps he will get,' he muttered to Michael, watching Heppel warm to his subject.

'Thorpe might be a coward for not coming immediately to see if the corpse was a member of his own college, but he is no lunatic. Can you tell me any more about Kenzie's death before we move the body to the church?'

'Only one thing.' Bartholomew took one of Kenzie's hands and pointed at the little finger. There was a thin, but stark, white band on the brown skin, showing where, until recently, a ring had been worn.

'The motive for his murder was theft?' asked Michael, staring down at the young man's hand.

Bartholomew shrugged. 'Possibly. You should ask Kenzie's friends whether the ring was valuable and whether they know if he was wearing it when he died. But, assuming he died during the night, the killer would need eyes like an owl to detect a ring on his victim's hand in the dark before he struck. There was no moon last night.'

'Perhaps he killed first and looked later,' said Michael. 'Although a young man who is so obviously a student in patched clothes is hardly likely to render rich pickings to justify so foul a crime.'

Bartholomew gave a brief smile without humour. 'We both know that people have been killed for far less than a ring in this town.'

The sun was casting long shadows across the High Street by the time they had ordered Kenzie's body to be taken to St Botolph's Church, and spoken to the servant, Henry the scullion, who had discovered the corpse. He could tell them nothing, other than to say that he had seen no one matching Kenzie's description hanging around the Ditch the day before.

'I must go to David's Hostel before someone else tells this young man's friends what has happened,' said Michael, squinting at the sun, a great orange ball in the cloudless sky. 'Come with me, Matt. I would be happier if there were two of us judging the reactions of Kenzie's compatriots when we give them the news of his death.'

Bartholomew started to object – he had planned to work on his treatise on fevers while there was still sufficient daylight in which to write – but Michael was right. If there had been some kind of falling out between the five friends that had resulted in the death of one of them, it would be better if there were more than one observer for guilty reactions. Neither Michael nor Bartholomew put much faith in Guy Heppel's powers of observation.

'You look tired, Guy,' said Michael solicitously to the Junior Proctor who trailed along behind them. 'Tell the Chancellor what has happened and then go home to rest.'

'I do feel weary,' said Heppel, stretching out a white hand to the monk's arm to support himself, as if even admitting to his weakness had suddenly sapped the remaining strength from his limbs.

'Shall I order you a horse to take you there?' asked Michael, eyeing the hand on his arm with disapproval. 'After all, it might be almost a quarter of an hour's walk by the time you retrace your steps from the Chancellor's office to your room in the King's Hall.'

Heppel seriously considered the offer, while Bartholomew turned away to hide his smile. 'I think I can manage to walk,' Heppel said eventually.

Michael and Bartholomew watched him walk away, a slender figure whose overlarge scholar's tabard hung in dense, cumbersome folds.

'You are supposed to be compassionate to your fellow men, Brother,' said Bartholomew. 'Not add to his already impressive list of ailments by telling him he looks ill.'

'The man is a weasel,' said Michael, unrepentant. 'And I do not believe him to be as self-obsessed as he appears. He heard every word of what you told me about Kenzie's corpse, and will report it all faithfully to the Chancellor.'

Bartholomew was confused. 'You think Heppel is spying on you for de Wetherset?'

Michael gave a short bark of laughter. 'De Wetherset would not dare – especially with an agent of Heppel's mediocre talents. But de Wetherset had some reason for appointing him over Father William, and it would not surprise me to learn that Heppel is his nephew or some other relative.'

'If that is true, then you will never find out from de Wetherset,' said Bartholomew with conviction. 'He is not a man to allow himself to be caught indulging in an act of flagrant nepotism.'

'True,' said Michael. 'But at least Heppel will be out of our way when we visit David's Hostel. The last thing we want as we gauge reactions to the news of Kenzie's death is Heppel offering special potions to ease grief.'

They began to walk along the High Street to Shoemaker Row. The intense heat had faded with the setting of the

sun, but the air was still close and thick with the smell of
the river and the Ditch. Carts rattled past them, hurrying
towards the Trumpington Gate and the villages beyond before
darkness fell and the roads became the domain of robbers and
outlaws. Although it was Sunday, and officially a day of rest, the
apprentices were active, darting here and there as they ferried
goods to and from their masters' storehouses along Milne Street
and the wharves. Bartholomew ignored the noise and bustle,
and thought back to his encounter with the David's students
the day before.

'Two of the Scots – Ruthven and Davy Grahame – seemed
well-disposed to study,' he said. 'But the others gave the
impression they would rather be anywhere other than making
a pretence of scholarship in Cambridge.'

'Really?' asked Michael thoughtfully. 'What else would they
rather be doing, do you think? Fighting? Rioting? Whoring?'

'Very possibly,' said Bartholomew. 'The one you grabbed by
the collar is called Fyvie. He has something of a temper, and
is perhaps over-sensitive to insults to his nation, whether real
or perceived. He is unwise to wear his emotions so openly: it
is asking for someone to taunt him into starting a brawl.'

He jumped as the doors of St Mary's Church were flung open
with a crash and troops of noisy, yelling scholars came out, jostling and shoving each other. One of them was leading a chorus
in Latin, the words of which made Bartholomew exchange a look
of half-shock and half-amusement with Michael. Bartholomew
smothered a smile when he noticed how much over-long hair
was bundled into hoods, and bright clothing was hastily covered
with sober scholars' tabards, as the students recognised Michael,
the Senior Proctor. He also noticed that one of his own students,
Sam Gray, was singing the bawdy Latin chorus as loudly as he
could, and saw that he had his tabard wrapped around a girl
he had obviously smuggled into the church.

The University, partly because of the large numbers of friars
and monks in its ranks, and partly to protect the local female
population, forbade its students any dealings with women. In
some ways, the rule was a wise one, for it went at least some
way in preventing potentially dangerous incidents involving
outraged husbands, fathers and brothers. Yet, with hundreds of
hot-blooded young men barely under the control of their masters, the rule was often impossible to enforce. If a headstrong
and disobedient student – like Sam Gray – decided to embark

on a relationship with a woman, there was little that could be done about it. Gray could be 'sent down' from the University in disgrace, but the plague meant that student numbers were low, and the University wanted to increase, not decrease them. The students were only too aware that the University's colleges and hostels were sufficiently desperate for their fees that they were prepared to overlook a good deal to keep them.

Gray saw Bartholomew, and his jaw dropped in horror. He hastily disentangled himself from the girl in a feeble attempt to make it look as though she were with someone else. Bartholomew favoured him with a reproving stare, and was gratified to see that Gray at least had the grace to look shamefaced. Fortunately for Gray, Michael's eyes were still fixed on the singer, who, seeing he had the unwanted attention of the Senior Proctor, slunk away through the churchyard. Once their leader had gone, the other students dispersed rapidly under Michael's authoritative glower, some with almost comical furtiveness.

'The students are always rowdy at the beginning of term,' said Michael, walking on. 'But I detect more than just rowdiness in them now. They seem dangerous to me, Matt. I have a feeling it would take very little to ignite them into doing something quite serious. I only hope one of those Scottish lads confesses that he has killed Kenzie. If these students think the townspeople have killed a scholar, they will riot for certain.'

'All former differences forgotten in the common cause,' mused Bartholomew. 'That only yesterday saw the beginnings of a brawl between the Scots and the friars will not prevent them fighting side by side against the townsfolk.'

They turned off the High Street into Shoemaker Row. David's Hostel was a half-timbered building, the rough plaster crudely covered in patchy white limewash that was stained with black rivulets running from some internal rot. The ends of the great wooden beams that formed the basic structure of the house were frayed and flaking, and bright orange fungus sprouted from the side of one window. Michael rapped officiously on a door that was new and strong, in contrast to the rest of the house, and waited.

Eventually, they heard footsteps, and the door was dragged open by a servant. He gave them a querying smile, and introduced himself as Meadowman the steward. He added shyly that Bartholomew had once treated him for river-fever, although

Bartholomew could not honestly say that there was anything familiar in the steward's homely face. Meadowman conducted them along the corridor, and into a spacious room at the back of the house, which served as dining room and lecture hall. Beyond the room was a kitchen, where a scullion crashed about noisily, preparing the next meal.

'Ivo!' called Meadowman, warning the scullion to silence his clattering while David's was the subject of a proctorial visit. The noise stopped, and Ivo's greasy head poked around the door to study the august personage of the Senior Proctor with undisguised curiosity.

'Greetings, Father Andrew,' said Michael, pushing past Bartholomew to stride into the room. Sitting at a large table with an open book in front of him was an elderly friar who smiled serenely as Michael entered. He had watery blue eyes, and his unlined, honest face reminded Bartholomew of a saintly hermit he had once met on a remote Spanish island. Also gathered around the table were several students, all wearing neat, black scholars' tabards, despite the heat.

As Bartholomew was introduced to Father Andrew, he had the distinct impression they were interrupting a lecture. He glanced at the book and recognised it as Porphyry's *Isagoge*, a basic undergraduate introduction to the philosophy of Aristotle.

'You will see David's Hostel has taken your warning seriously about our students' behaviour, Brother,' said Father Andrew in a voice that was soft and lilting with the accent of southern Scotland. 'We have been reading philosophy today, even though it is Sunday and term does not begin until the day after tomorrow. The Principal, Master Radbeche, will continue with Aristotle's *Praedicamenta* immediately after mass in the morning.'

'Master Radbeche?' asked Bartholomew, impressed. 'I had no idea Master Radbeche was Principal here.'

The old friar smiled. 'We are lucky to have such a notable scholar in our midst. Without wishing to sound boastful, there is no one who understands Aristotle like Master Radbeche.'

'Indeed not, Father,' said Michael. He cast a disparaging glance at the students. 'And it is unfortunate that his students do not seek to uphold his reputation and that of his hostel with scholarship and gentle behaviour.'

Bartholomew looked around the room. The fiery-tempered Fyvie sat staring morosely at the table, although whether his ill-humour resulted from the unwelcome proctorial visit or from being made to listen to Porphyry's dry text, Bartholomew could not determine. The cousins, Davy and Stuart Grahame, sat together at the end of the table, Davy with a quill in his hand and a pile of parchment scraps in front of him for making notes. Ruthven sat next to Father Andrew where he had evidently been peering over the friar's shoulder. Perhaps Father Andrew's reading had been too slow for him, and he was trying to read ahead. Three other students sat near the empty fireplace on stools, which were arranged in such a way that Bartholomew wondered whether they might have been playing dice out of Father Andrew's line of vision.

'Where were you all last night?' asked Michael, not wasting time on further formalities.

There was a startled silence until Father Andrew found his tongue.

'Why do you ask, Brother? Has there been more trouble in the town? I can assure you that after you spoke to the Principal yesterday, we kept all our students here. The front door was locked at seven o'clock last night, and no one left until mass at five this morning.'

'You said there were ten students at David's,' said Bartholomew to Ruthven. 'Where are the others?'

'Well,' said Ruthven slowly, casting a quick, nervous glance at Fyvie that neither Bartholomew nor Michael missed. 'There are the five of us from Edinburgh whom you met yesterday, and then there are the three Tarbert cousins from the Isles.' He gestured to the trio of students near the fireplace. 'We all have been here studying as you can see. Robert of Stirling is upstairs suffering from an ague, and his brother John is with him. That is all of us.'

Not exactly, thought Bartholomew, watching the faces of the others intently as Ruthven spoke. Fyvie sat motionless, his eyes fixed unblinking on the table. Davy Grahame held his quill with trembling hands, while his cousin flushed such a deep red, that the colour seemed to reach as far as his throat. However smooth Ruthven was trying to be, the others were very much aware that their comrade was missing, and might even know why.

'I can vouch for these young men,' said Father Andrew, waving his hand round at his charges. 'We have been here all day, and even took our meals here – despite the fact that Ivo, our scullion, has much still to learn about cooking. The students have not been out of the building at all. Robert of

Stirling and James Kenzie are ill upstairs, and John is looking after them. The others are all here as you can see.'

'What about last night?' said Michael. He looked at the four students who sat round the table. 'I think some of you know why we are asking.'

Father Andrew's expression was one of confusion, and he looked at his students in bewilderment. 'Tell the Proctor you were all here,' he said, looking at each one in turn. When none of them spoke up, his shoulders sagged suddenly in weary resignation. 'What are you hiding?' he asked in a tone that indicated he would tolerate no lies or half-truths. 'What have you done this time to bring shame upon David's Hostel?'

There was a silence during which the four looked from one to the other, knowing that they would have to tell what they knew, but none wanting to be the one to begin. Finally, Ruthven spoke.

'James Kenzie is gone,' he said miserably.

'James Kenzie is ill upstairs,' protested Father Andrew. 'I saw him asleep in his bed only a short while ago.'

'You saw his rolled up blankets,' said Ruthven apologetically to Father Andrew. 'Jamie is not here. He has gone.'

'Gone where?' demanded Michael.

'We do not know. We would have looked for him today, but we have been kept here studying. We did not wish to make a fuss and draw attention to the fact that he is absent, but now we are worried about him. We decided this afternoon that if he has not returned by nightfall, we would tell the Principal and Father Andrew.'

'Why wait?' asked Michael, unconvinced. 'Surely it would be better to tell them sooner, rather than later, if you are worried about your friend?'

Ruthven looked away, chewing on his lower lip in agitation.

Davy Grahame took a deep breath. 'Jamie has a woman,' he blurted out.

Father Andrew's jaw dropped in shock, and he regarded Davy Grahame aghast.

'Davy!' exclaimed Fyvie, starting to his feet. 'You did not have to tell them that!'

'Yes, I did,' said the younger Grahame, his firm tone of voice forcing Fyvie to sit again. 'I am worried. Supposing those two friars came across him last night and had him harmed? The Proctor might be able to help him.' He turned to Michael. 'Jamie has had a lover since last term. He occasionally slips out before the door is locked at night, and one of us makes up his bed to look as though it is occupied. He then joins us at mass at first light, and walks back with us to the hostel. Last night, it was more difficult than usual, because Father Andrew was with us constantly after he learned of our quarrel in the street yesterday. Anyway, Jamie feigned illness and said he was going to bed early. He must have slipped out while we were eating our supper. But this morning he did not appear at mass, and we have not seen him since. Do you know where he is?'

The others looked eagerly at Michael, and Bartholomew did not envy the fat monk his next task.

'I am afraid I do,' said Michael quietly. 'He is in St Botolph's Church.'

'St Botolph's?' echoed Fyvie, puzzled. 'What is he doing there?'

'Then why does he not come back?' demanded Stuart Grahame belligerently. 'We have been worried sick about him all day. He must surely know that! Why has he not sent word?'

'He will not be coming back,' said Michael, trying to be gentle.

Fyvie and Ruthven stared at him in disbelief, while Davy Grahame, quicker on the uptake than his elders, brought his hands quickly to his mouth in shock. Father Andrew's face was pale as the meaning of Michael's words became clear to him.

'Not coming back?' said Stuart Grahame. 'Why ever not? He has not decided to become a friar, has he? Has he been hurt in this love affair and sworn to forsake the world?' He stood abruptly. 'Let me see him. I will talk some sense into the fool!'

'Sit down, Stuart,' said Davy Grahame in a soft voice. 'Brother Michael is telling us that Jamie is dead.'

'What?' The colour drained from Stuart Grahame's face and he sat down suddenly with a jolt, as if his legs had turned to jelly.

'But he cannot be dead, Davy!' he said unsteadily. 'We saw him yesterday evening!'

Davy ignored him. 'How did he die?' he asked, looking from

Michael to Bartholomew, his expression one of dazed horror. 'Where?'

'Quickly,' said Bartholomew, 'and without pain. Near the King's Ditch at Valence Marie. Can you think of anyone who would want to harm him?'

'He was killed by another?' asked Father Andrew, appalled. 'You mean murdered?'

Michael nodded, and calmly blocked the door as Stuart Grahame suddenly lurched towards it. 'Those friars!' the Scot yelled. 'The friars killed him!'

Michael took him firmly by the elbow and led him to sit at the table again, where Father Andrew put a comforting arm around his shoulders. The biggest, oldest and toughest of the Scots began to weep uncontrollably. The others looked away, Ruthven scrubbing surreptitiously at his eyes with the back of his hand.

'We will speak to the friars, of course,' said Michael. 'But at the moment, we need you to think of reasons others might have for wishing Kenzie harm. We can start with his woman.'

Fyvie shook his head as if he were trying to clear it. 'She would not kill him – she loved him dearly! Her name is Dominica and she is the daughter of the Principal of Godwinsson Hostel.'

Ruthven seized Michael's sleeve. 'Tread carefully, though. She is a kindly girl, but her father is not well-disposed towards Scots. You could ruin her by indiscretion.'

The indiscretion was James Kenzie's, thought Bartholomew, if he had picked a lover whose father was so adverse to his nationality. But Ruthven's caution was obviously meant well – a final act of friendship in attempting to protect the reputation of his dead comrade's lover.

Michael appraised him coolly. 'We will not be indiscreet,' he said, 'although I trust no other of you is so flagrantly breaking the University's rule about women?'

Vigorously shaken heads met his inquiry, and Michael relented. 'Do you have anything more that might help us? Were you all here last night as you claim?'

Ruthven, still white-faced, answered. 'Yes. Father Andrew was with us until it was time for the door to be locked, but Jamie had already left by then. We told Father Andrew that Jamie was ill and was resting upstairs in bed, like Robert of Stirling. Father Andrew saw us all to our dormitory, and can vouch that we all accompanied him to mass this morning. The Principal stayed here with the two students from Stirling and Jamie . . . or so he thought.'

Father Andrew nodded. 'Seven students were with me at mass: these seven,' he said, gesturing at Kenzie's four friends and the trio by the fireplace. 'I thought Jamie was ill. Until now.' He looked sternly at the subdued students. 'You have been extremely foolish in aiding your friend to slip out at night, and you very possibly have contributed to his death. Think on that before you break more University rules.'

'I want to go home!' wailed Stuart Grahame suddenly. His younger cousin rushed to his side in an attempt to quell the tears. 'I do not like this violent town!'

'Did Jamie have a ring?' asked Bartholomew, watching Davy comfort his distraught kinsman. 'One that he wore on his little finger?'

For a moment there was silence, except for Stuart's soft weeping, and then Davy spoke up. 'Yes, he did. And although he never said so, I had the feeling that Dominica gave it to him. Why? Do you have it? I doubt it was valuable.'

Bartholomew shook his head. 'It was missing, and so we must consider theft as a possible motive for Jamie's murder. In the dark, it would have been difficult to tell whether or not something was valuable, and a thief might have stolen it believing it was worth more than it was.'

'Have there been others in his family to die violently?' asked Michael, addressing Ruthven.

'Of course there have,' said Ruthven, as surprised by the question as Michael was by the answer. 'At home we need constantly to defend our lands and property, sometimes from the English and sometimes from our neighbours. And, on occasions, we attack others. Of course Jamie has relatives who have died violently.'

'I see,' said Michael, bemused. 'But that is not what I meant.'

'He wants to know whether there is any possibility that the skeleton unearthed yesterday is related to Jamie,' said Davy. The student shrugged at Michael's surprise. 'You said Jamie died in the King's Ditch at Valence Marie, and rumour has it that a skeleton was found in the same location yesterday. It does not take three terms of Aristotle to guess why you posed such a question.'

'Of course Jamie is not related to those bones,' said Ruthven, bewildered. 'Why should he be? Do you know who the skeleton is?'

Michael shook his head. 'I am merely trying to ensure that I overlook nothing. As Davy has just noted, Jamie and the skeleton were found in the same area within a few hours of each other.'

Davy frowned. 'We have only been studying here for a year. Jamie was the first of his family to acquire learning – he constantly joked that he was the first of his clan to step on English soil without intending to steal the cattle. The skeleton cannot be any of his forebears.'

'What will happen to us?' asked Ruthven in a low voice, as Michael prepared to leave.

'You will remain in the hostel, and you will not leave it unless you are in the company of a master,' said Michael. 'If I hear that any of you has disobeyed me, I will arrest you at once.'

He turned abruptly and left the room, waiting for Father Andrew and Bartholomew to follow him into the corridor. As Father Andrew closed the door behind them, they heard Stuart Grahame begin to cry again, while Fyvie and Ruthven's voices immediately rose in a clamour of questions and self-recriminations.

Father Andrew shook his head wearily, and leaned against the door. 'I am so sorry, Brother. I had no idea they would be so stupid as to assist one of their number to spend nights out with his paramour. I should have realised that they would not be subdued as easily as they pretended to be. Do you know who killed Jamie? Was it these friars they mentioned, the ones with whom they brawled yesterday?'

'We do not know yet,' said Michael. 'His killer may have been a friend. Can you be certain that all four were here last night?'

Father Andrew nodded. 'I saw them into the dormitory. I was still furious with them – if we Scots are seen brawling in the streets, the townspeople may take reprisals. You probably noticed our new door? We were forced to buy that when our last one was kicked to pieces following an argument between the Principal and a baker about underweight loaves. People here still resent the Scots' victory over the English at Bannockburn in 1314, you know – some of the older townsmen were even in King Edward the Second's army at the time. Anyway, suffice to say that our intention is to remain aloof from conflict at all costs. It would not do if our landlord refused to rent us this building next year because we had earned a reputation for fighting.'

Michael gave him a sympathetic smile. 'I appreciate that maintaining a distance from brawls might prove difficult for these fiery lads,' he said. 'And I appreciate your efforts in attempting to control them. The continued good reputation of your hostel is even more reason why we must resolve James Kenzie's death as quickly as possible. We should take a quick look at his belongings to see if he left some clue regarding the identity of his killer. Where did he sleep?'

Father Andrew led the way up a narrow wooden staircase to the dormitory. Bartholomew saw that, as was the case in many hostels, the dormitory was converted into a common room during the day, when the straw mattresses that served as beds were rolled up and stacked against one wall. The room was reasonably tidy, although there was a strong smell of dirty clothes. Two large chests stood at one end of the room in which the students could store their few belongings.

Two mattresses were still out. A young man tossed feverishly on one, while another student sat anxiously at his side. The other mattress held nothing more than cunningly bundled clothing. Father Andrew clicked his tongue in disapproval.

While Michael conducted his search of the upper floor, Bartholomew went to the ailing student and rested his hand on the boy's forehead. It was burning hot, but the bed was heaped with blankets. The room was stuffy, too, and a quick glance around told Bartholomew that the poor lad was provided with nothing to drink to ease his fever. He sent for fresh water, and set about making him more comfortable. He prescribed a potion to ease the ague, and showed the student's anxious brother how to keep him cool. Dismissing Father Andrew's grateful thanks with a nod, he went to join Michael who was waiting at the door.

'Well, neither of them is the culprit,' said Bartholomew in a low voice, indicating the two lads in the dormitory. 'One would have been too sick, and the other has not left his brother's side.'

'And the mullions on the windows are so close together that I doubt even a slender student could squeeze through,' whispered Michael. 'The other room on the upper floor is where the masters sleep, and has similarly narrow windows. There is no back door: *ergo*, the only way out is through the front. And Kenzie was the only one who has been absent since last night, if we can believe what we have been told. I would guess they have been honest with us.'

He and Bartholomew left the hostel with relief, still conscious of Stuart Grahame's wails of grief, and the voices of his friends trying to offer him comfort.

'Well?' said Bartholomew. 'What now? It looks as though none of Kenzie's friends killed him. Do we go to see the friars?'

'We do indeed,' said Michael, his expression serious. 'Because, for one thing, I still have not spoken to their Principal about their behaviour in the High Street yesterday, and for another thing, they are members of Godwinsson Hostel, where Kenzie's lover is also the Principal's daughter.'

Godwinsson's door was answered by a gangling Welshman called Huw, who conducted them into a small, but comfortable, solar that glowed red with the last of the setting sun. The windows were glazed, an extravagance that had not been considered necessary for most of the house, which had only shutters to exclude winter winds and summer flies.

Bartholomew began to prowl restlessly as they waited for the Principal to see them. The steward had explained that Principal Lydgate lived with his wife in the adjoining house, while the students and other masters lived at the hostel proper. Godwinsson was a more pleasant house than David's – it was larger, cleaner, and did not smell of burning cabbage.

'It is odd how Lydgate's name has occurred so often of late,' said Michael, speaking mainly to distract Bartholomew, who was becoming impatient. 'First, two of his students are involved in a disturbance of the peace; then you reveal his childhood secret; and finally, it is his daughter who was receiving the attentions of the murdered man.'

'Lydgate was no child when the barn was fired,' said Bartholomew. 'He was at least eighteen: almost as old as Kenzie. But we should not speak of this, especially here. It will do no good to unturn such a stone, and he would probably deny it anyway.'

'Deny what, Bartholomew?'

Bartholomew jumped at the sound of Lydgate's voice so close

behind him. The Principal of Godwinsson had not entered by the same door through which Bartholomew and Michael had been shown, but from a second door in the opposite wall that Bartholomew had assumed was a cupboard. Glancing through it, he could see that it connected Lydgate's family house next door with the hostel. Had this been the route James Kenzie had used to meet Lydgate's daughter: either him to sneak to her room, or her to slip out to him?

'We are here to investigate the death of a student from David's,' said Michael, recovering from his surprise faster than Bartholomew, who was wondering, uncomfortably, how much of their conversation Lydgate had overheard.

'A student of David's is no concern of mine,' said Lydgate, shifting his small, hard blue eyes from Bartholomew and fixing them on Michael.

'The brutal murder of a member of the University should be the concern of every scholar,' Michael retorted superiorly. 'Especially now, in this climate of unease.'

'Who has been murdered?'

Bartholomew thought he had detected a shadow in the interconnecting corridor between the two houses, and so the unannounced entry of Lydgate's wife into their conversation did not startle him as Lydgate's had done.

'A David's student, Mistress,' said Michael, bowing politely to her. 'He was last seen alive yesterday evening at seven o'clock, and was found dead this afternoon.'

'Not one of our boys?' asked Cecily Lydgate. She sniffed dismissively. 'Then this has nothing to do with us.' She went to her husband, placing a proprietary hand on his arm. With undisguised irritation, he shrugged it off.

Bartholomew remembered the marriage of Cecily to Thomas Lydgate some twenty years or more before. It was not a love match, but a union designed to bring together two adjoining manors in Trumpington. When both fathers had died, Lydgate sold the Trumpington land within a week, and bought himself a pair of handsome houses in the town centre.

The physician studied Cecily Lydgate with interest. Although she had lived in the town for many years, he had seldom seen her. She had servants who did her shopping, and daily trips to church and the occasional outing to a fair or a banquet apparently satisfied any ambitions she had for entertainment outside her home. Lack of exercise and fresh air, however, were beginning to take their toll, for although her clothes were evidently made of cloth that was expensive, they did little to disguise the plumpness underneath. A fiercely starched wimple kept every hair from her face, making her eyes appear bulbous and her teeth too large.

By contrast, her husband had aged well, and still retained his hulking figure, although it was beginning to turn to fat around his waist. His hair remained jet black, with no traces of grey, and his clean-shaven face made him appear much younger than his wife, although Bartholomew knew they were the same age. Bartholomew had had nothing to do with Lydgate since his own studies had taken him to Peterborough, Oxford, and Paris, but dislike for the man, suppressed for many years, began to resurface, as fresh and crystal clear as when he had wronged Norbert.

Michael, uninvited, sat on the best chair in the room, and indicated, with an insolent flick of his hand, that Lydgate and his wife should sit on a bench opposite him.

Lydgate declined, and went to stand with his back to the last sunlight that streamed in dark gold rays through the window. A clever move, Bartholomew noted, for it was difficult to see his face with the light behind him.

'So, Brother. You have told me a David's scholar is dead. What would you have me do about it?' Lydgate asked coldly.

'Yesterday he was seen quarrelling in the street with two friars who live here,' said Michael, easing himself back comfortably in his chair, and folding his hands across his stomach.

Lydgate's response was aggressive. 'Rubbish,' he said, with a contemptuous toss of his head. 'Whoever claimed to have seen this was lying to you.'

'Really?' said Michael, with a pleasant smile. 'Then you will have no objections to us speaking to Brothers Edred and Werbergh.'

'I most certainly do have objections,' said Lydgate vehemently. 'You have no authority to come here harassing my students on the word of some lying townsman.'

'Oh? And who do you think has been lying to us, Master Lydgate?' probed Michael softly, raising his eyebrows and tapping one hand gently on the other.

'Labourers or guildsmen, they are all the same,' said Lydgate. He walked to the door and hauled it open to indicate that the interview was over. When Michael and Bartholomew did not move, Lydgate made an impatient gesture with his hand. 'I am a busy man. That is all, gentlemen.'

'I do not think so, Master Lydgate,' said Michael, standing to stroll casually across the room and close the door. 'You see, the witnesses you are so certain were lying are Doctor Bartholomew and me.' His tone lost its silkiness. 'I want to speak to Brothers Werbergh and Edred, and I want to do it now. And I can assure you that the authority I own was invested in me by the Chancellor from the King himself. If you do not consider the King's authority sufficient to answer my questions, tell me so, and I will relay the message to His Majesty myself.'

Disconcerted by Michael's sudden force of will and by the none too subtle threat of treason, Lydgate hurriedly sent his steward to find the friars, and fought to regain moral superiority by bluster.

'I will complain to the Chancellor about your attitude,' he said hotly. 'The King's authority does not give you the right to be offensive.'

Cecily Lydgate joined in with her nasal whine. 'You have been most rude.'

Michael rounded on her fiercely. 'How so, Madam? By requesting to speak to two men who were seen quarrelling with a student the day before he was brutally murdered? Do you have something to hide from me?'

'No! I . . .' protested Cecily, flustered. 'I have done nothing . . .'

'Then kindly refrain from meddling in University affairs, Madam,' said Michael in his most icy tones. 'Neither the Chancellor nor the King will be pleased if they hear that Godwinsson proved unhelpful – obstructive even – during the course of my inquiries into the foul murder of a member of the University.'

By the time Huw had ushered the friars into the solar, Lydgate and his wife were sitting side by side on the bench, while Michael stood in front of them, allowing his own considerable bulk to dominate them, as Lydgate had attempted to do to him.

'Where were you last night?' Michael snapped at the wary friars. 'Ah! Do not look at each other for the answer! Where were you? Come on, come on. I do not have all day!'

'Here,' ventured Werbergh, watching Michael fearfully.

'Here!' sneered Michael. 'Doctor, would you take Brother

Werbergh into the corridor and ask him for his movements since his quarrel in the street yesterday? I will talk to Brother Edred here, and then we will see whether their accounts tally.'

Bartholomew took Werbergh's arm before he had the chance to exchange the slightest of glances with the sullen Edred, and guided him outside, closing the door behind them. Huw the steward scuttled away from where he had evidently been listening through the keyhole.

Werbergh looked terrified, which was no doubt what Michael had intended. Bartholomew waited in silence for Werbergh to bare his soul. The physician had learned from Michael that uncomfortable silences frequently served to make people gabble, and, in gabbling, they often revealed more than they intended.

'After we . . . after you saved us from the Scots, Edred and I went to St Botolph's Church for vespers. We came straight home then, because the Senior Proctor told us to. We had to go out in the evening for compline, and after that I came back here. I walked home with Mistress Lydgate. You can ask her. She likes one of us to take her arm when she goes to church. Prefers us to her husband, I would say,' he added, with a sly grin at Bartholomew.

'What are you saying, Brother?' asked Bartholomew coldly, not liking the way in which the pale-faced friar was trying to ingratiate himself by tale-telling.

Werbergh began to talk quickly again, Bartholomew's hostility making him more nervous than ever. 'Mistress and Master Lydgate are not the loving couple they seem, and she prefers younger scholars to his company.'

'What has this to do with where you were last night?' asked Bartholomew, making no attempt to hide his disgust at the friar's transparent obsequiousness. Any fool could see that relations between the Lydgates were far from rosy, and Bartholomew resented Werbergh's attempt to distract him from his inquiries by plying him with malicious gossip. Mistress Lydgate could seduce all the young scholars she pleased, and it would be none of Bartholomew's business – unless she set her sights on any of his own students, but they were all perfectly capable of looking after themselves in that quarter, probably far more so than Bartholomew would be.

The student shook his head miserably, his attempt to distract

Bartholomew in tatters. 'I escorted Mistress Lydgate to her house and then followed the other students here. It was already getting dark, so most of us went to bed.'

'And what of Edred? Where was he?'

Werbergh licked dry lips. 'I did not notice where he was. We do not go everywhere together, you know,' he added with a spark of defiance. 'But I have been with other people from the moment we returned from our quarrel with the Scots until now. You can check.'

'Do you have any idea why we might be asking you this?' asked Bartholomew, watching the student carefully.

Werbergh shook his head, but two pink spots appeared on his cheeks, and the way in which his eyes deliberately sought and held Bartholomew's was more indicative of guilt than honesty.

'It is surely against the rules of your Order to lie?' said Bartholomew softly.

Werbergh's eyes became glassy, and the redness increased. 'Yes,' he said finally, tearing his gaze away, and studying his sandalled feet instead. 'I can guess why you are asking me these questions. But I was afraid such an admission might make you assume my guilt. You think Edred and I may have stolen his ring.'

'Ring?' echoed Bartholomew, taken off-guard.

Werbergh looked at him with an expression of one who has played cat-and-mouse for long enough. 'The Scottish student's ring,' he said wearily. 'He was waiting for us when we came out of compline. He accused us of stealing his ring while we were pushing at each other in the High Street.' He paused for a moment, oblivious to Bartholomew's confusion. 'He was very upset; I almost felt sorry for him. We professed our innocence, and he left quietly.' He looked up and met Bartholomew's eyes a second time, but this time with truthfulness. 'That is why you have come, is it not? Because he has accused us of stealing his nasty ring?'

'It is not,' said Bartholomew. 'James Kenzie was murdered last night. And if what you say is true, you may have been the last ones to see him alive, with the exception of his killer.'

Blood drained from Werbergh's face, leaving him suddenly white and reeling. Bartholomew, genuinely concerned that the friar might faint, took his elbow and sat him on a chest. Werbergh stared ahead of him blankly for a moment, before looking up at Bartholomew with eyes that were glazed with shock.

'You would not jest with me on such a matter?' he asked in a whisper. He studied Bartholomew's face. 'No. Of course you would not. What can I tell you? The Scot had been waiting in the churchyard, and he beckoned Edred and me to one side. Mistress Lydgate saw, I think. He sounded more hopeful that we might give his ring back to him, than angry that we might have stolen it. When we denied having it, he left. As I said, I felt almost sorry for him, even though he was so offensive earlier. He was alone – at least, I saw no one with him. I did not see anyone following him when he left.' He screwed up his face in what Bartholomew assumed was a genuine attempt to remember anything that might help. Eventually, he shrugged, and shook his head. 'That is all I can recall, I am afraid. We had a stupid argument in the street, but I did not wish any of the David's men dead because of it.'

The solar door flung open and Michael stalked out, the Lydgates and Edred, whose face was tear-stained, on his heels. Bartholomew bowed to Mistress Lydgate, and followed Michael, leaving Werbergh to make good his escape from his Principal by scuttling off in the other direction. Bartholomew was aware that Lydgate was pursuing him and Michael along the corridor and down the stairs to the front door, but was surprised to find his shoulder in a grip that was so firm it was almost painful. He spun round quickly so that Lydgate was forced to let go.

'I resent this intrusion into my affairs, Bartholomew,' said Lydgate in a low hiss. 'I have connections in the University. If I find you have been meddling in things that are not your concern, you will live to regret it.'

Had Lydgate overheard them talking about the burning of the tithe barn, Bartholomew wondered, as he met Lydgate's hostile glower with a cool stare of his own? Or was he merely referring to the rather insalubrious connection of two of his students with a murder victim?

'Leave well alone, Bartholomew,' Lydgate whispered with quiet menace when Bartholomew did not answer, and pushed the physician roughly towards the door.

Bartholomew slithered out of his grip, and thrust Lydgate away from him. The two stared at each other for a long moment of undisguised mutual loathing, before Bartholomew turned on his heel and strode after Michael. Lydgate watched him go and then closed the door. He leaned against the wall and his eyes narrowed into hard, vicious slits.

chapter 3

I N A SMALL, SECLUDED GARDEN BEHIND THE BRAZEN
George tavern later that evening, Michael sat at a wooden
table with a large goblet of fine red wine in front of him,
and watched Bartholomew pace back and forth in the gloom.
The physician's hard-soled shoes tapped on the flagstones of
the yard, and he tugged impatiently at his sleeve when it
snagged on a thorn of one of the rose bushes that added
their heavy scent to the still air of the night.

'We should not be here, Michael. You are a proctor and a
monk. It would not be good for you to be seen in a tavern,
especially drinking, and even more especially on a Sunday.'

Michael leaned back against the wall, where the stones still
held the warmth of the day. 'We will not be disturbed, and,
for your information, I conduct a good deal of business here
on behalf of the University and the Bishop.'

Bartholomew gave a huge sigh, and came to sit next to
Michael on the bench. He took a sip of the ale Michael
had bought him, and then another. 'This ale is not sour!'
he exclaimed in surprise. He peered into the heavy pewter
goblet, and realised the beer was clear enough to allow him
to see the bottom.

Michael laughed. 'There are advantages to conducting business outside Michaelhouse.' He sipped appreciatively at his rich
red wine. 'You should venture out more, Matt. You have become
far too used to that foul concoction brewed at Michaelhouse
for your own good health.'

They were silent for a while, listening to the beadles in the
street outside calling out the curfew, and, in the distance, the
excited yells and shouts of people who were apparently enjoying
some kind of celebration. The garden was dark, and the taverner
had provided them with a lantern that they shared with hundreds
of insects. Michael flapped them away from his wine.

'I had a letter last week,' began Bartholomew casually. 'Philippa, to whom I was betrothed, has married someone else.'

Michael was taken aback. Philippa had been the sister of a former room-mate of Bartholomew's, and had become betrothed to the physician after the plague. Some time ago, Philippa had declared herself bored with life in Cambridge and, seduced by the descriptions of fairs, pageants and feasts in her brother's letters, had set off to sample the delights of London. Three months had stretched to six, and Michael realised he had not seen Bartholomew's attractive fiancée since early summer of the previous year. The monk had not given her long absence a second thought. Neither had Bartholomew, apparently.

'Perhaps, since neither of you made the effort to visit the other during the time she was away, this would not have been a marriage made in heaven,' said the monk carefully, uncertain of his friend's feelings on the matter. 'You would not want to end up as a couple like the dreadful Lydgates.'

Bartholomew studied him in the darkness. 'I suppose not. Philippa married a merchant. She wrote that, at first, she thought that she would not mind being the wife of an impoverished physician, but realised that in time she might come to resent it. Then she said I would have taken rich patients to please her, and we both would have been unhappy.'

'You always paid more attention to your patients than to her,' said Michael, thinking in retrospect that Bartholomew might well have had a lucky escape. 'I cannot say I am surprised by her decision.'

'Well, I was!' said Bartholomew earnestly. 'I did not expect her to shun me quite so suddenly.'

'She has been gone more than a year; that is hardly sudden,' Michael pointed out practically. 'Women are like good wines, Matt. They need to be treated with care and attention – not abandoned until you are ready for a drink.'

Despite his melancholy mood, Bartholomew smiled at Michael's blunt analogy. 'And what would you know of women, monk?'

'More than you, physician,' replied Michael complacently. 'I know, for example, that since she was betrothed to you, it is illegal for her to wed another. You could take her to court.'

Bartholomew raised his eyebrows. 'And what would that achieve? I would acquire a wife who despised me on two counts: my poverty, and the fact that I wrenched her away from the husband of her choice.'

Michael shrugged. 'Then it is best you put the whole affair from your mind. And anyway, if you had married, you would have had to give up your Fellowship at Michaelhouse and your teaching. You like teaching, and you are good at it. Think of what you have gained, not what you have lost.'

'I would have lost the opportunity to investigate murders,' said Bartholomew morosely. 'And the chance to meet such charming people as the Lydgates, Edred and Werbergh.'

Michael chuckled. 'Such characters are not exclusive to the University, Matt. You would have encountered people just like them elsewhere, too. You might even have had to be pleasant to them, if they were your patients and you wanted them to pay you.'

Bartholomew grimaced with distaste at the notion. 'I miss her,' he persisted. 'I lie awake at night and wonder whether I will ever see her again.'

Michael eyed him soberly. 'So that is why you have been looking so heavy-eyed over the last few days. But if you do see her again, Matt, she will be someone else's wife and unavailable to you, so put such thoughts out of your mind. Perhaps you should consider becoming a monk, like me.'

'How would that help?' asked Bartholomew listlessly. 'It would make matters worse. At least now I am not committing a sin by thinking about women. If I were a monk, I would never be away from my confessor.'

'Oh really, Matt!' said Michael in an amused voice. 'What odd ideas you have sometimes! You are capable of great discretion, and that should be sufficient to allow you to choose your secular pastimes as and when you please. A monastic vocation would suit you very well.'

Bartholomew regarded him askance, wondering what kind of monk would offer a jilted lover that kind of advice. He took another sip of the excellent ale, and pondered whether he would ever know Michael well enough not to be surprised by some of his opinions and behaviour.

Michael took a noisy slurp of wine, and refilled his cup from the jug on the table. He stretched and yawned.

'It is getting late,' he said. 'We should be considering Godwinsson Hostel and its shady inhabitants, not discussing your sinful desires for another man's wife. Lydgate, Cecily,

Werbergh and Edred – what an unpleasant group of people to be gathered under one roof.'

'Two roofs,' said Bartholomew, forcing his thoughts away from Philippa. 'I forgot to ask about Kenzie's lover, Dominica. Did you?'

'I learned a little,' said Michael. 'But what did your nasty little friar tell you?'

Michael listened with growing interest as Bartholomew repeated his conversation with Werbergh, and gave a low whistle when he had finished.

'Well,' he said, 'one of them is lying. Edred's story coincides with Werbergh's until after compline. Then he says he walked back to the hostel in the company of Werbergh, but makes no mention of Mistress Lydgate.'

'Well, he would not,' said Bartholomew. 'He could scarcely claim his Principal's wife as an alibi with her sitting there and likely to denounce him as a liar. But neither story fits,' he continued thoughtfully. 'If Werbergh offered his arm to Mistress Lydgate, and Edred claims that he returned to the hostel with Werbergh, then all three must have been together. Edred makes no mention of Mistress Lydgate, while Werbergh makes no mention of Edred. Mistress Lydgate must surely have noted that it was she and not Edred who walked with Werbergh back to the hostel. Something is not right here, Brother.'

He could hear the rasp of Michael's nails against his whiskers as he scratched his chin in the darkness. 'And Edred did not mention Kenzie asking for his ring, even after I told him the lad had been murdered, and that I would appreciate any information he might have. I had a feeling he was not being honest with me.'

'Either Edred is remarkably stupid not to guess that Werbergh would tell me about meeting Kenzie, or it did not happen,' reasoned Bartholomew. 'Or Edred is hiding evidence of what he considers a minor incident, because he is involved in one that is more serious. I am inclined to believe Werbergh was generally truthful, which means that Edred is the one telling lies.'

'Edred and Cecily Lydgate both,' said Michael thoughtfully. 'If Werbergh is telling the truth and he walked home to Godwinsson with Cecily, then why did she not denounce Edred as a liar when he claimed *he* was with Werbergh? Something untoward is going on in that hostel. Give me the honest poverty at David's any day over the thin veneer of civilisation at Godwinsson.'

'So what about Dominica?' asked Bartholomew. 'What did you manage to find out about her?'

'Very little, I'm afraid,' said Michael. 'Only that on the night of Kenzie's murder she was staying with relatives – much against her will if I read correctly the set chin and determined looks of Mistress Lydgate the elder. Dominica is still with them. Which means that wherever Kenzie went last night, it was not Dominica's room, because she was not there.'

'Not necessarily,' said Bartholomew watching the bats flit around the garden. 'Perhaps that is exactly where he went, expecting to find her.'

'And instead found an angry father and a dragon of a mother,' said Michael. 'Which means that they killed him, and dumped his body in the Ditch to avoid suspicion falling on them.'

'That seems too easy,' said Bartholomew. 'There is something not right about all this.'

'Why should it not be easy?' asked Michael with a shrug. 'The Lydgates are hardly over-endowed with intelligence, and neither is Edred if he could not come up with a better story than the one he spun me – knowing that Werbergh would not support his alibi if pressed for the truth.'

Bartholomew sighed. 'I suppose you are right, but we cannot do anything about it, because we have no proof. All we know is that lies have been told.' He stood, feeling suddenly chilly in the cool night air. 'Perhaps the evidence we need will appear tomorrow. Lord save us! What was that?'

A tremendous crash, followed by yells and screams, shook the ground and made the leaves on the trees tremble. Flickers of orange light danced in the street outside, and the shouting suddenly increased dramatically.

The landlord of the Brazen George came hurrying into the garden, his face tight with fear.

'I know you do not like to be disturbed, Brother,' he said apologetically, 'but I thought you should know: the students are rioting. They have tied ropes to Master Burney's workshop and hauled the whole thing down. Now they are trying to set it on fire.'

Bartholomew and Michael raced out into the street. The

rickety structure, the upper floor of which had been Master Burney's tannery, now lay sprawled across the High Street with flames leaping all over it. Bartholomew knew that Burney, a widower since the plague, slept in the workshop, and started towards the roaring flames. Michael caught his arm and hauled him back.

'If Burney was in there when it fell, you can do nothing for him now,' he choked, eyes watering from the smoke.

Bartholomew saw that Michael was right: the searing heat from the flames was almost unbearable, even at that distance. He screwed up his eyes against the stinging fumes, and surveyed the wreckage. A tangle of limbs protruded from under a heap of smouldering plaster. Michael let out an appalled gasp and gripped Bartholomew's arm to point them out.

'Mistress Starre's son,' Bartholomew shouted, recognising the huge frame of the simple-minded giant among the twisted remains. 'I heard he died recently.'

'What are you talking about?'

'This building belongs to the Austin Canons of St John's Hospital,' Bartholomew yelled over the crackle of burning wood. 'They use the lower storey as a mortuary since they believe the smell from the tannery above will dispel the unhealthy miasma emanating from the corpses. The bodies you see were probably dead already – I know young Starre was.'

'Does their theory hold any validity?' asked Michael before he could stop himself. They should not be considering medical matters now, but attempting to order the rioting students back to their hostels and colleges – and if that failed, seek sanctuary somewhere before they became the victims of a town mob themselves. Fortunately for him, Bartholomew's attention was elsewhere.

'The fire is spreading!' he yelled, and Michael looked to where he was gesticulating wildly, seeing smoke seeping from the roof of the house next door. Seconds later, there was another dull roar, and a bright tongue of flames shot out of one of the windows.

'Mistress Tyler lives there with her daughters!' Bartholomew whispered, his horrified voice all but lost in the increasing rumble and crackle of the flames, greedy for the dry wood of the house.

'No. She lives next door. And anyway, look,' said Michael, indicating behind him with a flick of his head. Bartholomew saw with relief the frightened faces of the Tyler family huddled against the wall of the Brazen George opposite, clutching what few belongings they had managed to grab as they fled for safety.

Students were everywhere, flitting like bats in the dancing light of the flames in their dark tabards. Michael was shouting to them to put out the flames, but while some obeyed, others amused themselves by hurling missiles at the horn windows of the Brazen George. Townspeople, woken by the din, began to pour into the street, and small skirmishes began between them and the scholars. Backing up against the wall next to the terrified Tyler family, Bartholomew saw a group of apprentices kicking a student they had seized and knocked to the ground, while a short distance away, a group of University men were poking at a fat merchant and his wife with sharpened sticks.

A group of three students ran past, shouting to each other in French, but one, seeing the pretty face of the eldest Tyler girl, called to his friends and they came back. They seized her arms, and were set to make off with her, the expressions on their faces making their intentions perfectly clear. Mistress Tyler ran to the defence of her daughter, but stopped short as one of them jabbed at her stomach with a knife.

Bartholomew hit the student's arm as hard as he could, knocking the dagger from his hand, and wrenched the girl away from the others. With a quick exchange of grins, the French students advanced on him, drawing short swords from the arsenal they had secreted under their tabards. Bartholomew drew the small knife that he used for surgery from the medicine bag he always carried looped over his shoulder.

Seeing the tiny weapon compared to their swords, the students began to ridicule it in poor English. While one's attention strayed to his friends, Bartholomew leapt at him, inflicting a minor wound on his arm. The student gave a yell of pain and outrage, forcing Bartholomew to jerk backwards as a sword whistled towards him in a savage arc. Suddenly, the students were not laughing or jeering, but in deadly earnest, and Bartholomew was aware of all three taking the stance of the trained fighter. He knew he would not win this battle, armed with a small knife against three men experienced in swordsmanship. And then what would happen to the Tyler women?

'Run!' he yelled to them, not taking his eyes off the circling Frenchmen.

But the Tyler women had not managed to live unmolested on the High Street, with no menfolk to care for them since the plague, by being passive. Seeing Bartholomew's predicament they swung into action. The eldest hurled handfuls of sand and dust from the ground, aiming for the Frenchmen's eyes, while the mother and two younger daughters pelted them with offal and muck from a pile at the side of the road.

Bartholomew staggered backwards as one student, a hand upraised to protect his face from the barrage of missiles, lunged forwards. As Bartholomew stumbled, his foot slipped on some of the offal that the Tylers were hurling, and he had to twist sideways to avoid the stabbing sword that drew sparks from the ground as it struck. He continued to roll, so that he crashed into the legs of the second swordsman, and sent him sprawling to the ground. The third had dropped his weapon, and was rubbing at his eyes, where one of the handfuls of dust had taken a direct hit.

The second Frenchman grabbed Bartholomew around the neck, preventing him from rising. Bartholomew, struggling desperately to prise the arm away from his throat as he felt it begin to cut off his breath, realised that he had dropped his knife. The first student, his hand still raised to protect his eyes, advanced on the physician smiling evilly, assured that his quarry would now be easily dispatched. Bartholomew lunged forward with every ounce of his strength, and succeeded in breaking the hold that had pinned him to the ground. He scrambled to his feet, but found himself up against a wall with nowhere to move. The two Frenchmen moved apart by unspoken agreement, effectively eliminating any chance of escape.

Without warning, one of them dropped to his knees, his sword falling from his hand as he scrabbled at his back. His face wore an expression of shock that would have been comical in other circumstances. Then he pitched forward, and Bartholomew saw his own knife firmly embedded between the man's shoulder-blades, and Mistress Tyler standing behind him, her face white with shock and anger.

The third Frenchman, his eyes raw from the dust he had rubbed from them, called for the other one to come away, his voice becoming more urgent when he perceived their

friend's fate. The student ignored him, and advanced on
Bartholomew, his sword whistling in a series of hacking sweeps.
Bartholomew, seeing defence was useless, dived at him when
he was off-balance from a particularly vigorous thrust. Both
men fell to the ground in a frenzy of flailing arms and legs,
and Bartholomew's hands fumbled for the Frenchman's throat.
Ignoring the pounding of fists on his chest and arms, he began
to squeeze as hard as he could.

He was dimly aware of the other man coming to his friend's
rescue, and heard the Tylers renew their assault on him with any
missiles they could find. There was a heavy thud as he fell. The
student Bartholomew held was almost unconscious now, and
Bartholomew forced himself to release him. The man flopped
on to his side, concerned only with dragging sweet air down
his bruised throat, while his friend crawled towards him.

Breathing heavily himself, Bartholomew grabbed Mistress
Tyler's arm and hauled her from the street into the small
alley that ran down the side of the Brazen George, trusting
the daughters would follow. In the comparative peace, the five
of them regained their breath, the girls holding on to each
other for comfort. Mistress Tyler was the first to recover, while
Bartholomew leaned against a tall fence, hoping he would not
disgrace himself by being the only one to allow his shaking
legs to deposit him on the ground.

Although Oswald Stanmore had been to some trouble to
teach his young brother-in-law the rudiments of sword-play,
archery and boxing, Bartholomew had not taken easily or
happily to such training, preferring to seek out the company
of Trumpington's rector, and ply him with an endless barrage
of questions about natural philosophy and logic. Occasionally,
however, Bartholomew wished he had paid more attention to
Stanmore's lessons – the learning he had acquired over the
years would not save him from a sword thrust, and Cambridge
seemed to be growing ever more dangerous, with murders and
riots at every turn.

He winced as a student friar tore past the top of their
alleyway, screaming like an infidel. Students and townsfolk
alike ran this way and that, most in small groups for safety.
Distant yells indicated that the riot was spreading to other
parts of the town, and the dark night sky was glowing orange
in at least two places, suggesting that fires were not confined
to the High Street. Several riderless horses galloped by, adding

to the mayhem. Bartholomew wondered how the Sheriff would manage to control such widespread disorder with troops that had been sorely depleted during the plague and never replaced. Bravely, Mistress Tyler seized on a brief lull in the chaos to peer into the High Street, starting backwards when a shower of sparks danced across the road towards her.

'The fire is more or less out,' she called over her shoulder. 'But there are people inside our house – probably looting, although they will find precious little to take.' She put her arms around the elder girls' shoulders, while the youngest clung to her skirts. 'This is my treasure,' she whispered shakily. 'I will not risk it to save a few sticks of furniture.'

'Shall I try to drive the looters out?' asked Bartholomew, wondering whether his aching limbs would allow it, and regretting his offer the moment it was made.

Mistress Tyler looked at him aghast. 'Of course not! You have done enough for us already by rescuing my Eleanor from those French devils. But if you will do us a final kindness, Doctor, and escort us to my cousin's house, we would much appreciate it.'

Bartholomew agreed readily enough, but wondered whether his presence – a single, unarmed man – could do much to protect the Tyler women from further assault. He felt something pressed into his hand, and met the clear, grey eyes of Eleanor as she returned his knife to him, sticky and glistening black with blood. She must have retrieved it before following her mother to the alley. He was grateful, knowing that his knife found in the back of a corpse might well have been considered sufficient evidence to hang him for murder in one of the hasty and vengeful trials that often followed such disturbances, regardless of the fact that he was innocent.

He gave her a wan smile, and followed the women down the alley. They reached Shoemaker Row, where they kept to the shadows, avoiding the groups of apprentices that ran this way and that armed with a wicked assortment of weapons. At the Franciscan Friary, the stout doors were firmly closed: the friars obviously intended to keep well clear of the mischief brewing that night, and to protect their property from harm. One priest, braver or more naïve than his fellows, stood atop the gate, exhorting the rioters to return to their homes or risk the wrath of God. Few heeded his words, and he was eventually silenced by a well-aimed stone.

Finally, having pursued a somewhat tortuous route to avoid confrontations, Mistress Tyler stopped outside the apothecary's house.

'Is Jonas the Poisoner your cousin?' asked Bartholomew, using without thinking the usual appellation for the apothecary, following an incident involving confusion between two potions many years before.

'His wife is,' answered Mistress Tyler. She took Bartholomew's arm and, when the door was opened a crack in response to her insistent hammering, she bundled him inside with her daughters.

While she told her fearful relatives of their near escape, Bartholomew allowed himself to be settled comfortably in a wicker chair, and brought a cup of cool wine. As he took it, his hands shook from delayed fright, so that a good part of it slopped on to his leggings. Mistress Tyler's middle daughter – a young woman almost as pretty as her elder sister – handed him a wholly inadequate square of lace with which to mop it up. She was unceremoniously elbowed out of the way by Eleanor, and dispatched to fetch something larger, overriding Bartholomew's embarrassed protestations that it was not necessary.

'I did not thank you,' said Eleanor, smiling at him as she refilled his cup. 'You were more than kind to come to our rescue – especially given that you are clearly no fighting man.'

Such a candid assessment of his meagre combat skills was scarcely an auspicious start to the conversation, but he decided her comment was not intentionally discourteous. 'We were more evenly matched than the Frenchmen imagined,' he said, acknowledging the Tylers' own considerable role in the skirmish. 'And I should thank you for not running when I told you to.'

'Yes, or you would have been dead by now for certain,' she said bluntly. Bartholomew took a sip of wine to hide his smile, certain she was oblivious to the fact that many men would have taken grave exception to such a casual dismissal of their martial abilities.

She looked thoughtful. 'You are a scholar: tell me why the students are so intent on mischief this term. They are always restless and keen to fight, but I have never known such an uneasy atmosphere before.'

'We have discussed this at Michaelhouse several times, but we have no idea as to the cause,' he answered, setting his cup down on the hearth before he could spill it again. 'Should you discover it, please let us know. We must put a stop to it before any more harm is done.'

The middle daughter returned with water and a cloth with which to wipe up the slopped wine, and a slight, somewhat undignified tussle for possession of them ensued between the two sisters, a struggle that ended abruptly when the bowl tipped and a good portion of its contents emptied over Bartholomew's feet. Quickly, he grabbed the rest of it before they drenched him further. Across the room, Mistress Tyler tried to see what was happening.

'Hedwise, give the doctor more wine,' she called, before turning her attention back to the persistent questioning of her anxious relatives.

'No, thank you,' said Bartholomew hastily, as Hedwise tried to pour more wine into a cup that was already brimming. He did not want to return to Michaelhouse drunk.

Hedwise looked crestfallen, and Eleanor smiled enigmatically. 'Fetch some cakes, Hedwise. I am sure Doctor Bartholomew is hungry after his ordeal.'

The last thing Bartholomew's unsteady stomach needed was something to eat. He declined, much to Hedwise's satisfaction, and she settled herself on a small stool near his feet, still clutching the wine bottle so that his cup could be refilled the instant he took so much as a sip. Eleanor knelt to one side, leaning her elbows on the arm of his chair.

'When the weather is good, I sit outside to work – you know our family makes lace for a living – and students often talk to me. I will ask around to see if I can discover the cause of this unease for you.'

'Me too,' said Hedwise eagerly.

'It might be better if you were to stay inside,' said Bartholomew, concerned. 'Supposing those French students return?'

'Oh, they will,' said Eleanor confidently. 'They have been pestering me for weeks.'

'And me,' said Hedwise.

Eleanor ignored her. 'Our mother was forced to speak to their Principal about them.'

'Which hostel?' asked Bartholomew, feeling a strange sense that he already knew the answer.

'Godwinsson,' the women chorused.

'Do you know Dominica?' Bartholomew asked, looking from

one to the other. 'The daughter of Master Lydgate, the Principal?'

Eleanor smiled, her teeth white, but slightly crooked. 'Dominica is the only decent member of that whole establishment. She was seeing a student, but her parents got wind of it. They sent her away to Chesterton village out of harm's way.'

Hedwise giggled suddenly. 'They think she has chosen a student from their own poxy hostel, but the reality is that she has far too much taste to accept one of that weaselly brood. It is another she loves.'

'Her parents do not know the identity of her lover?' asked Bartholomew, surprised.

'Oh, no!' said Eleanor. 'But they would do anything to find out. They even offered money to their students to betray their fellows. A number of them did, I understand, but when stories and alibis were checked, the betrayals were found to be false, and stemmed from spite and malice, not truth.'

'What an unpleasant place,' said Bartholomew in distaste, recalling his own brief visit there – only a few hours ago, although it felt like much longer. 'Do you know who Dominica's lover is?'

'Dominica tells no one about her lovers, for fear their names would reach her father,' said Eleanor. 'She is clever though, never meeting in the same place twice, and ensuring there are no predictable patterns to her meetings.'

Had Dominica chosen the King's Ditch to meet Kenzie then, Bartholomew wondered, and the Scot had been killed as he waited for her to appear? If Dominica chose a different location each time she and Kenzie met, then she might well have been reduced to using a place like the shadowy oak trees near Valence Marie if the relationship had lasted for any length of time.

Feeling water squelch unpleasantly in his shoes, Bartholomew stood to take his leave of the Tylers and Jonas, declining their offer to stay the night. He wanted to return to Michaelhouse and sleep in his own bed.

Eleanor reached out to take his hand. 'We will worry about you until we see you again, Doctor Bartholomew. Visit us, even if it is only to say you arrived home safely.'

'Oh, yes,' said Hedwise, forcing her way between Bartholomew and her sister. 'Come to see us soon.'

Mistress Tyler looked from her daughters to Bartholomew

as she ushered him out of the door, first checking to see that it was safe. She touched his arm as he stepped into the street. 'Eleanor and Hedwise are right,' she said. 'You must visit us soon. And thank you for your help tonight. Who knows what might have happened to us had you not come to our aid.'

Bartholomew suspected that they would have thought of something. The Tyler women were a formidable force – resourceful and determined. Eleanor caught his hand as he left, and it was only reluctantly that she released him into the night.

The streets were alive with howling, yelling gangs. Some were scholars and some were townspeople, but all were armed with whatever they had been able to lay their hands on: a few carried swords and daggers, a handful had poorly strung bows, while others still wielded staves, tools, and even gardening equipment. Bartholomew, his own small knife to hand, slipped down the noisy streets hoping that his scholar's tabard would not target him for an attack by townspeople. There was little point in removing the tabard, for that would only expose him to an assault from scholars.

Here and there fires crackled, although none were as fierce or uncontrolled as the one that had destroyed Master Burney's workshop. In places, window shutters were smashed, and from one or two houses, shouts of terror or outrage drifted, suggesting that looting had begun in earnest. Bartholomew ignored it all as he sped towards Michaelhouse. He could do very little to help, and would only get himself into trouble if he interfered.

He felt someone grab his arm as he ran, pulling him off balance so that he fell on one knee. He brought his knife up sharply, anticipating another fight, but then dropped it as he recognised Cynric ap Huwydd, his Welsh bookbearer. Cynric was fleet of foot and possessed of an uncanny ability to move almost unseen in the night shadows; Bartholomew supposed he should not have been surprised that the Welshman had tracked him down in the chaos.

Cynric tugged Bartholomew off the road, and into the shadows of the trees in All Saints' churchyard.

'Where have you been, boy?' Cynric whispered. 'I have been looking for you since all this fighting started. I was worried.'

'With Mistress Tyler's family at Jonas the Poisoner's house. Is Michaelhouse secure? Are all our students in?' asked

Bartholomew, peering through the darkness at the man who, although officially his servant, would always be a friend.

Cynric nodded, looking through the trees to where a large group of students was systematically destroying a brewer's cart with stout cudgels. The brewer was nowhere to be seen, and his barrels of ale had long since been spirited away. 'All Michaelhouse students are being kept in by the Fellows – some by brute force, since they are desperate to get out and join in the looting. Only two are missing as far as I can see: Sam Gray and Rob Deynman.'

'Both my students,' groaned Bartholomew. 'I hope they have had the sense to lie low.' He coughed as the wind blew thick, choking smoke towards them from where a pile of wreckage smouldered. 'As should we. We must get home.'

Cynric began to glide through the shadows, with Bartholomew following more noisily. They had to pass the Market Square to reach Michaelhouse, and the sight that greeted them reminded Bartholomew of the wall paintings at St Michael's depicting scenes from hell. For a few moments he stood motionless, ignoring the rioters who jostled him this way and that. Cynric, ever alert to danger, pulled him to one side, and together they surveyed the familiar place, now distorted by violence.

Fires, large and small, lit the Market Square. Some were under control, surrounded by cavorting rioters who fed the flames with the proceeds of looting forays; others raged wildly, eating up the small wooden stalls from which traders sold their wares in the daytime. The brightly coloured canvasses that covered the wooden frames of the stalls, flapped in the flames, shedding sparks everywhere, and causing the fires to spread. Bartholomew saw one man, his body enveloped in fire, run soundlessly from behind one stall, before falling and lying still in his veil of flames. Bells of alarm were ringing in several churches, occasionally drowned by the wrenching sound of steel against steel as the Sheriff's men skirmished with armed rioters.

Here and there, people lay on the ground, calling for help, water or priests. Others wandered bewildered, oblivious to the danger they were in from indiscriminate attack. A group of a dozen students sauntered past, singing the Latin chorus that Bartholomew had heard sung outside St Mary's Church the previous day. One or two of them paused when they saw

Bartholomew and Cynric but moved on when they glimpsed the glitter of weapons in their hands.

Bartholomew saw the voluminous folds of Michael's habit swirling black against the firelight. Two of his beadles were close, all three laying about them with staves, as they fought to break up a battle between two groups of scholars – although, in their tabards and in the unreliable light of the fires, Bartholomew wondered how they could tell who was on whose side. He took a secure hold on his knife, and went to help Michael, Cynric following closely behind him.

He was forced to stop as one of the stalls in front of him suddenly collapsed in a shower of sparks and cinders, spraying the ground with dancing orange lights. By the time he was able to negotiate the burning rubble, he had lost sight of Michael. Then something thrown by a passing apprentice hit him on the head, and he sprawled forward on to his hands and knees, dazed. He heard Cynric give a blood-curdling yell, which was followed by the sound of clashing steel. With a groan another stall began to collapse, and Cynric's attackers were forced to back off or risk it falling on them. Once away, they obviously thought better of dealing with Cynric, a man more experienced with arms than any of them, and went in search of easier prey. Bartholomew crawled away from the teetering stall, reaching safety moments before the whole thing crashed to the ground in a billow of smoke that stung his eyes and hurt the back of his throat. Cynric joined him, his short sword still drawn, alert for another attack.

'The whole town has gone mad!' said Cynric, looking about him in disgust. 'Come away, boy. This is no place for us.'

Bartholomew struggled to his feet, and prepared to follow Cynric. Nearby, another wooden building, this one used to store spare posts and canvas, began to fall, the screech of wrenching wood almost drowned in the roar of flames. With a shock that felt as though the blood were draining from his veins, Bartholomew glimpsed Michael standing directly in its path as it began to tilt. He found his shouted warning would not pass his frozen lips, and was too late anyway. He saw Michael throw his arms over his head in a hopeless attempt to protect himself, and the entire structure crashed down on top of him.

Bartholomew's knife had slipped from his nerveless fingers before Cynric's gasp of horror brought him to his senses.

Ripping off his tabard to wrap around his hands, he raced towards the burning building. Oblivious to the heat, he began to pull and heave at the timber that covered Michael's body. Three scholars, on their way from one skirmish to another, tried to pick a fight with him, but when he whirled round to face them wielding a burning plank they melted away into the night.

Bartholomew's breath came in ragged gasps, and he was painfully aware that his tabard provided inadequate protection for his hands against the hot timbers. Next to him, Cynric wordlessly helped to haul the burned wood away. Bartholomew stopped when part of a charred habit appeared under one of the beams, and then redoubled his efforts to expose the monk's legs and body. But Michael's head was crushed under the main roof support; even with Cynric helping Bartholomew could not move it.

Bartholomew sank down on to the ground, put his face in his hands and closed his eyes tightly. He listened to the sounds of the riot around him, feeling oddly detached as he tried to come to terms with the fact that Michael was dead. Bells still clanged out their unnecessary warnings, people yelled and shouted, while next to him the pop and crackle of burning wood sent a heavy, singed smell into the night air.

'This is not a wise place to sit,' called a voice from behind him.

Bartholomew spun round, jaw dropping in disbelief, as Michael picked his way carefully through the ashes.

Cynric laughed in genuine pleasure, then took the liberty of slapping the fat monk on the shoulders.

'Oh, lad!' he said. 'We have just been digging out your corpse from under the burning wood.'

Michael looked from the body that they had exposed to Bartholomew's shocked face. Bartholomew found he could only gaze at the Benedictine, who loomed larger than life above him. Michael poked at the body under the blackened timbers with his foot.

'Oh, Matt!' he said in affectionate reproval. 'This is a friar, not a monk! Can you not tell the difference? And look at his ankles! I do not know whether to be flattered or offended that you imagine such gracile joints could bear my weight!'

Bartholomew saw that Michael was right. In the unsteady light from the flames, it had been difficult to see clearly, and the loose habits worn by monks and friars tended to make them look alike. Bartholomew had assumed that, because he had seen Michael in the same spot a few seconds before, it had been Michael who had been crushed by the collapsing building.

He continued to stare at the body, his thoughts a confused jumble of horror at the friar's death and disbelief that Michael had somehow escaped. He felt Michael and Cynric hauling him to his feet, and grabbed a handful of Michael's habit to steady himself.

'We thought you were gone,' he said.

'So I gather,' said Michael patiently. 'But this is neither the place nor the time to discuss it.'

When Bartholomew awoke in his room the next day, he was surprised to find he was wearing filthy clothes. As he raised himself on one elbow, an unfamiliar stiffness and a stabbing pain in his head brought memories flooding back of the previous night.

'Michael?' he whispered, not trusting which of the memories might be real and the others merely wishful thinking.

'Here,' came the familiar rich baritone of the fat monk from the table by the window.

Bartholomew sank back on to his bed in relief. 'Thank God!' he said feelingly. He opened his eyes suddenly. 'What are you doing here? What happened last night?'

'Rest easy,' said Michael, leaning back on the chair, and closing the book he had been reading. When Bartholomew saw the chair legs bow dangerously under the monk's immense weight, he knew he could not be dreaming. He eased himself up, and swung his legs over the side of the bed. There was a bump on the back of his head, and his hands were sore, but he was basically intact. He pulled distastefully at his shirt, stained and singed in places, and smelling powerfully of smoke.

'I thought it best to let you sleep,' said Michael. 'We virtually carried you home, Cynric and I. You should lose some weight, Doctor. You are heavy.'

'The rioting?'

Michael rubbed his face, and for the first time Bartholomew noticed how tired he looked.

'There was little we could do to stop it,' said Michael. 'As soon as we broke up one skirmish, the brawlers would move

on to another. We have some of the worst offenders in the
Proctors' cells, and the Sheriff informs me that his own prison
is overflowing, too. We even have three scholars locked up in
the storerooms at Michaelhouse. But even with at least twenty
students – and masters too, I am sorry to say – under arrest
and at least twice as many townspeople, I feel that we still
do not have the real culprits. There is something more to
all this than mere student unrest. I am certain it was started
deliberately.'

'Deliberately?' asked Bartholomew in surprise. 'But why?'

Michael shrugged wearily. 'Who knows, Matt?'

Bartholomew stood carefully, took off his dirty shirt, and
began to wash in the water Cynric left each night.

'Were many killed or injured?'

Michael shrugged. 'I do not know yet. Once I realised how
little we were doing to bring a halt to the madness, I decided
to seek sanctuary in Michaelhouse until it was over. I suspect
my beadles did the same, and there was scarcely a soldier to
be seen on the way home. When you are ready, I will go out
with you to see.' He nodded towards the gates, firmly barred
against possible attack. 'It has been quiet since first light, and I
expect all the fighting is over for now. Your skills will doubtless
be needed.'

Bartholomew finished washing in silence, thinking over the
events of the night before, blurred and confused in his mind.
From beginning to end, for him at least, it had probably not
taken more than two hours – three at the most. He hoped he
would never see the town in such turmoil again. He found
clean clothes, and shared a seedcake – given to him by a
patient in lieu of payment – with Michael, washed down with
some sour wine he found in the small chamber he used to
store his medicines.

Michael grimaced as he tasted the wine and added more
water. 'How long have you had this?' he grumbled. 'You might
do a little better for those of us you consider to be your friends.
Did you buy this, or did you find it when you moved here eight
years ago?'

Bartholomew, noting the bottle's dusty sides, wondered if
Michael's question was not as unreasonable as it sounded. He
glanced out of the window. The sun was not yet up, although
it was light. The College was silent, which was unusual because
the scholars usually went to church at dawn. Michael explained

that most of them had only just gone to bed – the students had milled around in the yard, fearful that the College would come under attack, and the Fellows had been obliged to stay up with them to ensure none tried to get out. The Master, prudently, had ordered that no one should leave the College until he decided it was safe to do so.

'You might not believe this,' Michael began, breaking off a generous piece of the dry, grainy seedcake for himself, 'but I heard some scholars accusing townspeople of murdering James Kenzie.'

'What?' said Bartholomew in disbelief. 'How can they think that? Our main suspects at the moment are the scholars of Godwinsson!'

'Quite so,' said Michael, chewing on the seedcake. 'But a rumour was put about that he had been killed by townsfolk. As far as I can tell, that seems to have been why the riot started in the first place. Meanwhile, the townspeople are claiming that the death of Kenzie was revenge for the murder – by scholars – of the child we found in the Ditch.'

'But that child has been dead for years!' cried Bartholomew. 'And there is nothing to say it was killed by a scholar.'

'Indeed,' said Michael. 'But someone has used the child's death, and Kenzie's, for his own purposes. There is something sinister afoot, Matt – something far more dangerous than restless students.'

'But what?' asked Bartholomew, appalled. 'Who could benefit from a riot? Trade will be disrupted and if much damage has been done, the King will grant the burgesses permission to levy some kind of tax to pay for repairs. No one will gain from this.'

'Well, someone will,' said Michael sombrely. 'Why else would he – or they – go to all this effort?'

Each sat engrossed in his own thoughts, until Bartholomew rose to leave.

'Are you sure you are up to going out and throwing yourself on the mercy of the town's injured?' Michael said in sudden concern. 'There are sure to be dozens of them and you are the town's most popular physician.'

Bartholomew waved a deprecatory hand. 'Nonsense. There is only Father Philius from Gonville Hall, Master Lynton of Peterhouse, the surgeon Robin of Grantchester, or me from which to choose. Philius's and Lynton's services are expensive, while Robin has a mortality rate that his patients find alarming. It does not leave most people with a huge choice.'

Michael laughed. 'You are too modest, my friend.' He grew serious again. 'Are you certain you feel well? You were all but witless last night.'

Bartholomew smiled. 'It was probably the shock of seeing you rise from the dead,' he said. His smile faded. 'It was not one of my more pleasant experiences. I lost my knife and tabard,' he added illogically.

'Cynric has your knife,' said Michael. 'It is not a good idea to leave an identifiable weapon at the scene of multiple murders you know. The Sheriff might find it and feel obliged to string you up as an example, despite the fact that he seems to consider himself your friend. We brought your tabard back but it was so damaged we had to throw it away. So get yourself another weapon, don your spare tabard, and let us be off.'

Bartholomew followed Michael across the yard of Michael-house, breathing deeply of the early morning air as he always did. Today, the usually clean, fresh wind that blew in from the Fens was tinged with the smell of burning.

Surprisingly, given the violence of the night's rioting, only eight people had been killed. The bodies had been taken to the Castle and Bartholomew promised the harassed Sheriff that he would inspect them later in the day to determine the cause of death for the official records. But there were many injured, and Bartholomew spent most of the day binding wounds, and applying poultices and salves. Some people were too badly hurt to be brought to him, and so Bartholomew traipsed from house to house, tending them in their homes. He was just emerging from the home of a potter who had been crushed by a cart, when he met Eleanor Tyler. Shyly, she handed him a neat package that rattled.

'Salves,' she explained. 'I thought you might need extra supplies today, given the number of people I hear have been injured. I packed them up myself in Uncle Jonas's shop.'

'Thank you,' said Bartholomew, touched by her thoughtfulness. 'That was kind, and I have been running low.'

She glanced at the potter's house with its sealed shutters. 'Will he live?'

Bartholomew shook his head. 'Father William should be here soon to give him last rites.'

She took his arm and led him away. 'I am sure you have done all you can for him but now you should look to your own needs. You look pale and tired and you should rest while you eat something. My mother has made some broth and we would be honoured if you would come to share it with us.'

'That would be impossible,' he said somewhat ungraciously, as he tried to extricate his arm. 'I have another six patients to visit, and I cannot just abandon them.'

'No one is asking you to abandon them,' she said, taking a firmer grip on his sleeve. 'I am simply advising you that if you want to do your best for them, you should rest. Uncle Jonas says it is dangerous to dispense medicines unless you are fully alert, and you cannot be fully alert if you have been working since dawn.'

'Eleanor, please,' he objected, as she pulled him towards the High Street. 'I am used to working long hours and none of the medicines I will dispense are particularly potent.' In fact, most of his work had involved stitching wounds and removing foreign bodies, work usually considered beneath physicians and more in the realm of surgeons.

They were almost at Eleanor's home, still marked with streaks of soot from the fire of the previous night. Mistress Tyler and her other two daughters were scrubbing at the walls with long-handled brooms, but abandoned their work when they saw Bartholomew. Before he could object further, he was ushered through a small gate to an attractive garden at the rear of the house. While the two older daughters pressed him with detailed questions about the town's injured, Mistress Tyler and the youngest child fetched ale and bread.

'I heard that Michaelhouse's laundress – Agatha – drove away a group of rioters from the King's Head virtually single-handed,' said Hedwise with a smile. Hedwise, like her older sister, had rich tresses of dark hair and candid grey eyes. She was slightly taller than Eleanor and had scarcely taken her eyes off Bartholomew since he had arrived.

'What was Agatha doing at the King's Head?' asked Bartholomew. 'She lives at Michaelhouse.'

'The King's Head is her favourite tavern,' said Eleanor, surprised. 'Did you not know? She can often be found there of an evening, especially when darkness comes early and there is nothing for her to do in the College. She says if Michaelhouse will not buy her any candles so that she can see to sew, then she will take her talents elsewhere.'

'Agatha?' asked Bartholomew, bemused. 'I had always assumed she went to bed after dark. I did not know she frequented taverns.'

'You see how these scholars fill their heads with books to the exclusion of all else?' asked Eleanor of Hedwise. 'Doctor Bartholomew probably has no idea about how Agatha earns herself free ale in the King's Head!'

'And I do not wish to,' he said hastily, embarrassed. The notion of the large and formidable woman, who ruled the College servants with a will of steel, dispensing favours to the rough male patrons of the King's Head was not an image he found attractive.

Eleanor and Hedwise exchanged a look of puzzlement before Hedwise gave a shriek of shocked laughter and punched him playfully on the arm. 'Oh, Doctor! You misunderstand! Agatha mends torn clothes for free ale. She is very good.'

'I see,' said Bartholomew, not sure what else he could say after what, in retrospect, indicated that he had a low opinion of the moral character of Michaelhouse's most powerful servant. He hoped the Tyler women were discreet, for Agatha was not a woman to suffer insults without retaliating in kind.

Eleanor dispatched her sister to help Mistress Tyler with the broth. Hedwise left Bartholomew and Eleanor alone with some reluctance, glancing backwards resentfully as she left. As soon as she was out of sight, Eleanor rested her hand on his knee.

'I hear Michaelhouse is due to celebrate its foundation next week,' she said.

'Yes, next Tuesday,' he said, grateful for the change in conversation. 'It is the most important day in the College calendar, and is the only time that its Fellows are allowed to bring ladies into the hall. We are each allowed two guests.'

'I know,' said Eleanor, smiling meaningfully, still gripping his knee.

Bartholomew looked at her, not certain what he was expected to say. He continued nervously. 'Our founder, Hervey de Stanton, provided a special endowment for the occasion, so that there will always be money to celebrate it. The Founder's Feast and the Festival of St Michael and All Angels the following Sunday – St Michael is the patron saint of Michaelhouse – come close together.'

'So, who have you invited to this feast?' asked Eleanor, raising her eyebrows.

'I had been planning to ask my sister and her husband, but I left it too late and they accepted an invitation from one of the commoners instead. So, I have invited no one.' It would have been pleasant, he thought ruefully, to have taken Philippa. The mere thought of her long, golden hair and vivacious blue eyes sent a pang of bitter regret slicing through him. He looked away.

'I am free on Tuesday,' said Eleanor casually. 'And I have never been to a Founder's Feast before.'

'Would you like to come?' asked Bartholomew doubtfully, wondering why a lively and attractive woman like Eleanor should want to sit through a long, formal dinner, with lengthy Latin speeches that she would not be able to understand, attended by lots of crusty old men whose aim was to eat enough to make themselves ill the following day and drink sufficient wine to drown a horse.

'Yes, I would,' she said happily, her face splitting into a wide grin. 'I would be delighted!'

'Good,' said Bartholomew, hoping she would not be bored. 'It begins at noon.'

Mistress Tyler arrived with the broth, and Eleanor's hand was withdrawn from his knee. Bartholomew ate quickly, concerned that he had already been away too long from his patients. It was excellent broth, however, rich and spicy and liberally endowed with chunks of meat that were edible. The bread was soft and white and quite different from the jaw-cracking fare made from the cheapest available flour that emerged from the Michaelhouse kitchens. Perhaps Michael had been right in the tavern the previous night, and Bartholomew did need to venture out of College more and sample what the world had to offer. Including the company of women, he decided suddenly.

As he took his leave, one of Jonas the Poisoner's children came to say that his father was inundated with requests for medicines after the riot, and that he needed Eleanor's help.

'You have some knowledge of herbs?' asked Bartholomew, impressed.

'She sweeps up,' said Hedwise with disdain.

'I do not!' Eleanor retorted, glowering at her sister. 'I have a good memory, and Uncle Jonas says I am indispensable to him in his work.'

'Then you had better go to him,' said Hedwise archly. 'I shall accompany Doctor Bartholomew to see his next patient.'

'There is no need for that,' said Bartholomew, not liking the way Eleanor's look had turned to something blacker.

Hedwise took his arm. 'Shall we be off, then? I shall return later,' she called to her family as she opened the garden gate and bundled him out.

'Do not be too long,' Eleanor shouted after her. 'You still have the pig to muck out, and I have that potion for the rash on your legs that you asked me to fetch from Uncle Jonas. You should apply it as soon as possible before it becomes worse.'

Hedwise laughed lightly and, Bartholomew thought, artificially, as she closed the gate behind her. 'Eleanor likes to jest, although mother is always berating her for being overly vulgar. But I have watched Uncle Jonas very carefully in his shop, and if I can be of service to you this afternoon, I shall be happy to oblige.'

'What about the pig?' asked Bartholomew, desperately trying to think of a way to reject her offer without hurting her feelings. It was not that he did not want her company, but some of the sights he had seen that morning had been horrific and he had no wish to inflict them on young Hedwise Tyler.

'The pig will manage without me for an hour or two,' said Hedwise, 'and I am sure I can do more good by assisting you than by dealing with that filthy animal.'

'Perhaps another time, Hedwise,' said Bartholomew gently, 'although I do appreciate your offer and the fact that you are prepared to subject yourself to some unpleasant experiences in order to help me.'

She looked away and, to his horror, he saw that her eyes brimmed with tears. At a loss, he offered her a strip of clean linen from his bag with which to wipe her eyes.

'I so seldom leave the house,' she said in a muffled voice. 'Eleanor, being the eldest, is always the first to go on errands and the like, while I have to stay at home with the pig.'

Bartholomew's discomfort increased, so, uncertain what to say, he said nothing. She gave a loud sniff.

'I never go anywhere,' she continued miserably. 'I have not even been to the Festival of St Michael and All Angels at St Michael's Church.'

'Oh, I could take you to that,' he said, relieved he could at least suggest something positive. 'It is the Sunday after next, although I cannot see that you would enjoy it – Michael's choir is going to sing, you see, and they are not what they were before the plague. Afterwards, Michaelhouse provides stale oatcakes and sour wine in the College courtyard. If it rains, we just get wet because the Franciscans outvote everyone else that the meal – if you can call it that – should be held in the hall. The Franciscans do not approve of townspeople in the hall except at the annual Founder's Feast.'

He realised he had not made the offer sound a particularly appealing one, and sought for something to say in the Festival's favour. Hedwise did not give him the chance.

'How wonderful!' she exclaimed, tears forgotten. 'Oh, thank you!'

'You can bring your mother,' he said, recalling that her elder sister had already inveigled an invitation to the Founder's Feast. He did not want Mistress Tyler thinking he was working his way through her entire family. Hedwise, however, had other ideas.

'Oh, no,' she said briskly. 'Mother will not want to sit in a damp church all day. But I will be delighted to accompany you. Just the two of us.'

'And a hundred other people,' he said. 'The church is always full for the Festival. Of course, it might not be so well attended if people hear the choir in advance. But if you have second thoughts about wasting a Sunday, you must tell me. I promise you I will not be offended if you find something better to do.'

'I can think of nothing better to do than to spend a Sunday with you at the Festival,' she announced. She gave him a huge grin and slipped away, dodging deftly out of the path of a man driving an ancient cow to the Market Square. A little belatedly, Bartholomew began to wonder what he had let himself in for.

chapter 4

BARTHOLOMEW'S FEARS FOR HEDWISE'S WELL-BEING WERE unfounded as it happened, and most of the cases he saw the afternoon after the riot comprised minor injuries, rather than serious wounds. He tended a merchant who had gashed his hand on glass when he tried to protect his home from looters, and then set off along Milne Street to where a baker with eyes sore from smoke awaited him. On his way, he was accosted by a shabby figure in dark green, with protuberant blue eyes and a dirty, unshaven look. His hands, Bartholomew could not help but notice, were black with dried blood.

'Good afternoon, Robin,' he said, involuntarily stepping back-wards as the surgeon's rank body odour wafted towards him.

'I hear you have been stitching and cutting,' said Robin of Grantchester in a sibilant whisper, pursing his lips and looking at Bartholomew in disapproval. 'Chopping and sewing.'

'Yes,' said Bartholomew shortly, walking on. He did not have the time to engage in a lengthy discussion with the surgeon about the techniques he used, despite the fact that Bartholomew thought the man could use all the help he could get: Robin of Grantchester was not noted for his medical successes. The surgeon scurried after him.

'Surgery is for surgeons,' hissed Robin, sniffing wetly. 'Physicking and reading the stars is for physicians. You are taking the bread from my mouth.'

Bartholomew heartily wished that were true, and that Robin would pack up his unsanitary selection of implements and look for greener pastures in another town. The more Bartholomew observed the surgeon in action, the more he was convinced that his grimy hands did far more harm than good, and shuddered to think of anyone being forced to pay him for any dubious services he might render. The fact that Robin always demanded payment in advance because of his high mortality rate did little to endear him to Bartholomew.

'My job is slitting and slicing,' said Robin venomously.

'Hacking and slashing, more like,' muttered Bartholomew, wondering whether the man had been drinking. His eyes were red-rimmed and he seemed unsteady on his feet.

'You are not a surgeon. You have no right,' persisted Robin. 'I do not profess to read the stars or inspect urine. Keep to your profession, Bartholomew, and I will keep to mine. I shall complain to the master of Michaelhouse if you continue to poach my trade.'

'Complain then,' said Bartholomew carelessly, knowing that Master Kenyngham would do nothing about it. 'I am duty bound to do whatever it takes to ensure the complete recovery of my patients. If that involves a degree of surgery, then so be it.'

'You can call me to do it,' said Robin, wiping his runny nose with a bloodstained finger. 'The other physicians do so, and I insist you do not poach my work.'

'All right,' said Bartholomew, stopping outside the sore-eyed baker's house. 'I promise you I will ask any patient I operate on whether they would rather have you or me. Will that suffice?'

Robin saw it would have to, and slunk away down a dark alley, his canvas sack of saws and knives clanking ominously as he went. Before Bartholomew could knock at the baker's door, he was hailed a second time, and turned to see Adam Radbeche, the Principal of David's Hostel and the man responsible for Father Andrew and his unruly Scottish students.

Radbeche was a distinctive-looking man, with a shock of carrot-coloured hair that reminded Bartholomew of a scarecrow. The Scot was a well-known figure in the University, famous for his brilliant interpretations of the works of Aristotle, and Bartholomew was pleased that Radbeche's scholarship had been rewarded by an appointment to Principal – even if it were only to the small, anonymous David's Hostel. Students and masters from the same part of the world tended to gather together, so it was not unusual that Radbeche had attracted fellow Scots to his establishment.

The philosopher's hand was bandaged; he explained that he had been burned while assisting a neighbour to extinguish a fire. The students had also helped to bring the fire under control, but, Radbeche said, at least three times he had counted them all back in again, so Bartholomew was inclined to believe that the Scots had played no part in the rioting. He led Radbeche across the road to sit on the low wall surrounding the little church of St John Zachary – decommissioned since the plague had taken most of its parishioners, and now with weeds growing out of its windows and its roof sagging dangerously.

While Bartholomew inspected and re-dressed the burned hand, Radbeche informed him that the ailing student Bartholomew had treated the day before at David's was recovering well. When Bartholomew waved away the offer of payment, impatient to attend the baker who had emerged from his house and was blinking at him anxiously, Radbeche suggested instead that he might like to borrow a medical book by the great Greek physician Galen. Bartholomew was surprised.

'Galen? But you have no medical students.'

Radbeche smiled. 'It was a gift from a man who could not read and who purchased the first book that matched the price he was willing to pay. It is the only book we own, actually. We borrow what we need from King's Hall or the Franciscan Friary.'

'Which book by Galen do you have?' asked Bartholomew with keen interest.

Radbeche seemed taken aback. '*Prognostica*, I believe.' He saw Bartholomew's doubtful look at his ignorance, and shrugged. 'I am a philosopher, Doctor. I have no interest in medical texts – even if they are all we have!'

Despite the fact that the University was a place of learning, and students were obliged to know certain texts if they wanted to pass their examinations, books were rare and expensive, and each one was jealously guarded. Michaelhouse only possessed three medical books and Bartholomew was delighted by Radbeche's generous offer. He gave the Principal a grateful grin and made his farewells so that he could attend to the agitated baker.

Later, as he was returning to Michaelhouse for more bandages, Bartholomew saw the untruthful Brother Edred limping up the High Street. Moments after, his colleague Brother Werbergh slunk past sporting a bruised eye, looking very sorry for himself.

Justice in Cambridge was swift and brutal, and, before evening, four men alleged to have been ringleaders in the rioting were hanged on the Castle walls as a grim warning to others who might consider breaking the King's peace. Other rioters were released when heavy fines had been paid, with warnings that next time, they too would be kicking empty air on the Castle walls. Whether the hanged men really were the ringleaders of the riot was a matter for conjecture. While Bartholomew imagined they might have been in the thick of the fighting – perhaps even urging others to do damage and harm – the evidence that they were the real instigators was, at best, dubious.

As the shadows began to lengthen, and the heat of the day was eased by a cooling breeze, Bartholomew finished his work. Sam Gray and Rob Deynman, the two students who had been missing from Michaelhouse the night before, had helped him with the last few visits. Deynman had shown an aptitude for bandaging that Bartholomew never realised he had; this offered some glimmer of hope that his least-able student might yet make some kind of physician.

'Where were you two last night?' asked Bartholomew as they walked home together.

The students exchanged furtive glances and Bartholomew, tired and hot, felt his patience evaporating. His students sensed it too and Gray hastened to answer.

'We were at Maud's Hostel. I know we are not supposed to frequent other hostels,' he added quickly, seeing Bartholomew's expression of weary disapproval. 'But Rob's younger brother is there, as you know.' He cast Bartholomew a sidelong glance. Bartholomew, struggling to teach Rob Deynman – not the most gifted of students – had seen within moments that the younger brother made Rob appear a veritable genius and had refused to teach him at Michaelhouse. The younger Deynman, therefore, had secured himself a place at Maud's, an exclusive establishment with a reputation for rich, but slow, students.

'It was my brother Jack's birthday,' said Deynman cheerfully, 'and we were invited to celebrate at Maud's. By the time the wine ran out and we were ready to leave, the riot had started. The Maud's Principal advised us to stay.'

'Very wise,' said Bartholomew, wondering whether the idea to stay was truly the Principal's, or, more likely, Gray's. Gray, with his loaded dice and silver tongue, would profit greatly from an evening among the wealthy, but gullible, students at Maud's. Deynman, slow-witted and naïve, was often an innocent foil to

Gray's untiring and invariably imaginative ploys to make money by deception. Still, Bartholomew was grateful that they had had the sense not to stray out on to the streets when the town was inflamed – whatever their motive. He was fond of Gray and Deynman, and had been relieved when they had reported to him unharmed earlier that day.

'Just the man I wanted to see,' came a soft voice from behind him, and Bartholomew felt his spirits sink. Guy Heppel, the Junior Proctor, sidled closer, smiling enthusiastically from under a thick woollen cap. He held out a hefty pile of scrolls to Bartholomew. 'I have all the information you will need to conduct a complete astrological consultation on me. Would now be a convenient moment?'

'No,' said Gray, before Bartholomew could think of a plausible excuse. 'There is a new moon tonight, you see, and Doctor Bartholomew, being born under the influence of Venus, is never at his best when the moon is new. You would be better off trying him next week.'

Heppel nodded in complete and sympathetic understanding. 'Then I shall do so,' he said, rubbing his free hand up and down the sides of his gown in the curious manner Bartholomew had noticed earlier. 'It is just as well you are indisposed, I suppose. The Chancellor has ordered me to march around the town with the beadles to warn scholars that anyone caught out after the curfew will spend the night in our cells. So, it is all for the best that you cannot entice me from my duties to spend the time with you on my consultation. When I finish announcing the curfew, I intend to go home to King's Hall and spend the evening by the fire.'

'Fire? In this weather?' asked Bartholomew before he could stop himself.

Heppel looked pained. 'For my chest,' he explained. 'You understand. And I find a fire so much better for reading after dark. Much better than a candle, don't you think?'

Since candles were expensive and firewood more so, Bartholomew had seldom had the opportunity to find out.

'I heard your brother-in-law's premises were attacked last night,' Heppel added as he rolled up his sheaf of parchments. 'I hope no damage was done.'

Bartholomew had not given his family a single thought that day, assuming that if any of Oswald Stanmore's household had been harmed they would have summoned him. He decided he should pay them a visit, reluctantly banishing from his mind the attractive alternative of a wash in clean water and a quiet supper in the orchard. He rubbed his hand through his hair wearily, nodding to Heppel as he took his leave.

'Thank you for getting me out of that, Sam,' he said when the Junior Proctor had gone. 'The last thing I feel like doing now is thinking about astrology. Did you make it all up?'

'Of course I did,' said Gray, surprised by the question. 'I certainly did not learn it from you, did I, bearing in mind your antipathy to the subject?'

'I have taught you some astrology,' said Bartholomew indignantly, 'including how to do consultations of the kind Heppel has in mind. In fact, you can do his next week and I shall listen to see how much you have remembered.'

Gray sighed theatrically. 'Never do a master a favour, Rob,' he instructed Deynman. 'It is seldom appreciated and often dangerous.'

'I will do Master Heppel's consultation,' offered Deynman enthusiastically. 'I recall everything you said about Venus and Mars.'

Bartholomew seriously doubted it, and had reservations about letting Deynman loose on anyone, even for something as non-invasive as a consultation about astrology. He might well inform Heppel that he only had a few days to live, or that a strong dose of arsenic would increase his chances of living to be a hundred years old. While Deynman's outrageous interpretations of planetary movements provided Bartholomew with an endless supply of amusing anecdotes with which to horrify Michael, it would scarcely be appropriate to inflict him on real patients.

Tiredly, Bartholomew sent his students back to Michaelhouse with orders not to go out again and went to find his brother-in-law. Soldiers were very much in evidence on the streets, sweating under their chain-mail, and armed to the teeth. Heppel and his group of beadles were marching around the town proclaiming that all scholars must be in their hostels or colleges by seven o'clock, and that any who were not would be summarily arrested. The Sheriff's men were issuing similar warnings to the townspeople.

It seemed to be working: the streets were emptier than usual. People had laboured all day in the sweltering sun to restore order to the town and, with luck, would be too exhausted for rioting that night. Burned wreckage had been moved into a large pile and other rubbish swept away. Bartholomew saw some of it being carted off in the direction of the King's Ditch, and wondered if, after all the dredging efforts by both town and University, the Ditch was to be blocked again so soon. He also wondered at the wisdom of collecting all the partly burned wood into a large pile in the Market Square: even to the most naïve of eyes, it looked like a bonfire waiting to be lit.

Stanmore's business premises were protected by a high wall and sturdy gates. No harm had come to them that Bartholomew could detect, although the house next door had been attacked and looted. Stanmore employed a small number of mercenaries to protect his ever-increasing trade and it would be a foolish man who would risk targeting his property. Bartholomew, with an ease born of familiarity, walked across the yard and ran lightly up the wooden stairs to the fine solar on the upper floor. Bartholomew had always liked the room Stanmore used as an office. A colourful assortment of rugs were scattered across the floor and it always smelled of parchment, ink and dyed cloth.

Stanmore sat at a table near the window, dictating a letter to his secretary. The merchant dismissed the clerk as Bartholomew poked his head round the door, then greeted his brother-in-law warmly. He sent for wine, and gestured that Bartholomew should sit on one of the cushioned window seats where he would be fanned by the breeze.

'Guy Heppel told me your premises had been attacked,' said Bartholomew, sipping at some fine red wine. He glanced down at it, noting how clear it was and the richness of its colour. He decided Michael was wrong after all – if Bartholomew acquired a taste for good wine, clear ale and edible food, he would starve to death at Michaelhouse.

'Guy Heppel was mistaken,' said Stanmore, sitting opposite him and offering him an apple from a large dish. 'I had my men posted on the walls with arrows at the ready; the rioters prudently went elsewhere – next door among other places.'

'Do you have any ideas about why the town is in such turmoil?' asked Bartholomew. Stanmore's wide network of informants meant that he was often party to information inaccessible to University men and it was always worth asking what he had heard.

Stanmore shook his head slowly. 'Ostensibly, the riots were

about the death of that student and the skeleton in the Ditch,' he said, 'but I cannot believe they were the only reasons. The whole town has been growing increasingly uneasy during the past two weeks or so. A student was killed by an apprentice last month in a street fight and his death did not provoke such a violent reaction.'

'Michael was thinking along the same lines this morning,' said Bartholomew. 'However, neither of us can imagine why anyone should want to instigate such chaos.' He rubbed a hand through his hair, staring down at the wine in his cup. 'Damage was done to both town and University property and there were arrests on both sides. It is difficult to see what anyone might have gained – scholar or townsperson. Do you have any ideas yourself?'

Stanmore blew out his cheeks. 'None that I can prove,' he replied. 'But Master Deschalers's house next door was systematically sacked last night – not looted on the spur of the moment, but carefully burgled and only items of the greatest value taken. Oh, things were broken and thrown around to make it look as if it had been sacked, of course. But the reality was that nothing was stolen except that which was most valuable and easily spirited away.'

'You think someone caused a riot to burgle Deschalers's house?' asked Bartholomew, startled.

Stanmore made an impatient sound. 'Of course not, Matt! But it would not surprise me if you discovered Deschalers's was not the only house looted last night. If several such burglaries took place, then someone might have benefited considerably.'

Bartholomew regarded him soberly, and finished his wine. 'If the word is spread that the riots were started to allow burglars to operate, then sensible people will hide their valuables. It might deter thieves from sparking off another night of chaos to do it again.' He set the cup down on the window-sill and stood.

'True,' said Stanmore, following Bartholomew down the stairs to see him out. 'And the threat of burglary might be enough to keep people off the streets. Who would be foolish enough to leave their homes, knowing that they were being enticed out deliberately?'

'I doubt it was the wealthy merchants, with houses worth looting, who were out rioting last night,' said Bartholomew, looking backwards at him. 'It was the apprentices and the poor people with little to lose. I do not think burglars would start a riot to steal a few cracked plates and a handful of tallow candles.'

'Times are hard, Matt,' said Stanmore primly. 'Since the Death, there is a shortage of everything – including plates and candles. Such items are valuable these days.'

'If you were poor, would you burgle Deschalers's mansion or Dunstan the Riverman's hovel?' asked Bartholomew. 'If caught, you would be hanged in either case.'

'True enough,' admitted Stanmore. 'Suffice to say I am glad I am not in the Sheriff's shoes today. I would not know where to start investigating all this.'

Bartholomew glanced up at the dusky sky, and swore softly. 'The Sheriff! Damn! I promised him I would go to the Castle and examine the bodies of those who died last night.'

'Better hurry, then,' said Stanmore, ushering him out of the gate. 'The curfew is early tonight, and I would not break it if I were you.'

Bartholomew walked briskly away from Stanmore's house towards the Castle. The land on which Cambridge stood was flat, but at the northern end, there was a small rise on which William the Conqueror had chosen to build a wooden keep in 1068. The small rise became Castle Hill, and the wooden keep had developed into a formidable fortress with a thick curtain wall and several strong, stone towers.

As he walked, Bartholomew saw the streets were virtually deserted, and cursed himself for agreeing to examine the bodies that day. He did not feel safe walking alone along streets that usually thronged with people, nor did he like the fact that the only people he did see were heavily armed.

'Matthew!' came a voice from the shadows. 'You should not be out so late. The curfew bell will sound in a few moments, and you are heading in entirely the wrong direction.'

'Good evening, Matilde,' said Bartholomew, turning with a warm smile to the woman who emerged from the house of one of the town's brewers. 'You should not be out, either.'

As soon as he had spoken, he realised how stupid his words were. Matilde was a prostitute, and the hours of darkness were, presumably, when she conducted much of her business. Known as 'Lady Matilde' because, according to popular rumour, she had once been a lady-in-waiting to a duchess but had been dismissed for entertaining one too many gentlemen in her chambers, she had come to Cambridge to ply her trade in peace. Unlike the other prostitutes, Matilde was well-spoken, and her manners were gentle. Bartholomew had never asked her whether the story were true – not because he thought she might not tell him, but because he liked her aura of mystery and enigma.

Matilde was, to Bartholomew's mind, the most attractive woman in Cambridge. She had long hair that reached her knees in a glossy veil, and a small, impish face that was simultaneously beautiful and mischievous. He found he was staring at her and had not heard a word she had been saying.

'I am going to the Castle,' he said, trying to mask the fact that he had not been paying attention. 'Can I escort you somewhere?'

'I have just told you that I am going home,' said Matilde, laughing at him. 'Have you not been listening to me?'

'Sorry,' said Bartholomew, beginning to walk towards The Jewry – the part of the town that had once been inhabited by a little community of Jews before their expulsion from England some sixty years before – where Matilde lived. It was on his way, and would not be an inconvenience. 'I have had a long day, Matilde, given the number of people who were injured last night.'

She gave him a sympathetic look, and they walked for a while in silence. Bartholomew was aware that he was dirty and dusty, but that she smelled clean and fragrant. Her hair shone, even in the faint light of dusk. Next to her the Tyler sisters paled into insignificance, like distant stars compared to the sun. Not for the first time in their friendship Bartholomew wished that she had chosen a different profession, and that he might ask her to accompany him for walks by the river, or even to the Founder's Feast. He was surprised when she replied, realising with a shock that he must have spoken the invitation aloud.

'I do not think that would be a good idea, Matthew,' she said. 'What would Master Kenyngham say when he saw you had invited a courtesan to dine at his college?'

Master Kenyngham would not know a courtesan if one appeared stark naked at his high table, thought Bartholomew, but his colleague Father William would, and then there would be trouble. But Bartholomew was tired, he was missing Philippa more than he thought possible, and he was about to go and inspect corpses in the dark for the Sheriff. He decided he did not care what Father William might say, and since the invitation had apparently been issued, he could hardly withdraw it.

'Please come,' he said. 'It is the only occasion in the year that Michaelhouse provides food fit for eating, and the choir are going to sing some ballads.' He hesitated. 'If you have heard them in church, that might put you off. But apart from the singing and the speeches, the day might be quite pleasant – much more so than the Festival of St Michael and All Angels will be.'

'I heard that you have already invited Eleanor Tyler to the Founder's Feast,' said Matilde. 'Are you sure that my presence will not be awkward for you?'

He gazed at her in astonishment. He had totally forgotten his invitation to Eleanor – not that it mattered, since he was allowed two guests – but it was remarkable that Matilde should know.

'She has been telling anyone who will listen that she is to be the guest of the University's senior physician for Michaelhouse's Founder's Feast,' said Matilde, smiling at his confusion. 'It is quite the talk of the town.'

'It is?' asked Bartholomew, bemused. 'To be honest, I think she more or less invited herself. I suppose she wanted to see the College silver, or hear the music.'

'That is what you think, is it?' asked Matilde, eyes sparkling with merriment. 'Oh, Matthew! You are a good man, but I do not think this University of yours is teaching you very much about life!'

'What do you mean?' asked Bartholomew, slightly offended. 'I have travelled as far as Africa and the frozen lands to the north, and I have seen great cathedrals and castles, and the aftermath of wars, not to mention—'

'That is not what I meant,' said Matilde, still smiling. 'I do not doubt your experience or your learning. You just seem to know very little of women.'

'I know enough,' said Bartholomew, although his recent experience with Philippa made him suspect Matilde was right. 'Some of my patients are women. But will you come? To the Founder's Feast?'

Matilde reached up and touched his cheek. 'Yes, I will. Although if you have second thoughts in the cold light of day, you must tell me. I will not be offended.'

Bartholomew had said as much to Hedwise Tyler after he

had invited her to the Festival of St Michael and All Angels. His head reeled. Had Philippa's rejection of him addled his mind? In the course of a single day, he had issued invitations to three separate women, one of whom was a prostitute, to visit Michaelhouse. While he might be expected to get away with one, three would certainly catch the eye of the fanatical Father William, not to mention the other Fellows. The best Bartholomew could hope for was that his colleagues would have some sort of collective fainting fit, only recovering their wits when the day was over and the women safely off the College premises. His mind still whirling, Bartholomew made his way to the Castle on the hill.

The Castle had the air of being in a state of siege. There was no soldier, inside or out, who was not fully armoured and armed. Archers lined the curtain walls in anticipation of an attack, and the great gates that normally stood open were closed, the wicket door heavily guarded. Bartholomew saw that there was a guard near the portcullis mechanism, ready to release it at a moment's notice. It was no secret in the town that the chains that held the portcullis needed to be replaced – such chains were yet another item impossible to buy since the plague – and it was generally believed that if the portcullis were lowered, the chains would not be strong enough to allow it to be raised again. Sheriff Tulyet, Bartholomew realised, must be anxious indeed if he were considering using it.

Bartholomew was allowed through the barbican, and then into the Castle bailey. Soldiers milled around restlessly, some preparing to leave on patrol, others returning. Every one of the towers that studded the curtain wall seemed to be a focus of frenetic activity. Ancient arms were being dragged out of storage to substitute for those that had been lost or damaged the night before; fletchers and blacksmiths laboured feverishly in the failing light to meet the Sheriff's demands for repairs and replacements.

The bodies Bartholomew had been asked to examine were in one of the outbuildings in the bailey. The building was little more than a shack; inside it was dank, airless and stiflingly hot. Bartholomew felt the sweat begin to prickle on his back after only a few seconds. There were no windows, and the Castle clerk who had been assigned to record Bartholomew's evidence brought a lamp so they would be able to see what they were doing.

'Five bodies were recovered from the burned houses on the High Street,' said the clerk as he sharpened an ancient quill. 'But they were all reclaimed by the Austin Canons from St John's Hospital on the grounds that they were already dead. The Canons use a house on the main street as a mortuary.' He paused in his sharpening, favouring Bartholomew with a look that indicated fervent disapproval.

'They think the smell from the tannery above might negate any ill-effects the odours from the bodies might produce,' said Bartholomew.

'I know what they think,' snapped the clerk. 'They were at great pains to explain it all to me when I complained. My wife's sister lives next door.'

Bartholomew stared at him. 'The building was burned to the ground last night. I hope . . .' He wondered what he could say. The clerk came to his rescue.

'The fire spread the other way, thank the Lord.' He crossed himself automatically, testing the tip of his quill for sharpness at the same time with his other hand. 'But she does not like living next to corpses. It is all very well for the Canons to say there are no ill-effects, but how would they know?'

Bartholomew suspected the clerk had a point, and had argued with the Canons at the time that the stench from the tannery probably masked dangerous odours, rather than neutralised them. But debating the point with the clerk would lead nowhere. He gestured for the man to kindle the lamp and lead him to the bodies that awaited their attention.

For a moment, both men stood together staring down at the neat row of sheeted figures that lay on the beaten-earth floor. Then, anxious to complete his task as soon as possible, Bartholomew knelt next to the first one, and drew back the rough cover. Memories surged forward unbidden as he found himself looking into the face of the French student he had fought, and whom Mistress Tyler had stabbed. He made a pretence at searching for other wounds, glad that the clerk's mind was on his writing, but feeling as if guilt must shine from every pore in his body. He muttered that the cause of death was due to a single stab wound in the back, covered the body, and moved on thankfully to the next one.

If anything, this was a worse encounter, for it was the corpse of the friar he had mistaken for Michael. He found his hands were shaking, and blinked the sweat from his eyes. For a moment he thought he might faint, and had to close his eyes tightly before he could regain control of himself.

'Have you identified this friar?' he asked, partly for information, but mainly because he wanted to hear the clerk's voice in this room of death.

'Brother Accra from Godwinsson,' said the clerk, consulting a list.

Godwinsson again! 'How can you be sure?' Bartholomew snapped, rattled. He continued a little more gently. 'His skull is crushed beyond all recognition.'

'He was identified by a scar on his knee,' said the clerk, apparently oblivious to Bartholomew's outburst. 'Principal Lydgate and a Brother Edred were the witnesses. They both claimed there was no doubt.'

Bartholomew covered the friar's mangled head with its blanket, and braced himself for the next one. It was the potter he had tended that morning. He glanced along the row of bodies and saw that there were nine, and not eight after all.

'This man is dead from crushing injuries caused by a cart,' he told the clerk. 'I saw him alive this morning, but did not think much to his chances.'

The fourth body was so badly burned that Bartholomew could not recognise the features. A sudden picture of old Master Burney came into his head as he remembered the tannery workshop collapsing in the High Street. Other visions flitted through his mind too: the Market Square alive with fire, and someone staggering across it as the flames leapt up his body until he fell. Bartholomew peered more closely at the corpse in the dim light, but there was nothing familiar in the hairless, blackened head. He moved on.

Of the next four, one was a student, and the others townsmen. All had died of knife wounds, great gaping red slashes that had splintered the bone beneath. The last was the body of a woman with long fair hair. Bartholomew was appalled to see that she had been much misused. Her face was battered beyond recognition, and she had been raped. He told the clerk who did not write it down.

'Better to write that she died from a head injury, Doctor. That is what you say killed her?'

Bartholomew frowned at him across the gloomy room. 'The wound to her head was the fatal one,' he said, 'but she has also been raped. What purpose is there in suppressing the truth?'

'The purpose is to prevent grounds for another riot,' said a voice from behind them. Bartholomew turned to see Richard Tulyet, the Sheriff, leaning against the door frame.

Tulyet, small, slight and efficient, gazed in distaste into the outbuilding and waited for Bartholomew to come out. The clerk remained behind to finish making a record of Bartholomew's findings, his pen scratching away in the small circle of light thrown out by the lantern.

'The townspeople might revolt again if we tell them one of their womenfolk was raped before she was murdered,' Tulyet said, closing the door and turning to look across the bailey. He made a sound of impatience as one of his men dropped a sword. The soldiers were nervous, and one of the sergeants strutted round them, yelling in a vain attempt to boost their courage. 'The town will automatically assume that the crime was committed by students, regardless of the truth.'

'I understand that,' said Bartholomew. 'But when her family comes to claim the body they will see for themselves what has happened. You do not need to be a physician to see how she was misused.'

'We have already considered that,' replied Tulyet. 'And so we are not releasing the dead to their families. The University will bury the students; the town will bury the others. In that way, no one will see the bodies, or attempt to instigate another riot to avenge them.'

'And that woman's attackers will go unpunished,' remarked Bartholomew disapprovingly. 'Perhaps they might commit such a crime again when the fancy takes them. Why not? No one bothered to investigate the first time.'

'Would you have me risk another riot and nine dead to avenge a rape?' asked Tulyet coldly.

'Yes I would,' Bartholomew returned forcefully. 'Because if you do not word will get round that any vile crime can be committed, and you will do nothing about it lest it interfere with the King's peace. Then, Master Tulyet, you will have a riot masking crimes that will make last night's business seem tame.'

Tulyet turned from him with a gesture of impatience. 'You scholars think you can mend the world with philosophy,' he said. 'I am a practical man, and I want to prevent another riot – whatever the cost.'

'And if your cost is too high?' demanded Bartholomew. 'What then?'

Tulyet tipped his head back, looking up at the darkening sky. Some of the anger went out of him and he grimaced. 'Perhaps you are right, Matt. But what would you have us do?'

Bartholomew contemplated. 'Make discreet inquiries. Find out who last saw her alive and with whom.' He gripped Tulyet's mailed arm, his expression earnest. 'You should at least try, Dick. Supposing some of the townspeople saw her raped and murdered and are expecting at least some attempt to catch the culprit? The last thing the town needs is a retaliation killing.'

'Is that not what last night was about anyway?' asked Tulyet, leaning against the dark grey stone of the curtain wall, and scrubbing at his fair beard. 'Scholars seeking to avenge the death of James Kenzie and townsfolk the poor child in the Ditch?'

'Oswald Stanmore does not think so,' said Bartholomew. 'And neither does Brother Michael. Both believe the riot to be part of some other plot.'

Tulyet's interest quickened. 'Really? Do they know what?'

Bartholomew shook his head. 'No. But both arrived at the same conclusion independently of each other: that the riot was a means, not an end in itself.'

Tulyet took his arm and guided him to his office in the round keep that loomed over the bailey. He glanced around before closing the door, ensuring that they could talk without being overheard. 'I have been thinking along the same lines myself,' he said, his expression intense. 'I cannot understand why the town should have chosen last night to riot – I do not see Kenzie's death or the discovery of the skeleton as particularly compelling motives to fight. It has been scratching at the back of my mind all day.'

Bartholomew rubbed at his temples. 'When Brother Michael and I found Kenzie murdered, it went through our minds that the students might riot if they believed he had been killed by a townsperson. We went to some trouble to keep our thoughts on the matter to ourselves. But neither of us anticipated that the scale of the rioting would be so great. It was terrifying.'

Tulyet puffed out his cheeks, and gave him a rueful smile.

'*You* were terrified! Imagine what it felt like to be the embodiment of secular law – for scholar and townsperson alike to single out for violence and abuse! These are dangerous times, Matt. Since the plague, outlaws have flourished and it is difficult to recruit soldiers to replace the ones we lost. Violent crime is more difficult to control and the high price of bread has driven even usually law-abiding people to criminal acts. But all this does not answer our basic question: what was the *real* cause of last night's violence?'

'Perhaps the way forward is to investigate the crimes that were perpetrated under its cover: for example the rape of that woman, and the burglary at Deschalers's home,' suggested Bartholomew.

'Those among others!' said Tulyet with resignation. 'I have had reports of three similar lootings – where only what was easily carried and of the highest value was stolen – and there are the nine deaths to consider.'

'Do you think one of those nine is at the heart of all this?' asked Bartholomew.

Tulyet shrugged. 'I think it unlikely. The only one of any standing or influence was the young friar from Godwinsson.'

Bartholomew told him about the visit he and Michael had paid to Godwinsson Hostel and the possible roles of the student friars, Edred and Werbergh, in Kenzie's death.

'Godwinsson,' mused Tulyet. 'Now that I find interesting.'

He went to a wall cupboard and poured two goblets of wine, inviting Bartholomew to sit on one of the hard, functional benches that ran along the walls of his office. Once his guest was settled as comfortably as possible on the uncompromising wood, Tulyet perched on the edge of the table. He swirled the wine around in his goblet, and regarded Bartholomew thoughtfully.

'We should talk more often,' he said. 'Not only are two of the dead from last night students of Godwinsson – a friar and a Frenchman – but this morning, the Principal of Godwinsson told me that his wife is missing.'

'So, Mistress Lydgate has flown the nest,' mused Michael, leaning back in his chair and smiling maliciously. 'Well, I for one cannot blame her, although I would say the same if it were the other way around, and Lydgate had taken to his heels.'

'A most charitable attitude, Brother,' said Bartholomew mildly. 'It is good to see that compassion is not dead and gone in the Benedictine Order.'

Tulyet was sitting on the chest in Bartholomew's room at Michaelhouse sipping some of the sour wine left from breakfast. Because it was dark, and therefore after the early curfew imposed following the riot, Tulyet had escorted Bartholomew back to Michaelhouse. The streets had been silent and deserted, but Bartholomew had been unnerved to detect a very real atmosphere of unease and anticipation. Doors of houses were not fully closed and voices whispered within.

'This is an unpleasant brew,' said Tulyet, looking in distaste at the deep red wine in his goblet. 'I would have expected better from Michaelhouse.'

'Then you must go to the Senior Fellow's chamber,' said Michael. 'He is the man with the taste, and the purse, for fine wines, not a poor Benedictine and an impoverished physician. But tell us about Mistress Lydgate. What happened at Godwinsson last night?'

Tulyet shrugged. 'Master Lydgate was out all night and discovered his wife was missing when he returned this morning.'

'Why was the Principal of a University hostel abroad on such a night?' demanded Michael. 'Why was he not at home, ensuring his students kept out of mischief, and protecting his hostel? And more to the point, why is he bothering you about his missing wife?'

Tulyet shook his head. 'It just slipped out. He came to the Castle this morning to identify a couple of the people killed last night. He was in quite a temper, and ranted on to me for some time about the audacity of his students to get themselves killed when it was so inconvenient for him. When I asked him what he meant he blustered for a while. Eventually he revealed that his wife had left him.'

'And where did he say he was last night, instead of locking up his wife and students?' asked Michael.

'I was told, begrudgingly – for I was assured his whereabouts were none of the Sheriff's concern – that he had been dining at Maud's Hostel and had remained there when he saw how the streets seethed with violence.'

'Maud's?' asked Bartholomew, pricking up his ears. 'Two of my students claimed they stayed at Maud's last night. I can ask them to verify Lydgate's alibi.'

'Can you indeed?' said Tulyet, fixing bright eyes on Bartholomew. 'Master Lydgate will not be pleased to hear that. It is no secret that the Master of Maud's – Thomas Bigod – is not kindly disposed to secular law, and would never confirm or deny an alibi to help me. Bigod recently lost title to a wealthy manor in the secular courts, and is said to have missed out on a fortune because of it. He holds me, as the embodiment of secular law in the area, responsible for his misfortune.'

'He is none too fond of University law, either,' said Michael gleefully. 'Guy Heppel arrested him the other night for being drunk and disorderly. Unfortunately, he ended up being our guest for longer than necessary because Heppel lost the keys to the cells.'

Tulyet roared with laughter and clapped his hands. 'Excellent! I wish I could have seen that! Heppel, for all his physical frailty, knows how to give a man his just deserts. Bigod has been a thorn in my side for months, using every opportunity to thwart the course of law and justice.'

'And I imagine Lydgate is only too aware of Bigod's antipathy to you,' said Bartholomew, 'which is why Lydgate chose him to provide an alibi.' He went to the door and told a passing student to fetch Gray and Deynman.

Tulyet stroked his fair beard thoughtfully. 'All this is most interesting. I told Lydgate to liaise with the University Proctors regarding his dead students' remains. He became abusive and said he did not want you near them because he was not convinced of your competence. I was rather surprised.'

'Well, I am not,' said Michael. 'Master Lydgate and I have had cause to rub shoulders once or twice recently, and the experience was not a pleasant one for either of us. The man is little more than a trained ape in a scholar's gown.'

'What makes you think he is trained?' asked Bartholomew.

'I heard he bought his way through his disputations when he was a student here,' said Tulyet. 'Is that true?'

'I would imagine so,' replied Michael, not in the least surprised by the rumour. 'I doubt he earned his degree by the application of intellect. Perhaps that is another reason why he did not want the Proctors looking too carefully into his affairs. Anyway, we certainly did not part on the most amicable of terms – he probably overheard us discussing the burning of the tithe barn yesterday, and resents his ancient crime being resurrected after so long.'

'What title barn fire?' asked Tulyet curiously. 'No fires have been reported to me.'

'It happened a long time ago,' said Bartholomew, fixing Michael with a reproving look for his indiscretion.

'Not the one at Trumpington twenty-five years ago?' persisted Tulyet, not so easily dissuaded. 'I remember that! It was the talk of the town for weeks! An itinerant musician is said to have started it, but he escaped before he could be brought to justice. My father was Sheriff then. Are you saying that Lydgate was involved? Was it Lydgate who let the culprit go?'

'No, Matt did that,' said Michael, laughing. 'Lydgate's role in the fire was a little more direct.'

'It was all a long time ago,' repeated Bartholomew, reluctant to discuss the matter with the 'embodiment of secular law'. He began to wish he had never broken his silence in the first place, and certainly would not have done had he known that the investigation into Kenzie's death would bring him so close to Lydgate and his Godwinsson students.

'Lydgate was the arsonist!' exclaimed Tulyet, laughing. 'Do not worry, Matt. I will keep this matter to myself, tempting though it would be to mention the affair at a meeting of the town council. But even the prospect of Lydgate mortified is not cause enough to risk another riot. If town and gown will fight over some ancient skeleton, they will certainly come to blows if the Sheriff accuses a University principal of arson!'

'That is true,' said Michael. 'But anyway, you can see why Master Lydgate is not exactly enamoured of the Senior Proctor at the moment. I can understand why he would rather keep me at a distance.'

'I also heard,' said Tulyet, reluctantly forcing his mind back to the present, 'that Mistress Lydgate's chamber was ransacked. A sergeant, who chased a Godwinsson student into the hostel after he was seen looting, told me her room was chaotic.'

'Really?' said Michael. 'I wonder why.'

'Hasty packing, I should think,' said Bartholomew. 'She probably did not know how long she had before her husband returned and gathered everything she could as quickly as possible.'

At that moment, Gray and Deynman knocked and entered, looking at Michael and Tulyet with such expressions of abject guilt that Bartholomew wondered uneasily what misdemeanours they had committed that so plagued their consciences.

'Who was at Maud's with you last night?' he asked.

'Master Bigod will vouch for us both,' began Gray hotly. 'And so will all the other students. I swear to you, we did not leave there, even for the merest instant!'

Bartholomew was amused at Gray's indignation – the student regularly lied or stretched the truth to get what he wanted, and there was an element of outrage in Gray that he was not believed when he was actually being honest. 'There is no reason to doubt you,' he said to mollify him. 'It is not your doings that concern us now, but someone else's. Can you remember who was there?'

Deynman relaxed immediately and began to answer, although Gray remained wary: Deynman's world was one of black and white, while Gray was a natural sceptic.

'All the Maud's students were there,' Deynman began. 'They all like my brother Jack and wanted to celebrate his birthday.'

Bartholomew did not doubt it, especially since the wealthy Deynmans were known to be generous and would have provided fine and plentiful refreshments for Jack's birthday party.

'How many?' asked Bartholomew.

'There are eight students including Jack,' said Deynman, screwing up his face in the unaccustomed labour of serious thought. 'We were all in the hall. Then there were the masters. There was one who does logic, another who teaches rhetoric, and the Principal, Master Bigod, who takes philosophy for advanced students.'

Bartholomew saw Michael smile at the notion that any of the students of Maud's were advanced and imagined that Master Bigod probably had a very light teaching load.

'Were there others?' asked Bartholomew. 'From different hostels or colleges?'

'No,' said Deynman with certainty. 'Jack invited me because I am his brother, and I invited Sam. There were no others.'

'During the time you were there, did anyone else visit? Did any master or student leave to see about the noise from the rioting?'

Deynman shook his head. 'We all ran to the window when we heard that workshop falling, but Master Bigod ordered the shutters closed and the doors barred immediately.' He grimaced. 'I started to object because it was hot in the hall and the open windows provided a cooling breeze. He told me I could leave if I did not like it.'

'But you told me he insisted you stayed once the riot had started,' said Bartholomew, looking hard at Gray. Gray shot his friend a weary look, and Deynman, suddenly realising that he had been caught out in an earlier lie, flushed red and became tongue-tied.

'What were you doing that made leaving so undesirable?' Bartholomew persisted. He eyed the full purse that dangled from Gray's belt. 'Cheating at dice?'

Gray gave Deynman an even harder glare and Bartholomew knew he had hit upon the truth. It was not the first time Gray had conned money from the unsuspecting with his loaded dice.

'We are getting away from the point,' said Tulyet impatiently. 'Did anyone else visit Maud's at any point last night, for however brief a time?'

Gray and Deynman looked at each other. Deynman's brows drew together as he tried to recall, while Gray appeared thoughtful.

'We were merry by dusk,' he said, 'but some time later, there was a knock on the door. I remember because Master Bigod was called out and he missed the end of one of my stories. It was a woman who came. She glanced into the hall, saw us all sitting round the table and withdrew hastily. She spoke for a few moments to Bigod before leaving. I heard the front door open and close again.'

'What was this woman like?' asked Tulyet. It was clearly not Lydgate.

'Small and dumpy with a starched white wimple that made her look unattractive,' said Gray unchivalrously.

'About fifty years old? With expensive, but ill-hanging clothes?' asked Michael, exchanging a glance with Bartholomew.

Gray nodded. 'Exactly! You must know her. That is all I can tell you, I am sorry. There were no other interruptions to our evening after she had gone. And there were no others in the hall with us. Master Bigod stayed up all night. I think he was afraid his students might disobey his orders and go out if he went to bed.'

Bartholomew dismissed them, and Gray cast a furtive glance at Michael before he left. Michael dutifully studied the ceiling in an unspoken message that the illegal dicing would be over-looked this time. Deynman beamed at him before following Gray out.

'So,' said Michael when the door had been closed and the students' footsteps had faded away. 'The visitor was Mistress Lydgate, but Thomas Lydgate was not there.'

'This is all most odd,' said Tulyet, rubbing at the bridge of his nose with a slender forefinger. 'Lydgate claims Bigod as an alibi but does not set foot in Maud's that night. Meanwhile, his wife, who has reached the end of her tether and is running away, does visit Bigod.'

'It will be no good us questioning Bigod,' said Michael, taking a careful sip of his wine. 'He will refuse to answer you, Dick, on the grounds that he does not come under the jurisdiction of secular law. And he certainly will not speak to me after Heppel's escapade with the cell keys. I suppose you could try Lydgate again – tell him you have witnesses prepared to swear he was not at Maud's as he claims, and see what he says.'

Tulyet sighed. 'I could. But I am not inclined to do so. I have more than enough to do without wasting my time on lying scholars. I need to concentrate on preventing another of these disturbances.'

'That should certainly be your first priority,' agreed Michael. 'And mine, too. Good luck to Cecily for fleeing that ignoramus of a husband. They are both better off without each other. But I am more concerned with Kenzie's killer at the moment. It is not pleasant to think of him free and laughing at us while the town is ripped to pieces about our ears by feeble-witted people filled with self-righteous rage.'

Tulyet picked up his goblet but put it down again with a shudder before he drank. He stood, peering out at the night through the open window shutters. 'I must be away,' he said. 'It is vital the patrols are seen tonight if we are to prevent more mischief. It has been most interesting chatting to you both. As I said earlier, the University and the town should talk more often. I am certain my crime rates would drop if we did.'

'Do you have any information at all about the woman who was raped?' asked Bartholomew as he walked with the Sheriff across the yard to the gate.

Tulyet shrugged. 'Very little. She was called Joanna, and she was a prostitute. Perhaps she was out plying her trade and got more than she bargained for.'

'That is an outrageous thing to say!' exclaimed Bartholomew. 'Because she is a prostitute does not give someone the right to rape her!'

Tulyet eyed Bartholomew in the darkness. 'I forgot,' he said. 'You have championed the town prostitutes on other occasions. Well, I am in sympathy with your point, Matt, but I need to concentrate on preventing further riots. I cannot spare the men to look into this Joanna's death. One of my archers says he saw Joanna in the company of some French scholars after the riot erupted. Tell Brother Michael it is a University matter and persuade him to investigate.'

He took the reins of his horse from the waiting porter and watched Bartholomew unbar the gate so that he could leave. As he led his horse out of the yard, he caught Bartholomew's arm. 'But if you do look into this death be tactful, Matt. It would be unfortunate if incautious inquiries sparked off another riot.'

Making certain that the gate was firmly closed and barred, Bartholomew strolled back across the courtyard to intercept Michael, who was heading towards the kitchens for something to eat before he, too, went to patrol the streets with his beadles. Bartholomew told the monk about Joanna but met with little enthusiasm.

'Dick Tulyet is right, Matt. There were many grievous crimes committed last night – nine dead and countless injured – which is why we cannot allow it to happen again. It is a terrible thing that happened to this whore, but it is done, and there is nothing we can do about it now.'

'We can avenge her death,' Bartholomew replied, disgusted that Michael should take such a view. 'We can find out who misused her and punish them for it.'

'But we have no idea who it may have been,' said Michael with a patent lack of interest.

'Tulyet said she was last seen with French scholars. French scholars tried to make away with Eleanor Tyler last night. Perhaps they had already committed one such crime.'

'Well, if so, then they are punished already,' said Michael dismissively, 'for you told me yourself that one already lies dead in the Castle, stabbed by Mistress Tyler. And you are being unfair. There are a lot of French scholars in the University; there is no reason to assume the Godwinsson trio are to blame.'

Bartholomew ran a hand through his hair and considered. 'There are not that many French students here. You could supply me with a list, since the University keeps records of such things. Then I could make some inquiries.'

'I will do no such thing,' said Michael firmly. 'First, it might be dangerous. Second, you are not a proctor and have no authority to investigate such matters. And third, even enquiring might strike the spark that will ignite another riot. No, Matt. I will not let you do it.'

'Then I will make inquiries without your help,' said Bartholomew coldly, turning on his heel and stalking back towards his room.

Michael hurried after him and grabbed his arm. 'What is the matter with you?' he asked, perplexed. 'I know you dislike violence, so why are you so intent on subverting the attempts of the Sheriff and the University to prevent more of it?'

Bartholomew looked at Michael and then up at the dark sky. 'The dead woman had hair just like Philippa,' he said.

Michael shook Bartholomew's arm gently. 'That is no reason at all,' he chided. He blew out his cheeks in a gesture of resignation. 'You are stubborn. Look, I will help you, but not tonight. I will get the list tomorrow and we can look into this together. I do not want you doing this alone.'

Bartholomew hesitated, then gave Michael a quick smile and walked briskly across the rest of the yard to his room. Michael was right: it was far too late to begin inquiries into Joanna's death that night and, anyway, he was weary from his labours with the injured all that day. He had surprised himself by revealing to Michael the overwhelming reason why he felt compelled to avenge Joanna and supposed he must be more tired than he guessed. Bearing in mind his ill-conceived invitation to Matilde as well, he decided to retire to bed before he made any more embarrassing statements. Thinking of Matilde reminded him of Philippa and he was disconcerted to find that the image of her face was blurred in his mind. Was her hair really the same colour as Joanna's? On second thoughts, he was not so sure that it was. He reached his room, automatically extinguishing the candle to save the wax. He undressed in the darkness and was asleep almost before he lay on the bed.

Michael watched his friend cross the yard and then resumed his journey to the kitchen. He knew from experience that he would be unable to prevent Bartholomew doing what he intended, and that it would be safer for both of them if Michael helped rather than hindered him. He gave a huge sigh as he stole bacon-fat and oatcakes for his evening repast

and hoped Bartholomew was not going to champion all fallen
women with fair hair like Philippa.

In an attempt to keep the scholars occupied and off the streets,
term started with a vengeance the following day. All University
members were obliged to attend mass in a church; lectures
started at six o'clock, after breakfast. The main meal of the
day was at ten, followed by more teaching until early afternoon. Since the plague, Michaelhouse food, which had never
been good, had plummeted to new and hitherto unimaginable
depths. Breakfast was a single oatcake and a slice of cold, greasy
mutton accompanied by cloudy ale that made Bartholomew feel
queasy; the main meal was stewed fish giblets – a favourite of
Father William – served with hard bread. Michael complained
bitterly and dispatched one of his students to buy him some
pies from the Market Square.

When teaching was over for the day Bartholomew and
Michael were able to meet. A light meal was available in
the hall but when Bartholomew heard it was fish-giblet stew
again – probably because it had not been particularly popular
the first time round – he went instead to the kitchens, Michael
in tow.

'And what is wrong with my fish-giblet stew?' demanded
Agatha the laundress aggressively, blocking the door with her
formidable frame, arms akimbo. 'If it is good enough for that
saintly Father William, then it should be good enough for you
two layabouts.'

'Father William is not saintly!' said Michael with conviction.
'If he were, he would not eat the diabolical fish-giblet stew
with such unnatural relish!'

'What do you mean?' demanded Agatha, looking from Michael
to Bartholomew with open hostility. 'There is no unnatural
relish in my fish-giblet stew, I can tell you! I only use the
finest ingredients. Now, off with you! I am busy.'

Agatha determined, and in a foul temper, was not a thing
to be regarded lightly, and Bartholomew was fully resigned
to returning to his room hungry. Michael, however, was less
easily repulsed, particularly where food was concerned.

'Everything you cook is delicious, Madam,' he said, attempting to ease his own considerable bulk past hers. She was
having none of that and stood firm. Michael continued suavely,
standing close enough so that he would be able to shoot past

her the moment a gap appeared. 'And the fish-giblet stew is
no exception. But a man can have too much of a good thing,
and, in the interests of my immortal soul, I crave something
a little less fine, something simple.'

Agatha eyed him suspiciously. 'Such as what?'

'A scrap of bread, a rind of cheese, a wizened apple or two,
perhaps a dribble of watered ale.'

'All right, then,' said Agatha reluctantly after a moment's
serious consideration. 'But I am busy with the preparations
for the Founder's Feast next week, so you will have to help
yourselves.'

'Gladly, Madam,' said Michael silkily, slipping past her and
heading for the pantry. Agatha glared at Bartholomew before
allowing him to pass, and he wondered what he could have
done to upset her. Usually, she turned a blind eye to his
occasional forays to the kitchens when he missed meals in
hall. He wondered whether the Tyler women had told her
that he believed she had dispensed amorous favours to the
rough men in the King's Head to earn free ale.

While she gave her attention to a mound of dead white
chickens that were piled on the kitchen table, he took a modest
portion of ale from the barrel in the corner. Michael clattered
in the pantry, humming cheerfully. Just when the monk had
taken sufficiently long to make Agatha start towards the source
of the singing with her masculine chin set for battle, Michael
emerged, displaying two apples and a piece of bluish-green
bread. Agatha inspected them minutely.

'Go on, then,' she said eventually. 'But that is all you are
getting, so clear off and keep out of my way.'

She gave Bartholomew a hefty shove that made him stagger
and slop the ale on the floor. He had darted out of the back
door before she noticed the mess, lest she was tempted to
empty the rest of the jug over his head. Michael followed more
sedately, heading for the fallen apple tree in the orchard. He
plumped himself down, turning his pasty face to the sun and
smiling in pleasure. His contentment faded when he saw the
ale Bartholomew had brought.

'There is wine by the barrel in the kitchens!' he cried in
dismay. 'All for the Feast. Could you not have smuggled us
some of that?'

'With Agatha watching?' asked Bartholomew, aghast. 'Suicide
is a deadly sin, Brother!'

'She has always liked you far better than the rest of us,' said Michael, reproachfully. 'You have only to hint and she will willingly give you whatever you want. If I were in such a powerful position, Matt, I would not squander it as you do. I would ensure you and I dined like kings.'

'She did not give the impression that she liked me just now,' said Bartholomew. 'She was positively hostile.'

'So I noticed,' said Michael, peering into the ale jug in disgust. 'What have you done to annoy her? Whatever it is, you are a braver man than me. I would not risk the wrath of Agatha!'

He stood, shaking his large body like some bizarre oriental dancer. Bartholomew was not in the least bit surprised when a large piece of cheese, a new loaf of bread, a sizeable chunk of ham, and some kind of pie dropped from his voluminous habit into the grass at his feet. The monk tossed the two apples and the mouldy crust away in disdain.

'Never eat anything green when there is meat to be had,' he advised sagely. 'Green food is a danger to the stomach.'

'And which medical text did this little pearl of wisdom come from?' asked Bartholomew, ripping a piece of bread from the loaf. It was nowhere near as fine as that he had eaten in Mistress Tyler's garden, but, even though it was hard and grey and made with cheap flour, it was an improvement on what he usually ate.

'You put too much store in the written word,' said Michael complacently. 'You should rely more on your instincts and experience.'

Bartholomew thought about Matilde's jibe the night before, and how she had laughed at his lack of experience with women. For the first time that day he considered the predicament he had landed himself in with his invitations.

'What is on your mind?' asked Michael, eyeing him speculatively as he broke the cheese in two, handing Bartholomew the smaller part. 'Something has happened to worry you. Is it this Joanna business?'

'Yes. No.' Bartholomew shrugged. 'Partly.'

'I always admire a man who knows his own mind,' said Michael dryly. 'You are not having second thoughts about taking that Tyler woman to the Founder's Feast, are you?'

Bartholomew gaped at him. 'How did you know that?' He

corrected himself. 'Is there anyone in the town who does not know?'

Michael gave the matter serious thought, cramming a slice of ham into his mouth as he did so. 'Father William, I should imagine, or he would have mentioned the matter to you with his customary disapproval. He would ban all women from the Feast, if he could.'

'What is wrong with women in the College for a few hours?' demanded Bartholomew, standing and pacing in agitation. 'They might give it a little life and make us see the world in a different perspective.'

'That is exactly what William is afraid of,' said Michael, chuckling. 'I am all for it, myself, and I would have them in for a lot more than a few hours. Sit down, Matt. This ham is delicious and you will not appreciate it striding up and down like a hungry heron.'

Bartholomew flopped on to the tree trunk, taking the sliver of ham Michael offered him. With his other hand, the monk crammed as much bread into his mouth as would fit and then a little more. Within a few moments, he was gagging for breath, forcing Bartholomew to pound him hard on the back.

'Eat slowly, Brother,' admonished Bartholomew mechanically. He had long since given up hoping that his advice would be followed. 'It is not a race and I promise to take none of your share.'

'You are not still pining after that Philippa, are you?' asked Michael when he had recovered his breath. 'Pining will do you no good at all, Matt. You need to go out and find yourself another one, if you decline to take the cowl. I suppose Eleanor Tyler is acceptable, although you could do a good deal better.'

'I also invited Matilde to the Feast,' Bartholomew blurted out. He stood again and resumed his pacing.

Michael's jaw dropped, and Bartholomew would have laughed to see the monk so disconcerted had he not been so unsettled himself.

'Matt!' was all Michael could find to say.

Bartholomew picked up one of Michael's discarded apples and hurled it at the wall. It splattered into pieces and some of it hit the monk.

'Steady on,' he objected. 'Does this uncharacteristic violence towards fruit mean that you are pleased or displeased by your appalling indiscretion?'

'Both,' said Bartholomew. 'Pleased because I think her a fine woman, and displeased because I am afraid of what the other Fellows might say to offend her.'

'They offend her?' gasped Michael. 'She is a prostitute, Matt! A whore! A courtesan! A harlot! A—'

'All right, all right,' said Bartholomew uncomfortably. 'I understood you the first time. But the invitation has been issued, so I can hardly renege.'

'Is this worth your Fellowship?' asked Michael. 'Your career?'

'On the one hand you tell me to go out and get a woman and on the other you tell me the ones I choose are inappropriate.'

'I recommended a discreet friendship with a respectable lady, not a flagrant dalliance with a prostitute *in the College!* And to top that, you even have a spare waiting on the side in the form of Eleanor Tyler.'

'Two spares, actually,' said Bartholomew. 'I have invited Hedwise Tyler to the Festival of St Michael and All Angels.'

This time he did laugh at the expression on Michael's face. Eventually Michael smiled too.

'It's all or nothing with you, isn't it? You never do things by halves. Perhaps I can have a word with the steward about the seating plan to see if a little confusion can be arranged. The last thing you want is a whore on either side of you. They might fight.'

'Eleanor Tyler is not a whore,' objected Bartholomew.

Michael sighed. 'No, she is not, although she is horribly indiscreet. Half the town knows that you have invited her to the Feast. Lord knows what she will say when she learns the identity of your second guest.'

It was something Bartholomew had not considered before. Michael was right – any respectable woman would baulk at the notion that she formed one of a pair with a prostitute.

Michael finished his repast, and led the way back through the kitchens towards the courtyard, still chuckling under his breath at Bartholomew's predicament.

'Out of my way, you two,' said Agatha sharply. 'I cannot have you under my feet all the time. I have a feast to organise, you know.'

'Yes, we do know,' said Michael. 'We have been invited.'

'And some of you have invited all manner of hussies,' said Agatha, fixing Bartholomew with an angry glare. 'Eleanor Tyler indeed! How could you stoop so low? I had expected better of you!'

So that was it, Bartholomew thought. Agatha disapproved of Eleanor Tyler. He exchanged a furtive glance with Michael and wondered what the robust laundress would find to say when she discovered whom he had asked as his second guest. Still fixing him with a steely glower, Agatha continued.

'That young woman is bragging to half the town about how she wrung an invitation from you to our Feast. She has all the discretion of a rutting stag!'

From Agatha, this was a damning indictment indeed. Seeing she had made her point, the laundress bustled Bartholomew out of the kitchens and began bellowing orders at the cowering scullions.

'What is wrong with Eleanor Tyler?' asked Bartholomew of Michael, a little resentfully. 'She is attractive, intelligent, witty . . .'

'Yes, yes,' said Michael impatiently. 'It is perfectly clear that you are smitten with the woman. But beware! Do not imagine that you will be allowed to render free services to poor patients if you marry either of the Tyler women. You will only be able to take wealthy clients who will pay you well enough to keep them in the lap of luxury.'

'Oh, really, Brother! I have invited them to a feast, not proposed marriage! Being crushed into a church, and then a hall, with dozens of other people can scarcely be considered romantic, can it!'

Michael pursed his lips primly and did not deign to reply.

While they had been in the orchard, Michael had sent Cynric to the Chancellor's office with a request for a list of all the French students in residence. The book-bearer was waiting with it in Bartholomew's room.

'You were right, Matt,' said Michael, scanning the list. 'There are only fourteen French scholars currently registered at the University. Of these, three are in Maud's, and have alibis in Gray and Deynman; three are in Godwinsson, although we know that one of them is now dead; two are in Michaelhouse – the only students missing from here were Gray and Deynman, so that lets them off the hook; one is in Peterhouse—'

'I know him,' interrupted Bartholomew. 'He cannot walk without the aid of crutches and his health is fragile. He cannot be involved.'

'There is one at Clare Hall,' continued Michael, 'but he is a Benedictine, who is at least seventy and would certainly not be out on the streets in the dark, let alone abduct and rape a young woman. Then there are two at St Stephen's, and two at Valence Marie.'

'So, the only possible suspects are the two at Valence Marie, the two at St Stephen's and the two surviving students at Godwinsson,' said Bartholomew.

Michael regarded him thoughtfully. 'I wonder if there are connections in any of this,' he said. 'We have Godwinsson and David's scholars quarrelling in the street, after which one of them is killed near Valence Marie; the same student of David's is having an affair with the Principal of Godwinsson's daughter, his identity unknown to her parents; French scholars from Godwinsson try to attack Eleanor Tyler, and one of them is killed in the process; and the Principal of Godwinsson wrongfully claims that he has been at Maud's all night. Meanwhile, his wife really did visit Maud's after the riot began; a skeleton is found at Valence Marie; and the dead prostitute is last seen with French scholars, which must have been those from Valence Marie, Godwinsson or St Stephen's.'

Bartholomew considered. 'There is nothing to suggest this skeleton can be linked with any of the other events.'

'Except that we have agreed that it is a strange coincidence that Kenzie should die so near where the skeleton had been found the day before, and in an identical manner.'

'We agreed no such thing!' said Bartholomew, startled. 'I said there was insufficient evidence to show that they died in the same way, although it is possible that they did.'

Michael flapped a flabby hand dismissively, before standing and stretching his large arms. 'I would like to make two visits this afternoon. I want to ask the Scottish lads at David's more about Kenzie, and then I want to have another word with those unpleasant Godwinsson friars. While we are there, we can drop a few questions about their part in the riot, and about the French louts that tried to kill you. If our inquiries proceed well, I might even ask a few questions of Lydgate himself – if he really was up to no good while the riot was in full swing, I doubt he has the brains to cover his tracks sufficiently to fool someone of my high intellectual calibre.'

'And on the way, we can stop off at St Stephen's and Valence Marie and see about these Frenchman, thus making the best possible use of the brilliant skills at detection you have just claimed,' said Bartholomew with a smile, ignoring Michael's irritable sigh.

The nearest hostel was St Stephen's, where the Principal told them, with some ire, that he had received a letter from France informing him that the two students he had been expecting would not be coming because of a death in the family. His anger seemed to result chiefly from the fact that bad weather had delayed the letter by more than a week, and he would have problems in finding students to fill their places now that most scholars were already settled in lodgings. There was no reason to doubt the authenticity of the letter, so Bartholomew's list of suspects was narrowed to those French students registered at Godwinsson Hostel and those at the Hall of Valence Marie.

The next visit was to David's, where the young Scots told Bartholomew and Michael that Kenzie had been becoming increasingly agitated about his affair because Lydgate was so intent on preventing it. Kenzie and Dominica had been forced to invent more and more ingenious plans to see each other, and they had begun to run out of ideas – much as Eleanor and Hedwise Tyler had suggested the night of the riot.

When Michael asked for more information about the missing ring, the students were unable to add anything, other than that they all believed Dominica had given it to Kenzie. It had been silver, they said, with a small blue-green stone. Ruthven, clearly embarrassed, revealed reluctantly that Kenzie had often waxed lyrical about Dominica's blue-green eyes, while playing with the ring on his finger.

As they made their way from David's to Godwinsson, Michael turned to Bartholomew.

'The last time we visited Godwinsson, Lydgate threatened you,' he said. 'I think you should wait outside.' He raised a hand to quell Bartholomew's objections. 'Lydgate does not like you, and nothing will be gained from antagonising him with your presence in his own home. Wait outside: listen at the window if you would, but stay out of sight. I will ask about the Frenchmen for you.'

Despite his misgivings, Bartholomew knew Michael was right, and as the fat monk knocked loudly on Godwinsson's front door, he slipped down a filthy alleyway by the side of the house and into the yard at the back. He glanced up and saw that, as last time, the window shutters in the solar where Lydgate had received them were flung open. The glazed windows also stood ajar to allow a breeze to circulate inside.

A sound from what he presumed to be the kitchen startled him, and he realised he was being foolish in prowling so openly around Godwinsson's back yard. There was a decrepit lean-to shed against the back of the house, a tatty structure that would not survive another winter. Its door was loose on decaying leather hinges and the roof sagged precariously. Heart pounding, Bartholomew slipped inside just as someone emerged from a rear door to pour slops into a brimming cesspool in a far corner of the yard.

The shed was stiflingly hot, and full of pieces of discarded wood and rope. Bartholomew picked his way across it until he was on the side nearest the solar. The warped wood created wide gaps in the walls that allowed him to see out, and, as long as Michael and Lydgate did not whisper, Bartholomew thought he should be able to hear much of what was happening in the solar without being seen.

He heard Huw, the Godwinsson steward, show Michael into the room as before and saw the monk lean out of the window to look into the yard as he waited for Lydgate. Bartholomew was about to signal to him when the kitchen scullion came out with another bowl of slops. Alarmed, Bartholomew jerked backwards, realising too late that sudden motion was more likely to give away his hiding place than his raised arm, half-hidden in shadows.

'You will find nothing of interest there, Brother,' came Lydgate's voice, clear as a bell, moments later. Bartholomew saw Michael's head withdraw and the scullion glance up at the window, distracted momentarily from his task. 'Unless you like cesspools.'

'Which brings me to your hostel, Master Lydgate,' came Michael's unruffled reply. 'I would like to see two of your students: the two French lads.'

'Why?' asked Lydgate. 'They have not been brawling with the Scots.'

The scullion in the yard gave his bowl a final scrape and returned to the kitchen.

'How do you know?' said Michael. 'Reliable witnesses saw them brawling with one member of the University and four defenceless women.'

Despite his tension, Bartholomew smiled at Michael's description: defenceless was certainly not a word that could truthfully be applied to the resourceful, independent Tyler women.

'How can you be sure of that?' snapped Lydgate. 'The night was dark and it was difficult to be certain who was who in the darkness with all those fires burning.'

'So you were out, too,' said Michael. It was a statement and not a question. Bartholomew could almost see Lydgate spluttering with indignation at having been so deftly fooled into admitting as much.

'My whereabouts are none of your concern!' Lydgate managed to grate finally. 'But for your information, I have people who can say where I was, whose word is beyond doubt.'

'But not in Godwinsson, Master Lydgate? To protect your family and students?' Michael continued smoothly.

'I was out!' Lydgate almost shouted.

'As were your students without you here to control them, it seems.'

Bartholomew heard the creak of floorboards and guessed that Lydgate was pacing to try to control his temper. 'All Godwinsson students were here. The other masters will testify to that.'

'I am sure they will,' said Michael, his tone ambiguous. 'Now, I would like to speak with these French students.'

As he spoke, the kitchen door opened again, and two students were ushered out by Huw the steward and the scullion. Speaking in low voices, and taking care to stay close to the walls where they would not be observed from the solar window, the students made for the alleyway that led to the road. Bartholomew pressed back into the shadows as they passed, although they were so intent on leaving that they did not so much as glance at the open shed door. Bartholomew was not surprised to hear them speaking French.

He watched them disappear up the alley before opening the door to follow. As the sunlight flooded into the gloomy lean-to, something glinted on the ground. Bending quickly to retrieve it, Bartholomew found a small, silver ring. Although there was no blue-green stone, there were clasps to show where such a gem might once have been. The ring was dirty, and its irregular shape indicated that it had been crushed, perhaps by someone stamping on it. He looked around quickly to see if he could see the stone, but there was no sign of it on the hard, trampled earth that formed the floor.

Slipping the ring into his pocket, Bartholomew left the shed and made his way quickly up the alley. As he emerged, he glimpsed the two students disappearing round the corner into the High Street. He ran after them, oblivious to the startled face of Huw the steward, who had come to the front of the hostel to watch their escape. Huw's surprise changed to artifice, and he rubbed at his whiskers, eyes glittering.

Bartholomew followed the two Frenchmen along the High Street towards the Market Square. It was more drab than usual: the colourful canopies that usually shielded the traders' wares from sun or rain had been burned during the riot. Here and there, skeletal frameworks had been hastily erected to replace those that had been lost, a few of them crudely covered with rough canvas, but for the most part, the traders were reduced to piling their goods on the ground. Ash and cinders had been trampled into the beaten earth, and to one side of the Square, a great mound of partially incinerated wood still loomed up where it had been piled the day before, waiting for someone to remove it and dump it all in the river.

It was nearing the end of the day, and, with the curfew fast approaching, the tradesmen's battle to sell the last of their wares was becoming frantic. Stories about how Cambridge had erupted in a welter of flame and violence had spread through the surrounding countryside, and many rural folk had elected not to risk coming to the town to buy supplies. Trade was poor so that potential customers were not permitted to escape easily; hands grabbed and pulled at Bartholomew as he tried to pass. Suddenly he could not see his quarry. Impatiently shrugging off a persistent baker, he dived down one narrow line of stalls, emerging at the opposite end of the Square. There was no sign of the French students. Bartholomew sagged in defeat, sweat stinging his eyes from the late-afternoon heat.

Suddenly, he spotted them again, surfacing from a parallel line of stalls eating apples. They walked at a nonchalant pace towards Hadstock Way. Bartholomew followed them a little further, although he now knew exactly where they were going. Without knocking, and with an ease born of a long familiarity, the two students casually strolled into Maud's Hostel.

There was nothing more Bartholomew could do without Michael's authority as Proctor, so he retraced his steps back to Godwinsson. He stopped to buy something to drink from a water-seller, but the larvae of some marsh insects wriggling about in the buckets gave him second thoughts. He remembered the foul wine he had shared with Michael and Tulyet, and went into the booth of a wine-merchant to buy a replacement. He purchased the first one that caught his eye, opened it, and took a large mouthful in the street.

'Not the best way to enjoy good wine,' came Michael's voice at his shoulder. 'But then again, judging from the wine you keep, what would you know of such things? Where have you been?'

He took the bottle from Bartholomew and took a hearty swig himself, nodding appreciatively at its coolness, if not its flavour.

Bartholomew told him what had happened, while Michael listened with narrowed eyes.

'Lydgate told me that the French students were at church,' he said. 'I thought it was a likely story. I learned little, I am afraid. Brothers Edred and Werbergh are taking part in a theological debate at the School of Pythagorus, and so were not available to talk to me. Since Lydgate knows I can check that excuse easily, he is probably telling the truth about that, at least. I will have to come back and speak to them later.'

Valence Marie was nearby, so they went there next, although Michael was reluctant. There was no porter on the door, no one answered their knocking, and they were forced to go inside to find someone to answer their questions. But the College appeared to be deserted. Putting his head round the door to the hall, the thought crossed Bartholomew's mind that, had he been a thief, he could have made off with all the College silver, which lay carelessly abandoned on the high table.

He shouted, but there was no reply. They left the hall and went to the Ditch at the side of Valence Marie where the skeleton had been found, but there was no one there either. Bartholomew flapped irritably at the haze of flies that buzzed around his head, disturbed from where they had been feasting on the foul-smelling muck that lined both sides of the near-empty canal. At the very bottom of the Ditch was a murky trickle that would turn into a raging torrent when the next heavy rains came. With a sigh of resignation, Bartholomew saw some unidentifiable piece of offal move gently downstream. Despite the cost and inconvenience of the dredging operations, people were still disposing of their waste in the waterways. They had learned nothing from the last time the Ditch had been blocked with rubbish and then flooded, causing some to lose their homes.

'We will have to return tomorrow,' said Michael, breaking into a trot in a vain attempt to escape the haze of flies that flicked around his head. 'The place is abandoned.'

The King's Ditch ran under the High Street and emerged the other side. Bartholomew always felt that, despite the distinct elevation in the road, the High Street did not have a bridge as much as the King's Ditch had a tunnel: its fetid, black waters slid through a small, dark hole, and oozed out into a pool on the other side. He crossed to the opposite side of the High Street, and stood on tiptoe to look over the wall that screened the western arm of the Ditch from the road. Here was a different story: the bank was alive with activity, but it was all conducted in total silence.

A dozen or so students stood in a line looking down into the Ditch, the monotony of their black tabards broken by the occasional grey or white of a friar's habit. A gaggle of scruffy children had also gathered to watch the proceedings; even their customary cheekiness had been subdued by the distinct aura of gravity that pervaded the scene.

'What are they doing?' Bartholomew whispered to Michael.

They edged closer, and saw Will and Henry, the Valence Marie servants, poking about in the vile trickle of water, watched intently by Thorpe, who stood with his Fellows clustered about him. Thorpe looked up and saw Bartholomew and Michael.

'Ah!' he announced, his voice almost sacrilegious in the self-imposed silence of the scholars. 'Here are the Senior Proctor and the physician. I am impressed with your speed, gentlemen. It has only been moments since I dispatched a messenger to the Chancellor's office to ask you to come.'

'Oh Lord, Michael!' exclaimed Bartholomew under his breath. 'Thorpe has found himself some more bones!'

Reluctantly, he moved towards Thorpe and his findings. The only sounds were Michael's noisy breathing behind him and the muffled rumble of carts from the High Street. As he walked, the students moved aside so he could pass, their faces taut with anticipation.

He met Thorpe's eyes for a moment, then looked down into the Ditch to where Will and Henry crouched in the muddy water. A distant part of Bartholomew's mind noted that the piece of offal he had observed shortly before had made its way downstream, and was now bobbing past Will's legs. It served to dissolve the feeling that he was attending some kind of religious ceremony, attended by acolytes who generated an aura of hushed veneration. He wondered how Thorpe had managed to effect such an atmosphere, disliking the way he felt he was being manipulated into complying with it. He saw that the mood of the onlookers was such that, even if they had discovered a donkey in the black, fly-infested mud, they would revere it like the relics of some venerable saint.

'What have you found this time, Master Thorpe?' he asked, his voice deliberately loud and practical.

Thorpe favoured him with a cold stare, and answered in subdued tones that had the scholars furthest away moving closer to hear him.

'We have discovered a relic of the saintly Simon d'Ambrey,' he said, clasping his hands in front of him like a monk in prayer. 'There can be no doubt about it this time, Doctor.'

He met Bartholomew's gaze evenly. Without breaking eye contact, he gestured to the Ditch, so that Bartholomew was the first to look away. Something lay on the cracking mud, carefully wrapped in a tabard to prevent the swarming flies from alighting on it. Bartholomew, aware that he was being watched minutely, clambered down the bank to examine it, while Michael, curiously silent, followed.

Bartholomew picked up the tabard and gave it a slight shake, causing what was wrapped inside it to drop out. There was a shocked gasp from the watching scholars at this rough treatment of what they already believed was sacred. Michael bent next to him as he knelt, and hissed furiously in his ear.

'Be careful, Matt! I do not feel comfortable here. These scholars are taking this nonsense very seriously. I imagine it would take very little for them to take on the role of avenging angels for any perceived insult to their relic. I do not wish to be torn limb from limb over a soup bone.'

Bartholomew glanced up at him. 'This is no soup bone,

Brother.' He looked back at the mud-encrusted object that had tumbled from the tabard. 'This is the hand of a man, complete with a ring on his little finger.'

chapter 5

ICHAEL PRETENDED TO LOOK CLOSER AT THE grisly object that lay on the bank so he could whisper to Bartholomew without being overheard.

'Hell's teeth, Matt! We have been desperate to avoid a situation like this! Now there will be gatherings of people to see the thing, and fights between town and gown will be inevitable. Are you sure this hand belongs to a man? Can you not say it is that of a woman?'

Bartholomew shook his head. 'It is far too big. You are stuck with this, I am afraid. These are the bones from a man's hand without question, and any other physician will tell you the same. Unfortunately, the thing even *looks* like a relic with that ring on its finger. What do you want me to do?'

Michael sat back on his heels, and watched Bartholomew wipe away some of the mud from the sinister hand. 'Take it to St Mary's Church,' he said. 'The Chancellor will be able to control access to it more easily there, and the beadles will be able to break up any gathering crowds.'

Bartholomew re-wrapped the hand in the tabard and called out to the servant, Will, who was still grubbing about in the ooze of the Ditch.

'Have you found anything else?'

Will shook his head. 'We shall continue to look, though, sir. The rest of the skeleton must be here somewhere since we have the hand.'

Bartholomew exchanged a brief glance of concern with Michael. Above them, the scholars muttered approval. Clutching the precious relic, Bartholomew began to climb back up the bank, followed by a puffing Michael.

'With your permission, Master Thorpe,' Bartholomew began,

'I will take this to St Mary's Church where I can examine it more closely . . .'

'You most certainly do not have my permission,' said Thorpe brusquely. He reached out his hand for the bones. 'It was found by Valence Marie scholars, and it will stay on Valence Marie land.'

Michael intervened smoothly. 'It will be treated with all reverence at St Mary's,' he said. 'If this really is a sacred relic, then it should be in the most important church of the University for all to see. The Chancellor will want to verify it himself. And doubtless the Bishop of Ely will want to see it, too.'

'It does not belong to the University or your Bishop, Brother,' said Thorpe with quiet dignity. 'It belongs to Valence Marie. We found it, and with us it will stay.' He looked around him, appealing to the watching scholars. Michael's fears had been justified and Bartholomew could detect that the atmosphere had undergone a rapid transition from reverent to menacing. Thorpe was a shrewd manipulator of crowd emotions.

Michael stepped forward as Thorpe tried to grab the bones from Bartholomew. 'It would be prudent to allow Doctor Bartholomew to examine them more closely, Master Thorpe, so that he can attest that they are genuine.'

'I need no such examination to convince me of the relic's authenticity,' said Thorpe, pulling himself up to his full height, and looking down his long nose at the monk. 'If you wish to satisfy your heathen curiosity, Brother, you may do so. But you will do so here, at the Hall of Valence Marie.'

Michael began to speak, but stopped as one or two scholars stepped forward threateningly. Bartholomew thought he heard the sound of someone drawing a dagger from its leather sheath, but could not be certain. The situation had become ugly: the scholars were convinced that Valence Marie now possessed a valuable relic and were prepared to go to extreme lengths to keep it. Bartholomew could already see the glitter of anticipated violence in the eyes of some students, their demeanour making it clear that if Bartholomew and Michael wished to leave the Ditch at all, it would not be with the bones.

Thorpe leaned forward and took the relic from Bartholomew's unresisting hands. He held the parcel in the air, and turned towards his scholars.

'The bones of a martyr have been entrusted to us,' he

announced in a strong, confident voice. There was a growl of approval. 'There will be many who will want to come to see them, and we must allow them to do so. But we have a sacred trust to ensure that they will always rest at Valence Marie!'

There was a ragged cheer. Some of the scholars began to follow Thorpe as he led the way back along the bank of the Ditch to his college. Others remained with Bartholomew and Michael, and formed a tight escort that almost immediately began to jostle and shove them.

Michael spoke rapidly in Latin to Bartholomew, trusting that his low voice and the speed of his words would render him incomprehensible to the students surrounding them. One or two moved closer to try to hear what he was saying, but most ignored him, their attention fixed on the silvery head of Thorpe leading his procession, and carrying his precious bones.

'We are in a fix, Matt. Examine the wretched thing, but say nothing of what you find. It seems Thorpe has already convinced them that they have the hand of a martyr – whether it is true or not.'

Bartholomew staggered as a hefty student crashed into him, almost knocking him over. With difficulty, he refrained from pushing him back, but almost fell again as someone gave him a hard shove from behind. He felt Michael's warning hand on his shoulder, and did nothing.

They reached Valence Marie, where Thorpe laid his bundle gently on the high table and unwrapped it. He called for water, and began to clean away the remaining mud. Underneath the filth, the bones gleamed yellow-white, and the ring on the little finger glittered in the golden rays of the early evening sun that lanced through the open windows. When Thorpe held up the relic for the scholars to see, there were murmurs of awe; one student even dropped to his knees, crossing himself.

Michael stepped forward, but Bartholomew's arms were seized before he could follow. Michael glanced round at the sounds of the ensuing scuffle.

'Might we examine the hand now that it is clean, Master Thorpe?' he asked politely. 'Then we will tell the Chancellor of your discovery.'

'There is no need for a medical examination,' said Thorpe, eyeing Bartholomew disdainfully. 'It is perfectly apparent what we have here.'

'But you said that any who wished to see it should be allowed to do so,' Michael pointed out. 'Does that courtesy not apply to Fellows of Michaelhouse?'

Thorpe was silent for a moment as he considered. He was aware that if he refused to allow the Chancellor's representatives to examine the bones, rumours doubting their authenticity would surely follow. But he was also aware that a negative verdict by the University's senior physician could be equally damning, as it had proved to be with the bones of the child. He rose to the occasion.

'You may examine the hand, as Fellows of Michaelhouse,' he said magisterially. 'But we will permit no unseemly treatment of it. No touching.'

Bartholomew was released reluctantly, stumbling as he tripped over a strategically placed foot. He heard one or two muffled snorts of laughter coming from the students.

'I see Michaelhouse has little to learn from the manners of the scholars of Valence Marie,' he remarked coolly to Thorpe, ignoring the way the Master's mouth tightened into a hard line. Out of the corner of his eye, he saw Thorpe glare a warning at the offending students, whose sniggering ceased instantly.

The now-cleaned bones lay on the muddy tabard. Bartholomew leaned forward to move them slightly but was not in the least surprised to feel Thorpe's restraining grip on his wrist. He was aware of the scholars edging towards him, mutters of anger and resentment rippling through their ranks.

'You are invited to look, but I said you are not to touch,' Thorpe said firmly.

Bartholomew pulled his arm away, peering closely at the hand. Although the bones appeared bright and clean, they were still joined together, mostly by brownish sinews. Thus they were not merely a disconnected collection of small bones, but a complete skeletal hand. He moved into a different position and inspected the ring. Finally, he straightened. Michael prepared to leave, but Thorpe blocked their way.

'Well?' he asked, his eyes flicking from one to the other.

Bartholomew shrugged. 'It is the hand of a large man,' he said simply.

'It is the hand of a martyr,' said Thorpe loudly, so that the hall rang with his words. 'Why else would it be wearing a ring so fine?'

Why indeed? wondered Bartholomew and followed Michael out of Valence Marie, into the fading rays of the evening sun.

He took a deep breath and began to walk quickly back along the High Street towards Michaelhouse, suddenly longing to be safe inside its sturdy walls. For once, Michael did not complain about the rapid pace, obviously as eager to put as much distance between himself and Valence Marie as Bartholomew.

After a few moments, when Michael was satisfied that they were not being followed by a crowd of resentful, antagonistic Valence Marie scholars, he repeated Thorpe's question. 'Well?'

Bartholomew slowed his pace fractionally and looked at Michael. 'You saw I was prevented from conducting a proper investigation but I can tell you two things. First, however much those Valence Marie servants root around in the mud, I will wager anything you please that no more of the skeleton will ever be found; and second, the hand does not belong to the martyred Simon d'Ambrey, unless he was considerably bigger than I recall and he died fairly recently.'

Michael stopped dead, but then glanced uneasily behind him and began walking again. They had reached St Mary's Church, near which the Chancellor had his offices. Michael took Bartholomew's arm and dragged him into the wooden building where Richard de Wetherset sat poring over documents in the fading daylight. He was a solid man, whose physical strength had largely turned to fat from a lifetime of sitting in offices. He had iron-grey hair and a hard, uncompromising will. Although Bartholomew appreciated de Wetherset's motives were usually selfless, and that he put the good of the University above all else, Bartholomew did not like the Chancellor, and certainly did not trust him. The Junior Proctor was with him, sitting on a stool and signing some writs, shivering in the pleasant breeze that wafted in from the window and snuffling miserably.

De Wetherset scowled as Bartholomew and Michael entered, none too pleased that he was being interrupted while there was still daylight enough to be able to read the last accounts of the day's business transactions. As Michael told him what had happened, the Chancellor flushed red with anger, his documents forgotten.

'This is the worst possible thing that could have happened,' he said, his voice low with barely restrained anger. 'What does that fool Thorpe imagine he is doing? He is putting the fame and wealth of his college above the peaceful relations of the

University with the town. There will be a riot for certain when this gets out: the town will demand this wretched hand for itself, and Valence Marie will refuse.'

He sat back in his chair, the muscles in his jaws bulging from his grinding teeth as he considered the University's position.

Heppel watched him anxiously. 'We must prevent another riot at all costs.'

'You are right. We must inform the Sheriff immediately lest the townspeople start to gather outside Valence Marie.'

De Wetherset stood abruptly and sent a clerk to fetch one of the Sheriff's deputies. He sat again, indicating that Bartholomew and Michael should take a seat on one of the benches that ran along the wall opposite the window. 'Did you examine this confounded relic?' he asked.

'Not as completely as I would have wished, but enough to tell me that the "confounded relic" no more belongs to a man twenty-five years dead in the King's Ditch than does my own,' Bartholomew replied. The Chancellor, not in the least surprised, gestured for him to continue.

'The hand was severed from the arm. There are cut marks on the wrist bones where the knife grazed them. And, think of the skeleton of the child, also in the Ditch for some years. It was stained dark brown by the mud. The bones on the Valence Marie hand are almost white, and I think it doubtful that they have been in the Ditch for any length of time. And finally, some care was taken to leave the sinews in place so that the collection of bones would be identifiable as a hand. Except for the little finger. There, the sinews must have broken or come loose, because the finger is held in place by a tiny metal pin almost hidden by the ring.'

'A pin?' exclaimed Heppel in astonishment. 'Are you suggesting, therefore, that someone planted this hand for Thorpe to find?'

Bartholomew ran his hand through his hair. 'It is possible, I suppose. It is equally possible that he planted it himself. But all I can tell you for certain is that the hand was taken from a man – a man larger than any of us, and whether alive or already dead I cannot say – and boiled to remove the flesh. When one of the fingers came loose, it was repaired expertly with a pin.'

Michael looked at him in concern. 'Another murder victim? Or someone desecrating the dead? How do you know that the bones were boiled?'

'Come now, Michael,' said Bartholomew. 'You have gnawed on enough roasted joints to know the answer to that. The bones of the relic are whitish-yellow, a colour they are unlikely to keep when embedded in the black mud of the King's Ditch, and they have a freshness about them that suggests careful preparation. You must have noticed how easily the mud washed off when it was cleaned. Moreover, think about the choice of relic: a hand is manageable, and easily prepared – ring and all. It is not so repellent as, say, a skull but more inspiring than a thigh-bone or a rib. I am willing to wager anything you please that no other parts will be found until there is a market for them.'

'And these bones belonged to a man larger than us?' asked de Wetherset, frowning. 'None of us is exactly petite!' He glanced at Heppel, swathed in a thick cloak against nasty draughts, and wiping his long, thin nose with a pale, white hand. 'Well, some of us are not.'

Bartholomew held up his own hands. 'The fingers were at least an inch longer than mine and the bones were dense and thick. I suspect a large hand was deliberately chosen to make it impossible for us to dismiss it as that of a woman.'

'Is it possible that Master Thorpe did all this?' wondered Heppel in revulsion. 'Selected a large corpse, stole its hand and boiled it up?'

Michael scratched his chin thoughtfully. 'He was desperate to find a relic in the Ditch and was most disappointed when Matt kept pronouncing that his finds were animal bones. Valence Marie is a new college and will benefit greatly from having a venerated relic on its premises, especially after the expense of dredging the Ditch in the first place.'

'Or perhaps someone is using Thorpe's desperation to play a cruel trick on him,' mused de Wetherset. 'It would not be the first time one scholar made a fool of another.'

'Or a townsman made a fool of the University,' pointed out Bartholomew.

De Wetherset glared at him for a moment, but then accepted his comment with a resigned nod. 'The real question is what are we to do?'

'Go to see Thorpe yourself, ask to see the hand and then point out the bright, new pin,' said Bartholomew promptly. 'He can hardly refuse to allow you to examine his relic, can he?'

De Wetherset agreed reluctantly and rose. 'Are you sure

about this pin?' he asked. 'I would not wish to be made a fool of either.'

'You will see it,' said Bartholomew, 'especially if you pick the hand up.'

As de Wetherset went to confront Thorpe, accompanied by a nervous Guy Heppel and two beadles, Bartholomew and Michael walked home. It was almost dark, and the curfew was in force. The streets were virtually deserted but, with relief, Bartholomew detected none of the atmosphere of anticipation he had sensed the night before. Doors were firmly closed, and although voices came from some of the houses, most were silent and in darkness. Dawn came early and the summer heat was exhausting for people who worked hard for their meagre livings. The Statute of Labour had been passed the year before, an edict that made it illegal for people to seek better-paid work by leaving their homes. The Statute had decreed that wages should remain at the pre-plague levels, despite the fact that food prices had soared since then. Unrest and bitter resentment festered, although the labourers were far too exhausted from scratching paltry livings from the land to do much about their miserable conditions.

'Thorpe was very masterly at manipulating the emotions of his scholars,' said Michael thoughtfully. 'I wonder if he could apply that talent to incite a mob to riot.'

Bartholomew raised his eyebrows, and nodded. 'There was one other thing neither of us mentioned to de Wetherset,' he said.

Michael nodded as they knocked on Michaelhouse's gates to be allowed in. 'I thought you had noticed,' he said. 'The ring on the relic had a blue-green stone, just like the colour of Dominica's eyes.'

The next day dawned in a golden mist that was soon burned away by the sun. By the main meal at ten o'clock, it was so hot that Bartholomew had to tend to two students who were sick and dizzy from dehydration. As a special dispensation, and, because he had no wish for his scholars to be fainting around him as he ate, the Master announced that it would not be necessary to wear tabards in the College during lectures or meals until the evening. The austere Franciscans pulled sour faces at the slackening of discipline, although Bartholomew found the Master's announcement eminently sensible.

By noon, the heat was so intense that Bartholomew, teaching in the College conclave, found it difficult to concentrate, and was very aware that his students were similarly afflicted. The conclave was a small room at the far end of the hall, and Bartholomew preferred teaching there than in the hall itself, where he had to compete for space with the other Fellows. The conclave, however, was bitterly cold in the winter when the wind howled through gaps in its windows, and unbearably hot in the summer when the sun streamed in. He tried blocking the sunlight by closing the shutters but that made the room unpleasantly stuffy. With the shutters open, the occasional breath of breeze wafted in, but students and master melted in the sunlight.

Gray drowsed near the empty fireplace, Deynman's attention alternated between the insects in the rushes and picking at a hole in his shirt, and even Tom Bulbeck, Bartholomew's best student, appeared uninterested. The topic of the day was Galen's theories about how different pulse rates related to the heavenly spheres – a subject that even Bartholomew found complex and overly intricate. Finally, he gave up, and, pulling uncomfortably at his sweat-soaked shirt, allowed the students their liberty for the rest of the day, accompanied with strict rejoinders about obeying the curfew.

Bulbeck hovered as the others left. Bartholomew smiled at him encouragingly.

'Even the great physician Bernard Gordon, who taught at Montpellier, found it difficult to distinguish between subtle variations of pulse beats,' he said, assuming Bulbeck was concerned that he was taking too long to grasp the essence of Galen's hypothesis.

Bulbeck gnawed at his lower lip. 'It is not that,' he said. He hesitated, aware that Gray and Deynman were waiting for him near the door. He made up his mind. 'It is this notion of heavenly bodies. I know you are sceptical of the role played by the stars in a patient's sickness – and the little I have seen of medical practice inclines me to believe you are right. So why must we waste time with such nonsense? Why do you not teach us more about uroscopy or surgery.'

'Because if you want to pass your disputations and graduate as a physician, you will need to show that you can calculate the astrological charts that can be used to determine a course of treatment. What I believe about the worth of such calculations is irrelevant.'

'The medical faculty at Paris told King Philip the Sixth of France that the Death was caused by a malign conjunction of Saturn and Jupiter,' said Gray brightly from the doorway.

'I know,' said Bartholomew. 'And this malign conjunction was said to have occurred at precisely one o'clock on the afternoon of 20 March 1345. The physicians at the medical school of Montpellier wrote *Tractatus de Epidemia*, in which they explained that the reason some areas were worse affected than others was because they were more exposed to evil rays caused when "Saturn looked upon Jupiter with a malignant aspect".'

'But you do not believe that,' pressed Bulbeck. 'You think there is some other explanation.'

Bartholomew thought for a moment, uncertain how much to tell his students of his growing dissatisfaction with traditional medicine. He had been accused of heresy more times than he could remember for his unorthodox thinking, and was ever alert to the possibility that too great an accumulation of such charges might result in his dismissal from the University. In the past, he had not much cared what his colleagues thought about his teaching, assuming that the better success rate he had with his patients would speak for itself. But he had moderated his incautious attitude when he realised that his excellent medical record would be attributed to witchcraft if he were not careful, and then his hard work and painstakingly acquired skills would count for nothing.

'No, I do not believe that heavenly bodies were entirely responsible for the plague,' he said eventually. 'And I do not think that consulting a patient's stars will make much difference to the outcome of his sickness. I have found that my patients live or die regardless of whether I consult their stars to treat them or not.'

'Father Philius at Gonville Hall believes astrology is the most powerful tool that physicians have,' said Gray, leaning nonchalantly on the door frame. 'He says treatment without astrological consultation is like treating a patient without seeing him at all.'

'I am well aware of Philius's views,' said Bartholomew irritably. 'I have debated them with him often enough. But Philius will be at your disputations, Tom, and if you cannot convince him that you know your astrology, you will not pass, even

if you are the best physician the world has known since
Hippocrates.'

Bulbeck looked despondent, and Bartholomew recalled how
he had felt when his Arab master in Paris had insisted that
he learned astrology, even though he had not believed in its
efficacy. So Bartholomew had learned his traditional medicine,
and answered questions about poorly aligned constellations
in his disputations. But he had also learned Ibn Ibrahim's
unorthodox theories on hygiene and contagion, and so his
patients had the benefit of both worlds.

Despite his scepticism, he was aware that the patient's mental
state played an important role in his recovery. On occasion,
Bartholomew's treatments had failed because a person had genuinely believed he could not be cured as long as Bartholomew had
failed to consult the planets. Guy Heppel, the Junior Proctor,
would probably prove to be one of them; the physician knew
that he would have to relent in the end, and at least make a
pretence of studying the man's astrology if he ever wanted to
pronounce him well. He said as much to Bulbeck, who looked
more glum than ever.

The student trailed out of the conclave and followed his
friends through the hall. By the time he had reached the
yard, however, Bartholomew saw he had already thrown off
his gloom and was arguing loudly with Gray about how much
a physician could justifiably charge for an extensive astrological
consultation. Bartholomew realised that if he let Gray loose on
Heppel's stars as he had planned, he would have to ensure
the Junior Proctor was not charged a month's wages for the
dubious privilege.

Bartholomew wandered back to his own room, which was not
much cooler than the conclave. He spent most winter nights
trying to invent new ways of keeping warm and now it seemed
as though he would also have to invent means to stay cool in
the summer.

He sat at the table and sharpened a quill to begin working
on his treatise on fevers, but no sooner had he written a few
words than his eyelids grew heavy and he began to dose.
He was awoken when Davy Grahame arrived to deliver the
book by Galen that the Principal of David's had promised
to lend him. Bartholomew was to keep it for as long as he
wanted, said Davy, and then enquired with ill-concealed envy
about the fine collection of philosophy and theology texts at

Michaelhouse. Bartholomew showed him where the books were chained to the wall in the hall, and left him happily browsing through them.

Bartholomew returned to his room, then pushed open the shutters to allow what little breeze there was to circulate. Abandoning his treatise, he sat again at the small table and opened the Galen. He smiled when he saw it was not the *Prognostica*, as Master Radbeche had thought, but the *Tegni*. He wondered whether anyone from David's had ever bothered to look at the book at all. But Bartholomew did not mind Radbeche's mistake. It was a luxury to have a book to read in the comfort of his own room, as opposed to begging an uncomfortable corner in another college, or listening to someone else reading aloud.

Unfortunately, David's Hostel's cherished tome was not a good copy of the *Tegni*, and the scribe's writing was difficult to decipher. But, a book was a book, and far too valuable a commodity to be judged harshly. Bartholomew began to read, slowly at first as he struggled with the ill-formed letters and frequent errors, but then faster as he became familiar with the clerk's idiosyncratic style, delighting in the richness of the language and the purity of Galen's logic.

Absorbed in his book, Bartholomew did not know Michael was behind him until a heavy hand dropped on his shoulder. He leapt from his chair, then slumped back again, clutching his chest and glaring at the chuckling Michael.

'Most sensible masters have decided no learning can be achieved in such heat,' said Michael, hurling himself on to Bartholomew's bed, which protested with groans from its wooden legs. 'I sent my lot away before noon. They are supposed to be thinking about the doctrine of *creatio ex nihilo*, although I doubt that much creation theology is running through their minds at this precise moment.'

'Mine are supposed to be learning about stomach disorders caused by dangerous alignments of the stars,' said Bartholomew, standing and stretching. 'Although I would rather tell them not to waste their time, and advise people not to drink from the river instead. It would save their prospective patients a good deal of suffering, and, in many cases, effect a quick cure.'

'You are mistaken, Matt,' said Michael. 'You may be happy to treat those who live in the hovels along the river banks, but your students will want to treat the rich, whose lips would

never deign to touch river water. Keep your heretic thoughts
to yourself and let the fledgling physicians learn about the
astrology of the wealthy who will expect more of them than
advice about water.'

Bartholomew opened his mouth to argue, but he knew that
Michael was right. He fetched the wine he had bought the day
before and poured some for Michael, who drank it quickly and
held out his cup for more.

'Have you seen de Wetherset since last night?' Bartholomew
asked, settling back on his chair and sipping distastefully at the
warm wine.

Michael nodded, pouring himself a third cup. 'Apparently
Thorpe has this damn hand in a glass case, all wrapped round
with satin. De Wetherset thinks the box is so elaborate that
it must have been made in advance, which suggests to me
that Thorpe is in the process of perpetrating some massive
fraud, not to mention the question of where the hand came
from in the first place. De Wetherset pointed out the pin, but
Thorpe maintains it must have become lodged there at some
point during its twenty-five year sojourn in the river. He even
intimated that the pin was put there by divine intervention, to
prevent the sacred bones from falling apart!'

He gave a snort of laughter, and looked to see if there was
more wine in the bottle. 'De Wetherset could do nothing to
convince Thorpe the thing was a fake and it is too late now
in any case. The rumours are abroad that a saintly relic is in
Valence Marie, and they are amassing a veritable fortune by
charging an entrance fee to see it.'

'It will all die down,' said Bartholomew. 'Give it time.'

'We do not have time,' snapped Michael suddenly. 'Thorpe
is a fool to make Valence Marie such a centre of attention with
the town so uneasy. It will be an obvious target if there is another
riot. And the damn thing is a fake! I would be charitable and
suggest it got into the Ditch by chance if it were not for the
ring and the pin.'

'The ring,' mused Bartholomew. He felt around in his pocket,
and pulled out the broken one he had found at Godwinsson. 'Is
this Kenzie's ring, do you think? Did he lose it when he was
skulking around Godwinsson waiting for Dominica to appear?
Or is Kenzie's ring now adorning the severed hand in Valence
Marie?'

Michael swilled the dregs of the wine around in the bottom

of his cup before draining it in a gulp. 'We could ask the Scottish lads to have a look at the one at Valence Marie,' he said. 'They might recognise it.'

'Would that be wise? Can we trust them not to start some rumour that Kenzie's severed limb is in Valence Marie? Then we might really have a problem on our hands. So to speak.'

'They might have a point,' said Michael.

Bartholomew shook his head firmly. 'Impossible. First, Kenzie's hands were not big enough to be the one at Valence Marie – believe me, I would have noticed if someone of Kenzie's height had hands the size of that skeleton's: it would have looked bizarre to say the least. Second, Kenzie was not wearing his ring when he was killed – he was asking Werbergh and Edred if they had it before he died.'

'Perhaps he found it after he had his conversation with Werbergh and Edred, and *was* wearing it when he was murdered,' said Michael with a shrug.

'I suppose he might,' said Bartholomew after a moment, 'although there is the ring I found in Godwinsson. That might have been the one Kenzie lost.'

Michael made an impatient click with his tongue. 'The ring you found is probably nothing to do with all this. It might have been in that derelict shed for weeks – even months – before you picked it up. There could be all sorts of explanations as to why it was there – not least of which was that it was thrown away precisely because it is broken. When I looked out of the window, I saw a scullion emptying waste there. The whole yard is probably a repository for rubbish.'

'It certainly smelled that way,' said Bartholomew, grimacing. 'But regardless of whether Kenzie did or did not have his ring when he died, the hand at Valence Marie does not belong to him. I will stake my reputation on it.'

'Well now,' said Michael, regarding his friend with an amused gleam in his eye. 'It is not often you are so absolutely unshakeable over the deductions you make from corpses. You usually insist on a degree of leeway in your interpretations. So, I suppose I will have to believe you. But I am not the issue here – the David's students are. And we have a problem: the David's lads are the only ones who might recognise the ring as Kenzie's, and yet we cannot risk them identifying it as his, because a riot would follow for certain.'

'Dominica would recognise it if, as Kenzie's friends suppose, it was a gift from her,' said Bartholomew.

Michael wrinkled his nose disdainfully at the notion. 'And how would we get the permission of her parents to let her come?' he said.

The sun went behind a cloud briefly, cooling the room for an instant, before emerging again and beating down relentlessly on the dried beaten earth of the courtyard.

Bartholomew leaned forward and thought. 'Let us assume she did give Kenzie the ring,' he said. 'Where would she have got it from? I doubt she had the money to go out and buy it herself. Therefore, she must have owned it already – it had probably been given to her by her parents. I am certain that Lydgate and his wife know exactly what jewellery their daughter owns, especially valuable pieces. If Lydgate or Cecily go to see this hand, they might recognise the ring.'

'That is even more outrageous,' said Michael. 'You are even less likely to get Lydgate to view this hand than his daughter. He would refuse outright if we asked. Sensible Cecily, meanwhile, has not yet returned to her husband, and if she has any intelligence at all, she never will. And not only that, neither of them knows that Kenzie was their daughter's lover, remember?'

Bartholomew was thoughtful for a moment. 'Your last point is irrelevant – it does not matter whether they know the identity of Dominica's lover or not for them to be able to identify the ring.'

'*Your* point is irrelevant,' Michael flashed back. 'Even if Lydgate can identify the ring as Dominica's, he would not tell us about it. And, as I said, sweet Cecily is still away. Lydgate has not exactly been scouring the countryside for his loving spouse; I have the feeling that he is as relieved to be apart from her as she, doubtless, is happy to be away from him.'

'I cannot make any sense out of all this, but one thing is patently clear.' Bartholomew fiddled with the laces on his shirt. 'If the ring on Valence Marie's relic really is the one that Kenzie lost – and I do not believe he miraculously found it after speaking with the Godwinsson friars only to die without it a few hours later – then the link between Kenzie and the fraud relating to this relic is beyond question.'

'I do not deny that,' said Michael. 'It is the nature of the link that eludes me.'

Both were silent as they reconsidered the few facts they had, until Bartholomew stood, and began to drag on his tabard.

'In all the excitement of finding that disgusting hand, we forgot the reason why we were at Valence Marie in the first place,' he said. 'We still need to talk to the French students about the rape and murder of Joanna.'

'We have managed to make enemies of the Principals of Godwinsson and Valence Marie both,' said Michael. 'I doubt very much if Thorpe will cooperate with you. He will assume you are still trying to prove his relic a fake – and after our experience earlier, I would be happier if you stayed well away from Valence Marie and their nasty bones.'

Bartholomew hesitated, recalling vividly the unmistakeably hostile atmosphere at Valence Marie. After a moment, he brightened. 'You are right about Thorpe, but there are others. One of the Fellows there is Father Eligius, and he is one of my patients. We have always been on friendly terms. He will help me if I ask.'

Michael eyed him dubiously. 'I know Eligius, too, and he looked to me like one of those most convinced of the hand's authenticity. He appeared positively fanatical. I cannot see that he would help you if he thought the outcome might be the discovery that the relic is a fake – regardless of your motives for asking the questions. And I cannot see him abandoning loyalty to his fellow members of College to allow you to prove some of them committed murder.'

'I will try anyway,' said Bartholomew, picking up his bag from the floor. He slipped the Galen into it so he would have something to read if Eligius kept him waiting. 'I have patients to see. I can try Eligius afterwards.'

'Try if you must,' said Michael, leaning back on the bed and closing his eyes, 'but be careful. I would go with you, but it is too hot, I am tired from patrolling last night, and I have no reason to believe you will be successful in discovering the murderer of this woman.'

Bartholomew shrugged off Michael's apathy and left the College for the High Street. Two of the more seriously injured riot victims still needed his attention, and he wanted to see Mistress Fletcher, one of the first people he had treated in Cambridge, now dying of a disease of the lungs despite all his efforts. He tapped lightly on her door and climbed the narrow wooden stairs to the upper chamber where she lay in her bed. Her husband and two sons sat with her, one strumming aimlessly on a badly tuned rebec. They stood as Bartholomew entered and Fletcher moved towards him.

'Please, Doctor,' he said. He gestured at his wife lying on the bed, her breathing a papery rustle. 'She needs to be bled.'

Bartholomew experienced a familiar feeling of exasperation at the mention of bleeding. It was an argument he had had with many of his patients, most of whom believed bleeding would cure virtually anything. He looked down at the sick woman with compassion, and his resolve hardened. She was dying anyway and invasive treatments now would merely serve to make her last few days miserable. He had brought a strong pain-killer that would help her through to the end without too much discomfort. He sent one of her sons for a cup of watered wine then crumbled the strong powder into it. Kneeling next to her, he helped her sip it until she had drunk it all. She lay back, the potion already easing the pain in her chest, and smiled gratefully.

'We could call Robin of Grantchester,' said Fletcher. 'He bleeds people for a penny, and applies leeches for two pennies.'

'It is very cheap,' added one of her sons hopefully.

'I am sure it is,' said Bartholomew, determined that the unsanitary surgeon would never set his blood-encrusted hands on poor Mistress Fletcher while he had breath in his body to prevent it.

The sick woman made a weak gesture and her husband bent to hear her. 'Please let Doctor Bartholomew treat me as he sees fit. He has already eased my chest. I want no leeches and no bleeding.'

Her husband stood again, awkwardly. 'I am sorry,' he said to Bartholomew. 'But this is difficult for us. I would do anything to give her a little more time.'

'She does not want it,' said Bartholomew gently. 'Not like this.'

Fletcher gazed down at his wife and said nothing. Seeing his patient asleep, her breathing less laboured than it had been, Bartholomew took his leave.

The street was almost as deserted as it had been the previous night: there were few who cared to venture out into the burning heat of the mid-afternoon sun. After only a short distance, the tickle of perspiration begin to prick at Bartholomew's back and he felt uncomfortably hot. He removed the tabard and shoved it into his bag. Guy Heppel could fine him for not wearing it, but the comfort of shirtsleeves would be worth it.

After visiting the two riot victims, Bartholomew walked towards Valence Marie, hoping to waylay Father Eligius as he left Valence Marie to attend terce at St Botolph's Church. Bartholomew was subdued because of his helplessness in treating Mistress Fletcher. He wondered what it was that caused wasting sicknesses in the chest and how they could be prevented. The more patients he saw and experience he gained, the more he realised how little he knew; the lack of knowledge depressed him.

When Father Eligius told him Valence Marie's French students had left that morning for London, Bartholomew grew even more dispirited. He walked past the town boundary, making his way across the meadows that led down to the river behind the Church of St Peter-without-Trumpington Gate. Reaching a cluster of oak trees, he stopped, dropped his bag, and sat with his back against one of the sturdy trunks. He squinted up into the branches, where the breeze played lazily with green leaves beginning to turn yellow. It was cooler in the meadow than in the town and the air smelled cleaner. It was also peaceful, with just the occasional raucous screech from a pair of jays that lived in one of the oaks and distant high-pitched chatter from children playing in the river to break the silence.

He thought about Kenzie, a young Scot who had had the misfortune to fall in love with a woman whose father would never accept him, and who was forced to keep his relationship secret. So who had killed him? Was it Dominica's angry father? Was it her mother? Since it did not take a great feat of strength to brain a man from behind, Bartholomew knew that a woman could have slain Kenzie as easily as a man. Perhaps Cecily's guilt was the real reason for her sudden flight from home. Were the killers the friars from Godwinsson, who were the last people known to have seen Kenzie alive? Was his death a random killing by someone intent on theft? And if so, was it Kenzie's ring that adorned Valence Marie's relic? But why had the two French students been ushered out of Godwinsson when Michael had asked to speak to them? Perhaps they were the murderers, and not the friars at all.

And what of poor Joanna? She had been buried at dawn

that morning in a cheap coffin paid for by the town, like the other town victims of the riot. Bartholomew had attended the funerals after mass at St Michael's, but he had been the only mourner for Joanna. While the family and friends of the other victims stood around the graves in St Botolph's churchyard, Bartholomew had stood alone, watching the verger shovel dry earth on top of Joanna. He wondered whether her friends and family even knew that she was dead. If no one had cared enough to attend her funeral, certainly no one cared enough to avenge her murder. Michael had said it was none of the University's affair, and anyway, the University was not in the business of hunting down its students for a crime on a victim that no one claimed; and Tulyet had neither the time nor the manpower.

Bartholomew stretched his legs out in front of him, and closed his eyes. Godwinsson, David's, Valence Marie and Maud's. All four seemed to be interconnected somehow with the murders of Kenzie or Joanna. And the dead child? Somehow he had been overlooked in all this. He had been buried the day before, his bones bundled up in a dirty sheet and thrust into a shallow grave in St Bene't's churchyard. A small mound of brown earth marked the site now, but in a few weeks it would be gone, and he would be forgotten again, just as he had been all those years before.

That thought brought a picture of Norbert into his mind, and Bartholomew smiled. It had been his only serious act of disobedience in Stanmore's household but one that he still felt was just. Did Lydgate know that Bartholomew had finally revealed his long-kept secret? Although the crime was twenty-five years old, there were still many who would remember it, and the hunt that had taken place for Norbert the following day. Bartholomew winced. That had been an unpleasant day for him, wondering whether vengeful villagers would return with Norbert captive to reveal who had let him escape.

Bartholomew wondered what he should do next. Should he follow the advice of Michael and Tulyet, and forget Joanna? The French students at Valence Marie had gone, so the only way forward was for him to talk to the two at Godwinsson. He knew their names and their faces, which meant he would not have to ask to see them through Lydgate. He stood up and reached for his bag, determining upon a course of action. The ailing Mistress Fletcher lived close enough to Godwinsson to allow Bartholomew to be nearby a good deal without arousing suspicion. He could even see Godwinsson from the windows on her upper floor. Starting tomorrow, he decided he would stay with Mistress Fletcher until he saw the Frenchmen leave, then follow until they reached a convenient place for him to confront them.

He retraced his steps through the meadow towards the High Street. Absorbed in thoughts of Mistress Fletcher's lungs and in ways to find Joanna's killer, he was so engrossed that he walked past Matilde without noticing her. It was only when she repeated his name, a little crossly, that he came out of his reverie and saw her.

'You are in a fine mood today,' she said, noting his grave face as he turned. 'I thought you were pretending not to know me!'

He smiled then. 'Oh no! Never that.'

But many men would, he knew. There were few who would converse openly with one of the town prostitutes in the middle of the High Street, at least, not during daylight hours. There were even fewer who would invite one to the most auspicious College event of the year, risking instant dismissal from their fellowships. He thrust that thought to the back of his mind, and listened to Matilde's amusing account about how a number of stray cats had raided the Market Square fish-stall while its owner had slipped away to view the relic at Valence Marie.

It occurred to Bartholomew, as he talked with Matilde, that she might very well know Joanna, the murdered prostitute with hair like Philippa. Bartholomew had no idea how many prostitutes worked in Cambridge, but he did know that they had an unofficial guild and held meetings during which they exchanged information and advice. When he asked her, Matilde looked taken aback.

'I know of no sister called Joanna,' she said. Bartholomew smiled to himself; he had forgotten Matilde referred to the other prostitutes as sisters. 'What did this Joanna look like?'

Bartholomew was at a loss for words. Joanna's face had been so battered that to describe it was impossible. He remembered in vivid detail the wounds she had suffered during the rape, and the savage blow to her head that had killed her, but telling Matilde that would get him nowhere. 'She was tall and had long, fair hair,' he said lamely.

Matilde spread her hands. 'None of the sisters is called

Joanna,' she repeated. 'I thought perhaps you may have been referring to one or two ladies in the villages who ply their wares here occasionally, but none of them has long, fair hair. Why do you want her? Perhaps I can help.'

Realising how her words might be interpreted, she blushed. Bartholomew, seeing her embarrassment also looked away, feeling the colour mounting in his own cheeks. After a brief silence they looked at each other again, and smiled, so that the uneasy atmosphere was broken.

'Joanna was killed in the riots,' he said. 'I wondered whether you might know her.'

Matilde looked shocked. 'No sister was foolish enough to be out when the riots were on, Matthew,' she said. 'All those men prowling around in gangs? Heavens, no! We may have been overwhelmed by business, but none of it would have been paid for. As soon as we saw what was happening, we put out the word that any sensible woman should remain indoors.'

'Do you know what all this rioting was about? Michael, Sheriff Tulyet, my colleagues at Michaelhouse, and even my brother-in-law, are at a loss as to why there is such an atmosphere of disquiet in the town.'

Matilde did not answer immediately, but looked away down the High Street. Bartholomew stared at her, admiring yet again her delicate beauty. She wore a plain blue dress that accentuated her lithe figure, and her unblemished skin, glossy hair and small, white teeth bespoke of health and vitality. She was also one of the few people Bartholomew knew who always seemed to have clean hands, and one of fewer still who did not have a perennial crust of dirt beneath her finger-nails. When she finally started to answer, Bartholomew found he had been so absorbed in looking at her, that he had all but forgotten what he had asked.

'In our profession,' she began, 'your hear things. Recently, I have been hearing a great deal.' She turned to look at him. 'I trust you, Matthew, which is why I will tell you what I know, although you must understand that I am breaking one of my own rules by breaching the confidence of a client. I would not do it for anyone else.'

'Are you sure you should?' Bartholomew asked. He found himself wishing yet again that she was not a prostitute and was angry at himself. Philippa's sudden rejection of him must have affected him more than he had originally appreciated;

he felt he was becoming like Brother Michael, full of secret lusts!

Matilde, unaware of the conflict within him, peered at him earnestly. 'Are you well, Matthew? You look pale.' At his nod, she continued. 'I have heard that the death of the Scottish student and the discovery of the child's bones were used to start the riot. Rumours said that both had been murdered and students and townsfolk alike were goaded with accusations of cowardice because they had done nothing to avenge them. The rumours started among the stall-holders in the Market Square, who are notorious as sources of gossip.'

Bartholomew rubbed his chin. So it seemed that Stanmore, Tulyet and Michael had been right after all – there was more to the riots than met the eye. Rumours had been deliberately started in a place where they would be sure to spread and inflame.

Matilde watched him. 'You had already guessed that much,' she said. 'I can see in your face you are not surprised. I heard that the rumour that the Scot was murdered by a townsman came from Godwinsson Hostel and the Hall of Valence Marie.'

Bartholomew stared at her. Godwinsson and Valence Marie yet again!

Matilde smiled, showing her even teeth. 'There! Now I have told you something you did not already know.'

Before he could stop himself Bartholomew asked, 'Was the person who told you all this responsible for starting the rumours? He must be, or how else would he know?'

Matilde pursed her lips. Bartholomew knew she was resentful that he should ask the name of her client when she had already overstepped her own personal code of conduct by talking about him in the first place.

'The riot was started in order to hide something else,' she continued, ignoring his question. 'Two acts were committed that night and the riot was contrived to hide them.'

'What two acts?' asked Bartholomew, nonplussed. 'The burglary of Deschalers's property? The burning of the Market Square?'

'I do not know,' said Matilde. 'I am only repeating what I have been told. The riots were contrived to mask the true purpose of two acts. Those were the exact words of my client.'

They talked a little more, before they parted to go separate ways. Bartholomew was mystified. He wished he knew the identity of Matilde's client, so that he could discover what these two acts were that necessitated such bloodshed and mayhem to mask them. The burglary at Deschalers's house had not been masked: several of Stanmore's apprentices had heard the house being ransacked and had seen dark-cloaked figures running away from the scene of the crime. Could one of the acts be the death of the woman called Joanna? But why? Bartholomew distinctly remembered her clothes. They were of good quality but not luxurious, suggesting that she had been comfortable but not rich. So, why would anyone need to spark off a riot to harm her? If she had committed some offence, it would have been far easier to have dispatched her in a dark alley with a knife.

Matilde was scarcely beyond earshot when Bartholomew was accosted by Eleanor Tyler, her dark hair bundled into a white veil and her grey eyes narrowed against the sun.

'Eleanor!' he exclaimed in genuine pleasure. 'Good evening!'

'Not so good,' she muttered, looking down the street to where Matilde picked her way gracefully through the ever-present rubbish and waste.

'Why? What has happened?' asked Bartholomew, concerned. 'Is your mother ill? One of your sisters? Hedwise?'

Eleanor pulled a sulky face at him and glanced back to where Matilde now stood talking to one of Stanmore's seamstresses. Eleanor's meaning suddenly struck home to Bartholomew. Did she believe he had been making arrangements for an assignation with Matilde?

'Matilde is a friend,' he began, wishing her to know the truth before it went any further. He hesitated. What more could he say without being offensive about Matilde —especially since it would not be long before Eleanor learned that Matilde was to be his other guest at the Founder's Feast?

'I heard you have a liking for her,' said Eleanor coldly.

'It is not like you imagine,' said Bartholomew, not certain that he was telling her the entire truth.

'You mean you do not engage her professional services?' said Eleanor bluntly. 'All very well, but it does your reputation no good to be seen chatting with her so confidently in the High Street. And now, since I am talking to you, my reputation is also being damaged.'

Bartholomew stared at her in disbelief. 'I hardly think—'

'For a man who has spent so much time travelling and seeing the world you have learned very little.' She raised her hand to silence his objections. 'I am not saying you have not learned your medicine. Indeed, you are generally regarded as the best physician in Cambridge, although you should know that many say your methods are dangerous, and disapprove of the fact that you are regularly seen in the streets talking to beggars, lepers – and now prostitutes!'

'But many of these are my patients—'

'And,' she continued, overriding him a second time, 'you should know that this woman – Lady Matilde, as you doubtless call her – should not be trusted. She makes up stories about her clients. See her if you must, but I would warn you against it for your own good.'

With that, she turned on her heel and stalked away, leaving Bartholomew bewildered in the middle of the High Street. A shout from a farmer with a huge cart saved him from being trampled by a team of oxen and, regaining his composure, he was suddenly angry. He hardly knew Eleanor Tyler and felt she had no right to talk to him about Matilde in the way she had. A veritable fountain of responses came into his mind, in the way that they usually did when the situation for using them had passed.

Then his anger faded. What did it matter? Eleanor had called him naïve. Perhaps he was – Matilde and Michael had both told him as much recently. It was clear that Eleanor strongly disapproved of Matilde and he should see her outburst for what it was: a simple, and not entirely surprising, dislike of prostitutes. He wondered whether Eleanor imagined she had some kind of claim on him following the invitation to the Founder's Feast. The thought also crossed his mind that his innocent discussion with Matilde might well give Eleanor cause to decline his offer, and then at least he would only have one woman to explain away to his chaste-minded colleagues.

He looked back to where Matilde was still speaking with the seamstress. Seeing him watching them, they both waved; self-consciously, he waved back. He hoped Eleanor's words were nothing more than jealousy, because he felt Matilde's information might prove helpful to Tulyet and Michael if it were true. But if Matilde were known to be untrustworthy, her clients might feed her false information, so her claim that the riot had been started to hide two acts might be meaningless.

Yet she had appeared to consider carefully before breaking the confidence of her client. But then perhaps she preceded all her gossip with this show of reluctance. He dismissed the whole affair from his mind impatiently, realising that mulling over what Matilde and Eleanor had said meant that he was merely raising yet more questions to which he had no answers. He decided to tell Michael what Matilde had revealed, but to advise him to use the information cautiously.

As he walked past St Bene't's Church, the doors opened and the students who had been to sext filed out. Since this was not one of the religious offices the students were obliged to attend, only those that wanted to pray were there. Thus it was a subdued crowd that emerged, in contrast to the high-spirited one he had seen three days before.

He saw a familiar figure and darted after him, stopping him dead in his tracks with a firm grip on his arm.

'You are hurting me!' whined the terrified Werbergh, looking in vain for help from his Godwinsson cronies. They, however, had more sense than to interfere in the dubious affairs of their untrustworthy colleague, and quickly melted away, leaving the friar and Bartholomew alone. Panic-stricken, Werbergh began to struggle, whimpering feeble objections about his rough treatment.

'Let me go! You cannot lay hands on a priest! I am one of God's chosen! I will tell Master Lydgate that you have been molesting a man of God!'

Bartholomew gave a small, humourless smile. 'Men of God do not lie. And you were not wholly honest with me, Brother Werbergh.'

Werbergh squirmed in Bartholomew's grip. 'I told you everything that happened. Please!'

'But when I discussed what you had told me with Brother Michael, your story and Edred's did not tally. You said you returned to Godwinsson with Cecily Lydgate after compline the night Kenzie was murdered, but Edred – with Cecily listening – claimed to have accompanied you. One, or both, of you is lying. What have you to say?'

Werbergh stopped struggling, his head and shoulders sagging. 'I told you the truth,' he insisted. 'I *did* go to compline with Edred and I *did* walk back with Mistress Lydgate. The Scot – Kenzie – *did* ask us if we had stolen his ring the night he was killed. But I suppose I did not tell you everything,' he added with a fearful glance at Bartholomew. 'That is to say, I only told you what I know to be true and what I understand.'

'Oh, for heaven's sake!' said Bartholomew, exasperated. 'Stop twisting words and tell me something honest.'

People on the High Street were beginning to notice them, wondering why he was holding the friar's arm so uncomfortably high. Bartholomew's tabard was in his medicine bag, so he looked like a townsperson abusing a student. He relaxed his hold on Werbergh to one that looked more natural, before some scholars took it into their heads to rescue the friar.

'I omitted only one thing,' said Werbergh miserably, looking up at Bartholomew. The physician in him noted the friar's shaking hands and unhealthy pallor. Werbergh was not a man at peace with the world or himself. 'I think Edred probably did steal the ring. I did not see him do it, but he has done it before. He jostles people, and afterwards, they discover that something is missing. I do not know how he does it. Anyway, he jostled the Scot, but it misfired and we ended up in that silly argument in the street.'

Bartholomew released Werbergh completely, watching him as he rubbed his arm. 'Anything else?'

'I was coming to see you anyway,' said Werbergh, glancing up and down the street nervously. 'That is why I was in the church – I was praying for guidance. I had just decided to come to talk to you and there you were, like an avenging angel.'

He looked at Bartholomew with glistening eyes, and Bartholomew wondered whether he had been drinking.

'I think Edred stole the ring. I think he knows more about Kenzie's death than he is telling,' said Werbergh in a rush. 'He was also gone all night when the riot was on and I believe he was out fighting. Perhaps he has a taste for violence; when I asked him where he had been the next day, he gave me this black eye.'

Bartholomew remembered Werbergh's bruised face the day after the riot and saw that his cheek remained discoloured. Edred had been limping. So what had the other duplicitous friar been doing?

'And where were you when the town was ablaze, Brother Werbergh?' Bartholomew asked.

'In Godwinsson, virtually alone,' said Werbergh unhappily. 'I have no taste for rough behaviour. I imagined I might get hurt if I went out fighting.'

'What about the French students at Godwinsson? Were they out that night?'

Werbergh, once he had started informing on his colleagues, was more than ready to continue. 'Of course. They love fighting, and they boast that they are good at it. Two came back later and said that their friend had been killed.'

'Did they say anything about what they had done that night?'

'Oh, yes. They spoke in great detail about the tremendous fight they had had with ten townsmen all armed with massive broadswords. They say they were lucky to survive but that Louis had been treacherously stabbed in the back before being overwhelmed.'

So, the Frenchmen's pride had been injured, Bartholomew thought, and they were unwilling to admit that Louis had been killed by a woman. Perhaps it was better that way. He did not like to think that the Godwinsson students might take revenge on the Tyler household for his death. Werbergh could tell him nothing more and Bartholomew let him go, watching him thoughtfully as he weaved his way through the throngs of tradesmen making their way home.

chapter 6

THUNDER ROLLED AGAIN, DISTANTLY, AND ANOTHER silver fork of lightning illuminated the darkened court-yard of Michaelhouse. Bartholomew sipped the sour ale he had stolen from the kitchens and watched through the opened shutters of his room. The night was almost dripping with humidity, even in the stone-walled rooms of the College and, from low voices carried on the still air, Bartholomew knew he was not the only person kept awake by the heat and the approaching storm.

He thought about Mistress Flecher. She would find the night unbearable with her failing lungs. She would be unable to draw enough air to allow her to breathe comfortably and would feel as though she were drowning. He considered going to visit her, perhaps to give her a posset to make her sleep more easily, but distant yells and the smell of burning suggested that a riot of sorts had broken out in some part of the town. The streets would be patrolled by the beadles and the Sheriff's men and he had no wish to be arrested by either for breaking the curfew.

Sweat trickled down his back. Even sitting in his room sipping the brackish ale was making him hot. He stood restlessly and opened the door, trying to create a draught to cool himself down. The lightning came again, nearer this time, lasting several moments when the College was lit up as bright as at noon. In the room above, he heard Michael's heavy footsteps pacing the protesting floorboards, and the muttered complaints of his room-mates for keeping them awake.

While the evening light had lasted, Bartholomew had read his borrowed book, then had fallen asleep at the table with his head resting on his arms. He had woken stiff and aching two hours later, his mind teeming with confused dreams involving Philippa, Matilde and Eleanor, and wild collections of bones arising from the King's Ditch.

Philippa. He thought about her now, humorous blue eyes and long tresses of deep gold hair. He had not realised how much he missed her until he knew she would not be returning to him. He wondered how he had managed to make for himself a life that was so lonely. A creak from the room above made him think of Michael, a Benedictine monk in major orders. Bartholomew often wondered, from his behaviour and attitudes, how seriously the monk took his vow of chastity. But Michael had deliberately chosen such a life, whereas Bartholomew had not, although he might just as well have done. He wondered whether he should take Michael's advice and become a friar or a monk, devoting himself entirely to his studies, teaching and patients. But then he would never be away from his confessor, because he liked women and what they had to offer.

He went to lie down on his bed to try to sleep, but after a few minutes, rose again restlessly. The rough blanket prickled his bare skin and made him hotter than ever. He paced the room in the darkness, wondering what he could do to pass the time and divert his mind from dwelling on Philippa. Since candles were expensive they were not readily dispensed to the scholars of Michaelhouse, and Bartholomew had used the last of his allowance that morning to read before dawn. When the natural light faded, most reading and writing ceased and the scholars usually went to bed, unless they took the considerable risk of carousing in the town. Then Bartholomew realised that he did have a spare candle, given to him in lieu of payment by a patient. He had been saving it for the winter, but why not use it now, to read the Galen, since he could not sleep?

He groped along the single shelf in his room, recalling that he had left it next to his spare quills. It was not there. He wondered if perhaps Cynric had taken it, or Michael. But that was unlikely. It was more probably Gray, who had taken things from Bartholomew without asking before. He took another sip of the warm ale, and then, in disgust at its rank, bitter flavour, poured it away out of the window.

'The Master has forbidden the tipping of waste in the yard. At your own insisting, Doctor,' came the admonishing tones of Walter, the night porter, through the open window. Bartholomew was a little ashamed. Walter was right: Bartholomew had recommended to Kenyngham that all waste should be tipped into the cesspool behind the kitchen gardens, following an outbreak of a disease at Michaelhouse that made the bowels bleed. Bartholomew had been proven correct: the disease had subsided when the scholars were not exposed to all kinds of unimaginable filth on their way from their rooms to meals in the hall.

'What do you want, Walter?' Bartholomew asked testily, setting the empty cup on the window-sill. 'It is the middle of the night.'

Walter's long, morose face was lit by a flicker of lightning and Bartholomew saw him squint at the brightness. Both looked up at the sky, seeing great, heavy-bellied clouds hanging there, showing momentarily light grey under the sudden flash.

'A patient needs you. Urgent.' It was no secret that Walter resented the fact that Master Kenyngham had given Bartholomew permission to come and go from the College during the night if needed by a patient. Such calls were not uncommon, especially during outbreaks of summer ague or winter fevers.

Walter glanced up at the sky again. 'You will probably get drenched when this storm breaks,' he added, in tones of malicious satisfaction.

Bartholomew looked at him in distaste, confident that Walter would be unable to make out his expression in the darkness of his room.

'Who is it?' he asked, reaching for his shirt and pulling it over his head, grimacing as it stuck unpleasantly to his back. He tucked it into his hose, and sat on the bed to put on his boots. Walter was right about the rain and Bartholomew had no intention of tramping about in a heavy downpour in shoes. He knew well what sudden storms were like in Cambridge: the rainwater would turn the dusty streets into rivers of mud; in the mud would be offal, sewage, animal dung and all manner of rotting vegetation. Wearing shoes would be tantamount to walking barefoot.

Walter rested his elbows on the window-sill and leaned inside, lit from behind by another flash of lightning.

'Mistress Fletcher,' he said. 'Does she have a son? It was not her husband who came.'

'Yes, she has two,' said Bartholomew, his stomach churning. Surely it was not time for her to die already? Perhaps the wetness of the air had hastened her end. He hoped the storm would break soon and that in her last moments she would breathe air that carried the clean scent of wet earth.

Bartholomew saw his door open, and Michael stepped inside,

clad in his baggy black robe with no cowl or waist-tie, while the wooden cross he usually wore around his neck had been tucked down the front of his habit. Michael had explained that it had once caught on a loose slat of his bed and all but strangled him in his sleep; now he slept with it inside his habit out of harm's way. He looked even larger than usual. Without the trappings that marked him as a monk, Bartholomew thought, he looked like one of the fat, rich merchants who lived on Milne Street.

'I heard voices,' Michael said. 'What has happened?'

'Mistress Fletcher needs me,' Bartholomew answered, struggling with his second boot. The hot weather seemed to have shrunk them somehow. Or perhaps his feet were swollen.

Michael shook his head. 'There were the beginnings of a riot tonight, Matt. It is not safe for you to go out.'

'Who was rioting?' Bartholomew asked, pulling harder at his boot.

'Some apprentices set light to that big pile of wood in the Market Square. The Sheriff's men put it down fairly easily, but I am sure small groups of youths looking for trouble are still roaming around, despite the patrols.'

The boot slid on at last and Bartholomew stood. He indicated his tabard folded on the room's single chest. 'Then I will leave that here and, if I meet any apprentices, they will think I am a townsperson.'

Michael sighed. 'They will see a lone man and will attack regardless of whether you are town or gown,' he said. 'Wait three hours until the curfew is lifted.'

Bartholomew shook his head. 'She might not be alive in three hours. She needs me now.'

Michael gave a resigned sigh. 'Then we shall go together,' he said. 'From the sound of it, she will be more in need of my skills than yours anyway.'

Bartholomew gave him a grateful smile in the darkness, and followed him into the yard. Once out, he realised how comparatively cool it had been in his room after all. The heat lay thick, heavy and still in the night air. It was slightly misty, where the fetid ditches and waterways were evaporating into the already drenched air. The smell was overpowering. Lightning cracked overhead, followed immediately by a growl of thunder. Quickly, Bartholomew led the way out through the wicket gate, up St Michael's Lane and into the High Street. Mistress Fletcher lived on New Bridges Street, almost opposite Godwinsson Hostel. On the way they had to pass the leafy churchyards of St Michael's, St Mary's, St Bene't's and St Botolph's, all stretching off into a dark abyss of overgrown grass and thick bushes.

As they reached St Bene't's the lightning flickered again and, out of the corner of his eye, Bartholomew thought he saw something glint briefly. He paused, peering into the gloom to try to make out what he had seen. Michael plucked at his sleeve.

'Let's not dally here of all places,' he said anxiously, then stopped short as someone came hurtling out of the row of trees running along the edge of the churchyard. He was knocked to his knees and someone leapt on his back with considerable force, pushing him flat on the ground. He was aware that Bartholomew had been similarly attacked and was angry with himself for not insisting that they were both armed before going out. Usually, the sight of Michael, monk and Senior Proctor, was enough to ward off most potential acts of violence, but he was not wearing his full habit tonight because of the heat.

He began to squirm under the weight of the man on top of him, and felt a second person come to help hold him down.

'Shame on you! Attacking one of God's monks!' he roared, a tactic that had worked successfully in the past. A snort of laughter met his words, indicating he had not been believed. He struggled again but his arms were pinned to his sides. The sound of a violent scuffle to one side told him in an instant what was happening. The message had been sent to lure Bartholomew out of the College. Michael had not been expected, and the two men holding him down were doing no more than that: he was not being harmed or searched for valuables, simply being kept from going to the aid of his friend.

The knowledge enraged him and he began his struggles anew, yelling furiously, hoping to raise the alarm. A heavy, none-too-clean, hand clamped down over his mouth, and he bit it as hard as he could. There was a cry of pain and the hand was removed to be replaced by a fistful of his own loose gown, rammed so hard against his face that he could scarcely breathe. He heard a shrill howl coming from the skirmish to his right and guessed that Bartholomew, unarmed or not, was putting up quite a fight.

'Where is it?' came a hissed question, more desperate than
menacing.

Michael heard the fight abate and Bartholomew ask, 'Where
is what?'

Loud cursing by an unfamiliar voice suggested that Bartholomew had taken advantage of the lull to land a heavy
kick. Michael, dizzy from lack of air, renewed his own efforts
to escape but stopped when he felt the cold touch of steel
against his neck.

'Tell us, or we will kill him.' On cue Michael felt the blade
move closer to his throat.

'I do not know what you want!' Bartholomew sounded
appalled. 'He is a monk. Kill him, and you will be damned
in the sight of God!'

Michael mentally applauded the threat of hell fires and
eternal damnation to get them out of their predicament,
but his brief flare of hope faded rapidly when he realised
Bartholomew's ploy had not worked.

'This is your brother-in-law, Oswald Stanmore,' the voice
hissed again, the knife pricking at Michael's throat. 'He is a
merchant, not a monk!'

Michael closed his eyes in despair. In the daylight, his habit
would be unmistakeable, tied and cowled or not, but in the
dark it was just a robe. He strained against his captors again,
but weakly because of the burning in his lungs, protesting at
the lack of air. Any moment now he would black out.

He was dimly aware that Bartholomew was still fighting but
the noise did not induce the people who lived in the houses
opposite the churchyard to come to their rescue. But why
should they? They were likely to be harmed, and almost
certain to be arrested for breaking the curfew.

'No!' someone yelled.

Then followed: 'Fool!'

Someone grabbed a handful of Michael's hair and wrenched
his head up, and he saw a knife flash in the darkness. He closed
his eyes again tightly and tried to remember the words of the
prayers for the dying.

Abruptly and unexpectedly, he was released. The weight that
had been crushing him lifted, and the handful of material that
had been slowly suffocating him dropped away. For a moment,
all he could do was suck in great mouthfuls of air. He scrabbled
at his throat to see if it had been cut and he was bleeding

to death, and felt instead the wooden cross that must have fallen out of his habit when his head had been pulled back. He looked up and down the High Street, glimpsing several dark shadows moving some distance away, and then they were gone. The road was deserted and as still as the grave.

Slowly, he crawled to Bartholomew. The first heavy drops of rain began to splatter in the dust, breaking the silence as they fell harder and faster. He pulled himself together and rolled Bartholomew on to his back, giving him a rough shake that made him open his eyes. After a moment Michael stood, reeling from his near strangulation, and hauled Bartholomew to his feet.

'Bring him here.'

Michael saw Mistress Tyler standing in the doorway to her house a short distance away, and they staggered towards her. The rain was coming down in sheets; by the time they reached her door they were drenched.

Wordlessly, Michael pushed past her into the small room beyond and Bartholomew sank gratefully on to the rush-strewn floor. Eleanor kindled a lamp, exclaiming in horror as she recognised them when the room jumped into brightness. Mistress Tyler dispatched her for wine, and bundled the younger girl away to bed.

'The commotion awoke us but we would have been able to do little to help,' said Hedwise, wringing her hands. 'We would have tried, though, had we known it was you, even if it had only been throwing stones from the window.'

'It is better that you stayed out of it,' said Michael. 'I doubt you would have been able to help and you may have brought reprisals upon yourselves. Did you ask us here without knowing who we were, then?'

Mistress Tyler nodded. 'We saw only two men attacked and needing help.'

Michael was impressed, certain that such open charity would not be available to anyone from Michaelhouse, especially if the morose Walter were on gate duty. He turned back to Bartholomew, and saw a large red stain on the front of his shirt. He took a strip of linen from Eleanor, bundled it into a pad, them pushed it down hard, as he had seen Bartholomew do to staunch the blood-flow from wounds.

Bartholomew looked at him in bewilderment. 'What are you doing?'

'Stopping the bleeding,' Michael answered assertively. Now the first shock of the attack was over, he was beginning to regain some of his customary confidence; the terrifying feeling of helplessness he had experienced when he was being suffocated was receding.

Bartholomew sat up, pushing Michael's hands away. 'What bleeding?' he asked, holding his head in both hands as it reeled and swam at his sudden movement.

'You are bleeding,' answered Michael, applying his pressure pad again firmly.

Bartholomew shook his head and instantly regretted it. He hoped he was not going to be sick in Mistress Tyler's house. He saw the red stain on his shirt but knew it was from no injury of his own. At some point in the struggle Bartholomew had scored a direct hit on one man's nose, and blood had splattered from him on to Bartholomew as they fell to the ground together.

Michael gazed at Bartholomew's shirt with wide eyes, looking so baffled that Bartholomew would have laughed had his head not ached so.

'Did you not check there was a wound first?' asked Bartholomew, his voice ringing in his head like the great brass bells at St Mary's Church.

Michael shrugged off this irrelevance. 'If the blood is not yours, what ails you?'

'A bump on the head,' Bartholomew replied.

'Is that all?' Michael sighed. 'Then we should stop pestering Mistress Tyler and return to Michaelhouse.'

'Stay a while,' insisted Eleanor, returning from the kitchen with a bottle and some goblets. 'At least wait until the rain stops.'

'And take a little wine,' said Mistress Tyler, filling a cup and offering it to Bartholomew. 'You look as though you need some.'

Michael snatched it and drained it in a single draught. 'I did,' he said, handing the empty goblet back with satisfaction. 'I was almost suffocated, you know.'

'We saw,' said Eleanor, with a patent lack of interest in Michael's brush with death. She knelt next to Bartholomew and offered him another goblet. 'Drink this, Matt. It is finest French wine.'

'He needs ale, not wine,' said Hedwise scornfully, appearing on his other side with a large tankard of frothy beer. 'I brewed this myself.'

'Rubbish!' snapped Eleanor, thrusting her goblet at Bartholomew. 'Everyone knows that wine is the thing for sudden shocks. Ale will do him no good at all.'

'With respect,' said Bartholomew, pushing both vessels away firmly, 'I would rather drink nothing.' He felt queasy and the proximity of alcoholic fumes was making his stomach churn. He struggled to stand, hindered more than helped by the sister on either side of him.

'Are you ready?' asked Michael archly, when the physician had finally extricated himself from their helpful hands.

Bartholomew nodded and followed Michael towards the door.

'See you next Tuesday,' said Eleanor, beaming as she opened it for him.

'And I shall see you the following Sunday,' said Hedwise, raising her chin in the air defiantly as she glowered at her sister.

Sensing an unseemly disagreement in the making, Mistress Tyler hauled them both back inside and closed the door quickly. Bickering voices could be heard through the open window.

Once they began to walk along the High Street, Bartholomew wished he had stayed longer. Walking made him dizzy and he wanted to lie down. He lunged across the road to retrieve his medicine bag that had been upended and searched during the fight. Michael took his arm and guided him away from some of the deeper potholes, some rapidly filling with rain.

'You are in for one hell of a day at the Founder's Feast,' remarked Michael unkindly. 'That Eleanor has set her sights on you and she will be none too pleased when she sees she has a rival for your affections.'

'Eleanor has done nothing of the sort,' muttered Bartholomew, rubbing his eyes to try to clear them. 'She is probably just interested in hearing your choir.'

Michael shook his head firmly. 'You want to watch yourself, Matt, dallying mercilessly with all these ladies. If you are not careful, you will end up like Kenzie – murdered in the King's Ditch. There is nothing as venomous as a woman betrayed.'

'Oh, really?' asked Bartholomew. 'Over the last four years

or so, I have seen a good deal more venom expended by the men of the town than by the women.'

'We should be considering what has just happened, not discussing your love life,' said Michael, suddenly serious, perhaps because he knew Bartholomew was right. 'What did those men want from you? Did you know them? It seems that Walter was right when he did not recognise the messenger as one of Mistress Fletcher's family. We were foolish to have walked into such an obvious trap.'

Bartholomew put his hand to his head in an effort to stop it spinning and closed his eyes. That was worse. He opened them again.

'They thought you were Oswald Stanmore,' he said, leaning heavily on Michael.

Michael caught him as he stumbled. 'Watch where you are going! I imagine my dark robe misled them.'

'They were from Godwinsson,' Bartholomew said, trying to concentrate on the way ahead, them wincing as a flash of lightning lanced brightly into his eyes. The rain was pleasant though, drenching him in a cooling shower and clearing the blurring from his eyes.

'Godwinsson? How could you see that in the dark?' queried Michael in disbelief.

'You should not ask me questions if you do not think I can answer them,' Bartholomew retorted irritably. 'There were lightning flashes and I saw their faces quite clearly. One was Huw the steward, and another was the servant I saw emptying the slops while I was hiding in Godwinsson's back yard – Saul Potter, I think he is called. And one of the ones who fought you was Will from Valence Marie – the fellow who keeps digging up bones.'

'That puny little tyke?' exclaimed Michael. 'Are you certain?'

Bartholomew nodded cautiously, his hand still to his head. 'And the one demanding to know where "it" was I think may have been Thomas Bigod, the Master of Maud's.'

Michael whirled around. 'Now I know you must be raving! Why would Master Bigod attack us in the street? Or rather, attack you, since I think this whole business has nothing to do with me – it was to you the message was sent. What did you say to Father Eligius when you went to Valence Marie this afternoon that has set the servant after you so furiously? Did you press him too hard about the Frenchmen?'

Bartholomew could not imagine he had said anything to Eligius, or anyone else, to warrant such a violent attack. 'I simply asked him if he knew where I might find his college's French students. He told me that they had gone to London.'

Michael looked sceptical. 'Just when term is beginning? It is an odd time for students to be leaving the University to say the least. Did you tell Eligius why you wanted them? Did you mention the relic and offend him by your rejection of it?'

Bartholomew skidded in something slippery. 'He would not have noticed if I had. He was too absorbed in his own devotion to the thing. It was difficult to persuade him to discuss anything else.'

Michael was silent, concentrating on steering himself and Bartholomew clear of the more obvious obstacles that turned the High Street into a dangerous gauntlet of ankle-wrenching holes, treacherously slick mud, and repellent mounds of substances the monk did not care to think about.

'But what about Master Bigod?' he said eventually. 'I cannot imagine why he would be out in the rain ambushing his colleagues.'

Bartholomew frowned, trying to concentrate. 'I may be mistaken – I did not see his face because it was hidden by a hood. But I am sure I recognised his voice. He is from Norwich, and his accent is distinctive, not to mention the fact that his voice is unusually deep.'

'Well, what do you think he wanted?' asked Michael, still dubious.

Bartholomew shrugged. 'I have no idea.' He stopped abruptly, turning to face Michael. 'Unless it could be that broken ring I found.'

Michael scratched his chin, the rain plastering his thin brown hair to his scalp, making his head seem very small atop his large body. 'It may have been, I suppose.'

'I think I may have broken the arm of one of our attackers: I was holding it when I fell and I heard it crack. He was wielding a knife, trying to stab me, and Bigod called for him to stop. I struggled and he missed, striking the ground instead – I heard it scrape the ground next to my ear. I suppose the sight of the blood on my shirt led Bigod to assume it was mine. I decided to play into their belief that I was dead so they would leave, but one of them, that Saul Potter I think, kicked my head.' He rubbed it ruefully. 'A tactical error on my part.'

'I do not think so, Matt,' said Michael soberly. 'They were certainly going to slit my throat. They only desisted at the last moment because they realised I really was a monk and not just Oswald Stanmore.'

Bartholomew tried to work out what the servants of Godwinsson and Valence Marie could possibly want from him. Or Master Bigod from Maud's. It proved their institutions were connected in some way. But how? To the murder of the child and James Kenzie? To the rape and murder of Joanna? To the mysterious movements of Kenzie's ring? Or to the 'two acts' that Matilde said the riot was instigated to hide?

Thinking was making him feel light-headed and he felt his legs begin to give way. They had reached St Michael's Church. He lurched towards one of the tombstones in the churchyard and held on to it to prevent himself from falling.

'I think I am going to be sick,' he said in a whisper, dropping to his hands and knees in the wet grass.

Feeling better, he was helped to his feet by Michael. 'May the Lord forgive you, Matthew,' the monk said with amusement. 'You have just thrown up on poor Master Wilson's grave.'

When Bartholomew woke, he sensed someone else was in the room with him. He opened his eyes and blinked hard. Above him the curious face of Rob Deynman hovered.

'At last!' the student said, his voice loud and unendearingly cheerful. 'I was beginning to think you would sleep for ever.'

'So I might, had I known I would wake to you,' Bartholomew muttered unkindly, sitting up carefully.

'What was that?' Deynman said, putting his ear close to Bartholomew in a grotesque parody of the bedside manner that Bartholomew had been trying to instil into him. Not receiving a reply, he pushed Bartholomew back down on the bed and slapped something icy and wet on his head with considerable force.

'God's teeth!' gasped Bartholomew, his eyes stinging from the violence of Deynman's cold-compress application.

'You just lie there quietly,' Deynman yelled, hauling the blanket up around Bartholomew's chin with such vigour that it all but strangled him. Bartholomew wondered why Deynman was shouting. He was not usually loud-voiced.

'Where is Michael?' he asked.

Deynman favoured him with an admonishing look. 'Brother

Michael is asleep, as are all Michaelhouse scholars. Tom Bulbeck, Sam Gray, and I – we three are your best students – are the only ones awake.'

'Not for long if you keep shouting,' said Bartholomew, feeling cautiously at his head. Someone had bandaged it, expertly, and only a little too tight.

Deynman laughed. 'You are back to normal,' he said. 'Crabby!'

Bartholomew stared at him in disbelief. Cheeky young rascal! 'Where is Sam?' he demanded coldly.

'Gone for water,' said Deynman, still in the stentorian tones that made Bartholomew's head buzz. 'Here he is.'

'Oh, you are awake!' exclaimed Gray in delight, entering Bartholomew's room and setting a pitcher of water carefully on the table. He knelt next to Bartholomew and peered at him.

'What is Deynman doing in my room?' Bartholomew demanded. 'What time is it?'

Gray sent Deynman to the kitchen for watered ale, and arranged the blanket in a more reasonable fashion.

'You should rest,' Gray said softly. 'It is probably somewhere near midnight and you have been ill for almost two days. We wondered whether you might have a cracked skull but now you seem back to normal, I think not. But your stars are sadly misaligned.'

'Two days?' echoed Bartholomew in disbelief. 'That cannot be right!'

But even as he said it, vague recollections of moving in and out of sleep, of his students, Michael and Cynric, hovering around him began to flicker dimly through his mind.

'Easy,' said Gray gently. 'The kick Brother Michael said you took in that fight must have been harder than you realised. And, as I said, your stars are not good. You were born when Saturn was in its ascendancy and the conjunction of Mars and Jupiter on Wednesday—'

'Oh really, Sam!' exclaimed Bartholomew irritably. 'You do not have the slightest idea when I was born. And if you had been to Master Kenyngham's lecture last week, you would know there was no conjunction of Mars and Jupiter on Wednesday.'

Gray was not easily deterred. 'Details are unimportant,' he said airily. 'But you were attacked on Wednesday night and it is late on Friday.'

'Two days wasted,' said Bartholomew, his mind leaping from

his neglected teaching to the inquiries he had been pursuing with Michael.

'We have not been idle,' said Gray, not without pride. 'While Deynman stayed with you, I read the beginning of Theophilus's *De urinis* to the first- and second-year students, while Tom Bulbeck read Nicholas's *Antidotarium* to the third, fourth and fifth years.'

Bartholomew regarded him appraisingly. 'It seems I am no longer needed,' he said, complimenting Gray's organisational skills.

Gray looked at him sharply to see if he were being facetious, but then gave a shy grin. 'I would claim it was all down to my talent for teaching but the students were only malleable because you were ill,' he said in an rare moment of honesty. 'Had you left me in charge and went drinking in the taverns all day, it would have been a different matter. We were all concerned for you. After all, since the plague, there is just you, Father Philius and Master Lynton who teach medicine. What would happen to us if you were to die?'

'Nicely put,' said Bartholomew.

'We have had to turn away hoards of anxious women who came to enquire after you,' announced Deynman, loud enough to be heard in every college in Cambridge as he returned with the watered ale. Tom Bulbeck slipped in behind him and came to squat next to Gray, inspecting his teacher anxiously. Deynman, choosing to ignore Gray's gesture to keep his voice down, continued with his oration.

'These ladies have been very persistent; we had a difficult job keeping them out of the College.'

'Oh?' said Bartholomew cautiously. 'Which ones came?'

'Which ones!' echoed Gray admiringly. He gave Bartholomew a conspiratorial wink. 'And all this time we thought you were destined to take the cowl, like Brother Michael. Now we find out you have a whole secret life that is positively teeming with some of the loveliest females in town.'

'I have nothing of the kind,' snapped Bartholomew testily. 'I simply invited one or two young ladies to the Founder's Feast.'

'And one to the Festival of St Michael and All Angels,' added Deynman helpfully. 'And she was the prettiest of them all.'

All? thought Bartholomew in horror. How many of them had there been? He sincerely hoped one of them had not been Matilde. Bulbeck, more sensitive to his teacher's growing discomfort than his friends, put him out of his misery.

'It was just the four Tyler women and your sister, Edith,' he said. 'They were concerned about you. And Agatha, of course.'

'That is no woman,' declared Deynman.

'You should keep your voice down,' advised Bartholomew. 'Or she might hear you and then I will not be the only one with a cracked head.'

The three students exchanged fearful glances, and Deynman crossed himself vigorously. Bartholomew smiled. He was beginning to feel better already. He was not at all surprised that the kick had rendered him insensible, especially given the sensations of sickness and dizziness he had experienced on the way back to Michaelhouse. He thanked his misaligned stars that astrology had been the subject of his recent discussion with his students, and not trepanation, or he might have awoken to find Gray had relieved him of a chunk of skull rather than simply predicted his horoscope. Dim memories began to drift back. Had Michael accused him of vomiting on Master Wilson's grave? If that were true, he really ought to do something to atone for such an act of sacrilege. When the pompous Master Wilson had died during the plague, he had made a deathbed demand that Bartholomew should oversee the building of his fine tomb. Three years had passed, and, apart from ordering a slab of black marble, Bartholomew's promise remained unfulfilled.

When he opened his eyes again, it was early morning and daylight was beginning to glimmer through the open window. On a pallet bed next to him, Gray slumbered, fully clothed, his tawny hair far too long and very rumpled. Bartholomew sat up warily, and then stood. Apart from a slight ache behind his eyes, he felt fine. So as not to wake Gray, he tiptoed out of his room, taking the pitcher of water with which to wash and shave. Then he unlocked the small chamber where he stored his medicines. Pulling off the heavy bandage he fingered the lump on the back of his head. He had felt worse, although not on himself.

He went back to his room for clean clothes, tripping over the bottom of Gray's straw mattress. The student only mumbled and turned over without waking. Bartholomew wondered at the usefulness of having him in a sick-room if he slept so heavily, but then relented, knowing he was a heavy sleeper himself. It was not the first time Gray had kept a vigil at Bartholomew's bedside, and he knew he should not be ungrateful to his student, whatever his motives for wanting his teacher hale and hearty.

Outside, the air was cool and fresh. The rain of two nights ago seemed to have broken the unbearable heat and the breeze smelled faintly of the sea, not of the river. Bartholomew looked at the sky, beginning to turn from dark blue to silvery-grey, ducked back inside to his room for his bag – noting that someone had thought to dry it out after the heavy rain – and walked across the yard to the front gates. Then he made his way to St Michael's Church. The ground was sticky underfoot, and here and there puddles glistened in the early light. He reached the church and walked furtively to Master Wilson's grave, relieved to see that nothing appeared to be amiss.

In the church, Fathers William and Aidan, Franciscan friars and Fellows of Michaelhouse, were ending matins and lauds. Bartholomew sat at the base of a pillar in the cool church and let Father William's rapid Latin echo around him. William always gave the impression that God had far better things to do than to listen to his prayers, and so gabbled through them at a pace that never failed to impress Bartholomew. However, if Bartholomew would ever be so rash as to put his observation to William, the friar would scream loudly about heresy and they would end up in one of the interminable debates that William so loved.

Aidan favoured Bartholomew with a surprised grin, revealing two large front teeth, one of which was sadly decayed. While Aidan fiddled about with the chalice and paten on the altar, William gave Bartholomew one of his rare smiles and sketched a benediction at him in the air. On the surface, Bartholomew and William had little in common and argued ceaselessly about what was acceptable to teach the students. Any display of friendship between them was usually unwillingly given, although beneath their antagonism was a mutual, begrudging respect.

In pairs and singly, Michaelhouse's scholars began to trickle into the church, and Bartholomew took up his appointed place in the chancel. Master Kenyngham arrived and gestured to the Franciscans to begin prime. The friars started to chant a psalm, and Bartholomew closed his eyes, relishing the way their voices echoed through the church, slow and peaceful. Roger Alcote, the Senior Fellow, stood next to him and enquired solicitously after his health. Bartholomew smiled at the fussy little man: he had no idea he was so popular among his colleagues – unless, like Gray, they knew that they would have a serious problem trying to find a replacement Regius physician to teach medicine at Michaelhouse.

During the morning's lectures, his students were uncommonly considerate, keeping their voices low, even during an acrimonious debate about the inspection of urine to determine cures for gout. Bartholomew was amazed to learn that they had been instructed to keep the noise down by Deynman of all people, which was especially surprising given his uncharacteristic loudness during the night. Apparently, he had thought Bartholomew might be deaf because the bandage had covered his ears. Bartholomew wondered what it was like to see the world in such black and white terms as Deynman.

When teaching was over for the day, Bartholomew sent for the town's master mason. While he waited, he read his borrowed Galen: although Radbeche's message had been that Bartholomew might use it as long as he liked, to be in possession of a hostel's one and only book was a grave responsibility, and he wanted to return it to them as soon as possible.

When the mason arrived, Bartholomew handed him the small box that contained the money Wilson had given him for the tomb. The mason opened the box and shook his head, clicking his tongue.

'Three years ago this would have bought something really fancy, but since the plague everything costs more – tools, wages ... Even with the stone already bought, I can only do you something fairly plain.'

'Really?' said Bartholomew, his spirits lifting. 'Master Wilson wanted an effigy of himself with a dozen angels, carved in the black marble and picked out in gold.'

The mason sucked in his breath and shook his head. 'Not with this money. I could do you a cross with some nice knots at the corners.'

'That sounds reasonable,' said Bartholomew and a deal was struck. He did not know whether to feel relieved that the hideous structure Wilson had desired would not now spoil the delicate contours of the church, or guilt that his intransigence had meant that Wilson's tomb-money had so devalued.

As he pondered, Michael sought him out, his face sombre. 'Mistress Fletcher died yesterday,' he said. He squeezed Bartholomew's shoulder and then went to sit on the bed. 'I went to her when word came that she was failing. She had fallen into a deep sleep in the afternoon and did not wake before she died some hours later. There was nothing you could have done and she would not have known whether you were there or not.'

Bartholomew looked away and said nothing. They sat in silence for a while. Michael played with the wooden cross around his neck, and Bartholomew stared out of the window into the sunny yard. He watched some chickens pecking about in the dirt and saw Deynman chase a hungry-looking dog away from them. Deynman spied Bartholomew gazing out of his window and waved cheerily. Absently, Bartholomew waved back.

'Damn Bigod!' he said in a low voice. 'I promised her I would be there.'

Michael did not reply. Bartholomew stood up, knocking something from the window-sill as he did so. As he stooped to retrieve it, he saw it was the candle he had been looking for the night he and Michael had been attacked. Pangs of guilt assailed him when he remembered thinking that Gray might have taken it. He replaced it on the shelf, wondering who had moved it in the first place. Cynric, perhaps, when he was cleaning.

Michael stood, too. 'I am going to talk to Tulyet about your notion of persuading Lydgate to look at the ring on Thorpe's skeleton,' he said. He raised his hands in a gesture of defeat. 'We have Kenzie murdered; a recently dead hand claimed to be a relic; riots possible every night and we do not know why; your raped and murdered prostitute; the attack against you in the night; and the child's skeleton. All unsolved mysteries, and I can think of no way forward with any of them. Tulyet will help us because he is as baffled as we are and I can think of nothing else to do.'

Bartholomew picked up his bag. 'I had planned to sit with Mistress Fletcher and watch Godwinsson at the same time. The French students were bound to go in or out sooner or later and I was going to follow them and question them about Joanna.'

'Forget them for now,' said Michael. 'We know where to find them.' He hesitated, then sat again, fiddling with the wooden cross that hung round his neck. Bartholomew waited, sensing the monk had something to say. He put the Galen in his bag, then perched on the edge of the table. Michael gave a heavy sigh.

'Two days ago, when you were indisposed, I went to see Master Bigod of Maud's Hostel. He denies totally the charge that it was he who attacked us in the street. I asked to see Will at Valence Marie but was told he was visiting a sick sister in Fen Ditton, and had been gone since the night the relic was found. Then I went to Godwinsson and, in the company of Guy Heppel, put the fear of God into Huw, their steward, and that scullion Saul Potter who you said kicked you. Do you know what I discovered?'

Bartholomew shook his head, setting his bag down on the table while he listened to Michael.

'Nothing!' spat Michael in disgust. 'Not even the tiniest scrap of information. Huw and Saul Potter claim they spent the evening cleaning silver, and went to bed by eight o'clock. I collared other Godwinsson servants, and they confirmed that the hostel was locked up and everyone was asleep long before the church clock struck nine. It was past midnight before we were attacked.' He turned to the physician. 'Are you certain that it was Will, Huw, Saul Potter and Bigod you recognised?'

Bartholomew thought back to the attack: Huw swearing at him in Welsh, Saul Potter's piggy eyes glittering as Bartholomew had torn away his hood, and Bigod demanding to know where something was.

'I injured one as we fell – his hand broke,' he said, the memory dim. 'Did any of the men you spoke to have injuries? What about Will from Valence Marie? Perhaps he left Cambridge to hide the fact that he was wounded.'

Michael looked pained. 'Damn! Your memory has played us false! You told me originally that the man had broken his arm, not his hand, and you said Will had been holding me down, not fighting with you. I inflicted no broken bones – although I certainly bit someone fairly hard – and so Will cannot be in hiding to cover his wounds.'

He banged his fist on the table in frustration. 'I wondered at the time whether you might not have been rambling. You were weaving all over the road like a drunk. When I went haring off to confront Bigod and the others, I had no idea your injury was so serious. Gray warned us you might lose some memory after he consulted your stars. I should have waited.'

'Stars!' spat Bartholomew in disgust. 'I *do* remember Bigod, Huw, Saul Potter and Will there. Others too. The lightning lit up their faces.'

Michael looked sceptical. 'How many were there?'

Bartholomew thought, struggling with the blurred images that played in his mind. 'Will and two others fought with you, while Huw, Saul Potter and Bigod fought with me.'

One of the Benedictines in the room above began to sing softly as Michael shook his head. 'Wrong again, Matt. Only two had been allocated to me; one sat on my back, while the other held my gown over my face and almost smothered me. But there were five men fighting you. I saw them. I had been taken by surprise and was knocked to the ground before I could react. You had more time to defend yourself and were able to fight harder. Do you remember any words they spoke?'

For a brief moment, Bartholomew considered not answering, feeling foolish and vulnerable at his lapse in memory. 'I heard Huw speak in Welsh, and Bigod asked me where something was,' he said reluctantly.

'I heard no Welsh,' said Michael, 'and I heard every word that was spoken, lying as I was immobilised. Damn! Should I apologise to Bigod for accusing him wrongly? The servants I do not care about but the Principal of a hostel is another matter.'

'I am certain I saw those four,' persisted Bartholomew. 'And I heard and felt the sharp crack of a bone breaking . . .'

He stopped, aware that Michael was regarding him unconvinced.

'I suspect I saw a good deal more than you, since I was pinned helplessly on the ground for several minutes while you fought,' said the monk. 'The faces of our attackers were very carefully concealed – I saw nothing. And I am sure they would not have left us alive had they the slightest suspicion that they might have been identified. Yet you claim to have recognised four of the seven. It must have been your imagination that led you to name Bigod, Will, Saul Potter and Huw. I can come up with no other explanation than that these were professional outlaws hired to collect something from you.'

'But what?' asked Bartholomew, uncomfortable at the way in which Michael was so blithely dismissing his recollections.

'And why me, not you? You are just as deeply involved in all this business as me – perhaps more so, since you are the Senior Proctor.'

'Perhaps it has nothing to do with "this business", as you put it,' said Michael. 'I have given the matter considerable thought. The attack was most definitely aimed at you, since you were the one who was lured out on the pretext of a medical emergency; I was merely incidental. No one knows you have that ring you found at Godwinsson, except me, so it cannot be that – unless you were seen picking it up. The only answer I can come up with is that these men were hired by a patient of yours to get something . . .'

'Such as what?' interrupted Bartholomew in disbelief. 'Medicine? Most people know I prescribe medicine perfectly willingly and do not need to be ambushed for it.'

'Perhaps you took something in lieu of payment that someone wants back,' suggested Michael. 'You are often given all manner of oddments when people have no money.'

'Exactly!' said Bartholomew. ' "Have no money." Which means that they also would not be able to afford to pay outlaws to get whatever it was back again. And I hardly think seedcakes, candle-stubs and the occasional pot of ink warrant such an elaborate attack. Anyway, as Gray will attest, I often overlook payment when a patient is in dire need.'

'Yes, yes,' said Michael testily. 'But I can think of no other reason why you alone should be enticed out of college and searched for something. You have some rich patients – they are not all beggars.'

'But they pay me with money,' said Bartholomew. 'And the motive for the attack was not theft, because neither of us was robbed.'

Michael was becoming impatient. 'Perhaps your misaligned stars have led you to forget something obvious. Some transaction with a patient?'

'I have not!' said Bartholomew angrily. 'And my stars are not misaligned!'

A distant screech of raucous laughter from the kitchens spoke of the presence of Agatha. For a frightening instant, Bartholomew, who had heard the laugh often, thought that it sounded alien to him. Gray's physical diagnosis had been right: it was only to be expected that some of his faculties might be temporarily awry following a hefty blow to the head.

Perhaps a clearer memory of the fight would emerge in time. Then again, perhaps it would not.

But Bartholomew knew that his stars had nothing to do with the fact that his memories were dim. Ironically, it seemed as though his reluctant adherence to teaching traditional medicine would backfire on him, if Gray was telling all and sundry that his master's stars augured ill. People would treat anything he said with scepticism until he, or better yet, Gray, showed that his stars were back in a favourable position. He almost wished he had been discussing trepanation rather than astrology, after all.

Bartholomew was torn between doubt and frustration for Michael's dilemma. The more he thought about it, the more he was certain that the men he had named were their attackers, but the details remained hazy. He rubbed his eyes tiredly.

'You should rest,' said Michael, watching him. 'And I must go to see Tulyet.'

Checking that the Galen was in his bag, Bartholomew followed Michael out of his room. He felt claustrophobic in the College, and wanted to be somewhere alone and quiet, like the meadows behind St Peter-without-Trumpington Gate. Ignoring Michael's silent glances of disapproval that his advice about resting was being so wilfully dismissed, Bartholomew walked purposefully across the courtyard, and up St Michael's Lane. Less decisively, he wandered along the High Street and began to notice things he had not seen before: there was a carved pig on one of the timbers of Physwick Hostel; one of the trees in St Michael's churchyard was taller than the tower; Guy Heppel had a faint birthmark on one side of his neck.

'I am delighted to see you up and about,' breathed the Junior Proctor, sidling up to him. He rubbed his hands up and down his gown in his curious way. 'I was most concerned to hear your stars are so unfavourable.'

'Thank you,' said Bartholomew shortly. 'But I can assure you that they are becoming more favourable by the hour.'

Heppel looked surprised at his vehemence. 'I am glad to hear it. I was hoping to have my astrological consultation from you soon. My chest is a little better with that angelica you gave me, but now I have a stiffness in my knees. I almost went to Father Philius at Gonville Hall when you were ill – I am told he does an adequate job – but now you are well again, I am glad I waited. Brother Michael informs me you are by far the best man in Cambridge for stars.'

Bartholomew's eyes narrowed and he walked away, leaving Heppel somewhat bewildered. He had not gone far when he saw Matilde. She approached him shyly and smiled with genuine pleasure.

'Agatha told me you were better,' she said. 'I was worried.'

'My stars are badly aligned, apparently,' he said, turning to glower at the retreating figure of Guy Heppel, who was still rubbing his hands up and down the sides of his gown.

'They have certainly put you in an ill-humour,' she said wryly. 'Or was that the doing of the Junior Proctor?'

'It was the doing of Brother Michael, telling people I am good at astrological consultations. If he spreads that tale around, I shall never be able to do any work.'

Matilde smiled. 'Then you should tell Heppel that his stars will augur well if he devotes himself to music, and persuade him to join Michael's choir. Heppel sings like a scalded cat and it will serve Michael right.'

Bartholomew regarded her doubtfully. 'Are you sure a scalded cat would not serve to improve Michael's choir? I cannot imagine it could be any worse than it is. It used to be quite good but he has not spent the time needed on it because of his extra duties as Senior Proctor.'

'Time has nothing to do with it, Matthew. It is not lack of practice that has made the choir what it is, but Michael's policy of providing bread and ale after each rehearsal. For many folk, it provides the only decent meal they have in a week.'

'I wondered why so many people were so keen to join,' said Bartholomew. 'I knew it had nothing to do with their appreciation for music.'

'Even so, I am looking forward to hearing it on Tuesday.' She looked at him anxiously. 'Unless you have changed your mind, or you feel too unwell, that is.'

'No, of course not,' he said quickly, although his predicament with his two guests had completely slipped his mind. He forced himself to smile. 'Just remember to bring something to stuff in your ears.'

After he had left Matilde, he met Oswald Stanmore, who asked whether his stars had improved. Bartholomew regarded him coolly and silently cursed Gray's enthusiasm for the subject. Puzzled by the uncharacteristic unfriendliness, Stanmore

changed the subject and told him about a fight in Milne Street
the night before between the miller's apprentices and students
from Valence Marie. Bartholomew barely listened, preoccupied
with how he might neutralise Gray's diagnosis. Stanmore put
up his hands in a gesture of exasperation when he saw his
brother-in-law was not paying him any attention, and let him
go. The merchant then strode to the small building where
his seamstress worked. She was there talking to Cynric, who
had been courting her slowly and shyly for more than a year.
Stanmore beckoned him over, and within moments Cynric
was slipping along Milne Street behind Bartholomew.

The sun was hot but not nearly as strong as it had been. White,
fluffy clouds drifted across the sky affording temporary relief
and there was a breeze that was still relatively free of odours
from the river. Bartholomew continued to walk, acknowledging
the greetings of people he knew but not stopping to talk to
them. He passed St Bene't's Church, where he and Michael
had been attacked, and reached St Botolph's. Glancing across
the churchyard to where Joanna and the other riot victims
were buried, he saw a figure emerge from where it had been
standing behind some bushes. Curious, and with nothing else
to do, Bartholomew climbed over the low wall and walked
towards the back of the church. He peered out round the
buttresses and saw that as he had thought, the person –
cloaked and hooded, even in the hot sun – was standing by
Joanna's grave.

Bartholomew abandoned stealth and approached the mourner
openly. The figure turned to see who was coming and then
looked away. It was a man of Bartholomew's height, taller even.
Bartholomew drew level and was about to address him, when
the man spun round and shoved Bartholomew so hard that
he fell back against the wall of the church. Then he raced off
along the path back towards the High Street. Bartholomew's
feet skidded on wet grass as he fought to regain his balance.
But as the man ran his hood fell away from his face and
Bartholomew, for the briefest of moments, was able to recognise him.

Bartholomew tore after him but on reaching the High Street
saw that the man had disappeared into the mass of people
walking home from the market. As he looked up and down the
road in silent frustration, he saw that Cynric had materialised
next to him.

'Did you see him?' Bartholomew gasped. 'It was Thomas Lydgate, standing at Joanna's grave-side.'

Cynric looked at him perplexed. 'You are still addled, lad,' he said gently. 'There was no one here other than you.'

chapter 7

BARTHOLOMEW WAS GROWING EXASPERATED, WHILE Michael and Cynric listened to him with a sympathetic patience that only served to make him feel worse. He rubbed his head and flopped down into the large chair next to the kitchen hearth from which Agatha oversaw the domestic side of the College.

'So, you say you saw Lydgate at Joanna's grave,' said Michael. 'And that Lydgate is her father.'

'Not quite,' said Bartholomew tiredly. 'I think Joanna must be Dominica and it is she who lies in the grave.'

'But Joanna is a prostitute,' said Michael. 'How can she be Dominica?'

Was Michael trying to force him to give up his theory by being deliberately obtuse? Bartholomew wondered. Michael was not usually so slow to grasp the essence of his ideas. He rubbed the back of his head again, trying to ease the nagging ache there, and tried again. 'Joanna is not a prostitute known to Matilde,' he said. '*Ergo,* I believe Joanna was not a prostitute at all. I think someone deliberately misled Tulyet with a false name, and that Joanna's real identity is Dominica, whom no one has seen since she was sent to these mysterious relatives in Chesterton.'

'But she was sent to them before the riots, to keep her away from her lover – *before* you think she was killed,' said Michael. 'She is probably still there with them. In Chesterton.'

'Then check. I will wager you anything you like she will not be there,' said Bartholomew. 'Her death the night of the riot explains the curious actions of her parents. Cecily went to Maud's, and stayed briefly talking to Master Bigod. Perhaps she was asking him if he had seen Dominica. Why else would a respectable lady, who seldom leaves her house anyway, be out on the night of massive civil unrest? Meanwhile, Thomas

Lydgate was missing all night, and gave a false alibi to Tulyet. He was probably also searching for her. The next day he and Edred went to the Castle to identify the friar who died, whom I thought was you' He faltered. That memory at least was burned indelibly into his mind.

'And you think that while Lydgate and Edred were at the Castle, they also had a look at this Joanna and satisfied themselves it was Dominica?' finished Michael.

Bartholomew nodded. 'Why else would Lydgate be at her grave?'

He saw Michael and Cynric exchange glances, but was too tired to be angry with them. Cynric had not seen Lydgate, but that did not mean he had not been there. Because Michael doubted Bartholomew's memory over the events of two nights ago, the monk was prepared to doubt him now. How long would he continue to doubt? A few days? Weeks? For ever? Bartholomew rubbed his eyes, trying to clear his blurred vision.

He wondered how Cynric had happened to be so close to hand all of a sudden, appearing at the church so fortuitously? It occurred to him that Cynric must have been following him. Probably not from Michaelhouse, but from Milne Street, where he had been alerted by Stanmore. Gray's insouciant diagnosis – made when the student did not have the most basic information necessary to allow an accurate prediction – was impinging on every aspect of Bartholomew's life. If only he had been teaching something else that week! He wondered whether he could bribe his fellow physician Father Philius to provide a more favourable astrological reading. But Philius and Bartholomew opposed each other on virtually all aspects of medicine, and Philius would probably seize on the notion that his colleague was unbalanced with the greatest of pleasure.

Michael was speaking, and Bartholomew realised he had not heard anything the monk had said. When he asked him to repeat it, Michael stood abruptly.

'I was saying that there might be all manner of reasons why Lydgate might visit Joanna's grave. Perhaps she was his personal prostitute, which might be why Matilde did not know her – it would mean she remained exclusive to him and did not tout for business on the streets. Perhaps he thought he was at the grave of his friar and not Joanna's at all. And if you persist in your theory that Dominica was Joanna, who do you think raped and killed her? It would hardly be the French students of Godwinsson!'

Bartholomew was too weary to try to reason it all out. 'Did you speak to Tulyet about asking Lydgate to identify the ring?' he asked, partly for information, but mostly so that he would not have to answer Michael.

The monk nodded. 'He advises – and on reflection, I believe he is right – that we should ease up on our inquiries into Kenzie's death until the town is more peaceful. Inflaming a man like Lydgate by suggesting his daughter's ring is on Valence Marie's relic will serve no purpose other than to risk more violence.'

'So the next time I wish to murder someone, all I need to do to make sure I get away with it is to start a riot,' said Bartholomew bitterly. 'It is a good thing to know.'

Michael sighed theatrically. 'We are simply being practical, Matt. I would rather one murderer went free than another nine innocents – including someone like your Joanna – die in civil unrest. But we should not be discussing this while you are incapable of drawing rational conclusions. You should rest and perhaps the planets will be kinder to you tomorrow.'

Cynric agreed. 'You look tired, boy. Would you like me to see you to your room?'

'I am not one of Oswald Stanmore's seamstresses,' said Bartholomew, trying not to sound irritable when Cynric was attempting to be kind. 'I do not think I am likely to be accosted by ruffians while walking from the kitchens to my room.'

'You never know,' said Michael, smiling. 'You might be if Father William has caught wind of all your dalliances with these women!'

Bartholomew trailed across the courtyard to his room as the last orange rays of sun faded and died, still feeling helpless and angry. He took a deep breath, scrubbed at his face, and went over to the chest for the pitcher of water that usually stood there. It was on the floor. He frowned. He never kept it on the floor because he was likely to kick it over when he sat at the table. He looked around more carefully. The candle he had replaced on the shelf that morning now lay on its side, and one of his quills was on the floor. He picked it up thoughtfully, and looked in the chest. He was tidy in his habits and kept what few clothes he owned neatly folded, but the shirts in the chest had been moved awry.

He took the key from his belt to the tiny chamber where he kept his medicines, and tried to unlock the door. It was open already. He entered the room cautiously and peered around in the gloom. Several pots and bottles had been moved, attested by the stain marks on the benches. When he crouched to inspect the lock, there were small scratches on it that he was certain had not been there before, suggesting that someone might have picked it.

Locking the door carefully, he went back to his room. Only he had the key to the medicines room, on the grounds that he necessarily kept some potions that, if administered wrongly, might kill. Gray and Bulbeck were allowed in, Deynman was not, for his own safety. Could Gray or Bulbeck have entered the medical store while he was ill? It was possible, although neither of them was likely to rummage through his chest of clothes: they had no earthly reason to do so since Bartholomew probably owned fewer clothes than either of them, and those he did own were darned and patched and could scarcely be coveted items, even to impecunious students.

So, the only logical conclusion was that someone else had been in his room and the medicines store. Could this person have been looking for the object Bigod was so keen to have? Bartholomew thought again. He knew that either Gray, Bulbeck or Deynman had been with him the whole time he had been ill, so the first opportunity for anyone else to search his room would have been that day, either while he was teaching, or when he had gone out later. He frowned and rubbed the back of his head. He had been unable to find the candle stub the night of the thunderstorm; the notion crossed his mind that his room must have been searched before he was attacked, too.

He saw a shadow on the stair outside and saw Michael pause to glance in at him, before going upstairs to his own room. 'What is the matter?' asked the monk. 'What are you doing?'

'I think my room has been searched,' Bartholomew replied. 'Several bottles have been moved in the storeroom, and the water pitcher . . .' He stopped when he saw the expression on Michael's face.

'Good night, Matt,' Michael said and climbed the stairs to his room.

A light rain was falling when Bartholomew awoke the next morning, the clouds after the previous clear days making dawn seem later than it was. Bartholomew had slept well, feeling better than he had done for days as he washed, shaved, dressed and walked briskly across the courtyard towards the gates. Walter eyed him speculatively.

'Where are you going?' he demanded rudely.

Bartholomew was nonplussed. Where did Walter think he was going? Where did scholars usually go at this hour in the morning? Then it struck him. It was Sunday and the morning service was later on Sundays. Something in Walter's gloating look made him reluctant to admit his mistake and give the porter proof that he was mentally deficient as well as astrologically lacking.

'I am going visiting,' he replied briskly, lifting the bar from the gate himself since Walter apparently was not going to do it for him. 'As I often do on Sundays.'

'In the rain?' queried Walter. 'Without a cloak?' Suspicion virtually dripped from his words.

'Yes,' said Bartholomew, opening the gate and stepping out into the lane. 'Not that it is any of your affair.' He closed the gate, and then opened it again moments later, catching Walter halfway across the yard. 'And I do not need Cynric to follow me,' he shouted.

He walked quickly towards the river, following a sudden desire to be as far away from Michaelhouse as possible. There was a thick mist swirling on the dull waters, rolling in from the Fens. He began to walk upstream, thinking that he would visit Trumpington and have breakfast with Stanmore and Edith. Abruptly, he stopped. They would be as bad as the scholars of Michaelhouse: they would see him arriving early, having walked to them in the rain, and would doubt his sanity.

So, downstream then, he thought, and struck out enthusiastically along the towpath that led behind the Hospital of St John. Once he saw a spider's web encrusted with more tiny drops of water than he thought it would have the strength to hold and stopped to admire it. Further on, past the Castle and St Radegund's Convent, he came face to face with a small deer, which stared at him curiously before bolting away into the undergrowth. After a while he came to the village of Chesterton, where Dominica Lydgate, the unfortunate daughter of the Master of Godwinsson, was supposed to be staying with her mysterious relatives.

The bell in the church was beginning to toll for the

early morning service. Bartholomew waded across the river, still shallow from weeks of dry weather, and made his way through a boggy meadow towards it. He opened a clanking door and slipped inside as the priest began to say mass. One or two children regarded him with open interest and Bartholomew wondered how he must appear to the congregation: cloakless, tabard dripping wet, shoes squelching from fording the river. One child reached up and patted his bag, giggling afterwards with her sister at her audacity. Bartholomew smiled at them, increasing their mirth, until a nervous mother moved them away.

The Chesterton priest apparently had better things to do with his morning than preaching, for he raced through the mass at a speed that would have impressed Father William. The quality of his Latin, however, was appalling, and once or twice he said things that Bartholomew was certain he could not mean. As he intoned his unintelligible phrases, he eyed his few parishioners with what was so obviously disdain that Bartholomew was embarrassed.

After the brief ceremony, the priest stood at the door to offer a limp hand and a cold nod to any who paused long enough to acknowledge him. Bartholomew loitered, taking his time to finish his prayers, and then pretending to admire the painted wooden ceiling. When he was certain everyone else had left, he headed for the door.

The priest nodded distantly at him, and almost jostled him out of the building so that he could lock the door.

'Nice church,' said Bartholomew as an opening gambit. The priest ignored him and began to stride away. Bartholomew followed, walking with him up the path that led to the village – a poor collection of flimsy cottages clustered around a square, squat tower-house.

'Have you been here long?' he asked politely. 'It seems a pleasant village.'

The priest stopped. 'I do not like scholars in my church,' he growled, eyeing Bartholomew with open hostility.

'I am not surprised, given your atrocious Latin,' Bartholomew retorted. Since the polite approach had failed, Bartholomew considered he had little to lose by being rude in return.

'What do you want here?' said the priest. 'You are not welcome – not in my church and not in the village.'

He made as if to move on but Bartholomew stood in front

of him and blocked his path. 'And why would that be?' he asked. 'On whose orders do you repel travellers?'

'Travellers!' the priest mocked, looking hard at the tabard that marked Bartholomew not only as a scholar of the University of Cambridge but as one of its teachers. 'I know who you are, Doctor Bartholomew.'

Bartholomew was startled when the priest gave his name. The man looked smug when he saw Bartholomew's astonishment.

'They said you would come,' he said. 'You or Brother Michael. You will find nothing to interest you here.'

'I wish the answers to two questions,' said Bartholomew, 'and then I will go. First, where is the house where Dominica Lydgate is supposed to be staying? And second, who told you to expect us?'

The priest sneered and started to walk away. 'You will learn nothing from me, Bartholomew. And do not try to cow me with threats because I know you have been ill and your stars are unfavourable. I was a fighting man once, and could take you on with one hand behind my back.'

Could you indeed? thought Bartholomew. 'Perhaps you might like to repeat that to the Bishop when I bring him here to celebrate mass with you next week. The Bishop is also a fighting man, especially after hearing bastard Latin in his churches.'

The man turned back, and Bartholomew saw him blanch. 'The Bishop would not come here,' he said, but his voice lacked conviction. Although he could not be sure that a scholar like Bartholomew would have sufficient influence with the Bishop of Ely to induce him to visit Chesterton, he was certainly aware that the Bishop could have him removed from his parish in the twinkling of an eye. It was clear the priest was not popular with his parishioners and it seemed unlikely that any of them would speak in his favour.

Bartholomew shrugged. 'You will know next week,' he said, and began to walk back the way he had come. He heard the priest following him and turned, uneasy with the man so close behind.

The priest sighed and looked out towards the meadows. 'First, Dominica was in the tower-house, but she is no longer here. Second, this manor is owned by Maud's Hostel, so I need not tell you on whose instructions we are bound to silence.'

The man's arrogance had evaporated like mist; Bartholomew

suddenly felt sorry for him in his shabby robes and dirty alb.

'Who lives in the tower-house?' he asked.

'That is your third question,' said the priest, some of the belligerence bubbling back. 'It belongs to Maud's, and Mistress Bigod lives there. Now, please leave.'

'What relation is she to Thomas Bigod, the Master of Maud's?' asked Bartholomew before he could stop himself. He looked apologetically at the priest, who grimaced.

'Since I have already told you what I was expressly forbidden to reveal, what can other questions matter?' he asked bitterly. 'Mistress Bigod is Thomas Bigod's grandmother.'

'His grandmother? Thomas Bigod is no green youth, so she must be as old as the hills. Does she live there alone?'

'She has a household of servants and retainers,' said the priest. 'And she is probably eighty-five or eighty-six now. I have given her last rites at least four times over the past two years.'

Bartholomew reflected. So much for the Lydgates' claim that Dominica had been staying with relatives. She had been left in the care of a kinswoman of none other than the surly Master of Maud's Hostel – a man whose name seemed to crop up with suspicious regularity whenever Bartholomew and Michael discovered something odd. The last time Bartholomew had encountered Master Bigod had been when the man had tried to rob him on the dark street during the thunderstorm.

The priest was growing restless. He was keen to be away from the person to whom he had been forbidden to speak, but was still afraid that Bartholomew might have the influence to persuade the Bishop to visit Chesterton's church. The physician promised not to reveal the source of his information, although it would not be difficult for anyone to guess, given that several villagers had watched him speak with the priest, and gave his word never to mention Chesterton and miserable Latin in the same breath to another living soul. The priest remained uneasy but there was little Bartholomew could do to convince him further that he had far better things to do than to hang around in Ely waiting for an audience with a busy bishop, who would not be interested in a remote and unimportant parish anyway.

Finally tearing himself away, Bartholomew walked towards the untidy collection of shacks that comprised the village, but left quickly, unnerved by the hostility that brooded in the eyes of the people he met. A short distance away, certain he was not observed, he found a suitable vantage point, and settled in the long grass to watch the tower-house for any indication that Dominica might still be there. There was little to see, however, and he soon grew chilled from sitting still.

Perhaps around ten o'clock, the church bell rang for mass again. The occupants of the tower-house evidently preferred the later sitting, for a large number of people trudged through the drizzle to the dismal church. In the midst of them, carried in a canopied litter, was the old lady. Bartholomew's professional eye could detect no signs of senility, no drooling or muttering. If anything, she seemed to exercise a rigid control over her household, and her sharp, strong voice wafted insistently to where Bartholomew listened.

When the church doors had been closed to block the draughts, probably on the old lady's orders, Bartholomew left his hiding place and made for the tower-house. He skulked around the outbuildings, attentive for signs that someone had remained behind, but heard nothing. It seemed Mistress Bigod's entire household was obliged to attend the ten o'clock service: the tower-house and its stables and sheds were deserted. He walked quickly into the yard and looked up at the keep. It was a simple structure, based on the Norman way of building: a flight of steps outside led up to the main entrance on the middle floor; the upper floor had glazed windows and was probably the old lady's private apartments; the lower floor was virtually windowless and was doubtless used for storage.

Climbing the stairs, Bartholomew found that the heavy, metal-studded door was shut but not locked. He pushed it open and walked lightly into the large room that served as a hall. He glanced around quickly but there was nothing much to see: trestle-tables had been set up ready for the midday meal and trenchers laid at regular intervals along them.

Quelling his nervousness, Bartholomew tiptoed across to the narrow spiral staircase in the far corner and ascended to the upper floor. This was divided into two smaller rooms, each with a garderobe passage and a fireplace. One room was unmistakeably masculine, and a scholar's tabard thrown carelessly over a chest indicated that Thomas Bigod probably used it when he visited his grandmother. Bartholomew's heart began to thump, as his fear of being caught grew with each door he opened. But there was nothing in the hall, or the chambers above, of remote interest to him, and no sign that Dominica had been kept there.

He crept back down the staircase to the hall. At the far end, opposite the hearth, was a screen, behind which stood a long table for the servants to use when preparing meals – like many houses, the kitchens were in an outbuilding to reduce the ever-present risk of fire. Under the table was a trapdoor with a ladder that led to the lower floor. The basement was lit by narrow slits, and smelled musty and damp. The dankness suggested that it was not used for storage and was usually empty. A quick glance round told Bartholomew there was nothing to see whatsoever, that he should give up his wild notion of locating where Dominica had been and leave the tower-house before he was apprehended.

Suddenly he became aware of voices and froze in horror. Surely the mass could not be over yet, bad and fast Latin notwithstanding! He felt his stomach churn in anticipation of being discovered, realising that he had been foolish to enter the tower-house alone. What if Bigod found him? His henchmen could easily knock him on the head, dump him in the river and no one would ever know what had become of him. And even if Bigod did baulk at cold-blooded murder, Bartholomew would be hard-pressed to explain to the Sheriff what he was doing prowling around the house of someone he had never met while she was at church.

He fought down his panic. The voices were not coming closer. In fact, they seemed to be emanating from underneath him. Cautiously, he peered around in the gloom until he saw a second trapdoor leading to another chamber – like a bottle-dungeon below ground level that he had once seen in a castle in France. He eased the trapdoor up a fraction, noting that the hinges were well oiled, and that the wood was new. The voices came clearly through the gap now. A woman's voice, remonstrating with a man. Dominica?

He eased the trapdoor up a little more, so that he could see down into the lower storey. What he saw was not a bottle-dungeon, deep and dark and rank-smelling with offal, but a well-lit, pleasantly decorated room. A wooden ladder led up to the trapdoor and there were no locks to seal it from without. This arrangement was obviously not to keep someone prisoner but to allow its occupant to come and go at will. He glanced around the chamber in which he knelt. Piles of rushes were heaped around the walls and a heavy-looking chest stood nearby. Doubtless the rushes could be spread and the chest dragged across the trapdoor to hide it, should the underground chamber need to be kept from prying eyes.

The speakers were out of sight; Bartholomew looked down at the tapestries on the walls and the rich woollen rugs on the floor with astonishment. Delicate silver drinking vessels stood in a neat line across a table draped with a lace cloth; the remains of what had probably been a fine breakfast sat in a tray nearby. By changing position, Bartholomew saw that the underground chamber housed two compartments. The second was probably a bedroom.

The voices suddenly grew louder as the speakers moved into the room immediately below Bartholomew. Thomas Bigod's distinct accent wafted up first, accompanied by the unpleasant nasal wheedling of Cecily Lydgate. So that was where she had been hiding from her husband, thought Bartholomew, mystified.

Bigod put his foot on the bottom rung of the ladder to climb up it, as, in the same instant, voices came from the hall above. Lowering the trapdoor in panic, Bartholomew looked round desperately for somewhere to hide. There was only one possible place and he was relieved beyond measure to find the chest was empty. He had just managed to close the hefty lid with unsteady hands when, simultaneously, he heard footsteps on the ladder from the hall and Bigod pushing open the lower trapdoor.

Inside, the chest was airless and pitch black. Bartholomew dared not try to lift the lid a fraction, lest it make a noise and give him away. His heart was thumping so much that he wondered if it were shaking the chest. He closed his eyes, took a deep breath and tried to concentrate on what was being said in the basement outside.

Bartholomew deduced, from her characteristic whine, that Cecily Lydgate had followed Bigod up the ladder. Did that mean that she was with Dominica in the hideous underground boudoir? Bartholomew strained his ears but with the chest sturdily made, it was difficult to hear much at all.

'Edred did,' he heard Cecily say, 'with Thomas.' Which Thomas? Bartholomew wondered: her husband Thomas Lydgate or Thomas Bigod?

'. . . relic is in Valence Marie.' Bigod again, talking about the skeletal discovery that would make Valence Marie rich.

Bartholomew tried to ease the lid open to hear better, but felt the hinges judder and knew it would squeak if he tried to raise it further.

'Thomas does not know yet . . . Werbergh has been told not to tell him . . .' Cecily's whine. She must be referring to her husband now, since she was referring to a Godwinsson student. Bartholomew determined to talk to the untruthful Brother Werbergh again as soon as possible – if he ever escaped from his predicament.

There was a long pause, during which Bartholomew thought he heard the trapdoor being lowered into place, and Cecily, in childishly giggling tones, bid Bigod farewell as she went back down to her underground hideaway. Bartholomew was so tense that his palms were slippery with sweat and stung where his nails had dug into them; his shoulders and neck ached. If Bigod were to pull the chest across the trapdoor to hide it now, Bartholomew's weight would surely betray him! Or perhaps Bigod would just snap shut the sturdy lock that hung on the side of the chest, and leave him there. That thought made the saliva dry up inside Bartholomew's mouth and he felt as if he could not breathe. He bit his lower lip hard and tried to control his rising hysteria.

'Dominica dead . . .' came Bigod's Norfolk-accented voice, a few moments later. So Dominica was dead after all, and he had been right. He wondered if the identity of her killers was what Werbergh was not to tell Thomas Lydgate. Unless it was Thomas Lydgate who had killed her, with Edred. But that seemed unlikely, for if so, why would Lydgate then risk going to his daughter's grave?

'And the next riot will be on Thursday night,' came a new voice, loud and clear, with a note of finality. The voice was familiar but Bartholomew could not place it.

He heard footsteps climbing the ladder to the hall, then the chamber was silent. Cautiously, he pushed up the lid of the chest, his stomach flipping over for an unpleasant moment when it stuck. There was a low, but very audible, groan from the protesting hinges as it rose and Bartholomew was glad he had not tried to raise it when Bigod and his co-conspirators were in the room. He listened carefully. Cecily was now safely ensconced within her underground chamber with the trapdoor closed. Some of the rushes had been scattered, so that, unless someone knew where to look, the lower trapdoor was concealed from casual observers. The upper trapdoor remained open.

It had been closed when Bartholomew had entered the basement. Was someone planning to come back? Were the servants and the old lady back from mass yet? He listened, but could hear nothing. Just as he was about to climb out, the trapdoor darkened and someone began to descend the ladder, whistling as he came. Bartholomew swore softly to himself, ducked inside the chest, and eased the lid back down. This time, to give himself some air and to allow him to see and hear what was happening, he groped around for something to wedge between the rim of the chest and the lid. His fingers closed on the handle of an old pottery jug that had been lying in the bottom of the chest with sundry other bits of rubbish: some rags screwed up into balls, a rusty knife, and some flowers withered to a crisp brown.

Legs paused in front of the chest, and Bartholomew reached silently for the rusty knife, bracing himself for the lid to be thrown open. What would he do if it were? His legs were numb from crouching and he doubted whether he would be able to react fast enough to prevent the man from raising the alarm. Bartholomew held his breath, feeling sweat begin to form on his face and back.

With a small thump, something landed on the chest. The man had tossed something on to it. Bartholomew released pent-up breath slowly: someone would hardly put something on the lid if he intended to open it. He forced himself to relax and watched as the man began to walk around the chamber. The man began to whistle again. Bartholomew saw him wrench an old sconce from the wall with a creak of ancient metal and try a new one for size. It evidently did not fit, for there was an irritable pause in the whistling and one or two grunts could be heard as force was applied.

The man came back to the chest and Bartholomew heard the clink of metal. It had been his tools he had put there. A few moments later, there came the sound of metallic rasping as something was filed into shape. The sconce was tried again, but to no avail. The man advanced on the chest once more, then sat on it heavily.

A loud snap exploded in Bartholomew's ears as the pottery handle broke under the man's weight. Bartholomew heard him curse and stand to inspect the chest. By now, Bartholomew almost wished he would be discovered, just to end the unbearable tension. The lid had been forced down over the broken handle, which was now wedged firmly between the lid and the side of the chest. With horror, Bartholomew saw the man's fingers curl under the lid as he attempted to prise it open.

Fortunately for Bartholomew, the attempt was a half-hearted one; with a grunt, the man gave up and sat down again, forcing the lid to jam further shut with his weight. The whistling was resumed, accompanied by filing in time with the rhythm of the tune. It seemed to go on for ever. Bartholomew eased himself into a slightly more comfortable position and waited.

After an age, a voice drifted down into the chamber. The workman called back, and Bartholomew heard them share a joke about the eccentricity of a mistress who wanted new sconces fitted in rooms that nobody used. At last, the man seemed happy with the sconce's fitting, and his whistle receded as he climbed the ladder. There was a deep thump as the upper trapdoor was dropped into place and then there was silence.

Taking a deep breath, Bartholomew pressed his back to the lid of the chest and pushed. Nothing happened. He tried again but the lid was stuck fast. Bartholomew felt his heart begin to pound and his mouth go dry. What could he do? He could hardly call for help! He took several deep breaths and concentrated on using every ounce of his strength in forcing the lid to open. Just when it seemed the task was impossible, and he was on the verge of giving up in despair, it flew up with a tremendous crash that reverberated all around the small chamber. Bartholomew winced at the noise and stood shakily, his legs wobbling and burning with cramp and tension. And came face to face with Cecily Lydgate.

As Cecily opened her mouth to scream, Bartholomew raised his hands in a desperate gesture to beg her silence, and saw that he still clutched the rusty knife that had been at the bottom of the chest. In the light from the lamp in the new sconce – that Cecily had evidently been in the process of lighting – he saw that it was not rusty at all, but thickly coated in dried blood.

Cecily saw the knife, too, and the scream died before it reached her throat. She looked at Bartholomew with a rank fear that sickened him. Unsteadily, he climbed out of the chest and walked towards her. His blood began to circulate again, sending unpleasant buzzing sensations down his arms and legs. He longed to be away from this dank cellar and its vile secrets.

'What will you do with me?' Cecily asked, her bulging eyes flicking from Bartholomew's face to the knife in his hand.

'Nothing, if you do not shout,' Bartholomew replied, wondering how he could extricate himself from the situation without harm to either of them.

They were both silent while Bartholomew moved his weight from foot to foot to try to speed up the process of easing his cramp.

'Master Bigod's retainers are looking for you outside,' she said finally.

Bartholomew grimaced. 'Because the villagers told them I had come?'

Cecily nodded, her eyes fixed on the knife. 'But they will not think to look here. My husband said you were clever.'

Not a great compliment from one whose intellect Bartholomew did not rate highly. He said nothing, but closed the chest so he could sit on it. Cecily stayed where she was.

'Why are you here, Mistress?' he asked, gesturing around the gloomy basement. 'It can scarcely compare with your handsome house in the town.'

Her pale grey eyes suddenly filled with tears that dropped down her wrinkled cheeks. 'I am safe here.'

'Safe from whom?' asked Bartholomew, although he had already guessed at the answer.

'Safe from him. From Thomas.'

'Do you think your husband would harm you?' Bartholomew asked. He was not surprised she was afraid: Lydgate seemed to be a man who might resort to violence if it suited him.

'He killed Dominica!' she said in a sudden wail, muffling her face in one of her wide sleeves. Bartholomew cast a nervous glance up at the trapdoor. If she carried on so, someone would come to investigate. He thought about her accusation. Could it be true? Lydgate had no alibi for the night that Dominica had died. Indeed, he had worse than no alibi: he had given one that had proven to be false. Could Lydgate have killed his daughter? Was his appearance at her grave remorse, rather than grief? He glanced at the knife in his hand, some of the dried blood staining his palm, and wondered whether it had been used on Dominica. He almost cast it away from him in disgust, but if he were unarmed, Cecily would certainly raise the alarm.

Once the matter was out in the open, Cecily began to talk with evident relief. 'As soon as the riots started most of the students left, spoiling for mischief. I was grateful Dominica was safe, away from the town. Then Edred came back, breathless and limping and said he had seen her in the company of a man near the Market Square. Thomas was furious. He knew she had been seeing a student but she would not tell us which one. Thomas set out into the night, and I followed, hoping to find her first so that I could warn her.'

She paused, wiping first her eyes, then her nose, on the ample material of her sleeves. 'I went to all the places where I thought she might be – her friends, a cousin, the church. And then I saw Thomas, standing with his dagger dripping, and Dominica lying there with her clothes all drenched in blood. There was a man there, too, also dead – her lover, I presume. Thomas did not see me. I ran to Maud's, and Thomas Bigod ordered one of his servants to bring me here.'

'Is this where you kept Dominica before she died?' Bartholomew asked, gesturing to the underground chamber and trying to force his bewildered mind to make sense of the details.

'Yes, with the chest across the trapdoor. But she got out when a servant brought her food. The servant claimed she stabbed him but I do not believe Dominica could do such a thing.'

Bartholomew and Cecily simultaneously looked at the blood-stained knife. Cecily's hands flew to her throat. But the poor girl had been kept a prisoner in the painted dungeon, so who could blame her for using violent means to escape? Bartholomew thought Dominica must have disposed of the knife in the chest before she left.

Bartholomew did not doubt that Cecily believed the story she had related to him, but was what she saw really what had happened? He had seen no stab wounds on Dominica – assuming she was Joanna, of course – and so if Lydgate had killed her, it had not been with his blood-dripping knife. But two students had died from knife wounds that night, although, whatever Cecily might believe, neither of them could have been Dominica's lover because James Kenzie had been murdered the night before. And who had raped Dominica? Surely not Lydgate!

Bartholomew was certain that Lydgate might kill given the right circumstances – for a short while he had given serious consideration to the possibility that Lydgate might have killed Cecily, and was only claiming she had left him to explain her sudden absence. And he definitely had something to hide, or why would he be so hostile to Michael and his inquiries, and give Tulyet a false alibi? Bartholomew recalled Tulyet saying that Cecily's room had appeared to have been ransacked. When he asked her about it, thinking she would confirm his suspicion that she had done it herself in her haste to pack up a few belongings, she denied that she had returned to the hostel after seeing the dead Dominica. In fact, she was horrified.

'Did you see it?' she cried. 'Did they take anything?'

'What do you mean? Who?'

'Those thieving students, of course! They all know I have one or two paltry jewels in my room, and they must have been looking for them! Did they get them?'

'I have no idea; I did not see your room. But your husband would have noticed whether anything was missing, surely?'

She calmed down somewhat. 'That is true. He would not let a stone lie unturned if he thought we had been relieved of any of our meagre inheritance.'

Her reactions seemed a little more fervent than a 'meagre inheritance' should warrant, and Bartholomew wondered what riches the Lydgates had secreted away in their house. If Dominica had silver rings with blue-green stones to give away to casual lovers, then their fortune was probably substantial. But there seemed no point in pursuing that line of thought any further, so he let it drop.

'Has Bigod lost something, or want something he does not have?' he asked instead, thinking about the attack on him in the High Street and hoping Cecily might be able to shed some light on it. He fiddled with the knife in his hands. 'Something important?'

'Such as what?' she asked, her voice unsteady as she fixed her eyes on the blood-stained weapon.

'Such as a ring?' Bartholomew suggested.

She looked confused. 'Dominica lost a ring. Well, it was my ring, really, but she took it without asking and then lost it.'

'With a blue-green stone?' Bartholomew asked.

Cecily's eyes narrowed and Bartholomew saw her fear mingle with suspicion. 'How do you know that? Did Thomas tell you?'

Bartholomew shook his head slowly, but decided there was nothing to be gained by telling this embittered woman that her daughter had given the ring to her lover, whose identity Cecily still did not know. He thought for a while, information and clues tumbling around in his mind in a hopeless muddle, while Cecily watched him like a cornered rat.

'When Brother Michael asked Edred where he had been the night James Kenzie – the Scot from David's Hostel – was murdered, you did not contradict him when you knew he was lying,' he said after a few moments. 'You knew Edred did not return to Godwinsson with Werbergh because Werbergh accompanied you. Why did you not expose him?'

Cecily wiped her nose again. 'When Huw, our steward, said you wanted to see us, Thomas told me to say nothing, even if I heard things I knew were not true. He said you and the Benedictine wanted to destroy our hostel and that unguarded words might help you to do it.'

Bartholomew supposed her answer made sense. 'Who knows you are here, besides Master Bigod?' he asked.

'No one,' said Cecily, surprised by the question. 'It would be too risky to trust anyone else.'

'Then who was Bigod speaking with just now? He mentioned that there would be a riot on Thursday.'

'There was no one here except Thomas Bigod and me,' she said, genuinely bewildered. 'You must have imagined it, or perhaps he was speaking to a servant. None of them know I am hiding here.'

Bartholomew knew he had imagined nothing of the sort, but then recalled that the voice he had half-recognised had joined the conversation after he had heard Cecily return to her bottle-dungeon. He looked down at the knife in his hand.

'So, what do we do now?' he wondered aloud. 'If I leave you here alive, you will raise the alarm and Bigod will come after me. If I bind and gag you, you will tell them I was here when they release you, and they will have little problem in hunting me down in the town.'

Her eyes flew open, wide with terror. 'No! I will help you escape! I will create a diversion that will allow you to slip away, and I will tell them nothing!'

Bartholomew raised his eyebrows at this unlikely proposition. 'Did you love your daughter, Mistress?' he asked.

She blinked, confused by the sudden change in direction. 'More than she believed,' she answered simply.

'Would you like to see her killer brought to justice?'

Her eyes glittered. 'More than you can possibly imagine.'

'Then you must trust me, and I must trust you. I do not think your husband killed Dominica.' He quelled her stream of objections with a steady gaze. 'I do not doubt what you saw but I examined what I believe was Dominica's body and there was no knife wound on it. She was killed by a blow to the head. Whoever's blood was dripping from your husband's knife, it was not Dominica's. I suspect Dominica was already dead when Lydgate found her. Perhaps the blood came from the body of the man you said was next to her. Last night, I saw Lydgate at what I think is Dominica's grave . . .'

'She is buried then? Where?'

'St Botolph's Church. I will show you where when this is over. Officially, she is recorded as a woman called Joanna and no one wants to investigate why she died lest it spark another riot. But I will try to find her killer, Mistress.'

Her face was chalky white as she tried to come to terms with the new information. 'Why?' she asked eventually. 'What makes you want to avenge my Dominica?'

Bartholomew was unable to find an answer. He could hardly say her hair reminded him of Philippa's. In truth, he did not know why finding her killer had become important to him. Perhaps it was merely because he had been told not to. He shrugged.

Oddly, this unpleasant, vindictive woman seemed to accept that his motives were genuine without further explanation. She nodded, and came to perch next to him on the chest. Bartholomew let the knife clatter to the floor. An understanding had been reached. They sat silently for a while, until Cecily spoke.

'Since I have been here, I have asked myself again and again why Thomas should have killed Dominica. She was the only person he has ever truly loved – we both did. If it had not been for her, I suspect Thomas and I would have embarked upon separate lives many years ago. Although I saw him standing over her with the knife, a part of me has always been reluctant to accept that Thomas would destroy the most important thing in his life, and this is why I am prepared to accept your reasoning. Perhaps it was not Dominica's blood I saw on the weapon, but that of her lover laying next to her. I am sure Thomas would have no compunction in slaying *him*.'

'Perhaps,' said Bartholomew carefully.

'But even if Thomas is innocent of Dominica's death, I fear him still,' said Cecily, her expression a curious mixture of defiance and unease. 'How can I be sure that you will not tell Thomas where I am?'

'Why would I? I do not like him.'

'You do not like me either.'

That was certainly true. 'But if I informed your husband of your whereabouts, you could have your own revenge by telling Bigod that I overheard part of his conversation.'

She nodded, appreciating his point. 'So, we have a bargain,' she said. 'I allow you to leave unmolested and keep from Master Bigod that you were hiding here, while you do not tell anyone where I am, and will investigate the death of my daughter. It seems evenly balanced, would you not say?'

Bartholomew agreed cautiously. 'Evenly enough. But when I return to Michaelhouse, I will write a letter to Thomas Lydgate telling him of our conversation and of your whereabouts. I will seal it, and leave it with a trusted friend with orders that in the event of my unexplained death or disappearance, it is to be given to him.'

Anger glittered in her eyes for a moment and then was gone. She nodded, begrudgingly accepting his wariness. 'Then be careful, Doctor Bartholomew. Do not disappear or die in your investigations. Although I am well hidden here, there is only one way out, and I do not relish the idea of being trapped in this dungeon if Thomas were to discover my whereabouts.'

'Nor would I,' said Bartholomew with a shudder. 'What an unpleasant place. Could Bigod not have found you somewhere more conducive?'

Cecily looked away, and Bartholomew detected an unsteadiness in her voice when she spoke. 'I wondered whether he might allow me to share the chamber he has on the upper floor but he insists this one is safer for me. I am grateful for his help but I sense I am more of a hindrance to him than a welcome guest. I am not sure I would have fled to him had I known he would recommend I stay here. It reminds me too much of Dominica.'

Personally, Bartholomew would have asked Bigod to lend him some money and left the area for good had he been in Cecily's position, but he imagined she was probably afraid to stray too far from the place where she had lived all her life. Bartholomew was unusual in that he had travelled quite extensively: most people did not if they could help it, considering it an unnecessary risk.

Cecily looked at the open trapdoor in the floor and gave a short, bitter laugh. 'This place was never intended to be a prison, you know. Before this house came into the possession of the Bigod family, it was owned by Jewish merchants. They built this secret chamber during the events that led to their expulsion in 1290, intending it to be a refuge if they were ever attacked. But it has become a prison now. First for Dominica and now for me. And both, ultimately, because of Thomas.'

One part of Bartholomew's mind had been listening for sounds from the hall above. It had been silent for some time now. Cecily saw him glance up at the trapdoor, and nodded.

'On Sundays, the old lady likes a tour of her manor. The entire household is obliged to be in attendance and the whole affair might take several hours. Go now, Bartholomew. To the north of the house, behind the stable, you will find a path that leads to the river without passing through the village. Wait! Take this!'

She held out her hand. A silver ring lay there, with a blue-green stone. He looked at her bewildered. How many of these things were there?

'There were two,' she said, as if reading his thoughts. 'Lover's rings and identical, except for the size.' She gave a wry smile. 'I am not a fool, Bartholomew. I know why Dominica claimed she lost one ring and clung so dearly to the other. And you mentioned that Master Bigod may have been looking for a ring – perhaps Thomas asked him to look for the one Dominica says she lost.' She dropped the ring in Bartholomew's palm. 'I took that from her the night I sent her here. I have worn it since her murder. Take it. It might help you find the foul beast who killed her – perhaps this lover of hers that she went to such extremes to conceal from us. Who knows? Perhaps he may be foolish enough to wear her ring still, and now you will be able to recognise it from its fellow.'

Bartholomew put the ring into one of the pouches in his medicine bag. He climbed the ladder, and opened the trapdoor a crack. Cecily waited below. She was right: the hall was abandoned. He clambered out, and helped her to follow. In the gloom, he glimpsed her face, white and shiny with tears. She looked away, embarrassed. He left her behind the service screen and slipped stealthily across the hall towards the door.

'Hey!'

Bartholomew froze in horror as a group of men entered the hall. He ducked under one of the trestle-tables, but it was an inadequate hiding place at best, and his heart pounded against his ribs in anticipation of being dragged out. The men were not servants, but mercenaries, probably the ones who, according to Cecily, had been looking for him earlier.

'Just stop that!' came the voice again, loud in indignation as a conical helmet bounced on the floor. The speaker stooped to retrieve it, so close that Bartholomew was treated to a strong waft of his bad breath. It was all over now! It had to be!

A piercing scream tore through the air, and all eyes were drawn to the screen at the end of the hall. Bartholomew rubbed ran a hand through his hair wearily. It had not taken Mistress Lydgate long to renege on their agreement. But what else could he have done? He could not have killed her in cold blood, and locking her in the underground chamber would only have given him a few hours at most until Bigod came to seek him out. Perhaps he should have done just that and fled Cambridge for London or York. Now he was about to be dispatched by Cecily instead – not by her own hand it was true, but the outcome would be the same.

The screamed petered out. 'A rat! A rat!' came a wavery voice.

The soldiers looked at each other and grinned or grimaced, depending on their tolerance.

'A rat!' muttered the one whose helmet had been knocked from his head. 'Blasted woman.'

'There it goes! After it!' Cecily screeched. 'Oafs! Catch it!'

With rebellious mutterings, the men shuffled in the direction she was pointing up the spiral stair, until the hall was empty. Bartholomew emerged, still shaking, from his hiding place and slipped out of the door. As he left, he raised his hand in a silent salute of thanks to Cecily, who gave him a weak smile, and followed the men up the stairs.

Outside, the yard was empty; Bartholomew easily found the

path Cecily had told him to take. He forced his stiff legs into a
trot, continuing to run until he reached the river. He splashed
across it, his haste making him careless, so that he missed his
footing on one of the slippery rocks in the river bed and fell.
Coughing and choking, he regained his feet and continued
across, grateful he did not have the copy of Galen in his bag
as he had done for the past few days. The water was very cold
and the path had led him to a deeper part of the river than
where he had crossed that morning.

He scrambled up the opposite bank, and crashed through the
undergrowth until he reached the path that led to Cambridge.
He began to race along it, hoping that the vigorous movement
would restore some warmth to his body, but then slowed.
He should be more careful. Bigod was also likely to use
this path if he intended to return to town. Perhaps he was
already on it, and Bartholomew had no wish to run into
him. He stopped and listened intently, but heard nothing
except for the dripping of leaves from the morning's rain,
and the soft gurgle of the river. Cautiously, he began to
move forward again, stopping every few steps to listen. Voices
carried on the still air forced him to hide in the dripping
undergrowth twice, but the only travellers on the path on
a wet Sunday afternoon were three boys returning from a
fishing trip, and a small party of friars bound for a retreat
in the woods.

The light was beginning to fade when the high walls of
Michaelhouse came into view. He tried the small back door
that led into the orchard, but it was firmly barred. The Master,
wisely, was taking no chances of unwanted visitors in his grounds
while the town was in such a ferment of unrest. Bartholomew
knocked on the front gates to be allowed in, ignoring the
interested attention of the day porters as he squelched across
the yard to his room.

'Matt! Where have you been?' demanded Michael, standing
up from where he had been reading at Bartholomew's table.
'What a state you are in! What have you been doing?'

'What are you doing here?' Bartholomew responded with a
question of his own, slinging down his bag and beginning to
remove his wet clothes.

'Waiting for you! What does it look like? Where were you?'

'Out walking,' said Bartholomew non-committally. He had
not yet considered how he would tell Michael what he had

discovered without breaking his promise to Cecily to keep her whereabouts a secret.

'Out swimming more like!' retorted Michael, looking at Bartholomew's sopping clothes and dripping hair. 'What have you been doing?'

Bartholomew swung round to face him, irritated by the monk's persistent prying. 'Do you think the Proctor should know the comings and goings of all?'

Michael looked taken aback by his outburst, but then became angry himself. 'Walter said you left before dawn to go walking in the rain with no cloak. What do you expect me to think? We know about your badly aligned stars. I was worried.'

Bartholomew relented. 'I am sorry. I did not mean to cause trouble. But there is no need for all this concern, from you or anyone else. You are constantly demanding my expertise as the University's senior physician, so listen to me now – there is nothing wrong with me. Gray has never yet made the correct calculations for an astrological consultation – quite aside from the fact that he does not have the necessary information about me even to begin such a task. And you know I doubt the validity of astrological consultations, anyway. I cannot imagine why you are so ready to believe Gray over me.' He went to the water jug, but it had not been refilled that day. 'Where is Cynric?'

'Looking for you,' Michael said waspishly. 'And keep your voice down if you must hold such unorthodox views, or Father William will hear you, and then you will be in trouble.' He sat down again. 'Have you been looking into the death of that prostitute? I thought you may have gone to see Lady Matilde, but she said she has not seen you since yesterday, while the Tyler women complain bitterly that they have not set eyes on you since the night you were attacked. What have you been doing? You have certainly been up to more than a walk. Will you tell me?'

Bartholomew shook his head impatiently. He was tired and needed to think first, to work some sense into the jumble of information he had gathered before passing it to Michael. Such as the identity of the man whose voice was familiar, who had decreed that there will be a riot on Thursday.

'Then go to bed, Matt!' said Michael, throwing up his hands in exasperation. 'We will talk again in the morning.'

He left, and Bartholomew slipped his hand into his medicine bag, withdrawing the ring that Cecily Lydgate had given him.

He looked at it for a moment, before feeling in the sleeve of his gown for the broken ring he had found at Godwinsson. He put them together. They were almost identical, except for the missing stone and the size. What did that tell him? That the light-fingered friar Edred had stolen Kenzie's ring and ground it under his heel in anger when he realised it belonged to his Principal's wife? That Kenzie had lost it while he waited in Godwinsson's shed like a moonstruck calf, hoping for a glimpse of his lover through the windows of her house? That Kenzie had somehow found his ring, only to have it stolen again after his death, and placed on the skeletal hand at Valence Marie? But Werbergh had said that Kenzie had come to him and Edred to ask if they had it. Werbergh believed Edred had taken it, and the fact that Kenzie was prepared to risk a confrontation with the friars to ask for it led Bartholomew to deduce that he could not have been wearing it when he died.

Bartholomew rubbed the bridge of his nose. He was tired, and the time spent crouching in the chest had taken a greater toll on him than he realised. He washed away the smell of the river as best he could in the drop of water left from the morning, and lay down on the bed, huddling under the blankets. He was on the edge of sleep when he remembered he had left the rings on the table. Reluctantly, he climbed out of bed, and dropped them both back into the sleeve of his gown. It was not an original hiding place but one that would have to do until he found a better one.

He was asleep within moments. Michael waited until his breathing became regular then stole back into the room. He smiled when he saw Bartholomew's gown had been moved slightly, and slipped his hand down inside the sleeve. It would not be the first time that his friend had used the wide sleeves of his scholar's gown to hide things. He froze as Bartholomew muttered something and stirred in his sleep, although Michael was not seriously worried about waking him. There were few who slept as heavily as the physician, even when he was not exhausted from a day's mysterious labours.

The rings glinted dimly silver in Michael's palm. He stopped himself from whistling. The broken one he had seen already and had dismissed as something of little importance. But it was important now, with a second, virtually identical, ring beside it. He looked to where Bartholomew slept and wondered how he had come to have it. He shrugged mentally letting the rings fall back inside Bartholomew's sleeve. He would ask him tomorrow, when he told him that there had been more trouble at Godwinsson Hostel that day, and that Brother Werbergh lay dead in St Andrew's Church.

chapter 8

I N THE PARISH CHURCH OF ST ANDREW, WERBERGH LAY ON a trestle-table behind the altar. A tallow candle spluttered near his head, adding its own odour to the overpowering scent of cheap incense and death. Michael had been told that Werbergh's colleagues had agreed to undertake a vigil for him until his funeral the following day, but the church was deserted.

It was late afternoon, the day's teaching was completed, and the students had been given their freedom. Orange rays slanted through the traceried windows making intricate patterns on the floor, although the eastern-facing altar end of the church was gloomy. Bartholomew picked up the candle so that he could see the body better, while Michael wedged himself into a semicircular niche that had been intended to hold a statue before the church-builders had run out of money.

Someone had been to considerable trouble to give Werbergh a modicum of dignity during his last hours above ground. His hair had been brushed and trimmed and his gown had been carefully cleaned. Bartholomew inspected the friar's hands and saw that they, too, had been meticulously washed and the nails scrubbed.

'Where was he found?' Bartholomew asked.

Michael regarded him in the dim light. 'Tell me what you discovered yesterday and I will tell you about Werbergh.'

Bartholomew dropped Werbergh's hand unceremoniously back on the table. 'I will be able to tell you little of any value if you do not provide me with the necessary details,' he said irritably. 'In which case, we are both wasting our time.'

Michael stood. 'I am sorry,' he said reluctantly. He gave a sudden grin, his small yellow teeth glinting in the candlelight. 'But it was worth a try.'

Bartholomew raised his eyebrows and returned his attention to Werbergh's body.

'He was found dead in the wood-shed in the yard of Godwinsson yesterday afternoon,' said Michael. 'Apparently, he had been looking for a piece of timber that he might be able to make into a portable writing table. Huw, the Godwinsson steward, said he had been talking about the idea for some weeks. The shed is a precarious structure and collapsed on top of him while he was inside.'

Bartholomew thought of his own visit to the ramshackle shed in Godwinsson's back yard. It had definitely been unstable but he had not thought it might be dangerous, and certainly not dangerous enough to kill someone who went inside.

'When did you first see the body?'

'Lydgate sent word to the Chancellor as soon as it became clear that Werbergh was in the rubble. No one thought to look until he was missed some hours later. Why do you ask?'

Bartholomew picked at the tallow that had melted on to the table. 'So, Werbergh has been dead for at least an entire day. I would expect the body to be stiffer than it is, given the warm weather.'

Michael came to stand next to him as Bartholomew began a close inspection of the body. The physician ran his hands through Werbergh's hair, then held something he had retrieved between his thumb and forefinger. Michael leaned forward to look but shook his head uncomprehendingly.

'It is a piece of dried river weed,' said Bartholomew, dropping it into Michael's outstretched palm. He forced his hands underneath the body while Michael looked increasingly mystified. Bartholomew explained.

'Feel here, Brother. The body is damp underneath.'

'It looks to me as though his friends may have washed his habit,' said Michael, indicating Werbergh's spotless robe. 'Perhaps they washed it in the river so it would be clean for his funeral. People do launder clothes there, you know, despite what you tell them about it.'

'Give me time,' said Bartholomew. 'I need to inspect the body without the robe. Can we do that? Will it give offence?'

'Oh, doubtless it will give offence,' said Michael airily, 'especially if you can show that our friar's death is not all it seems. Examine away, Matt, with the Senior Proctor's blessing, while the Senior Proctor himself will guard the door and deter prospective

visitors. After all, there is no need to risk offending anyone
if your findings are inconclusive.'

He ambled off to take up a station near the door, while
Bartholomew began to remove Werbergh's robe. The task
was made difficult by the fact that the table was very narrow.
Eventually though he completed his examination, put all back
as he had found it and went to join Michael, slightly out of
breath and hot from his exertions.

Michael was not at the door, but outside it, engaged in a
furious altercation. Bartholomew shrank back into the shadows of the church as he recognised the belligerent tones of
Thomas Lydgate, poor Werbergh's Principal. Bartholomew
had never heard him so angry, and, risking a glance out,
saw the man's face was red with fury and his eyes were starting from his head. The physician in Bartholomew wanted
to warn him to calm down before he had a fatal seizure,
but he hung back, unwilling to become embroiled in the
dispute.

'You have no right!' Lydgate was yelling. 'The man is dead!
Can you not leave him in peace even for his last few hours
above ground?'

'Like your students have done, you mean?' asked Michael
innocently. 'The ones you told me would keep a vigil over him
until tomorrow?'

Lydgate's immediate reply was lost in his outraged spluttering,
and Bartholomew smiled to himself, uncharitably gratified to
see this unpleasant man lost for words.

'If I hear that you have let that witless physician near him, I
will complain in the strongest possible terms to the Chancellor
and the Bishop.' Lydgate managed to grate his words out
and Bartholomew imagined his huge hands clenching and
unclenching in his fury. 'I will see you both dismissed from
the University!'

'Why should you object so strongly to Doctor Bartholomew
examining your student's body, Master Lydgate?' asked Michael
sweetly. 'You have no reason to fear such an examination,
surely?'

Once again came the sounds of near-speechless anger. 'There
are rumours that he is not himself,' Lydgate managed eventually. 'I would not wish his feeble-minded ramblings to throw
any kind of slur on my hostel!'

'Can a slur be thrown, or should it be cast?' Michael mused.

Bartholomew smiled again, knowing that Michael was deliberately antagonising Lydgate. 'But regardless of grammatical niceties, Master Lydgate, I can assure you that my colleague is no more witless than you are.'

Bartholomew grimaced, while Lydgate appeared to be uncertain whether Michael was insulting him or not. He broke off the conversation abruptly and pushed past Michael towards the door. Bartholomew edged behind one of the smooth, round pillars and waited until Lydgate had stormed through the church to the altar before slipping out to join Michael. Michael took his arm and hurried him to a little-used alley so that no one would see them emerge from the churchyard.

'So, you think I am as witless as Lydgate, do you?' said Bartholomew, casting a reproachful glance at the fat Benedictine.

'Do not be ridiculous, Matt,' Michael replied. 'Lydgate is a paragon of wit compared to you.' He roared with laughter, while Bartholomew frowned, wondering whether there was anyone left in Cambridge who was not intimately acquainted with the alignment of his stars – even Lydgate seemed to know all about them. Michael saw his expression and his laughter died away.

'Witless or not, I would sooner trust your judgement than that of any other man I know,' he said with sudden seriousness. 'Even that of the Bishop. And as for your stars, I have far more reason to trust your judgement in matters of physic than Gray. If you say you are well, why should I doubt you?'

Bartholomew smiled reluctantly. Michael continued.

'So I am inclined also to believe you over the matter of the identities of our attackers, despite my reservations the day before yesterday when you gave me answers that I thought conflicted with what you had said earlier. What you say makes no sense, but that is no reason to assume you were mistaken. We will just have to do more serious thinking.'

Bartholomew was more relieved than he would have thought possible. Some of his irritability began to dissipate and he found himself better able to concentrate on Werbergh.

'So,' said Michael cheerily, 'tell me what your witless mind has seen that the genius of Lydgate has sought to hide.'

'The evidence is crystal clear,' began Bartholomew. 'I judge, from the leakiness and swelling of the body, that Werbergh has been dead not since yesterday morning, but a day or two earlier.

He probably died on Friday night or Saturday morning. At some point, he was immersed in water, although he did not die from drowning. His robe is still damp, the skin is slightly bloated which is consistent with his body being in water after death, and in the hair on one arm I found more river weed. Although there are marks on the body that are consistent with the shed collapsing on him, the fatal wound was a blow to the back of the head – like Joanna, Kenzie, and possibly the skeleton of the child.'

Michael's face was grave. 'You believe Werbergh was murdered then?'

'Well, it was certainly not suicide.'

'Could the wound have been caused by the falling shed?'

'It could,' said Bartholomew, 'but in this case it was not. There is no doubt that the shed collapsed, or more likely was arranged to fall, on Werbergh: there are wounds where slivers of wood can be found, but they were inflicted some time after he died. The injury to the back of his head was caused by something smooth and hard – the pommel of a sword perhaps, or some other metal object – and has no traces of wood in it. Had that wound been caused by the falling shed, I think it would have contained splinters, given the fact that the timber was so rotten.'

Michael scratched at his cheek with dirty finger-nails, his face thoughtful. 'Well, this explains all too clearly why Lydgate did not want you to examine Werbergh. Few would know these signs, or think to look for them, if the death appeared to be an accident.'

'Do you think Lydgate killed him?' asked Bartholomew. 'His actions are certainly not those of an innocent man.'

'They most assuredly are not,' agreed Michael. 'But if we try to report our findings to the Chancellor now, Lydgate will claim you are incompetent to judge because of your unfavourable stars.' He resumed scratching his cheek again. 'So, we will keep this knowledge to ourselves. And thinking he has managed to fool us might lead the killer – whether it is Lydgate or someone else – into making a mistake. I spoke to the Godwinsson scholars yesterday and all had alibis for the alleged time of Werbergh's death, but now we need to know what they were all doing on Friday night, not Sunday.'

'Kenzie first and now Werbergh,' said Bartholomew. 'I wonder where those Scottish lads were on Friday night. Perhaps they grew tired of waiting for justice and took it into their own hands to avenge Kenzie's death.'

'True,' said Michael, nodding slowly as he ran through the possibilities in his mind. 'Since Master Lydgate seems to have an aversion to you, I will go alone to chat informally to the scholars of Godwinsson, to see if I can find out what was afoot on Friday night. Meanwhile, how would you like to visit David's to see how our Scottish friends are?'

Bartholomew shrugged assent. Michael rubbed his hands together and then clapped Bartholomew on the back. 'We will outwit whoever is responsible for these crimes, my friend, you and I together.'

Despite the cooler weather of the last two days, David's Hostel was stifling. The shutters were thrown open but the narrow windows at the front of the house allowed little air to circulate: the large windows at the back allowed the sun to pour in but faced the wrong direction to catch the breeze. Bartholomew imagined that the decrepit building, although unhealthily hot in the summer, would be bitterly cold in the winter.

Meadowman, the David's steward, showed Bartholomew into the large room that served as the hostel's hall, while Fyvie hurried away to fetch the Principal. Davy Grahame and Ruthven were seated at the table with a large tome in front of them, while the older Grahame played lilting melodies on a small pipe in a corner with one or two other students.

Through the window, Bartholomew could see the brother of the student who had been ill. He was stripped to the waist and was splashing around happily with a brush and a bucket of water. From the envious eyes of some of the others, Bartholomew could see that cleaning the yard and escaping from academic studies was regarded more as a privilege than a chore. Ivo the scullion clattered about noisily in the kitchen as usual, and Meadowman went back to polishing the hostel pewter.

Robert of Stirling, the brother of the student cleaning the yard, rose when he saw Bartholomew and began fumbling in the scrip tied around his waist. Shyly he offered Bartholomew a silver coin, muttering that it was for the medicine he had been given. Bartholomew, who could not recall whether he had been paid or not, waved the money away with a shake of his head. The student pocketed his coin again hurriedly, giving Bartholomew a quick grin.

'Have you found Jamie's murderer yet?' he asked, the smile fading.

Bartholomew was aware that, although no one had moved, everyone in the room was listening for his answer.

'Not yet,' he said. What more could he say? They were really no further forward than they had been when he and Michael had first imparted the news of Kenzie's death to his friends several days before. And now there was a second death, similar to the first.

He looked up as Father Andrew entered. The friar's benign face was slightly splattered with ink, and his hands were black with it. He noticed Bartholomew's gaze and smiled apologetically.

'I am having problems with a new batch of quills,' he explained in his soft, lilting voice. 'I am a theologian, Doctor, and I am afraid such practical matters as cutting quills elude me.'

Bartholomew returned his smile, and Andrew perched on a stool next to him, clasping his stained hands together.

'Ivo!' he called to the noisy scullion. 'We have visitors, boy! Meadowman, can you not give Ivo a task he might complete more quietly?' He turned to Bartholomew. 'David's is severely limited in whom it can afford for servants,' he said in a low voice, so he would not be overheard and hurt Ivo's feelings. 'Meadowman is efficient enough but our scullions must be supervised constantly. But enough of our problems. What can we do for you, Doctor?' A smile crinkled his light blue eyes as he saw Ruthven and Davy Grahame return to their reading and he nodded approvingly at their diligence. 'I am afraid Master Radbeche is out at the moment but I will help you if I can.'

'I am afraid we are making little headway in this business concerning James Kenzie,' said Bartholomew. 'I really came to ask if there was anything else you might have heard, or remembered, since the last time we met that might help.'

The smile left Andrew's eyes and his face became sad. 'Poor Jamie,' he said softly. 'He would never have made a good scholar but he was a decent lad: truthful and kind. It was a terrible thing that he died such a death. His parents will be devastated.' He shook himself. 'But my eulogies will not help you catch his killer. In truth, I have thought of little else during these last few days, but I have been unable to come up with the merest shred of information that could be of use to you. I did not know he had a secret lover, and I certainly did not know it was Dominica Lydgate, or I would have dissuaded him immediately.'

'Why?' asked Bartholomew. 'Did you not like her?'

Andrew shook his head vehemently. 'You misunderstand,' he said. 'I have never met her. But I can see no future in a relationship between a poor student and the daughter of a wealthy principal. I would have dissuaded him for his own ultimate happiness. It is not for nothing the University has strict rules about women!'

'Who do you think might have killed Jamie?' Bartholomew asked.

Andrew spread his hands. 'I wish I knew. As it is, I do not even know why. You asked his friends about a ring Jamie was supposed to have had. Perhaps he was killed for that, if his killer assumed it was of value. I cannot imagine what he was doing near the Ditch at Valance Marie, but maybe that is not a safe place to be of an evening. Perhaps a group of apprentices were looking for trouble and killed him for simple mischief.'

'Do you think it possible that he may have been killed by students from another hostel?' asked Bartholomew. 'For example the friars with whom he argued the day before he died?'

Andrew spread his inky hands again. 'It is possible, I suppose, but it seems an extreme reaction on the part of the friars. Students of different hostels are always quarrelling with each other, but such altercations seldom result in murder – at least, not cold-blooded, premeditated slaying; we all know they kill each other in the heat of the moment.'

Although they were pretending to be doing other things, Bartholomew knew that the students were listening intently.

'Do you think the friars killed Jamie?' he asked Stuart Grahame.

Stuart Grahame looked up and flushed red at the sudden attention. 'I did to begin with,' he said, 'but not now. The friars would have been more likely to have killed me or Fyvie, since we were the ones who reacted the most strongly to their insults. Jamie did not antagonise them enough so that they would want to kill him.'

And how much would that be? Bartholomew wondered. He watched the others carefully but could see nothing in the wide,

guileless eyes of Davy Grahame that suggested guilt, while
Ruthven nodded wisely at Stuart Grahame's words, so that
Bartholomew suspected that Grahame was merely repeating
Ruthven's own logic. Fyvie, however, stared moodily at the
rushes and his face revealed nothing.

'And what do you think, Fyvie?' asked Bartholomew, watching
him intently.

Fyvie said nothing for a few moments, and then stood. He
loomed over Bartholomew, who would have felt threatened
had Father Andrew not been present. He slowly pointed a
finger at the physician.

'I have no reason to dismiss anyone from my list of suspects,'
he said. 'Perhaps Stuart Grahame is right about the friars and
perhaps he is not. But who else had a reason to kill him?'

Who indeed? thought Bartholomew. If Werbergh had been
telling the truth about Kenzie appearing at the church to ask
if the friars had stolen his ring, then Edred might well have
been presented with the perfect opportunity to follow and
kill him. His motive might simply have been that he did not
want the Scot to be alive to accuse him of theft. The more
Bartholomew considered it, the more the evidence seemed to
stack against Edred.

They all jumped as water hit one of the window shutters
with a crash, splattering in over the sill and spraying Ruthven
and Davy Grahame. The two students ducked away, grinning
at each other as they shook droplets from their hair and wiped
their faces with their sleeves. From the yard, there was a gale of
laughter and a moment later the smirking face of the student
who had been working there appeared. His mischievous delight
vanished when he saw David's had a visitor.

'John!' admonished Father Andrew. 'Where are your manners,
lad?'

'Have you got him?' asked John of Bartholomew, leaning
earnestly through the window. 'Is that why you are here? To
tell us you have caught Jamie's murderer?'

'He has not,' said Father Andrew. 'Go back to your chores,
John, and no playing with the water or I will tell your brother
to take over your duties.'

While John reluctantly went back to his cleaning, the friar
spoke gently to Fyvie, urging him to sit down. 'Perhaps Jamie's
murder was a random crime. Many deaths occur without a
reason. You must brace yourself for the possibility that his

killer may never be caught, despite the best efforts of the Senior Proctor and his colleagues.'

Fyvie looked up at him and then his glower abated somewhat. 'I am sorry,' he wailed suddenly, making Bartholomew start nervously. 'But we are cooped up here day and night, not allowed to go out unless we are accompanied, and all the while Jamie's murderer is laughing at us! I am not saying I wish to kill the man myself,' he said, with an apologetic glance at Father Andrew, 'but I do wish to bring him to justice.'

The friar patted his arm consolingly. 'The Proctor is doing all he can. Meanwhile, you would not wish to upset your family by becoming embroiled in things you should not.'

He sighed and called to the open window. 'There is no need to eavesdrop, John. Come in if you insist on listening.'

John's begrimed face appeared immediately, and he leaned his elbows on the window-sill.

'A shed collapsed on Brother Werbergh yesterday morning,' said Bartholomew somewhat abruptly.

Students and master looked at each other in confusion. 'Is Brother Werbergh one of the Godwinsson friars with whom our students argued?' asked Andrew. Bartholomew nodded. 'Is he badly hurt?'

'He is dead,' said Bartholomew.

There was a deathly silence. 'Is that why you are here?' asked Andrew. 'To see where David's Hostel students were at the time of his death?' His eyes became sad. 'You might have been a little more straightforward with us, Doctor. I assure you, we have nothing to hide, and you have no need to resort to this trickery. Yesterday morning, you say? We were either at church or here.'

'What about Friday and Saturday?' Bartholomew asked.

'You said he died yesterday,' Andrew pointed out. 'But it makes no difference. Since this dreadful business began we have kept our students here, or out under supervision. As I told you earlier we cannot afford to be seen brawling, or we will lose our hostel. Either I, or the Principal, can vouch for every one of our students at any time since. And I can assure you that none of them has fooled us with rolled-up blankets this time.'

Bartholomew rose to leave. 'I am sorry to have wasted your time, Father,' he said, 'but these questions needed to be asked – to clear your names from malicious gossip if nothing else.'

Andrew's mild indignation abated somewhat. 'I am sorry, too, Doctor. We have nothing to be ashamed of, so we do not resent your inquiries. We will answer any questions that will bring Jamie's killer to justice.' He rubbed at the ink on his hands. 'Have you finished with our Galen yet? Although we have no medical students at David's, a book is a valuable thing, and we would like it back soon.'

Bartholomew, who had been under the impression from Principal Radbeche that there was no immediate urgency for him to finish with it, was embarrassed that he had taken his time to read it. He offered to return it immediately. Andrew gave Bartholomew an apologetic smile.

'It is the only book we own outright,' he said again. He gestured at the tomes that were piled on the table. 'These others are borrowed from King's Hall. While I am delighted that you have found our Galen useful, I would feel happier in my mind knowing it is back here.' His grin broadened, and his voice dropped as he leaned towards Bartholomew so the students could not overhear. 'I show it to the illiterate parents of prospective students, so they know that we are serious about learning. Even though our book is a medical text, it serves an important function at David's!'

Bartholomew said he would send Gray round with the book as soon as possible. He offered his hand to Father Andrew, who clasped it genially before settling down at the table to read with Ruthven and Davy. Robert of Stirling leapt to his feet to see him out and Bartholomew followed him along the stuffy corridor. The student removed the bar from the gate, all the while gabbling about the attack several weeks before in which the old door had been kicked down. Bartholomew sensed the lad was chattering to hide his nervousness.

As Bartholomew stepped past him, Robert took his arm, casting an anxious glance back down the corridor. He made as though to speak but then closed his mouth firmly. Sweat beaded on his upper lip and he scrubbed at it irritably with his shirt-sleeve.

'What is wrong?' Bartholomew asked, wondering whether Robert had fully recovered from his fever. Perhaps he needed more medication and was afraid he would not have enough money to pay for it.

'Jamie's ring,' the student blurted out. 'I admired it. My father is a jeweller, you see. I know about good stones.' His words were jerky and he gave another agitated glance down the corridor.

'If it will put your mind at ease, I will tell no one we have spoken,' said Bartholomew gently, giving the nervous student a reassuring smile.

Robert swallowed hard. 'I persuaded Father Andrew to take me and my brother John to see the relic at Valence Marie on Saturday,' he said. He paused again and Bartholomew forced himself to be patient. 'Jamie's ring was on that horrible thing!' Robert's words came in a rush.

'I noticed the hand wore a ring similar to the one Jamie is said to have owned,' said Bartholomew carefully. One thing they could not afford was for Robert to claim Kenzie's ring was at Valence Marie: Valence Marie would start a fight with David's for certain. 'It is not necessarily the same one.'

'It *is* the same!' said Robert, his voice loud, desperate to be believed. Bartholomew grew anxious and wondered how he might dissuade Robert from his belief.

'Easy now,' he said. 'I will ask Brother Michael to inspect the ring, and—'

'You do not understand!' interrupted Robert, shaking off Bartholomew's attempt to placate him. 'I am not telling you it is similar. I am telling you it is the same one.'

'How can you be sure?' asked Bartholomew with quiet reason. 'I have seen at least one other ring identical to the one at Valence Marie myself recently.'

Robert looked pained. 'You recognise different diseases,' he said. 'I recognise different stones. My father is a jeweller, and I have been handling jewels since I was old enough not to eat them. It was the same ring, I tell you!'

His point made, he became calmer, although he kept casting anxious glances towards the hall.

'Why did you not tell me this when you were in the hall with the others?' asked Bartholomew.

Robert shook his head violently and fixed Bartholomew with huge eyes. 'I could not explain how I know,' he whispered.

Bartholomew was puzzled. 'But you said your father is a jeweller. Is that not explanation enough?'

Robert lowered his gaze. 'No one but you knows that. John told a lie when we first arrived two years ago. We have been living it ever since. We cannot reveal that we are the sons of a merchant.'

Bartholomew shook his head, nonplussed. Many merchants'
sons studied in Cambridge and he was unaware that any of them
faced serious problems because of it. Looking at Robert's dark
features, he suddenly realised the physical similarity between
him and the Arab master with whom he had studied in Paris.
In a flash of understanding, it occurred to him that Robert
and John might be Jewish, that their father was a money-lender
rather than a jeweller. In France, the Jewish population had
been accused of bringing the plague, and the situation was
little better in England. If Bartholomew's supposition were
true, he did not blame Robert and John for wishing to keep
their heritage a secret.

Robert continued. 'Master Radbeche and Father Andrew
think my father owns a manor near Stirling.'

'They will not learn otherwise from me,' said Bartholomew.
'But this matter of Jamie's ring . . .'

Robert became animated again. 'It is his ring! There is no
doubt! I pretended to examine the hand closely but really I
was looking at the ring.'

Bartholomew felt in the sleeve of his gown. 'But what about
this?' he asked, handing the ring Cecily had given him to
Robert. Robert took it and turned it around in his fingers,
smiling faintly.

'Ah, yes, lovers' rings. I wondered if Jamie's might be one
of a pair. But this is not the ring he had.' He gave it back to
Bartholomew. 'He had the gentleman's; this is the lady's.'

Bartholomew showed Robert the other ring, the one he had
found on the floor of Godwinsson's shed. The shed that killed
Werbergh, he thought, although obviously Werbergh could not
have been looking for the ring, since he was already dead when
he was put there.

Robert was talking, and Bartholomew forced his thoughts
back to the present. 'This would once have held a stone about
the same size as the ones in the lovers' rings, although the
craftsmanship on this is very inferior. See the crudeness of
the welding? And the arms of the clasp are different sizes.'
His nervousness seemed to abate as he talked about something
he knew. 'This is a nasty piece. I would say it belonged to a
whore, or someone who could not afford anything better. In
fact, I would go as far as saying there was no stone at all, but
perhaps coloured glass.'

He looked up, dark brown eyes meeting Bartholomew's. 'I

cannot say how Jamie's ring came to be on that horrible hand, but it is his without a doubt. The matching ring you have is the other half of the pair; I imagine you got it from Dominica. The third ring is nothing – a tawdry bauble. Do you think they might have some connection to why Jamie was killed?'

Bartholomew slipped them back into his sleeve and shrugged. 'The one on the relic definitely does. You have helped considerably by telling me what you have, and I promise you, no one will ever know where I came by the information. Perhaps you will return the favour by keeping your knowledge of the matter to yourself.'

Robert looked at Bartholomew as though he were insane. 'I feel I have risked enough just talking to you. I will not tell another soul – not even my brother John. John does not share my interest in precious stones, and found the hand sufficiently repulsive that he did not look at it long enough to recognise Jamie's ring.'

Bartholomew felt in his bag, pulling out a small packet. 'Take this. It is a mixture of herbs I give babies when they are teething and will do you no harm. If anyone should ask why you have been talking with me for so long, tell them you still feel feverish and wanted some medicine.'

The student gave Bartholomew a grin and took the packet. 'I should go,' he said, with another glance over his shoulder. 'I am glad I could help. I want you to catch Jamie's killer.'

As Bartholomew left, he heard Robert slide the bar into place behind the door, and frowned thoughtfully. Assuming Robert was not mistaken, Kenzie's ring on the hand found at Valence Marie lent yet more evidence to the fact that Thorpe's relic was a fake: if Kenzie had worn the ring a few days before, there was no legitimate way the bony hand could have been wearing it for the last twenty-five years. Bartholomew walked slowly, his head bent in concentration. Will, the Valence Marie servant, might have been near the place where Kenzie had died. Had he discovered Kenzie's body, stolen the ring, and then decided to adorn the hand with it?

Bartholomew sighed. He was back to a question he had asked before: who else would recognise the ring? Kenzie would have done, certainly, but he was dead. Dominica, assuming Bartholomew was right in his assumption that she was Joanna, was also dead. Thomas and Cecily Lydgate would know it, especially Cecily. Had Kenzie been killed just so that the ring

could be put on the hand for the Lydgates to see? It seemed
a very elaborate plot and there was nothing to say that the
Lydgates would ever go to view the hand. Also, it necessitated
a high degree of premeditation: Kenzie was killed several days
before the relic appeared, and it was surely risky to kill for a
ring, then just toss it into the Ditch on a skeletal hand in the
hope that it might be found by the dredgers.

Try as he might, Bartholomew could make no sense of it all.
Only one thing was clear. His left sleeve had a small tear in it
that he had been meaning to ask Agatha to mend. Because of
this, he had been careful to put the two rings into his right
sleeve the night before. But when he had shown the rings to
Robert, they were in his left sleeve. Although the hiding place
was perhaps an obvious one, there was only one person who
might guess that he would use it. Bartholomew frowned again,
wondering why Michael had searched not only his gown the
previous night as he slept, but also his room the day before.

The day of the Founder's Feast dawned bright and clear. All
the scholars of Michaelhouse rose long before dawn to help
with the preparations for the grand occasion. Agatha, who
had not slept at all the night before, bellowed orders at the
frantic kitchen staff and at any scholars who happened to
be within bawling range. Bartholomew smiled when he saw
the dignified Senior Fellow, Roger Alcote, struggling irritably
across the courtyard with a huge vat of saffron custard, trying
not to spill any on his immaculate ceremonial gown.

'Sam Gray!' yelled Agatha from the door of the kitchen, loud
enough to wake half of Cambridge. Gray's tawny head appeared
through the open window shutters of his room, looking anxious.
'Run to the Market Square and buy me a big pewter jug for the
cream. That half-wit Deynman has just cracked mine.'

'How can he have cracked a pewter jug?' called Gray, startled.
'They are supposed to be unbreakable.'

Bartholomew heard Agatha's gusty sigh from the other side
of the courtyard. 'That is what I always thought but Deynman
has managed it. So, off to the market with you. Now.'

Gray rubbed his eyes sleepily. 'The market stalls will not be
open yet,' he called. 'It is still dark.'

'Then go to the metal-smith's house and wake him up!'
shouted Agatha, exasperated. Even the wily Gray knew better
than to disobey a direct order from Agatha, and he scuttled

away, running his fingers through his hair in a vain attempt
to tidy it. Meanwhile, Agatha had spotted Bartholomew who,
with Father William, was draping one of Alcote's luxurious
bed-covers over the derelict stable that teetered in one corner
of the yard.

'And what do you think you are doing?' she demanded in
stentorian tones to Father William. He looked taken aback,
apparently considering that the purpose of their task was
obvious to any onlooker.

'Father Aidan said he thought these crumbling walls were an
eyesore and he suggested we cover them.' He shook his head in
disapproval. 'All vanity! We should be saving our guests from
the eternal fires of hell, not pandering to their earthly vices
by disguising ramshackle buildings with pieces of finery!' He
gave the bed-cover a vicious tug as though it were personally
responsible for Father Aidan's peculiar recommendation.

'I meant why are you forcing Doctor Bartholomew to help
you?' she roared. 'He should not be cavorting about with you
when his stars are bad.'

Bartholomew closed his eyes in despair, wondering yet again
how much longer Gray's diagnosis would continue to haunt
him. Still, he thought, trying to look on the positive side, at
least his recent accident had meant that Agatha had forgiven
him for inviting Eleanor Tyler to the Feast, and he was now
back in her favour. When he opened his eyes again Father
William was regarding him uneasily.

'I can finish this, Matthew,' he said. 'You go to your room
and lie down.'

'I am perfectly healthy,' Bartholomew snapped, pulling the
bed-cover into place with unnecessary roughness. 'In fact, much
more so than you.'

'Me?' asked William, surprised. 'How can you tell that?'

'You keep rubbing your stomach and you are as white as
snow. Did you eat that fish-giblet stew that has been making
an appearance at every meal since last week?'

William winced and looked away queasily. 'It tasted much
stronger than usual and I should have known not to eat
it when some of it spilled and the College cat would not
touch it.'

Bartholomew stepped back, satisfied that the unsightly, tumble-
down stable would not now offend the sensibilities of Michaelhouse's august guests. Of course, some of them might well

wonder why a bed-cover was draped over one of the buildings in the yard, but that question could be dealt with when
it arose.

'I can give you some powdered chalk mixed with poppy
juice. That should settle it down. But if you take it you must
avoid drinking wine today.'

'I was not planning to indulge myself in the sins of the flesh,'
said William loftily. 'A little watered ale is all I shall require at
the Feast. And I certainly shall not be eating anything.'

'Good,' said Bartholomew, setting off towards his room,
Father William in tow. He stopped abruptly. 'Oh, Lord! There
is Guy Heppel. I hope he has not found another body in the
King's Ditch.' It crossed his mind, however, that investigating
such a matter might be a perfect opportunity for him to
extricate himself from the delicate situation he faced with
his two female guests that day.

William snorted. 'That canal is a veritable cemetery! I cannot
see that either the town or the University will be keen to dredge
it again after all it has yielded this time.'

He watched Heppel making his way delicately across the
uneven yard, holding his elegant gown high, so that it would
not become fouled with the mud, some hard and dry but some
sticky and thick, that covered it.

'That man is a disgrace! To think he was appointed over
me to keep law and order in the town!' William drew himself
up to his full height and looked down his nose as the Junior
Proctor approached. 'And I think he wears perfume!'

Heppel arrived, breathless as always. He was apparently
to be someone's guest, perhaps Michael's, for he wore ceremonial scarlet and a pair of fine yellow hose. Uncharitably,
Bartholomew could not but help compare the skinny legs that
were thrust into them with those of a heron.

'Thank the Lord you are awake,' said Heppel to Bartholomew
in relief. 'I must have this astrological consultation before I
enjoy the pleasures of your Founder's Feast today. After the last
one I attended, I was ill for a week. I must know whether my stars
are favourable, or whether I should decline the invitation.'

Father William gave a sudden groan and clutched at
Bartholomew to support himself. 'Oh, I do feel ill, Matthew,'
he whispered hoarsely. 'I think I might have a contagion.'

'A contagion?' squeaked Heppel in alarm, moving backwards
quickly. 'What manner of contagion?'

'One that is both painful and severe,' said William, holding his stomach dramatically. 'I do hope its miasma has not affected Matthew. You might be better waiting a while for this consultation, Master Heppel, in case he passes it to you.'

Heppel took several more steps away, and shoved a vast pomander to his nose.

'Saturn is still ascendant,' said Bartholomew, thinking he should at least try to ease Heppel's obvious concern for his well-being. 'So take a small dose of that angelica and heartsease I gave you and eat and drink sparingly today. That should see you safely through the ordeal. And avoid anything that might contain fish giblets.'

'Are fish giblets under the dominion of Saturn, then?' asked Heppel, puzzled and taking yet another step backwards as William reeled.

'Yes,' said William before Bartholomew could reply. 'Say a mass before you come to the Feast, Master Heppel, and pray for me.'

Heppel bowed briskly to Bartholomew and William and walked out of the yard a good deal more quickly than he had walked in. Bartholomew took Father William's arm, although the ailing friar made a miraculous recovery once Heppel had been ushered out of the front gate by the porters.

'Did you smell it?' William growled to Bartholomew. 'Perfume! Like a painted whore! And God knows whores have no business in a place of learning!'

Bartholomew swallowed hard and hoped Michael had ensured that Matilde was not seated anywhere near Father William at the Feast. He unlocked the little storeroom where he kept his medicines and mixed a draught of chalk and poppy syrup. William gulped it down and pulled a face.

'God's teeth, Matthew, that is a vile concoction! You should give a dose to that reprehensible Heppel. That would stop him coming after you for his astrological consultations.'

'Remember,' Bartholomew warned as the friar left. 'No wine.'

'I am not one of your dull-witted students, Matthew,' said William pompously. 'I only need to be told something once for it to sink in. No wine.' He looked Bartholomew up and down disparagingly. 'I do hope you are going to change into something a little more appropriate. You look very scruffy this morning.'

'But wearing fine clothes would be indulging in the sins of the flesh,' Bartholomew pointed out to the man who professed to have no wish for material goods and to care nothing for appearances.

Aware that he had been caught out in an inconsistency, Father William pursed his lips. 'You have my blessing to indulge yourself today, Matthew. After all, we cannot have Fellows of other colleges thinking that Michaelhouse scholars are shabby, can we? I, of course, as a lowly friar, own no fine clothes, but Agatha washed my spare habit specially for the occasion. Unfortunately, it shrank a little and is now a lighter shade of grey than it should be, but it is spotlessly clean.'

'Are you telling me that this is the first time it has ever been washed?' asked Bartholomew, disgusted. 'You have had the same two habits since before I became a Fellow here and that was eight years ago!'

'Grey does not show the dirt, Matthew. And anyway, I was afraid laundering might damage them. I am well aware of your peculiar notions about washing, but I personally believe that water has dangerous properties and that contact with it should be avoided at all costs.'

'So I see,' said Bartholomew, noticing, not for the first time, that the friar's everyday habit was quite stiff with filth. He imagined there was probably enough spilled food on it to keep the College supplied for weeks.

'Well, I must go and prepare the church for prime,' said William. He raised a hand to his head. 'The burning in my stomach has eased but I feel a little giddy. Is it that potion you gave me?'

'It might be,' said Bartholomew. 'Of course, it might equally well be the terrifying notion of wearing a clean habit. You will need to take another dose, probably just before the Feast. I will leave it for you on my table, so you can come to get it when it is convenient. Only take half of it, though. The rest is to be drunk before you go to bed.'

William nodded and was gone. Alone, Bartholomew washed and shaved and donned a clean shirt and hose, although both were heavily patched and darned. Cynric slipped into the room with Bartholomew's ceremonial red gown that he had painstakingly brushed and ironed. Bartholomew took it reluctantly, guessing that Cynric had been to some trouble to render it so smart. The physician was careless with clothes, and knew it would be only a matter of time before something spilled on it or it became crumpled.

'It should be a fine day,' said Cynric, nodding to where the sky was already a clear blue. 'I hope you have a good time with that Eleanor Tyler.'

His good wishes did not sound entirely sincere and Bartholomew glanced at him, puzzled. 'First Agatha and now you. What is wrong with Eleanor Tyler?'

'Nothing, nothing,' said Cynric hastily. He hesitated. 'Well, she is a touch brazen, boy, if you must know the truth. And she is after a husband. With no father to negotiate for them, those Tyler daughters are taking matters into their own hands. That is what makes them brazen.'

But not as brazen as a prostitute, Bartholomew thought, wondering what Cynric would say when he found out about Matilde. It crossed his mind that Cynric, Agatha and even Father William, might excuse his choice of guests on the grounds that his stars were misaligned, assuming, of course, that they did not discover that the invitations were issued long before he was hit on the head.

The day was already becoming warm as the scholars assembled in the yard to walk to the church for prime. Bartholomew found he was uncomfortable in his thick gown, and warned Cynric that watered ale might be required at some point of the proceedings if someone fainted. Master Kenyngham, the gentle Gilbertine friar who was head of Michaelhouse, beamed happily at his colleagues, blithely unaware of Gray scampering late into his place near the end of the procession. Agatha approached Gray nonchalantly, and a large pewter jug exchanged hands, even as the line of scholars began to move off towards the church.

Michael walked next to Bartholomew, behind the Franciscans, his podgy hands clasped reverently across his ample stomach. He wore his best habit, and the wooden cross that usually hung around his neck had been exchanged for one that looked to be silver. His thin, brown hair had been trimmed, too, and his tonsure was, as always, perfectly round and shiny.

'You look very splendid today, Brother,' Bartholomew remarked, impressed by the fact that, unlike everyone else, the monk had escaped being involved in the frantic preparations that morning.

'Naturally,' said Michael, raising a hand to his hair. 'A good many important people will be at this Feast, not to mention your gaggle of hussies. I must make a good impression.'

'Did you ask the steward to make sure Matilde was not near William?' asked Bartholomew anxiously.

The monk nodded. 'Eleanor will be next to Father William. Matilde will sit between you and our esteemed Senior Fellow, Roger Alcote.'

'Are you insane?' Bartholomew cried. The Franciscans looked round to glower at him for breaking the silence of the procession. He lowered his voice. 'Alcote will be worse than William, if that is possible, and William will be horrified to find himself next to Eleanor!'

'That cannot be helped,' said Michael primly. 'You should have considered all this before inviting a harem to dine in our College.'

The church was gloomy in the early morning light but candles, lit in honour of the occasion, cast wavering shadows around the walls. The procession made its way up the aisle and filed silently in two columns into the chancel, Fellows in one and students in the other. The body of the church was full of townspeople and scholars from other colleges. Eleanor Tyler was standing at the front and gave Bartholomew a vigorous wave when he saw her. Michael sniggered unpleasantly and then slipped away to join his choir.

'What in God's name is Father William wearing?' hissed Roger Alcote from Bartholomew's side. 'Has he borrowed a habit from Father Aidan? It is far too small for him – you can virtually see his knees! And the colour! It is almost white, not grey at all!'

'He washed it,' explained Bartholomew, smiling when he saw William's powerful white calves displayed under his shrunken habit. 'He said he thought that water might be dangerous to it, and, from the state of it, I would say he was right!'

Michael cleared his throat, and an expectant hush fell on the congregation.

'Let us hope he has chosen something short,' muttered Alcote, as Michael raised his hands in the air in front of his assembled singers. 'Or we may find we have fewer guests for the rest of the day than we had anticipated.'

His uncharitable words were not spoken lightly. As one, the congregation winced as the first few notes of an anthem by the Franciscan composer Simon Tunstede echoed around the church. What Michael's singers lacked in tone was compensated for by sheer weight of numbers, so that the resulting sound was deafening. Michael gesticulated furiously for a lowering of volume but his volunteers were out to sing for their supper and their enthusiasm was not to be curtailed. The lilting melody of one of Tunstede's loveliest works was rendered into something akin to a pagan battle song.

The door of the church opened and one or two people slipped out. Bartholomew saw his sister standing near the back of the church, her hand over her mouth as she tried to conceal her amusement. To his horror, he saw Eleanor Tyler had no such inhibitions and was laughing openly. Next to her, Sheriff Tulyet struggled to maintain a suitably sombre expression, while his infant son howled furiously, unsettled by the din. Only Master Kenyngham seemed unaffected, smiling benignly and tapping his hand so out of time with the choir that Bartholomew wondered if he were hearing the same piece.

To take his mind off the racket, Bartholomew looked at the space that had been cleared for Master Wilson's tomb. The mason had said the whole contraption would be ready before the end of autumn, when Wilson's mouldering corpse could be removed from its temporary grave – recently desecrated by Bartholomew – and laid to its final rest under his black marble slab. The notion of exhuming the body of a man who had perished in the plague bothered the physician. Some scholars believed that the pestilence had come from graves in the Orient, and Bartholomew had no desire to unleash again the sickness that took one in every three people across Europe. He decided that he would exhume the grave alone, wearing gloves and mask, to reduce the chances of another outbreak. Anyone who felt so inclined could come later and pay their respects – although he could not imagine that the unpopular, smug Master Wilson would have many mourners lining up at his grave.

When the long Latin mass was over, the scholars walked back to Michaelhouse and prepared to greet their guests in the courtyard. There was a pleasant breeze – although it had blown the bed-cover hiding the stable askew – and the sun shone brightly. Agatha's voice could be heard ranting in the kitchens, almost drowned out by the church bells. The gates were flung open and the guests began to arrive.

One of the first was Eleanor Tyler, who flounced across the courtyard, looking around her speculatively. She looked lovely,

Bartholomew thought, dressed in an emerald-green dress with her smooth, brown hair bound in plaits and knotted at the back of her head. She beamed at Bartholomew and took his arm. Her face fell somewhat when she saw a patched shirt-sleeve poking from under his gown.

'I thought you were all supposed to be wearing your best clothes,' she said, disappointed.

'These are my best clothes,' protested Bartholomew. 'And they are clean.'

'Clean,' echoed Eleanor uncertainly, apparently preferring grimy finery to laundered rags. But her attention was already elsewhere. 'Why is there a bed-cover on that old wall?' she asked, pointing to Bartholomew and William's handiwork. 'If it is being washed, you might have taken it in before your guests arrived.'

'Your choir put their hearts and souls into that anthem by Simon Tunstede,' remarked Bartholomew as Michael came to stand next to him. 'It must have been heard fifteen miles away in Ely Cathedral.'

Michael winced. 'More like sixty miles away in Westminster Abbey! Once their blood is up, there is no stopping those people. My only compensation is that my guest, the Prior of Barnwell, told me he thought it was exquisite.'

'But he is stone deaf,' said Bartholomew, startled. 'He cannot even hear the bells of his chapel any more.'

'Well, he heard my choir,' said Michael. 'Here he comes. You must excuse me, Madam.' He bowed elegantly to Eleanor, lingering over her hand rather longer than was necessary.

Eleanor's indignation at the monk's behaviour was deflected by the magnificent spectacle of the arrival of Sheriff Tulyet and the Mayor, both resplendent in scarlet cloaks lined with the softest fur, despite the warmth of the day. Sensibly, Tulyet relinquished his to a servant, but the Mayor knew he looked good and apparently decided that sweating profusely was a small price to pay for cutting so fine a figure. Master Kenyngham approached, smiling beatifically, and introduced himself to Eleanor, asking her if she were a relative of Bartholomew's.

At that moment, Bartholomew spotted his sister and her husband, and excused himself from Eleanor's vivid, and not entirely accurate, description of how Bartholomew had saved her on the night of the riot. Kenyngham, Bartholomew noted, was looking increasingly horrified; he hoped Eleanor's account of the violence that night would not spoil the gentle, peace-loving Master's day.

'Matt!' said Edith Stanmore, coming to greet him with out-stretched arms. 'Are you fully recovered? Sam Gray tells me your stars are still poorly aligned.'

Bartholomew raised his eyes heavenwards. 'I am perfectly well, Edith.' He fixed his brother-in-law with a look of reproval. 'And I have no need of Cynric following me everywhere I go.'

Stanmore had the grace to look sheepish. 'This is Mistress Horner,' he said, turning to gesture towards an elderly woman who stood behind him. Mistress Horner was crook-backed and thin, wearing a dowdy, russet dress that hung loosely from her hunched figure. A starched, white wimple framed her wind-burned face, although her features were shaded by a peculiar floppy hat. A clawed, gloved hand clutched a walking stick, although she did not seem to be particularly unsteady on her feet. Bartholomew had not seen her before and assumed she must be someone's dowager aunt, wheeled out from some musty attic for a day of entertainment. He bowed politely to her, disconcerted by the way she was staring at him.

Stanmore caught sight of the Mayor standing nearby, and was away without further ado to accost him and doubtless discuss some business arrangement or other. Edith was watching her brother with evident amusement.

'You have met Mistress Horner before,' she said, her eyes twinkling with laughter.

'I have?' asked Bartholomew, who was certain he had not. He looked closer and his mouth fell open in shock. 'Matilde!'

'Shh!' said Matilde, exchanging a look of merriment with Edith. 'I did not go to all this trouble so that you could reveal my disguise in the first few moments. What do you think?'

She smiled up at him, revealing small, perfectly white teeth in a face that had evidently been stained with something to make her skin look leathery, while carefully painted black lines served as wrinkles. Bartholomew was not sure what he thought; there was no time anyway because Eleanor had arrived to reclaim him, and the bell was chiming to summon the scholars of Michaelhouse and their guests into the hall for the Feast. His heart thudded painfully as he escorted Eleanor and Mistress Horner through the porch, in the way that it had not done since he was a gawky youth who had taken a fancy to one of the kitchen maids at his school. He heard his sister informing Eleanor, who was not much interested, that Mistress Horner was a distant relative.

When they reached the stairs, Eleanor grew impatient with Mistress Horner's stately progress, and danced on ahead, eyes open wide at the borrowed tapestries that hung round the walls of Michaelhouse's hall, and at the yellow flicker of several hundred candles – the shutters were firmly closed to block out the daylight, although why Michaelhouse should think its guests preferred to swelter in an airless room to dining in a pleasant breeze, Bartholomew could not imagine. On the high table, the College silver was displayed, polished to a bright gleam by Cynric the night before. Bartholomew solicitously assisted his elderly guest towards it, alarmed when Father William stepped forward to help. Matilde, however, was completely unflustered and accepted the friar's help with a gracious smile that she somehow managed to make appear toothless.

Despite the fact that there were perhaps four times as many people dining in College than usual, only one additional table had been hired for the occasion. The scholars and their guests were crammed uncomfortably close together, particularly given that the day was already hot, and hundreds of smoking candles did not make matters any easier. Squashed between Eleanor on the one side and Matilde on the other, Bartholomew felt himself growing faint, partly from the temperature, but mainly from anticipating what would happen if Matilde's make-up should begin to melt off, or Eleanor Tyler display some of the indiscretion that his friends seemed to find so distasteful. He reached for his goblet of wine with an unsteady hand and took a hefty swallow. Next to Eleanor the misogynistic Father William did the same, sweat standing out on his brow as he tried to make himself smaller to avoid physical contact with her.

Father Kenyngham stood to say grace, which was perhaps longer than it might have been and was frequently punctuated by agitated sighs from behind the serving screen, where Agatha was aware that the food was spoiling. And then the meal was underway. The first course arrived, comprising a selection of poultry dishes.

Eleanor clung to Bartholomew's arm and chattered incessantly, making it difficult for him to eat anything at all. Father William was sharing a platter with the voluptuous wife of a merchant that Father Aidan had invited, and was gulping at his wine as his agitation rose with the temperature of the room. Bartholomew could only imagine that the College steward, who decided who sat where, must have fallen foul of William's quick tongue at some point, and had managed his own peculiar revenge with the seating arrangements. Meanwhile Roger Alcote, another Fellow who deplored young women, was chatting merrily to the venerable Mistress Horner and was confiding all kinds of secrets.

'I hear you have had little success in discovering the killer of that poor student – James Kenzie,' said Eleanor, almost shouting over the cacophony of raised voices. She coughed as smoke from a cheap candle wafted into her face when a servant hurried by bearing yet more dishes of food.

'We have had no success in finding the murderers of Kenzie, the skeleton in the Ditch, or the prostitute, Joanna,' said Bartholomew, taking a tentative bite of something that might have been chicken. It was sufficiently salty that it made him reach immediately for his wine cup.

Further down the table Father William did the same, although, unlike Bartholomew, the friar finished his meat, along with another two cups of wine to wash it down. Bartholomew was concerned, knowing that wine reacted badly with poppy juice, as he had warned that morning. So much for William's claim that he only needed to be told something once, thought the physician. He tried to attract the friar's attention, but then became aware that Eleanor had released his arm and was regarding him in a none-too-friendly manner.

'Why are you bothering with this whore?' she demanded, loud enough to draw a shocked gasp from Alcote, two seats away. 'No one in the town cares about her, so why should you?'

'I feel she was badly used,' said Bartholomew, surprised by the venom her voice.

'So were the other eight people who were killed in the riot, but none of them has a personal crusader searching for their killers.'

'But they all had someone who cared about them at their funerals,' Bartholomew pointed out. 'Joanna had no one.'

'That was probably because she was unpopular,' said Eleanor coldly.

'Did you know her then?' asked Bartholomew, startled.

'Of course not! She was a whore!'

Bartholomew glanced uneasily at Matilde, but if she was paying any attention to Eleanor, she did not show it. Her head was turned in polite attention towards Roger Alcote, who had recovered from his shock at the mention of whores and was informing her, in considerable detail, about the cost of silver on the black market. Bartholomew wondered how Alcote knew about such matters, but realised that Alcote was not the wealthiest of Michaelhouse's Fellows for nothing.

'You must desist with this ridiculous investigation,' Eleanor announced firmly. 'This harlot's killer is long gone and you will only waste your time. Not only that, but think how it looks for a man of your standing and reputation to be fussing about a prostitute!'

'Because she was a prostitute does not give someone the right to kill her,' reasoned Bartholomew quietly.

'No, it does not, but you are wrong in applying yourself so diligently to her case. Why can you not look into whose cart crushed that poor potter instead – he was a good man and well-liked. Or what about the scholars who were slain? That friar from Godwinsson, for example.'

'I do not think I will be able to make much progress with Joanna's murder anyway,' said Bartholomew in a placatory tone, reluctant to discuss the matter with Eleanor if she was going to be hostile. It was none of her business and she had no right to be telling him what he could or could not do in his spare time. 'I have discovered nothing at all, except that the two Frenchmen from Godwinsson are the most likely suspects, and they are never at home.'

'Are you mad?' asked Eleanor in horror. She dropped her voice to a whisper when Alcote leaned forward to gaze disapprovingly at her. 'My mother killed their friend to save you! Have you not considered that your prying might force them to reveal her as the killer? And then she will be hanged, and it will be all your fault!'

She had a point. Eleanor had already told him that the French students had often pestered her while she sat outside to sew, and the surviving pair would know exactly who had killed their friend. In fact, Mistress Tyler was probably fortunate that they had not retaliated in some way already, although the fact that the students had told all and sundry that they were attacked by a crowd of well-armed townsmen seemed to indicate that they were prepared to overlook the matter in the interests of appearances.

'All right,' he conceded. 'And as I said, I think there is little more I can do anyway.'

Eleanor gazed at him sombrely for a moment, before turning her attention to the portion of roast pheasant in front of her.

'Thank you,' she said, as she ripped the bird's legs off. 'But we should not spoil this wonderful occasion by quarrelling, Matt. Pass me some of that red stuff. No, not wine, addle-brain! That berry sauce.' She took a mouthful, and quickly grabbed her goblet. 'Pepper, flavoured mildly with berries!' she pronounced, fanning her mouth with her hand. 'That is spicy stuff!'

Father William evidently thought so too, for Cynric stepped forward to refill his cup three times in quick succession. By the time the second course arrived, the friar was distinctly red in the face, and was considerably more relaxed than he had been when the Feast had begun.

'I advised you to drink no wine, Father,' Bartholomew whispered to him behind Eleanor, who was giving her entire attention to stripping the pheasant to the bone with her teeth. 'It does not mix well with the medicine you took.'

'Nonsense,' said William expansively. 'I feel in excellent health. Try some of this meat, Matthew, lad. I do not have the faintest idea what it is, but what does that matter, eh?'

He elbowed Eleanor hard in the ribs and Bartholomew regarded him aghast. The Franciscan slapped a generous portion of something grey on top of the mountain of gnawed bones on her trencher, and then peered at it short-sightedly.

'That should probably do you,' he said finally. 'Put some flesh on you, eh?'

He gave her another nudge and burst into giggles. Amused, Eleanor grinned at him, and he slapped his hand on her knee, roaring with laughter. Bartholomew groaned.

'Cynric! Do not give him any more to drink. Fetch him some water.'

'I told you this morning, I do not approve of water,' bellowed William jovially. 'Bring me wine, Cynric and bring it quickly! Now, Mistress, I do not believe I have seen you in our congregation very often. I hope you are not bound for the old fires and brimstone of hell, eh?'

William would have fires and brimstone in his stomach

the next day if he did not moderate his wine consumption, Bartholomew thought, astonished as the friar brought his face close to Eleanor's and began to regale her with a tale of how he had once sought out heretics in the south of Spain. It was not a pleasant story, nor one that was appropriate for such an occasion, but Eleanor was spellbound, her food forgotten as she listened to the Franciscan's account of what amounted to wholesale slaughter in the name of God.

As dessert was being served, Bartholomew noticed that Father William had not been the only one who had drunk too much too quickly. Alcote, next to Matilde, had the silly, fixed grin on his face that told all those who knew him that he was on the verge of being insensible. With relief, Bartholomew was able to give Matilde his full attention. Like the physician, she had eaten and drunk little, and was one of the few people left in the hall in full control of her faculties. She watched the guests and scholars around her with delight, laughing when the Mayor's fine hat fell into his custard because he was trying to maul Edith Stanmore who sat across the table from him, and enthralled by the way Michael's choir went from appalling to diabolical as they became steadily more intoxicated. When one of the tenors passed out, taking a section of the altos down with him, she turned to Bartholomew with tears running down her cheeks.

'Oh, Matthew! I do not think I have laughed so much in years! Thank you for inviting me. I was uncertain about coming at first – after all, a feast in a University institution attended by a crowd of debauched, drunken men, is not really an occasion respectable women should attend – but now I am glad I came. The sisters will love hearing about all this!'

It was ironic, Bartholomew thought, that one of the most auspicious occasions in the University calendar should be seen in terms as a source of mirth for the town's prostitutes. But looking around him, it was difficult to argue with her. Alcote had finally slipped into oblivion, and was asleep in his chair with his mouth open; Father Aidan, Bartholomew was certain, had his hand somewhere it should not have been on the person of the St Radegund's Convent cellarer who sat next to him; Michael, virtually the only one in the hall still eating, was choking on his food, and was being pounded on the back by a trio of young ladies; Father Kenyngham had blocked out the racket around him and was contentedly reading a book;

William was on his feet, unsteadily miming out some nasty detail about his days in the Inquisition while Eleanor listened agog; and in the body of the hall, scholars and guests alike were roaring drunk or on the verge of passing out.

Those that were still able were beginning to leave. Edith gave Bartholomew and Matilde a nod before she picked her way out of the hall, followed by Oswald Stanmore who walked with the unnatural care of those who have over-imbibed. Judging from Edith's black expression, her husband was not in her good graces for enjoying the wine and carelessly abandoning her to the unwanted attentions of the Mayor. Bartholomew would not have wanted to be in Stanmore's shoes the following morning.

'So, did you dress as a grandmother to save your reputation, or mine?' he asked, turning away from the chaos to look at Matilde.

'Both,' she said. 'But mainly yours. It was your sister's idea, actually, although of course her husband knows nothing about it. He thinks I am some distant cousin you invited, and lost interest in me as soon as he learned I had nothing to sell and didn't want to buy anything.'

Bartholomew laughed, then raised an arm to protect her as Father William, now describing some fight in which he had emerged victorious, snatched up a candlestick and began to wave it in the air, splattering wax everywhere and landing the voluptuous merchant's wife on his other side a painful crack on the back of the neck.

'And so I managed to escape from those evil-doers, stealing back all my friary's sacred relics to protect them from pagan hands,' he finished grandly, slumping back down into his chair.

'You escaped from these heathens with *all* the relics?' asked Eleanor, impressed. 'All alone, and with no weapon other than a small stick and your own cunning?'

'And the hand of God,' added William, as an afterthought. He wiped the sweat from his face with the edge of the tablecloth. 'The relics are now safe in Salamanca Cathedral. We later returned to the village and charged everyone with heresy.'

'The whole village?' asked Eleanor, eyes wide and round. 'What happened?'

William seized the candlestick again and lurched to his feet. 'There was a fight, of course, but I was ready for them!'

The merchant's wife received another crack on the head as William girded himself up for action. Before he could do any more damage, Bartholomew wrested the object from him and he and Cynric escorted him, none too willingly, to his room. The fresh air seemed to sober the friar somewhat.

'That damned medicine of yours,' he muttered. 'You gave me too much of it.'

Bartholomew looked sharply at the friar. 'Did you take all that I left on the table? You were supposed to have saved some of it for later.'

'Then you should have told me so,' growled William, trying to free his arm from Cynric to walk unattended. 'It was powerful stuff.'

'So was the wine,' remarked Bartholomew. As soon as the friar was on his bed, he began to snore. Bartholomew turned him on his side and left a bucket next to the bed, certain he would need it later.

Meanwhile, back in the hall, Bartholomew's place had been taken by Sam Gray who was deep in conversation with Eleanor. When the physician offered to walk her home, she waved him away impatiently, and turned her attention back to Gray.

'I will see her home,' Gray volunteered, far more readily than he agreed to do most things. He proffered an arm to Eleanor, who took it with a predatory grin. Side by side, they picked their way across fallen guests, scraps of food and empty bottles, and left the hall.

'Eleanor will be safe enough with him,' said Matilde, seeing Bartholomew's look of concern. 'It is still daylight outside and she is a woman well able to take care of herself.'

'Then, perhaps I can escort you home.'

'No, Matthew. The sisters will be waiting to hear all about this Feast, and they will want to see me in my disguise. I shall go to them now, so that they have my tale before they start work tonight.'

'Why are they so interested?'

'Why should they not be? These men, who lie in drunken heaps, are the great and good of the town, who use us for their pleasures on the one hand, but who are quick to condemn us on the other. The sisters will enjoy hearing about how they have debased themselves. My only regret is that I have no suitable words with which to describe the choir.'

'I could think of some,' said Bartholomew, looking across to where a few of them were carousing near the screen. Whether they were still singing, or simply yelling to make themselves heard, he could not decide.

'Thank you again,' she said, touching him on the arm. 'You will be busy tomorrow, dealing with all these sore heads and sick stomachs, so go to bed early.'

With this sound advice, she took her leave, making her way carefully across the yard and out of the gates, a curious figure whose matronly attire and walking stick contrasted oddly with her lithe, upright posture and graceful steps. Bartholomew heaved a sigh of relief, aware that a combination of good luck, Matilde's ingenuity and strong wine had extricated him from his delicate situation with no damage done. Wearily, still smiling about the spectacle William had made of himself, Bartholomew headed for his room.

No one at Michaelhouse was awake before sunrise, and the Franciscans, to a man, missed their pre-dawn offices. Father William looked gaunt and pale and roundly damned the perils of over-indulgence. Notwithstanding, he helped himself to a generous portion of oatmeal at breakfast, so Bartholomew supposed that he could not feel too ill.

Before lectures started, Robin of Grantchester appeared at the gates, informing the scholars of Michaelhouse that he was prepared to offer them a collective discount on any leeching or bleeding that was required. No one took advantage of his generosity, although a number of Fellows and students availed themselves of Bartholomew's services, which tended to be less painful, less expensive, and more likely to work. Unkindly, Bartholomew suggested that Robin should visit the Mayor, who was last seen being carried home in a litter, singing some bawdy song that, rumour had it, Sam Gray had taught him.

Once teaching was finished, Bartholomew found he had a large number of patients to see. A few of them were people suffering the after-effects of the previous night's excesses, but others were ill because food was scarce following the plague, and not everyone could afford to buy sufficient to keep them in good health. The irony of it did not escape the physician.

Michael meanwhile, after a day's break from his duties, announced that he was going to pay another visit to Godwinsson Hostel to try to wring more information from its students about their whereabouts at the time of Werbergh's death. His previous attempt had proved unsuccessful because no one had been at home. Concerned for his friend entering what he considered to be a lion's den, Bartholomew offered to accompany him but Michael waved him away saying that the physician might be more hindrance than help in view of Lydgate's antipathy towards him. They walked together to the High Street and then parted, Michael heading towards Small Bridges Street, and Bartholomew to St Mary's Church where the Chancellor was paying for his greed over a large plate of sickly marchpanes the day before.

It was late by the time Bartholomew had completed his rounds, and the evening was gold and red. He knew he should return to Michaelhouse, and send Gray to return the Galen to David's Hostel that he had forgotten about the day before, but it was too pleasant an evening to be indoors. There were perhaps two hours of daylight left – time enough for him to walk to the river and still be back at Michaelhouse sufficiently early to send Gray to David's with the book before curfew.

He decided to visit two of the old men who lived near the wharves on the river. Both were prone to attacks of river fever and, despite Bartholomew's repeated advice against drinking directly from the Cam's unsavoury depths, they were set in their ways; because they had been using the river as a source of drinking water since they were children, they saw no reason to change. They were old and each new bout of illness weakened them a little further, especially in the summer months. Bartholomew visited them regularly. He enjoyed sitting between them on the unstable bench outside their house, watching the river ooze past, and listening to tales of their pasts.

A cool breeze was blowing in from the Fens and the setting sun bathed the river in a soft amber light. Even the hovels that stood in an uneven line behind Michaelhouse looked picturesque, their crude wattle-and-daub walls coloured pale russets and rich yellows in the late daylight.

The two old men, Aethelbald and Dunstan, were sitting in their usual place, their backs against the flimsy wall of their house, and their dim-sighted eyes turned towards the wharves where a barge from Flanders was unloading. They greeted Bartholomew with warm enthusiasm and, as always, made room for him to sit between them on the bench that was never built to take the weight of three.

Bartholomew sat cautiously, ever alert for the sharp crack

that would pre-empt the three of them tumbling into the dust. There was nothing more than an ominous creak and, gradually, Bartholomew allowed himself to relax.

They chatted for a while about nothing in particular. Aethelbald was recovering well from his last attack of river sickness, and both claimed that they were now only drinking from the well in Water Street. They told him about a fox that was stealing hens, that there were more flies now than when they were young, and that one of Dunstan's grandchildren was suffering the pangs of his first unrequited love.

The two old men talked while Bartholomew listened. It was not that he found chickens, flies and adolescent crushes fascinating, but there was something timeless about their gossip that he found reassuring. Perhaps it was that what they told him was so unquestionably normal and that there were no hidden meanings or twists to their words. Their lives were simple and, if not honest, then at least their deceptions were obvious ones, and their motives clear – unlike the devious twisting and reasoning of the University community.

Dunstan was chuckling about his grandson's misfortunes in love because, apparently, the lady of his choice was a prostitute.

'Which one?' asked Bartholomew curiously.

'Her name was Joanna,' said Dunstan, still cackling.

Bartholomew stared at him. 'Joanna? But there is no prostitute in the town by that name!'

The two men stared back, their laughter giving way to amused disbelief. 'You seem very sure of that, Doctor,' said Dunstan with a wink at his brother.

Bartholomew was chagrined to feel himself flush. 'I was told,' he said lamely.

Now it was Aethelbald's turn to wink. 'I'm sure you were, Doctor,' he said.

Dunstan saw Bartholomew's expression and took pity on him. 'She is not from these parts. She was visiting relatives here from Ely when she met my lad. She has gone back now.'

'When did she go? What did she look like?' asked Bartholomew, sitting straight-backed on the rickety bench, oblivious to the protesting cracks and groans of its flimsy legs.

The brothers exchanged a look of surprise but answered his questions. 'She went back the morning after the riot,' said Dunstan, 'She was a big lass with a good deal of thick yellow hair.'

Fair hair, mused Bartholomew. Could Joanna have been the body he had seen in the castle after all? Was it Joanna that Cecily had seen dead at the feet of her husband, and not Dominica? He recalled his own experiences of mistaken identity that night in relation to Michael and winced. It was not easy to be certain in the dark, with only the flickering light of uncontrolled flames to act as a torch. Perhaps Cecily Lydgate had seen only fair hair and had jumped to the wrong conclusion. Which would mean that Michael had been right all along and that Dominica and the mysterious Joanna were different people.

'Did you see her after the riot?' Bartholomew asked.

Dunstan shook his head. 'Our lad had a message the morning after, bidding him farewell. That is how we came to know about it. She wrote our lad a note and he cannot read, so he had to bring it here because Aethelbald has some learning – providing the words are not too long, and they are all in English.'

Aethelbald looked proud of himself, and explained that he had spent a year at the Glommery School next to King's Hall and had learned his letters. Bartholomew's thoughts tumbled in confusion. If Joanna, and not Dominica, had been killed during the riot, then why had there been no one except Bartholomew at her funeral service? What of the people she had come to the town to visit?

As if reading his thoughts, Dunstan began telling him about the relatives Joanna had come to see.

'It was that family on the High Street,' he began unhelpfully.

'That family of women,' added Aethelbald. 'A mother and three daughters.'

For the second time in the space of a few minutes, Bartholomew gazed from one to the other of the brothers in bewilderment.

'Mistress Tyler and her daughters?'

Dunstan snapped his fingers triumphantly. 'That's it!' he exclaimed. 'Agnes Tyler.' He was silent for a moment, before he began to chuckle again. 'And, although she said she was delighted to have a visit from her Ely niece, I know for a fact from Mistress Bowman that she did not take kindly to Joanna running some unofficial business from Agnes's home!'

The two old men howled with laughter, then returned to the business of the fox and the chickens, while Bartholomew's thoughts whirled in confusion. Joanna had not been with the

Tylers in the riot. Surely Mistress Tyler would not have left her inside the house? He chewed on his lower lip as he recalled the events of that night. He had offered to go back to oust looters from the Tyler home after the fire had died out, but Mistress Tyler had asked him to escort them to Jonas the Poisoner's house instead. If Dunstan was right, then Joanna would still have been in Cambridge and had left the following morning.

But if it had been Mistress Tyler's niece that had been murdered, why were her aunt and cousins not at her funeral service? Was it because they did not know she was dead? But surely that was not possible? The names of the riot victims had been widely published and Tulyet had gone to some trouble to ensure the families of the dead were informed. And even if Mistress Tyler had believed Joanna had already left for Ely, the name Joanna on a list of town dead must surely have raised some question in her mind?

He closed his eyes, seeing again the events of that night: students and townsmen running back and forth, shouting and brandishing weapons; Master Burney's workshop alive with flames and the fire spreading to the Tyler home nearby; Mistress Tyler saying there were looters in the house after the French students' attack had been thwarted. Bartholomew had not seen or heard the looters: he only had Mistress Tyler's word that they had been in her house. And then he thought about the house when Michael and he had recovered from the attack; it had been pleasant, clean and fresh-smelling, and the furniture was of good quality and well kept. There was no evidence that the room had been ill-used or damaged by fire.

He felt sick as the implications began to dawn on him. Had Mistress Tyler left Joanna in the house deliberately, to be at the mercies of the supposed looters? Did that explain why she wanted him to escort her to Jonas's house – even though the family had already shown they were more than capable of looking after themselves, and his presence would not make a significant difference to their chances – to keep him from knowing Joanna was still in the house? And did it explain why Eleanor had been so keen to dissuade him from his investigations when he had told her that he was looking for Joanna's killer during the Feast?

Also, the night he and Michael were attacked, Agnes Tyler

had invited them into her house as an act of charity without knowing who they were. Would she have invited them so readily had she known, aware that any signs of looters in the house only a few nights before were essentially invisible? When Eleanor had invited him to eat with them the day after the riot, he had been taken to the garden, not to the house itself. Or was it simply that the Tylers had been to some trouble to eradicate quickly any signs of what must have been an unpleasant episode in their lives?

Slowly, feeling that the frail bench was beginning to give way under their combined weight, he stood to take his leave of the old men. He walked slowly back along the river bank in the gathering gloom, aware that the curfew bell must have already sounded because the path was virtually empty. His thoughts were an uncontrolled jumble of questions and he tried to sort them out into a logical sequence. First and foremost was the revelation that Joanna had existed, while Bartholomew had wrongly assumed that she was Dominica. Second was that Matilde had been certain that Joanna had not been a prostitute, which had misled him: Joanna had not been a prostitute who lived in Cambridge.

He rubbed at his temples as he considered something else. Eleanor Tyler had seen Bartholomew talking in the street with Matilde and had chided him for it. What had she said? That Matilde was not to be trusted, and that she revealed the secrets of her clients. At the time, he had been disturbed more by the slur to Matilde than by what she might have meant. Eleanor's was an extreme reaction but one he had put down to the natural dislike of prostitutes held by many people. But in the light of what he had just learned from Dunstan and Aethelbald, it could mean that she had guessed that he might be asking about Joanna, and wanted to ensure that any information given to him by Matilde would be disregarded.

Matilde had also told him that the riots had been started to hide two acts. Perhaps one of the acts was the murder of Joanna – getting rid of the unwelcome visitor that had been bringing shame to Mistress Tyler's respectable household.

He raised his eyes heavenward at this notion. Now he was being ridiculous! How could Mistress Tyler possibly have the influence, funds or knowledge to start riots? And surely it was not necessary to start a riot merely to be rid of Joanna? Why not simply send her home to Ely?

All Dunstan's information had done was to muddy already murky waters. Now Bartholomew did not even know whether Dominica was alive or not, whereas before he had been certain she had been dead. But he was sure Lydgate had been at the grave. Why? Had he, like Cecily, mistaken Joanna for Dominica in the dark? Was his graveside visit to atone for a life taken by mistake?

The shadow of a cat (or was it a fox?) flitting across the path brought him out of his reverie. He realised that he had been so engrossed in his thoughts that he had walked past the bottom of St Michael's Lane and was passing through the land that ran to St John's Hospital. With an impatient shake of his head, he turned to retrace his steps, quickly now, for the daylight was fading fast, and he did not wish to be caught outside the College by the Sheriff's men or the beadles without a valid excuse.

As he turned, he saw another shadow behind him. This time, it was two- not four-legged and made a far less competent job of slipping unobtrusively into the bushes than the animal. Bartholomew was after him in an instant, diving recklessly into the undergrowth and emerging moments later clutching a struggling student. He hauled him upright to see if he could recognise the scholar's face in the rapidly fading light.

'Edred,' he said tonelessly. He released the Godwinsson friar and watched him warily.

Edred made a quick twitching movement and Bartholomew thought he might dart away. But he stayed, casting nervous glances at his captor.

'Well?' asked Bartholomew. 'Why were you following me?'

Edred's eyes slid away from Bartholomew's face looking off down the river.

'To see where you were going.'

'That is no answer,' said Bartholomew impatiently. 'Did someone tell you to? Master Lydgate?'

The name produced a violent reaction, and Edred shook his head so vigorously that Bartholomew thought he might make himself sick. Bartholomew had seen many soldiers before they went into battle and knew naked fear when he saw it. He took the young friar's arm and escorted him firmly back towards Michaelhouse.

Michael had been waiting at the gates. Relief showed clearly

in his face when Bartholomew shouted to be let in. He was
surprised to see Edred but said nothing while Bartholomew
led the student to the kitchen, and asked Agatha to give him
a cup of strong wine. While Edred drank, colour seeped back
into his pinched white features. Michael nodded to Agatha to
keep her matronly eye on him and beckoned Bartholomew
out of earshot in the yard.

Venus was twinkling way off in the dark blue sky and
Bartholomew wondered what it was that made it shine first
red, then yellow, then blue. When he had been a child, he
had imagined it was about to explode and had studied it
for hours. He had watched it with Norbert, too, many years
before, both wanting to witness what they imagined would be
a dramatic event. The last time they had seen it together had
been at the gates of Stanmore's house in Trumpington, before
Norbert had disappeared into the night to flee to the safety of
Dover Castle.

'I was beginning to be worried,' Michael was saying. 'I was
back ages ago and I thought you may have run into trouble,
given that your attackers are still on the loose. I was about to
go out to look for you.'

Bartholomew raised apologetic shoulders and gave his friend
a rueful smile. 'Sorry. I did not think you might be anxious.' He
ran his fingers through his hair. 'What did you discover at the
Hostel from Hell?'

Michael laughed softly at his appellation for Godwinsson.
'Very little, I am afraid. There was some kind of celebration at
Valence Marie on Friday night because of finding the relic. The
scholars of Maud's and Godwinsson were invited. Some went,
others did not, but by all accounts it was a drunken occasion
and those that did attend are unlikely to recall those who did
not. It will be almost impossible to check alibis for anyone. Just
about anybody could have knocked Werbergh over the head
and hidden his body. Including Lydgate.'

'Not so for David's Hostel,' said Bartholomew, recalling his
visit there two days before. 'Master Radbeche has his students
under very strict control – perhaps too strict for such active
young men. Anyway, none of them are ever out of the sight
of either Radbeche or Father Andrew.'

He had a pang of sudden remorse as he remembered the
Galen. He considered sending Gray with it, but it was almost
dark and he did not wish to be the cause of his student's

arrest by the beadles. Father Andrew would have to wait until morning.

'The only thing I managed to ascertain,' continued Michael, 'was that Edred has not been seen since Werbergh's body was found. And, as I was beginning to wonder whether he might have gone the same way as his friend, you bring him to Michaelhouse.'

Bartholomew told him how he had encountered Edred, and Michael listened gravely. He decided to keep his thoughts about Joanna until later, when he and Michael had the time to unravel the muddle of information together.

When they returned to the kitchen, Agatha had settled Edred comfortably at the large table with some of her freshly baked oatcakes. He looked better than he had done when he first arrived, and even managed a faint smile of thanks at Agatha as she left the kitchen to go to bed. Bartholomew was aware of a slight movement from the corner, and saw Cynric sitting there, crouched upon a stool, eating apples which he peeled with a knife. He raised his eyebrows to ask whether he should leave, but Bartholomew motioned for him to stay.

Bartholomew sat opposite Edred and leaned his elbows on the table. Michael went to Agatha's fireside chair and the room was filled with creaking and puffing sounds until the fat monk had wriggled his bulk into a position he found satisfactory.

'Why did you steal James Kenzie's ring?' asked Bartholomew softly.

Edred's gaze dropped. 'Because Master Lydgate offered money for the student who returned it to him,' he said, his voice little more than a whisper. 'We were all looking for it, mostly on each other. Then I saw it on the Scot. It was me who started the argument in the street that day. I wanted to get closer to him to make sure it was the right ring.'

He looked down, unable or unwilling to meet the eyes of his questioners.

'How did you steal the ring from Kenzie's finger?' asked Bartholomew, more from curiosity than to help with solving the riddle of Kenzie's death.

Edred shrugged. 'I have done it before,' he said. 'I jostled him and we pushed and shoved at each other. I pretended to fall and grabbed at his hand. When I released it, I had his ring and he did not.'

'A fine talent for a friar,' said Bartholomew dryly.

Edred favoured him with a superior smile. 'It is a skill I learned from a travelling musician in exchange for a basket of apples when I was a child. It is a trick, nothing more.'

'Not to James Kenzie,' said Michael. 'Why did you lie about this when I asked you about it later?'

Edred's eyes became frightened again and he seemed to lose some of the colour from his face. 'Because I took the ring to Master Lydgate and he told me if I ever mentioned to anyone what I had done, he would kill me,' he said.

'So, why are you telling us now?' asked Michael, unmoved by the friar's fear.

'Because he made a similar threat to Werbergh. Werbergh spoke to you,' said Edred, looking at Bartholomew with large eyes, 'and now he is dead.'

'But if you think Werbergh died because he spoke to me,' said Bartholomew reasonably, 'why are you now doing the same?'

'Because I do not know what else to do,' said Edred. Bartholomew had expected him to break down into tears and wail at him, but Edred was made of sterner stuff. He swallowed hard and met Bartholomew's gaze evenly. 'I thought if I told you what I know, you might be able to sort out this mess and offer me some kind of protection.'

Michael sighed. 'It all sounds most mysterious,' he said cynically. 'But let us start at the beginning. We will consider your protection when we better know what we must protect you against.' He leaned back into his chair again, ignoring the creaking wood. 'Proceed.'

Edred looked from one to the other, his face expressionless. 'Master Lydgate killed Dominica and a servant from Valence Marie that she was with the night of the riot. He also killed Werbergh and James Kenzie. And if he knows where I am he will kill me too.'

chapter 9

I N THE SILENCE THAT FOLLOWED EDRED'S ANNOUNCEMENT, Bartholomew was aware of small sounds in the kitchen: Michael's heavy breathing, a student laughing in one of the rooms, the purring of the College cat as it rubbed around his legs.

'How do you know all this?' asked Michael, the first to regain his tongue.

Edred studied an oatcake, then began to crumble it in his fingers. 'On the night of the riot, I was out with some of the other students. I was only there to administer to those that might need me, and to try to stop needless fighting,' he said, looking at Michael.

'Of course you were,' said Michael flatly. 'Pray continue.'

'Then I saw Dominica Lydgate in the company of two men. I knew she was thought to be safe in Chesterton, and so I ran back to Godwinsson to tell Master Lydgate that she was in Cambridge.'

Bartholomew nodded. That accorded with what Cecily had told him. He thought of Joanna and the uncertain light. 'Are you certain it was Dominica? Could you have been mistaken?'

Edred looked surprised. 'Yes, I am certain,' he said. 'It was Dominica I saw.'

'Did you recognise the men she was with?' asked Michael, looking at the small pile of crumbs on the table from Edred's oatcake.

Edred hung his head and swallowed noisily.

'Come now, Brother Edred,' said Michael firmly. 'You are safe here. Tonight you can sleep in Michaelhouse and tomorrow we will see about getting you away from Cambridge altogether. But only if you are honest with us now.'

Edred nodded miserably. 'I thought I recognised who she was with,' he said, 'although I am still uncertain. I think one of the men was called Will – he is a grubby little man who works at Valence Marie and who has been trawling the King's Ditch for relics recently. The other was his brother, Ned, who died in the riot.'

Bartholomew thought back to the bodies lying in the castle outbuilding. One may well have been Will's brother.

He looked up to find Edred staring at him intently. 'Master Lydgate has killed four people already. My conscience will not allow him to kill again.'

'But what evidence do you have that he has killed these four people?' asked Bartholomew, denying himself the satisfaction of asking the arrogant friar why his conscience only started to prick after four deaths.

Edred began to push the oatcake crumbs into a heap with his index fingers. 'When I told Master Lydgate I had seen Dominica the night of the riot, he left to find her. He was in a rage such as I have never seen before.' He looked up briefly. 'And, believe me, I have witnessed a fair few of his rages during my time at Godwinsson. Anyway, after he had gone Mistress Lydgate said she was going, too. I did the only thing an honest friar could do and accompanied her.'

Michael and Bartholomew exchanged a wry look in response to the friar's claimed motive. Edred, his attention fixed on his pyramid of crumbs, did not notice.

'We searched for some time and then we found Dominica. But Master Lydgate had arrived before us and Dominica already lay dead. He had also killed Ned. He was standing over the bodies with his dagger dripping. Of Will there was no sign. He must have managed to escape, for I have seen him alive since.'

'But did you actually see Lydgate kill them?' persisted Bartholomew. Although Edred's story corroborated Cecily's, there remained a small thread of doubt in his mind.

Edred gave a short bark of laughter. 'No, I did not. But a man hovering over two corpses with his dagger dripping blood? What else would you imagine had happened? Mistress Cecily was all for rushing forward to Dominica, but I prevented her. Master Lydgate stood over his victims for a while, looked around him as though he expected the Devil to snatch him away, and then slunk off. We had seen enough. Mistress Lydgate asked me to escort her to Maud's and I left her there. By the time I returned to the scene of the murder, Dominica's and Ned's bodies had been removed by the Sheriff's men.'

Michael looked at Bartholomew as he asked his next question. 'Do you know where Cecily Lydgate is now?'

Bartholomew avoided his eyes while Edred continued. 'I cannot say what happened after I left her at Maud's. She did not return to Godwinsson, but apparently someone had made a terrible mess of her room – perhaps when it was searched.'

'Searched for what?' asked Michael.

'Her jewellery, I suppose. It is widely known that she possesses a great deal of priceless jewellery.'

'Was this jewellery missing after her room was searched?' Michael asked.

Edred's mouth lifted at one corner in a disdainful sneer. 'Of course not. She does not keep it on display. It is all hidden away in places known only to her and Master Lydgate.'

'Not Dominica?' asked Bartholomew.

Again the sneer. 'One or two places, perhaps, but not all. The Lydgates are not a trusting couple where their wealth is concerned.'

Around Edred's neck was a delicate golden crucifix that Bartholomew had not seen him wear before. Since Edred seemed to know about Cecily's hidden treasure, Bartholomew supposed it was not too much of a leap in logic to suppose that Edred had taken the opportunity to ransack her room himself. It would certainly explain why he had taken so long to return to the scene of Dominica's murder – long enough so that the Sheriff had removed the body – after he had seen Cecily safely to Maud's Hostel.

'The day after all this, you went to the Castle to identify the body of the Godwinsson friar who died during the riot, did you not?' asked Bartholomew. 'In the company of Master Lydgate?'

Edred nodded. 'Several students were missing after the riot and Master Lydgate wanted to see whether any of the dead were ours. Two were: the friar and the French student. The friar's head was crushed but we saw the scar on his knee where he was injured at the Battle of Crécy. Or so he always claimed. Master Lydgate insisted on viewing all the dead, although I only looked at ours.'

Bartholomew caught Michael's eye, wondering if he would consider this evidence that Lydgate had been looking for

Dominica among the dead. Except that now, Bartholomew was no longer certain whom Lydgate had been seeking – or even which of the women had lain dead in the makeshift Castle mortuary. Edred went back to his pile of crumbs.

'Now, tell us why you also think Lydgate killed Werbergh?' asked Michael, leaning back in his chair and folding his arms across his considerable girth. 'His death was an accident, was it not? The shed fell on him when he went to find timber to build a writing desk. Why do you think Werbergh was murdered?'

Edred looked pained. 'Because Master Lydgate told us that if we talked to you, he would kill us. Werbergh was seen talking to you and he disappeared, only to reappear dead under the shed.'

'And you think this suspicious?' asked Michael.

Edred gave another of his short, explosive laughs. 'I most certainly do! Oh, it looked convincing enough, and our servants, Saul Potter and Huw, both claimed that Werbergh had told them he was going out to look for wood to build a desk, but it seemed too convenient. A man disappears and suddenly returns only to die in a fluky accident? No! That is too coincidental.'

'But you did not actually see Lydgate kill Werbergh,' pressed Bartholomew. It was a statement and not a question.

'It is not necessary to have seen him plunge the dagger into his victims in order to make sense of the evidence,' retorted Edred, his temper ruffled. He suddenly put his head in his hands, scattering the crumbs. 'I should have known it was a mistake to come to you. Why should you believe me?'

Why indeed? thought Bartholomew. Edred had really given them very little new information, and most was in the form of supposition and conjecture. But Bartholomew's compassion was aroused when he saw the young man's shoulders shaken by a sob. Edred obviously believed what he was telling them was the truth and was frightened by it.

'And what about James Kenzie?' he asked in a gentler tone. Edred shook his head, unable or unwilling to answer, so Bartholomew answered for him. 'You stole the ring from him during the street brawl and took it to Lydgate to claim your reward. Lydgate was simultaneously pleased to have such a clue regarding the identity of his daughter's lover, but angry when you told him it was a Scot. He is a man who blusters and threatens. He vowed to kill Kenzie, and hurled the ring from the window in his anger. Then he threatened to kill you if you confessed that you had stolen the ring.'

Edred looked at him with a tear-stained face. 'No. It did not happen quite like that. I gave the ring to Master Lydgate and he became furious. But not with the Scot, with me. He said the ring was a fake, a cheap imitation of the original. He accused me of having it made so that I could claim the reward from him. He hurled it to the floor and stamped on it. Then he said that if I ever told anyone what I had done, he would kill me. He said having a friar who was a confessed thief and liar would bring Godwinsson Hostel into disrepute. After he had gone I picked up the ring and I could see that he was right. What I had thought was silver was cheap metal. I flung it through the window in disgust.'

'So the ring you took from Kenzie was a fake?' said Bartholomew thoughtfully. He reached into his sleeve and brought it out. 'Is this it?'

Edred took the broken ring and examined it briefly. 'Yes. That's the wretched thing that brought me so much trouble. I don't know the Scot came to have it, rather than the original. He came later that night to ask if I had taken it, but since it was already broken, and it had landed me in so much trouble, I told him I had not.'

But what was Kenzie doing with a ring that was a fake? wondered Bartholomew. Dominica had definitely given one of the original pair to Kenzie – Robert had identified it quite clearly as the one at Valence Marie – while the other, the one Dominica had kept, had remained with Cecily. But Kenzie had not worn the real ring in the street brawl, he had worn a cheap imitation. Meanwhile, the real ring was on the finger of the relic at Valence Marie. It made no sense. How did the real ring get from Kenzie to the hand found at Valence Marie?

'So, if Lydgate knew that the ring you had taken from Kenzie was a false one, why do you think Lydgate killed him?' Michael was asking.

'That evening, after I had shown the false ring to Master Lydgate, Dominica was sent away to relatives in Chesterton to keep her from seeing her lover,' said Edred. 'I was restless after the scene with the Scot, and knew I would be unable to sleep, so I stayed out. As I was returning, much later, I saw someone throwing pebbles at Dominica's window. He threw perhaps three or four before he realised he was not going to be answered, and then he stole away.'

'And did you recognise this person?' asked Michael.

'Oh yes, I recognised him by the yellow hose under his tabard, which was obvious, even by moonlight. It was the Scot – James Kenzie you say his name was. A few moments after, I saw Master Lydgate leave the house and follow him up the lane. I went to bed, and the next day, you came to say that Kenzie was murdered. I made the reasonable assumption that Lydgate had also seen Kenzie throwing stones at Dominica's window, guessed him to be her lover, followed him and killed him.'

'Why did you not tell us this before?' asked Michael. 'And why did you lie to us when we asked where you were that night?'

Edred looked frightened again, but also indignant. 'How could I do otherwise? By telling you, I would have admitted to theft and lying, two virtues not highly praised by my Order. I would have been thrown out of the University. And anyway, how could I accuse the Principal of murder? Who would you have believed: the poor, lying thief of a friar who had been seen by the Proctor arguing with the murdered man the day before his death, or the rich and influential Lydgate?'

Michael inclined his head, accepting the young man's reasoning. 'But by hiding your own lesser sins, you have protected the identity of a murderer. And you now say that this murderer has struck thrice more and will do so again.'

Edred looked away. 'I did not know what to do. I did not think you would believe me, because I had already lied to you. But I was afraid, too. The Lydgates know I was absent from the hostel the night of Kenzie's death, and Mistress Lydgate could have accused me of lying when I used Werbergh as my alibi that night. But she did not, and I think she guessed I saw her husband leaving to follow Kenzie. Perhaps she saw me returning through her window. Anyway, the message was clear: if I maintained my silence about what I had seen, so would they.'

It made sense logically, thought Bartholomew, casting his mind back to the information they had been given the day of Kenzie's murder. Edred's story and Werbergh's had not tallied and Bartholomew had wondered whether Edred was lying about the theft of the ring to mask a far more serious incident. The incident had been that he believed his Principal had committed murder. It tallied with Cecily's story, too. She had been told not to contradict anything said to protect Godwinsson from the unwelcome inquiries of Brother Michael. But were Edred's suspicions to be believed? It was all so simple: Lydgate killed Kenzie, then his daughter and Ned from Valence Marie, then Werbergh, whom he thought might be passing information to Bartholomew and Michael. Was Lydgate a man who could kill four people with such ease? Cecily certainly feared her husband sufficiently to flee from him, so perhaps he was.

'Two more questions,' said Bartholomew, seeing the student's shoulders begin to sag with tiredness, 'and then you should sleep. First, do you know who attacked Brother Michael and me in the High Street?'

Edred shook his head. 'I heard about that from Master Lydgate. He was delighted that you had received your just deserts, but he did not know who would attack you, and neither do I.'

Bartholomew nodded, satisfied with the answer, especially given the very plausible response reported from Lydgate. But that did not mean that Godwinsson was uninvolved. Bartholomew remained convinced that it had been Saul Potter and Huw's voices he had heard that night, despite his hazy memory.

'And second,' he continued, 'where are Godwinsson's French students?'

Edred looked frightened again. 'One was killed in the riot. But when Master Lydgate had the truth from the other two that they had been involved in a brawl with you – and not with ten heavily armed townspeople as they initially claimed – he grew angry. They left to return to France. Huw and Saul Potter helped them escape.'

Escape from their Principal, thought Bartholomew. What a terrible indictment of his violent and aggressive character. No wonder Cecily had left him.

As if reading his thoughts, Edred added. 'He hates you. That is one of the reasons I came. Any man who has earned such hatred from Master Lydgate must surely be the man whom I can trust with my life, and who will protect me from him.'

Bartholomew nodded absently, and indicated for Cynric to show Edred where he might sleep. The Welshman fetched a spare blanket from the laundry and led the weary scholar out of the kitchen towards Bartholomew's room. When they had gone, Bartholomew and Michael sat in silence.

'Do you believe him?' asked Bartholomew after a while.

Michael nodded. 'I am certain he thinks he is telling the truth. But that is not to say I agree with his interpretation of it.'

Bartholomew concurred. 'All his evidence – such as it is – suggests that Lydgate killed Dominica, Kenzie, Ned and Werbergh. But there is something not right about it all, something missing.'

'But what? The motives are there in each case, and the opportunity.'

'I know, but there is something I cannot define that does not fit,' said Bartholomew insistently.

'I would have thought you would have been pleased with Edred's evidence. It adds weight to your theory that Joanna was really Dominica.'

'Oh, that,' said Bartholomew dismissively.

Michael leaned forward in his chair, while Bartholomew repeated the conversation he had had with the old rivermen. Michael listened gravely.

'And there is something more, is there not?' he asked when Bartholomew had finished. 'About Mistress Lydgate's disappearance? I know you have another ring like the one on the relic in your sleeve. I found it while you were asleep a couple of nights ago. So, you may as well tell me what else you have learned.'

'Did you search my room?' asked Bartholomew, remembering the moved candle and jug.

'Of course not!' said Michael indignantly. 'And I did not really search for the rings. I just knew where you would hide them.' He paused. 'Are you certain your room was searched?'

Bartholomew nodded. 'Twice. And if it was not you, it must have been those who attacked us, looking for whatever it was they wanted me to give them.'

Michael picked at a spot on his face. 'Perhaps. But tell me what happened on Sunday when you were out. Perhaps the two of us can make some sense out of all these clues.'

Bartholomew hesitated, wondering about his agreement with Cecily regarding her hiding place. But unless he told Michael all he knew, they would never get to the bottom of the mystery and more people might die. Michael was a good friend and Bartholomew knew he could be trusted with secrets, so he told Michael about his visit to Chesterton. When he had finished, Michael sat back thoughtfully.

'This is an odd business,' he said. 'Is the dead woman Joanna or Dominica? And whichever one it is, where is the other? And did Lydgate really kill all these people? I see no reason to suppose he did not, although, like you, I have doubts niggling in the back of my mind. And now we know there is a riot planned for tomorrow night, we can deduce for certain that the recent civil unrest is not random. I will send a messenger to Tulyet tonight. He might be able to avert trouble if he has warning of what is planned.'

Bartholomew, recalling the scenes of violence and mayhem a few nights before, sincerely hoped so. Michael fingered the whiskers on his cheek, thinking aloud.

'I do not like Bigod's involvement in this affair. You say he was one of those who attacked us – although he denies it – and it is he who secretes Mistress Lydgate away from her husband. His role is even more puzzling when you consider that not only does he provide Cecily with a haven, but that he is Lydgate's alibi for the night of the riot. It is odd, I would think, for someone to be such a good friend to both parties simultaneously – most friends would side with either one or the other.'

Bartholomew frowned in thought. 'I wondered at the time why Cecily chose Bigod, of all people, to flee to that night. He is clearly a loyal intimate of Lydgate. But then she said she had hoped he would allow her to share the upper chamber at Chesterton tower-house with him. It became clear – he is her lover and Lydgate's best friend.'

Michael's eyes were great round circles. 'You never cease to amaze me, Matt,' he said. 'That seems something of a leap of faith, given the evidence you have.'

Bartholomew grinned, accepting Michael's caution. 'I know. But it would explain some of Bigod's actions – he is prepared to risk a good deal by offering Lydgate an alibi for the night of the riot. At the same time, he is willing to hide away the man's wife. And Werbergh told me the first time we visited Godwinsson that Cecily was more interested in students than in her husband.'

'All right, then,' said Michael. 'Let us assume you are correct. But we are not finished with Bigod yet. The conversation you overheard in the basement at Chesterton shows he knows when there is to be a riot. Extending this logically, it can be assumed that he knew about the last riot too, which explains why Maud's students were all safely inside at a birthday party.'

'Of course,' said Bartholomew. 'But the Godwinsson students were out, so it seems Lydgate was not party to Bigod's plans.'

'Maybe,' said Michael. 'I wonder if these "two acts" that Matilde told you about were the murder of Lydgate's wayward daughter and her lover. Lydgate was out all night, after all, and we have not the faintest idea what he was up to when he was not standing over corpses with dripping daggers.'

Bartholomew rubbed the back of his head, becoming disheartened at the way every question answered seemed to pose ten more. 'But even Cecily has her doubts about Lydgate's role in the murder of Dominica. She is reluctant to believe he would kill the person he loved most.'

'People do the most peculiar things for the most bizarre of motives, Matt,' said Michael in a superior tone of voice. 'But one of the oddest aspects about this whole business is these damned rings. How did one of Whining Cecily's rings find its way on to the relic at Valence Marie? And I wonder who that other person was that you heard in the basement, the one whose voice you could not place. Have you considered who it might be? This is important.'

'Not really,' said Bartholomew, closing his eyes as he recalled the clear tenor. 'It was familiar but I cannot place it at all.'

'Was it someone from Valence Marie?' asked Michael to prompt him along. 'Father Eligius, perhaps. Or that fellow who looks like a toad – Master Dittone? Robert Bingham is ill with ague, so it cannot be him. Or one of the merchants, maybe?'

Bartholomew racked his brains but the identity of the voice eluded him still. 'Cynric is a long time,' he said eventually, standing and looking out of the window.

'Probably looking for a pallet bed,' said Michael, standing also. 'It is too late to do anything tonight. First thing in the morning, I suggest we talk to Mistress Tyler and see if we can discover the whereabouts of Joanna. Then, unpleasant though it might be, I must tackle Lydgate. I do not want you there but I will ask Richard Tulyet to accompany me. Perhaps afterwards, Mistress Lydgate will find it safe to come out of her self-inflicted imprisonment.'

They walked across the courtyard together, Michael still speculating on Lydgate's guilt. Cynric had lit a candle in

Bartholomew's room, and the light flickered yellow under the closed shutters. Bartholomew wondered why Cynric was wasting his only candle when he knew his way around perfectly well in the dark. As he turned to listen to Michael, he heard the faint groan of the chest in his room being opened. Michael stopped speaking as Bartholomew darted towards the door.

His attention arrested by Edred's hands in the chest, Bartholomew did not see Cynric sprawled across the floor, until he fell headlong over him. He heard Michael yell, and Edred swear under his breath. Bartholomew struggled to his knees, his hands dark with the blood that flowed from the back of Cynric's skull. Blind fury dimmed his reasoning and he launched himself across the room at the friar with a howl of rage.

Edred's hands came out of Bartholomew's storage chest holding a short sword. It was one Stanmore had given him many years ago that Bartholomew had forgotten he had. Edred swung at him with it, and only by dropping to one knee did the physician avoid the hacking blow aimed at his head. Edred swung again with a professionalism that suggested he had not always been in training for the priesthood. Bartholomew ducked a second time, rolling away until he came up against the wall.

Edred came for him, his face pale and intent as he drew back his arm for the fatal plunge. His stroke wavered as something struck him hard on the side of the head, and Bartholomew saw shards of glass falling around him. Michael was not standing helplessly in the doorway like some dim-witted maiden but was hurling anything that came to hand at Edred.

While the friar's attention strayed, Bartholomew leapt at him, catching him in a bear-like grip around the legs. Edred tried to struggle free, dropping the sword as he staggered backwards. Michael continued his assault and Bartholomew could hear nothing but smashes and grunts. Suddenly, Edred collapsed.

Bartholomew squirmed to free himself from Edred's weight. Michael came to his aid and hauled the unresisting friar to his feet. Edred's knees buckled and Michael allowed him to slide down the wall into a sitting position. Bartholomew scrambled across the floor to where Cynric lay.

The Welshman's eyes were half open and a trickle of blood oozed from the wound on the back of his skull. Bartholomew cradled him in his lap, holding a cloth to staunch the bleeding.

'So, I am to die from a coward's blow,' Cynric whispered, eyes seeking Bartholomew's face. 'Struck from behind in the dark.'

'You will not die, my friend,' said Bartholomew. 'The wound is not fatal: I have had recent personal experience to support my claim.'

Cynric grinned weakly at him and closed his eyes while Bartholomew bound the cut deftly with clean linen, praying it was not more serious than it appeared.

'Matt!' came Michael's querulous voice from the other side of the room. Bartholomew glanced to where the monk knelt next to Edred.

'I have killed him,' Michael whispered, his face white with shock. 'Edred is dying!'

Bartholomew looked askance. 'He cannot be, Brother. You have just stunned him.'

'He is dying!' insisted Michael, his voice rising in horror. 'Look at him!'

Easing Cynric gently on to the floor, Bartholomew went to where Michael leaned over the prostrate friar. A white powder lightly dusted Edred's black robe and the smell of it caught in Bartholomew's nostril's sharply. The powder was on the friar's face too, it clung to the thin trail of blood that dribbled from a cut on his cheek and stuck around his lips. Bartholomew felt for a life-beat in the friar's neck and was startled to feel it rapid and faint. Puzzled, he prised open Edred's eyelids and saw that the pupils had contracted to black pinpricks and that his face and neck were covered in a sheen of sweat.

'Do something, Matt!' said Michael desperately. 'Or I will have brought about his death! Me! A man of the cloth, who has forsworn violence!'

The noise of the affray had disturbed those scholars whose rooms were nearby and they clustered around the door as Bartholomew examined Edred. Gray and Bulbeck were among them, and he ordered them to remove Cynric to his own room, away from the strange white powder that seemed to be killing Edred. He grabbed the pitcher of water that stood on the window-sill and washed the powder from the cut on Edred's face and from his mouth. The friar was beginning to struggle to breathe.

'What is happening? What have you done?' Roger Alcote, still a little pale from the aftermath of the Founder's Feast, forced his way through the scholars watching at the doorway, and stood with his hands on his hips waiting for an answer.

'I threw a jar,' said Michael shakily, backing away from where Edred was labouring to breathe. 'It struck him full in the face and broke, scattering that powder everywhere.' He turned on Bartholomew suddenly. 'What was it? Why do you keep such deadly poisons lying so readily to hand?'

'I do not,' protested Bartholomew. He went to considerable trouble to keep the few poisons he used under lock and key in his storeroom. He shook his head in disbelief. 'The powder is oleander, judging from its smell. I keep a small quantity locked in the chest in the storeroom but I used the last of it several days ago.'

'So where did it come from?'

Bartholomew ignored Michael's question. More important at that moment was that he did not understand why Edred was reacting to the poison so violently. Edred's breathing was becoming increasingly shallow, and Bartholomew forced his fingers to the back of the friar's throat to make him vomit. He doubted whether it would help, since the oleander had also entered the friar's body through the cut in his head and had probably been inhaled when the jar had smashed, but he had to try. He dispatched Michael to fetch the charcoal mixture he had used successfully against oleander poisoning – although admittedly a very mild dose – in the past, and forced Edred to swallow it. But it was all to no avail. Bartholomew felt the friar's heartbeat become more and more rapid, and then erratic. He tried to ease him into positions where the student might be able to breathe more readily, but he was fighting a lost battle.

'Matt! He is dying!' pleaded Michael. 'Do something else! Make him walk. Let me fetch eggs and vinegar. That worked with Walter last year.' Without waiting for Bartholomew's reply, he thrust himself through the silent group of watching scholars at the door and they heard him puffing across the yard towards the kitchens.

Bartholomew stood and turned to face them. 'It is too late.'

'How did this happen?' asked Master Kenyngham, shocked. 'Who is he? And what is he doing in our College?'

Bartholomew wondered how he could begin to explain, but at that moment Michael returned, his hands full of eggs and a pitcher of slopping vinegar. He sagged when he saw Edred's half-closed eyes and waxen face.

'Is he dead?' he asked hoarsely.

Bartholomew nodded. 'Oleander is a powerful poison. There was nothing I could do.'

Alcote elbowed him out of the way to look at Edred. 'I wonder you ever have any patients, Matthew. You always seem to be losing them. First Mistress Fletcher, and now this friar.'

Bartholomew flinched. While he had a better rate of success with his cures than most of his colleagues, he was only too aware that there were diseases and injuries when a patient's demise was inevitable, no matter what treatment he might attempt. Knowing that his skills and medicines were useless in such cases was the part of being a physician he found most difficult part to accept.

'You did not even consult his stars,' Alcote was saying, kneeling next to the dead man, and preparing to give him last rites.

'He had no time,' Kenyngham pointed out, rallying to Bartholomew's defence. 'It all happened rather quickly. And how could the man answer questions about his birth-date anyway, when he lay fighting for his last breath?'

Alcote declined to answer, and traced vigorous crosses on Edred's forehead, mouth and chest. The sudden movement created a puff of the white dust and Alcote raised his hand to his mouth as he prepared to cough. Bartholomew leapt forward and dragged him away.

'Wash your hands, Roger,' he said firmly. 'Or you will be discovering first-hand how my medical skills cannot save a man from poisoning.'

Colour drained from Alcote's face and he scurried hastily from the room to act on Bartholomew's advice. Kenyngham ushered everyone out and closed the door behind him.

'There is nothing more to see,' he said to the still-curious scholars. 'Go back to your chambers. Fathers William and Aidan will pray for this man's soul.' He watched them disperse to do his bidding and turned to Bartholomew. 'It is clearly not safe to be in your room with that white poison floating around, so we will deal with the friar's earthly remains in the morning when we can see what we are doing.'

Bartholomew leaned against the door wearily, wondering what nasty turn the investigation would take next, and whether he and Michael would live to tell the tale. Meanwhile, Michael was trying to explain to Kenyngham what had happened. The placid Gilbertine listened patiently to Michael's brief summary of his inquiries into the death of Kenzie and the involvement of Lydgate, but refused to allow the monk to dwell too deeply on the details of Edred's death. He took the distressed Benedictine firmly by the shoulder.

'No good will come of thinking about the matter before we have made a thorough examination of the facts. You did not seek to kill this man, Michael: it was an accident. And who can say that if you had not thrown the poison jar, this friar would not have slain Matthew? Or both of you? It seems to me he was bent upon some kind of mischief. It grieves me to see such evil in a man of the cloth, but if you are determined to be a proctor you must inure yourself to such matters.'

It was sound advice, although Bartholomew was surprised to hear it from Kenyngham, a man whose gentleness and reluctance to believe ill of anyone sometimes proved a liability to his College.

Kenyngham continued. 'It is too late and too dark to begin inquiries into this mysterious powder now. Sleep in Michael's room tonight, Matthew. I will send a porter to inform the Chancellor of what has happened immediately.'

Bartholomew followed Michael up the creaking stairs. Michael was strangely subdued, and Bartholomew's mind whirled with questions as he lay under the coarse blankets of his borrowed bed. What had Edred been doing? Was his confession merely an excuse to get into the College to search Bartholomew's room? What was so important that he had been prepared to kill? And perhaps more important to his own peace of mind, why had Edred died so quickly and violently from his slight exposure to the oleander powder?

When Bartholomew awoke the next morning, the room was unfamiliar. The wooden ceiling was brightly painted and the bed was lumpy. He raised himself on one elbow, and in a rush the events of the previous night came back to him. Michael snored softly in his own bed, while Gray was on another, his tawny hair poking out from under the blanket. Gray had been concerned that some of the oleander might have landed on

Bartholomew and had insisted on staying with him to be on hand lest he began to show symptoms of poisoning. After all, he had added, his blue eyes wide, Master Lynton and Father Philius had full classes already, so who would teach him and his friends medicine if Bartholomew were to die? Trying not to disturb them, Bartholomew stood up as quietly as he could.

Michael, a light sleeper, woke immediately.

Bartholomew pointed to the lightening sky. 'It is time for us to be about our business,' he whispered. 'We have a lot to do today, and there may be a riot tonight.'

Michael swung his large legs off the bed and sat up with a yawn.

Their voices woke Gray, who uncurled himself and watched Bartholomew. 'I will don a mask and gloves and clean the poison from your room,' he offered, rubbing the sleep from his eyes.

Bartholomew thanked him. 'But do not let Deynman help – he is not to be trusted around poisons for his own safety. Ask Tom Bulbeck to assist you. I suppose someone will arrange for Edred to be returned to Godwinsson today?'

Michael shook his head. 'The Master heard from de Wetherset last night after you were asleep. He recommends that Edred be buried discreetly in St Mary's churchyard. He is afraid that the death of a scholar in a college other than his own might start another riot, and I believe he is right. I do not trust Lydgate to be sensible about this and so he shall not be told. Not yet, anyway. Master Kenyngham will call a meeting of all our scholars this morning and order that last night's events are not to be discussed outside Michaelhouse. He will appeal to their sense of College loyalty in dangerous times, and I am sure they will comply.'

'But what did Edred want?' asked Bartholomew, his bewilderment of the night before surging back to him. 'What do I have that causes people to search my room – three times now – and lure us out in the depths of the night to attack us?'

'Medicines? Poisons?' suggested Gray, who had been listening with interest to their conversation.

'I have nothing that Jonas the Poisoner, Father Philius or Hugh Lynton do not have,' said Bartholomew, 'not to mention the infirmarians at Barnwell Priory and the Hospital of St John's.'

'The rings in your sleeve?' asked Michael, ignoring Gray's look of incomprehension.

Bartholomew shook his head. 'Edred saw me take the broken ring from my sleeve in the kitchen. Why bother to look in my room when he knew where they were?'

'Do you have letters from anyone, or documents?' said Gray, racking his brains.

'Not that I can think of,' said Bartholomew. 'I have records of the treatments given to patients and of medicines dispensed. But these cannot be important to anyone but me.'

'Whatever it was, Edred was prepared to kill for it,' said Michael. 'And he died for it. Are you certain it was the oleander that killed him?' Bartholomew saw the silent appeal in his friend's eyes and looked away.

'I am afraid so. He was most definitely poisoned, and I am sure the white powder that coated him was oleander from one of the jars you threw. His symptoms matched those usual in such cases, although Edred succumbed very rapidly to the poison's effects.'

'But why do you need such a foul powder?' cried Michael, suddenly agitated. 'You are a physician, not a poisoner! And you are usually so careful with toxins. Why did you leave this one lying so readily to hand?'

'I use a diluted form of oleander for treating leprosy,' said Bartholomew. 'It works better on some forms of the disease than other potions. But it *is* a very diluted form and, as I said last night, I used the last of it several days ago.'

'You ordered more oleander from Jonas the Poisoner before your stars became so sadly aligned,' said Gray helpfully. 'It came yesterday while you were out. I could not lock it in the storeroom because you were out with the key, so I put it on the shelf in your chamber so it would not be lying around too obviously. But it was powerful stuff, this oleander – much more so than the stuff you usually use. It seems to me that this friar died more quickly than he would have done had he been killed with your normal-strength powder.'

At his words, Bartholomew's stomach started to churn with a sudden, vile realisation. He sat down abruptly and looked up at Michael with horrified eyes. 'The Tyler family!' he said in a whisper. 'They are related to Jonas's wife!'

'So? Are you saying that the Tyler women are trying to poison you?' asked Michael, astounded.

'They may have sent me some kind of oleander concentrate, instead of the diluted powder I usually order from Jonas. It would be easy enough to do, given that they would look the same.'

Michael thought for a moment and then sighed, raising his shoulders in a gesture of defeat. 'It is possible, I suppose. They are involved in all this business somehow, through Joanna. Maybe they felt you were coming too close to the truth about her and wanted you out of the way.'

'But I take great care with powerful medicines,' said Bartholomew, thinking uncomfortably of how Eleanor had tried to dissuade him from looking any further into Joanna's death. 'I am unlikely to be poisoned by them.'

'Perhaps they did not want to kill you at all,' said Gray. He stiffened suddenly as a thought occurred to him. 'Not me, either! I swear to you that I did not lay a finger on her! Well, perhaps a little kiss, but she was willing enough for that.'

'What is this?' asked Michael, bewildered.

'Sam escorted Eleanor home after the Founder's Feast,' said Bartholomew. 'Are you sure you did nothing to anger her? Or her mother?'

'Nothing!' cried Gray. 'Honestly! I thought she had set her sights on you but you had put her off somehow during the Feast. I was singing your praises and she told me, rather sharply, to keep them to myself. That's when I decided to make a move. Well, just a kiss. Perhaps they wanted you to dispatch one of your patients for them. That would make sense.'

'But I only use oleander for treating leprosy,' objected Bartholomew. 'And all the lepers I attend are poor, pathetic creatures who have long since ceased to deal with affairs outside their own community.'

'Why should the Tylers know what you use oleander for?' said Michael. 'None of them are physicians or even apothecaries.'

Bartholomew spread his hands. 'We may be wronging them terribly,' he said. He thought back to the events of the previous night. 'Did Edred say anything to you after he was stricken?' he asked, recalling Michael kneeling next to the friar as Bartholomew attended to Cynric, before Michael realised that Edred's sudden collapse was more serious than a jar breaking in his face.

Michael rubbed his cheeks with his hands. 'Nothing,' he said softly. 'Not so much as a whisper.'

Gray stood to pour him a cup of watered wine from the supply on the window ledge. As he flopped back on the bed again, he winced as he sat on something hard. He pulled it from underneath him and shot Bartholomew a guilty glance.

'Master Radbeche's Galen,' said Bartholomew, recognising the rough leather binding. 'I must return that today.'

'I saw it yesterday afternoon when I put the package from Jonas in your room,' said Gray, defensively. 'I thought I might borrow it since you were out. I brought it here to read last night, but I fell asleep,' he finished lamely.

'You should ask before you take things,' said Bartholomew mildly, pleased that Gray was prepared to undertake voluntary reading, but concerned that he should borrow David's Hostel's precious tome without permission.

'It is an interesting text,' said Gray, detecting that Bartholomew's admonition held an underlying note of approval and keen to turn it to his advantage. 'Although I must say that the last chapter was the most interesting of all. And not by Galen,' he said with a laugh.

'How do you know it is not by Galen?' asked Bartholomew. Although Gray was a quick student, he rarely used his intellectual talents to the full and was far too lazy to instigate a debate that would mean some hard thinking. 'Are you so familiar with his style and knowledge of medicine that you are able to detect mere imitation from the master himself?'

'Oh, no!' said Gray hastily, knowing that he would never be able to take on Bartholomew in a debate about the authenticity of Galen. 'But the last chapter is not about medicine at all. Have you not read it? It is a collection of local stories – like a history of the town.'

Michael made a sound of irritation at this irrelevance and drained the wine from his cup. 'So what? Parchment is expensive and scribes often use spare pages at the end of books to record something else so as to avoid waste. If you are surprised by that, Sam Gray, then you are revealing that you have read far fewer books than you should have done at this point in your academic career.'

'I was not surprised by it,' said Gray hotly. 'I was just pointing out to you that the last chapter was considerably more interesting than boring old Galen.'

He scrambled to his feet and brought the book over to Bartholomew. 'Your marker is here,' he said, indicating a point about three-quarters of the way through, where Bartholomew had reached. 'And the interesting chapter is here.'

He opened the book to the last few pages. The text was in the same undisciplined scrawl that characterised the rest of the book, complete with spelling errors, crossings out and ink blots. Gray was right about the content: there was nothing medical about the subject of the last chapter and parts were illustrated with thumb-sized sketches. The drawings were good, and Bartholomew suspected that the anonymous scribe derived a good deal more pleasure from his illustrations than his writing.

'See?' said Gray. 'Here is a bit about how William the Conqueror came in 1068 and ordered that twenty-seven houses should be demolished so that the Castle could be built. And here is a description of the fire that almost destroyed St Mary's Church. My uncle remembers that very well.'

'Does he?' asked Bartholomew, startled. The fire in St Mary's, he knew, had been in 1290, and Gray's uncle was certainly no more than forty years old.

'Oh, yes,' said Gray. 'He often tells the story about how he dashed through the flames to save the golden candlesticks that stood on the altar.'

'So, it runs in the family,' muttered Michael, also aware of the date of the fire. 'That explains a lot.'

'What do you mean?' demanded Gray. 'My uncle is a very brave man.'

'What else is in this history?' asked Bartholomew quickly, before tempers could fray. While Michael's sharp, sardonic wit might best Gray in an immediate argument, Michael would then be considered fair game for all manner of Gray's practical jokes, not all of them pleasant or amusing.

'There is a bit about the hero Hereward the Wake, who fought against William the Conqueror in the Fens,' continued Gray, giving Michael an evil look. 'And a paragraph about Simon d'Ambrey who was shot in the King's Ditch twenty-five years ago and whose hand is in Valence Marie. The whole thing ends with a tale about some Chancellor called Richard de Badew who funded Clare College before the Countess came along and endowed it with lots of money in the 1330s.'

Intrigued, now that the University and not the town was the subject of the text, Michael came to sit next to them, peering at the book as it lay open on Bartholomew's lap.

'The rest of the book is undoubtedly Galen,' said Bartholomew, flicking through it. 'I have read it before, although this is by far the worst copy I have ever seen.'

'It was the book!' exclaimed Gray suddenly, grabbing Bartholomew's arm. 'The attack in the street, your room searched. It was the book they wanted!'

'Whatever for?' asked Bartholomew, unconvinced. 'It is a poor copy of Galen at best and certainly not worth killing for.'

'Not for the Galen. For the bit at the end,' insisted Gray, eyes glittering with enthusiasm. 'Perhaps it contains information about the town that no one knows.'

'Perhaps Hereward the Wake is alive and well and wants to read it,' said Michael, laughing. 'Or maybe this long-dead Chancellor, de Badew.'

'It was no apparition that brained me in the High Street,' said Bartholomew firmly. 'That was Will, Huw, Saul Potter and Bigod. And it was Edred who searched my room.'

He leaned back against the wall and began to study the book with renewed interest. Were the local stories significant, or was the copyist merely using up leftover paper at the end of his book, as Michael suggested? The leather covers of the tome were thick and crude, and inside, an attempt had been made to improve their appearance by pasting coloured parchment over them. Bartholomew ran his fingers down them and then looked closer. He was wrong – the parchment had not been placed there to make the inside cover look neater, but to hide something. He picked at it, uncertain. Michael watched silently. Both were scholars with a love of learning and of the books that contained it. Damaging one of these precious items was an act alien to both of them.

Gray took it from him, and with a decisive movement of his hand, ripped the parchment away. Bartholomew and Michael, as one, winced at the sound of tearing, but looked with interest at what spilled out into Gray's hands. While Gray performed a similar operation with the front cover, Bartholomew and Michael read the documents that had fallen from the back.

Bartholomew felt sick. 'These are copies of letters sent by Norbert to me after he fled to Dover,' he said in a low voice. 'They date from a few weeks after he left, to the last message I had about fifteen years ago and are signed with the name of his sister, Celinia.'

'Who is Norbert?' asked Gray, intrigued.

Bartholomew sighed. 'He was accused of burning the tithe barn at Trumpington when we were children. I helped him escape.'

'And this,' said Michael, waving another document in the air, 'is a list of times and dates suggesting meetings, along with names and addresses. They include Mistress Tyler, Thomas Bigod, Will of Valence Marie, Cecily Lydgate, and the Godwinsson servants Saul Potter and Huw, to name but a few. You were right, Matt. It was Bigod, Will, Potter and Huw who attacked us – for these parchments.'

'Do you think they are involved in starting the riots, then?' asked Gray, his eyes alight with excitement.

Bartholomew turned the letters over in his hands. 'That seems something of a leap in logic, but does not mean that you are wrong. The only thing finding these documents has made clear to me is that Norbert may have returned to the area. Why else would his letters be here?'

Mistress Tyler's house was silent and still. Tulyet's sergeant kicked at the door until it gave way and forced his way in, shouldering aside the splintered wood to stand in the small chamber on the ground floor. Bartholomew peered in. The room was bare except for a heavy chest, a table and some shelves. Tulyet pushed past him and began to climb the ladder that led to the upper chamber where the women had slept. He shook his head in disgust as he descended.

'Gone,' he called. 'And swept so clean that a spider could not hide.'

'This will confound your plans for the Festival of St Michael and All Angels on Sunday,' remarked Michael to Bartholomew leeringly. 'Whom will you ask to escort you now Hedwise Tyler has fled? I doubt you will get away with Matilde a second time. You might be reduced to taking Agatha given that you are so intent on being surrounded by women!'

Bartholomew pretended to ignore him, wondering how such things could occur to the fat monk when the situation was so grave.

'Why clean a house you are abandoning for ever?' he mused, looking around him.

'I will never understand women,' agreed Tulyet. 'What a waste of time!'

'Perhaps not,' said Bartholomew, frowning. Watched by the others, he began a careful examination of the room. Finally, he stopped and pointed to some faint brownish stains on one of the walls. When he moved some cracked bowls and pots that had been left, there was a larger stain on the wooden floor.

'Cooking accident?' asked Michael, nonplussed.

'Hardly, Brother,' said Bartholomew. 'Only people who do not mind their houses going up in flames cook so close to the walls. This stain is blood. It splattered on the wall and then pooled on the floor.'

'Whose blood?' asked Tulyet, staring at it. 'This Joanna's?'

'Probably,' said Bartholomew, thinking again of Mistress Tyler leading him away from her house the night of the riot. 'There is enough of it to suggest that a serious, if not fatal, wound was inflicted and there was simply too much blood to be cleaned away.'

Michael puffed out his cheeks, and prodded half-heartedly at the stone jars and bowls that had been left. Bartholomew leaned against the door frame and thought. He had been hoping that there had been some mistake, and that they would discover the Tylers' part in the affair was coincidental, or innocent. But how could he hold to that belief now? They had fled the town, taking everything that was moveable with them. He wondered if Eleanor had been given the idea by Father William while at the Feast, since he had regaled her with stories of how he had run away laden with monastic treasures.

Hope flared within him suddenly. Perhaps they had been taken by force; abducted and taken away against their will. The hope faded as quickly as it had come. What abductor would take the furniture with him and sweep the upstairs chamber before making away with his prizes? Not only that, but Bartholomew very much doubted that the Tyler women could be abducted anywhere they did not want to go.

Michael bent to one of the bowls and Bartholomew saw him run his finger around its rim. He held it up lightly coated with a gritty, white powder and raised the finger to his lips to sniff at it. With a bound, Bartholomew leapt at him, knocking Tulyet sideways before slapping Michael's hand away from his face and wiping the powder from his finger with his shirt-sleeve.

Michael looked puzzled. 'How will we know what this is unless

we smell it?' he said. 'I have watched Jonas the Poisoner smell
and taste his medicines often enough.'

'Then Jonas is a fool,' snapped Bartholomew. 'If, as you
believe, that powder is the same kind that killed Edred, it is
in a highly concentrated form.'

'But you told me last night that the poison might have
worked more quickly on Edred because it entered a wound
or because he inhaled it in. A small amount on my hand will
not harm me.'

'It might,' said Bartholomew. 'Can you feel your finger
now?'

Michael rubbed his finger cautiously. 'It is numb. I cannot
feel it,' he added with a slight rise in pitch, and his eyes
widening with horror.

Bartholomew pursed his lips. 'Go and rinse it off,' he said.
'The feeling will return eventually.'

Tulyet crouched next to the bowl, poking at it with his dagger.
'Is it the same concentrated powder that killed the friar in your
room?' he asked, glancing at Bartholomew as Michael hurried
from the house in search of water.

'It would seem so,' said Bartholomew. 'Even a small amount
has taken the feeling from Michael's fingertip.'

Tulyet stood. 'I will send men after Mistress Tyler and her
devious daughters to see what she has to say for herself.' He
looked down at the bowls again. 'Although, all we can prove
is that she had the same powerful poison in her house that
Jonas sent to you.'

'I will go to see if Jonas knows where she might have gone,'
said Bartholomew. 'If he has any ideas I will send you a
message.'

Wringing and flexing his afflicted finger, Michael followed
Bartholomew to the apothecary's shop, while Tulyet went to
organise men to search for the Tyler family, although they all
knew that they would be long gone.

Jonas's shop was empty of customers, and the apothecary
was mixing potions on a wide shelf that ran along one side
of the room. He was humming to himself, his bald head
glistening with tiny beads of sweat as he applied himself to
pounding something into a paste with considerable vigour. His
two apprentices were hanging bunches of herbs to dry in the
rafters of an adjoining room.

'You sent me a powerful poison, Jonas,' said Bartholomew

without preamble, watching the apothecary jump at the nearness of the voice behind him. Colour drained from Jonas's usually pink-cheeked face. He cast a nervous glance at his apprentices and closed the door so that they should not hear.

'Please, Doctor,' he said. 'That matter was finished with a long time ago and I paid dearly for my mistake. Do not jest with me about poisons!'

'I am not jesting about the events of years ago,' said Bartholomew. 'I am talking about the events of yesterday. You sent me oleander so concentrated that Brother Michael's finger is numb from touching a few grains of it.'

Michael held up his finger, an even more unhealthy white than the rest of him. Jonas's eyes almost popped from their sockets. Cautiously, like a bird accepting a much desired crumb, Jonas inched forward to examine Michael's finger. He put out a tentative hand and touched the pallid, puckered skin.

As though he had been burned, he snatched his hand back again.

'Oleander without a doubt,' he said. 'But why were you touching it?'

'That was caused by the same oleander you sent to me for the physic I use for leprosy,' said Bartholomew.

Jonas backed up against the wall, as though faced with a physical threat. 'Not me, Matthew,' he said. 'You know I am careful with such poisons. Have I ever made a mistake in the measurements and doses I send to you? Everything that leaves this shop, even down to the mildest salve, is checked. First by me, then by my apprentices and then by my wife.'

'But nevertheless, this powerful oleander was sent to me,' said Bartholomew persistently. 'Yesterday afternoon.'

Jonas's confusion increased. He pointed to a package on one of the wall shelves. 'There is your order of oleander, Matthew. It is ready but, as I said, all potions leaving my shop are checked. Your order has not yet been checked by my wife, which is why it is waiting.'

Now it was Bartholomew's turn to be confused. 'But you sent my order yesterday.'

Jonas bristled. 'I did no such thing. You can look in my record book if you doubt me.'

Bartholomew exchanged a puzzled look with Michael. 'Were Eleanor or Hedwise Tyler here yesterday?' he asked.

Jonas smiled suddenly. 'Both were here. Eleanor has been most helpful these last few weeks. The outbreak of summer ague has meant that we have been busier than usual and she has been a valuable assistant. She helped to prepare some of the orders yesterday, and even offered to deliver them, so that my apprentices would not have to leave their work.'

The smile slowly faded and he swallowed hard. 'Oh no!' he said, backing away from them. 'You are not going to tell me that Eleanor sent the poison?'

'Does she have access to your poisons?' asked Bartholomew.

'Not access as such,' said Jonas, his small hands fluttering like birds about the front of his apron in his agitation. 'But she was interested in my work and I showed her what was where.'

'I assume you store your oleander in its concentrated form and sell it diluted for medicines?' asked Bartholomew. It was standard practice among apothecaries and there was nothing untoward in it. Jonas nodded. 'Did Eleanor know this?'

'I showed her how I diluted it yesterday,' said Jonas, his hands fluttering even more wildly. 'For you as a matter of fact. You ordered some for the lepers at Barnwell Priory.'

'Do you know Eleanor and her family have gone?' asked Bartholomew.

'Gone where?' asked Jonas, bewildered. 'Not far, surely. She said she would help me this afternoon and I have come to rely on her. And her family is coming for dinner this evening.'

'I do not think so,' said Michael. 'The Tyler house is abandoned and all removeable items gone.'

Jonas shook his head. 'They are coming to eat with us tonight. Meg!' he yelled suddenly, making Bartholomew leap out of his skin. Immediately, there were footsteps on the wooden stairs, and Jonas's wife appeared.

'They say Agnes has left town, Meg,' said Jonas, still wringing his hands. 'I told them that was impossible because she and the family are coming to dinner tonight.'

Meg's eyes grew huge and flitted from Bartholomew to Michael in terror.

'Tell us what you know, Mistress,' said Michael, watching her reaction with resignation.

Meg's fearful eyes danced back to her husband, who smiled at her, encouraging her to support his statement.

'I went round to Agnes's house yesterday afternoon and they had everything piled up in the middle of the room,' she said. 'They made me promise not to mention they were leaving until they had gone.'

'Gone where?' asked Bartholomew. 'And why?'

Meg shook her head. 'I begged them to stay. They are my only relatives here but they were insistent that they should go.'

'Do you know that Eleanor sent me a powerful poison yesterday, in place of the diluted oleander I use for treating leprosy?'

'No!' Meg cried. 'She did not!'

'Oh, but she did, Mistress,' said Michael. 'And I suspect you know far more than you are telling us. Now, we do not have all day, so tell us the truth and hurry up with it.'

Meg's eyes flitted to her husband's horrified face and she burst into tears.

'This oleander has caused the death of someone,' Michael pressed. Jonas's legs gave out and he plopped on to a low bench on top of a bunch of dried mint. Within moments, the herb's pungent odour filled the shop.

'Oh no!' he groaned. 'Who has died? Not that saintly Master Kenyngham? My business will be finished for ever if this gets out!'

Meg wailed louder, so that Michael had to raise his voice to be heard. 'I am sure your part in all this will be overlooked if you tell us what we need to know.'

Meg fought to bring her sobs under control. 'Eleanor said that Doctor Bartholomew had been asking questions about Joanna,' she said, after a few moments of serious sniffing. 'She was terribly distressed because she said she did not want him, of all people, to be the cause of her mother's downfall. I am not sure what she meant. I thought it was Joanna's prostitution and that Eleanor was worried for the good name of her mother's household, but I think now that it was more than that.'

She paused to scrub at her nose with the back of her hand. 'I saw Eleanor in the poisons cupboard yesterday and she told me she was preparing your order of oleander. Later, I remembered that Jonas always keeps the diluted oleander for you in a separate jar, but that Eleanor had been using the concentrated powder.'

'So it is true!' wailed Jonas in horror. 'We did send concentrated oleander to Doctor Bartholomew! This is just too
dreadful!'

'Please continue, Mistress,' said Michael, silencing the apothecary with a disdainful glance.

Meg took a deep breath. 'I was appalled that she might
inadvertently have sent you the wrong thing, and rushed to
her house so we could put all to rights before Jonas found
out, or anyone was harmed. Agnes and Hedwise had all their
belongings piled in the middle of the floor while Eleanor sat
in a corner and wept. They would not tell me what was amiss.
I asked Eleanor about the powder but she said it was still on
the shelf with the other orders awaiting delivery.'

She gestured to the package above her head with Bartholomew's
name written on it, a certain defiance in her eyes. 'And
there it is.'

'But she was lying, Mistress,' said Michael harshly. 'Eleanor
had already dispatched one package to Doctor Bartholomew –
the one she had prepared at home containing the concentrated
oleander she had stolen from Jonas. She hoped it would
have done its job before he received the real package and
became suspicious. And you suspected all was not well by her
behaviour.'

'No!' shrieked Meg, weeping afresh. 'I did *not* know. I came
home, and there was the package, just as she said it would be.
I threw it away and prepared another in its place – with diluted
oleander.'

'And do you know what Eleanor's motives were in all this?'
persisted Michael, his grim expression making it abundantly
clear that he did not believe her for an instant.

'Motives for what?' cried Meg. 'She did nothing wrong!
She accidentally used the wrong powder in your order but I
discovered her mistake and corrected it before anyone came
to harm. I do not know how poor Master Kenyngham died
but it was not with anything from our shop!'

Michael said nothing, and regarded her long and hard.
Bartholomew had known Jonas and Meg for years and knew
they would not risk their livelihood so rashly: he was therefore
inclined to believe they were telling the truth. But Eleanor
was another matter. Clearly, she had stolen the concentrated
oleander and prepared if for Bartholomew in the safety of her
own home, as attested by the residues in the bowl Michael

had touched. But was Mistress Tyler aware of her daughter's actions? Or Hedwise? Surely, Bartholomew's feeble investigation concerning Joanna could not warrant Eleanor trying to kill him? He decided that he might be wise to stay away from future involvements with women – at least until he had learned a little more about them.

Meg wiped her nose. 'Eleanor told me some days ago that Doctor Bartholomew had some odd notion that Joanna had been murdered during the riot. Of course, nothing of the kind had happened and we all know that Joanna had left because she found Cambridge too violent.'

'So, Joanna is in Ely?' asked Michael. Meg nodded and Michael continued. 'In that case, surely it would be a simple matter to summon her back again and prove that she is alive and well, living a life of sin near the greatest Benedictine House in East Anglia. Why did Mistress Tyler not do that?'

Meg looked bewildered, as though such a notion had not occurred to her before. 'I do not know,' she stammered. 'Perhaps because they were so relieved when she left. Joanna was definitely not the demure and gentle niece we remembered from years ago.' She pursed her lips in disapproval. 'She had become a harlot.'

Bartholomew studied the frightened woman soberly. She did not possess the quick intelligence and courage of her Tyler relatives and Bartholomew was in no doubt that she had believed what she had been told. Meg's crime was nothing more than gullibility. But Bartholomew was now certain that Joanna had played a part in some plot – whether willingly or unwillingly he did not know – and that Eleanor had sent him the poison in order to prevent him coming any closer to the truth. The more he thought about it, particularly in relation to the bloodstains in the house, the more he sensed that there was most definitely something untoward about Joanna's sudden departure, and that Eleanor had taken it upon herself to protect her family from the consequences.

'Did you see Joanna after the riot?' asked Bartholomew, already guessing what the answer would be.

Meg shook her head. 'Agnes said Joanna did not want to help with the clearing up afterwards. It is typical of her. She has become a lazy woman. Agnes saw her off early that morning.'

But Joanna, if Joanna it were, was already dead in the Castle mortuary that morning and Agnes Tyler herself was staying at Jonas's house because her own had been looted.

'Where did Agnes see Joanna?' pressed Bartholomew.

'I do not know,' said Meg. 'She was up early and went off to inspect the damage done to her house. I did not question where they met.'

If they ever met, thought Bartholomew. There was no evidence to suggest that they did, and quite a bit to suggest that they did not.

'One last question,' he said. Meg nodded cautiously, still sniffling. 'Could Joanna write?'

Meg looked taken aback. 'Of course not,' she said. 'Her mother always planned for her to follow in her footsteps and become a dairy-maid at the Abbey. She had no need to learn her letters.'

But Eleanor could write, thought Bartholomew. And someone had written a note, purporting to be from Joanna, to Dunstan's lovesick grandson, perhaps so that her sudden disappearance would not arouse the lad's suspicion, and cause him to go to Ely to find her. If Joanna was illiterate, it was unlikely that she would have written a note – or even bother to dictate one – to a moonstruck adolescent who could not read. Eleanor Tyler's role in the affair was becoming increasingly suspect.

Bartholomew made his farewells to Meg and the agitated apothecary. As he turned to leave the shop the doorway darkened. Against the bright sunlight, a figure stood silhouetted.

'Doctor Bartholomew,' said the hulking shape in a loud, confident voice that dripped with loathing. 'And Brother Michael. I have been searching for you two. We should talk. Meet me at St Andrew's Church at sunset tonight.'

The figure moved away, leaving Bartholomew and Michael staring at the empty doorway.

'Well,' said Michael. 'Do we obey this summons and meet Master Lydgate tonight?'

'A summons from the Devil?' asked Bartholomew dubiously.

chapter 10

I N A FLAMING BALL OF GOLDEN ORANGE THE SUN BEGAN TO dip behind the orchard walls, bathing the creamy stone of Michaelhouse in a deep russet-red. Shadows lengthened, or flickered out altogether and in the distance carts clattered and creaked as farmers and merchants made their way home at the end of the day.

Michael stood and stretched. 'Ready?' he said, looking down to where Bartholomew was still sitting comfortably on the fallen tree, his back against the sun-warmed stones of the orchard wall.

Reluctantly, Bartholomew climbed to his feet, and followed Michael through the trees to the back gate. They let themselves out and walked quickly towards the High Street. It thronged with people heading for home. Horses and donkeys drew carts of all shapes and sizes and weary apprentices hastened to complete the last business before trading ceased for the day. One cart had lost a wheel in one of the huge pot-holes, and a fiery argument had broken out between the cart's owner and those whose path he was blocking. A barking dog, children's high-pitched taunting of the carter and a baker's increasingly strident calls to sell the last of his pies, added to the general cacophony.

Bartholomew and Michael ignored the row, squeezing past the offending cart. As they emerged the other side, Bartholomew heard something thud against the wall by his head. Someone had thrown a stone at him! He turned, but Michael's firm hand pulled him on.

'Not a place to linger, my friend,' he muttered. Bartholomew could not but agree. Any large gathering of townspeople, already riled by an incident such as the blockage caused by the broken cart, was not a place for University men to tarry. Bartholomew glanced backwards as they hurried on, glimpsing the owner of the broken cart howling in rage as three or four hefty apprentices tried to shoulder it out of the way.

He paused briefly, frowning at the carter as something clicked into place in the back of his mind, but yielded to Michael's impatient tug on his sleeve. They reached St Andrew's Church without further incident and slipped into its cool, dark interior. Here, the shadows lay thick and impenetrable and the only light was from a cluster of candles near the altar. Michael closed the door, blocking out the noise of the street, while Bartholomew prowled around the church looking for Lydgate.

Bartholomew had not wanted to come to this meeting. He did not trust Lydgate and did not understand why, after so many protestations of dislike, the man should suddenly want to meet them. Inadvertently, his hand went to the dagger concealed under his tabard, which he had borrowed from the ailing Cynric. He rarely carried weapons but felt justified in bringing one to the meeting with Lydgate, although surely even Lydgate would be loath to commit murder in a house of God? But desperate or enraged men would not stop to consider the sanctity of a church. Even the saint, Thomas à Becket, had not been safe in his own cathedral.

The door gave a sudden creak and Bartholomew instinctively slipped into the shadows behind one of the pillars. Lydgate entered alone, pulling the door closed behind him with a loud bang. He stood for a moment in the gloom, accustoming his eyes to the dark after the brightness of the setting sun outside. Michael approached him and Bartholomew left his hiding place to join them.

Before any greetings could be exchanged, Lydgate pointed a finger at Bartholomew.

'You have many questions to answer, Bartholomew,' he hissed belligerently.

Bartholomew eyed him with distaste. It was not an auspicious start. Even the Principal of a hostel had no authority to speak to him so. But nothing would be served by responding with anger, especially with the blustering Lydgate.

'We have much to discuss with you,' he replied as pleasantly as he could.

Lydgate regarded him with his small blue eyes. 'First,' he began, 'where is Edred?'

Michael spoke before Bartholomew could answer. 'Where

is your daughter, Master Lydgate?' he asked. 'Is she still with your relatives away from Cambridge?'

Bartholomew looked at him sharply. He did not want Michael to mention Cecily's hiding place at Chesterton, even in connection with something else. Although he did not have an overwhelming respect for Lydgate's powers of reasoning, he did not wish Michael to give him even the most obtuse clue that might betray her.

Lydgate seemed nonplussed at Michael's question, and stood looking from one to the other in confusion, his hands dangling at his sides. How could such a man, a lout with poor manners and worse self-control, ever have become the Principal of a hostel? wondered Bartholomew. The University clearly needed to review its selection procedures.

'She is . . .' Lydgate began. He seemed to remember himself. 'Tell me where Brother Edred is lurking. He did not return home this morning.'

'This morning?' Michael pounced like a cat. 'Why this morning and not last night? Surely, you do not expect your scholars to return at dawn when they should be safely tucked up in bed all night, Master Lydgate?'

Again the confused look. Bartholomew began to feel tired. It was like having an argument about logic with a baby. Lydgate was incapable of subtlety: he was too brutal and impatient. Bartholomew looked at the great hands hanging at Lydgate's sides. They were large, red and looked strong. Had those hands committed all the murders that Edred had claimed?

'We have much information that might be of interest to each other,' said Michael, relenting. 'Let's sit and talk quietly. Come.'

He led the way to some benches in the Lady Chapel. Lydgate sat stiffly, unafraid, but wary and alert to danger. Bartholomew sat opposite him, the hand under his tabard still on the hilt of his dagger. Michael sat next to Bartholomew.

'Now,' the monk said. 'I will begin and tell you what Edred has told us. Then, in turn, you can tell us what you know and together we will try to make sense of it all. Is that fair?'

Lydgate nodded slowly, while Bartholomew said nothing. The beginnings of a solution, or at least part of one, were beginning to form in his mind, and the implications bothered him. They centred around the carter who had been blocking the High Street.

'Edred came to us last night saying he was in fear of his life,' Michael began. 'He claimed you had killed young James Kenzie, then your daughter Dominica and a servant from Valence Marie and finally your student Brother Werbergh.'

Lydgate leapt to his feet. 'That is not true!' he shouted, his voice ringing through the silent church. 'I have killed no one.'

Michael gestured for him to sit down again. 'I am merely repeating what we were told,' he said in placatory tones. 'I did not say we believe it to be true. Indeed, Edred's claims were all based on circumstantial evidence and conjecture, and he had nothing solid to prove his allegations. We arranged for him to sleep in Michaelhouse last night, since he seemed afraid. While Matt's bookbearer made his bed, Edred struck him from behind and began a search of the room. Do you have any idea what he might have been seeking?'

Lydgate shrugged impatiently. 'No. What was it?'

'We are uncertain,' said Michael. Bartholomew was grateful that Michael had decided to be less than open with Lydgate although, hopefully, Michael was providing him with sufficient information to loosen his tongue.

Michael continued. 'When we caught Edred rummaging, he drew a sword and threatened us. In the ensuing struggle, Edred was killed.'

Lydgate's mouth dropped open, and Bartholomew swallowed hard. The Chancellor and Master Kenyngham had advised against telling Lydgate of Edred's death and Bartholomew wondered whether Michael had not committed a grave error in informing him so bluntly. He sat tensely and waited for an explosion.

He waited in vain. 'You killed Edred?' said Lydgate, his voice almost a whisper. He scrubbed hard at the bristles on his face and shook his big head slowly.

Michael flinched. 'I did not kill him deliberately. Which cannot be said for the murderer of Werbergh.'

'Werbergh?' echoed Lydgate. 'But he died in an accident. My servants, Saul Potter and Huw saw it happen.'

'Werbergh did not die in the shed,' said Bartholomew. 'I hope this will not distress you, Master Lydgate, but I took the liberty of examining Werbergh's body in the church. I think he died on Friday night or Saturday, rather than Sunday morning under the collapsing shed. And he died from a blow to the head, after which he fell, or was pushed, into water.'

Lydgate scratched his head and let his hands fall between his knees. He looked from one to the other trying to assimilate the information.

'How can you be sure?' he asked. 'How can you tell such things? Did you kill him?'

'I most certainly did not!' retorted Bartholomew angrily. 'I was not up and about until Saturday, as anyone in Michaelhouse will attest.'

Michael raised his hands to placate him. He turned to Lydgate. 'There are signs on the body that provide information after death,' he said. 'Matt is a physician. He knows how to look for them.'

Lydgate rubbed his neck and considered. 'You say Werbergh died on Friday night or Saturday? Friday was the night of the celebration at Valence Marie. A debauched occasion, although I kept from the wine myself. I do not like to appear drunk in front of the students. Virtually all of them were insensible by the time the wine ran out.'

'Was Werbergh there?' asked Bartholomew. 'Was Edred?'

Lydgate scowled, and Bartholomew thought he might refuse to answer, but Lydgate's frown was merely a man struggling to remember. 'Yes,' he said finally. 'Both were there. Werbergh was drunk like the others. Edred was not. They left together, late, but probably before most of the others.' He looked from Michael to Bartholomew. 'Do you think this means Edred killed Werbergh?'

Bartholomew ran a hand through his hair. 'Not necessarily. I think he genuinely believed Werbergh had died by your hand sometime on Sunday morning, not from a blow to the head on Friday night.'

'No,' said Michael, shaking his head. 'That is false logic, Matt. He may have killed Werbergh on Friday, but claimed Master Lydgate had killed him on Sunday lest any should remember that it was Edred who accompanied the drunken Werbergh home on the night of his death.'

Lydgate scratched his scalp. 'What an unholy muddle,' he said.

'Unholy is certainly the word for Edred,' said Bartholomew feelingly. 'What was his intention last night? What did he think he could gain by blaming the murders on his Principal?'

'Oh, that is simple,' said Lydgate. 'It is the only thing I understand in this foul business.' He gave a huge sigh and looked Bartholomew in the eye. 'But I do not know why I should trust you. You have already tried to blackmail me.'

Bartholomew gazed at him in disbelief. Michael gave a derisive snort of laughter.

'Do not be ridiculous, Master Lydgate! What could Matt blackmail you about?'

But Bartholomew knew, and wondered again whether Lydgate had overheard him and Michael discussing the burning of the tithe barn during their first visit to Godwinsson.

After a few moments, Lydgate began to speak in a voice that was quiet and calm, quite unlike his usual bluster. 'Many years ago, I committed a grave crime,' he said. He paused.

'You burned the tithe barn,' said Bartholomew, thinking to make Lydgate's confession easier for him.

Lydgate looked at him long and hard, as though trying to make up his mind. 'Yes,' he said finally. 'Not deliberately, though. It was an accident. I . . . stumbled in the hay and knocked over a lantern. It was an accident.'

'I never imagined it was anything else,' said Bartholomew. 'Nothing could have been gained by a deliberate burning of the barn – it was a tragic loss to the whole village. That winter was a miserable time for most people, with scanty supplies of grain and little fodder for the animals.'

'You do not need to remind me,' said Lydgate bitterly. 'I was terrified the whole time that you would decide to tell the villagers who was the real cause of their misery – me and not that dirty little Norbert you helped to escape.'

'You knew about that?' asked Bartholomew, astonished.

Lydgate nodded. 'I saw you let him go. But I kept your secret as you had kept mine. Until the last few weeks, that is, when you threatened to tell.'

'I have done nothing of the sort,' said Bartholomew indignantly. 'The whole affair had slipped my mind and I did not think of it again until the skeleton was uncovered in the Ditch. Edith thought the bones might be Norbert's and I told her that was impossible.'

'How do you know?' asked Lydgate curiously.

'Because I received letters from him,' said Bartholomew. He looked at Michael. 'Copies of which were concealed in a book I have recently read,' he added.

'Then it must be Norbert who is trying to blackmail me and not you at all! He has waited all these years to claim justice! I see! It makes sense now!' cried Lydgate.

Various things became clear in Bartholomew's mind from this tangled web of lies and misunderstandings. Lydgate must have already been sent blackmail messages when Bartholomew and Michael had gone to speak to him about Kenzie's murder, which was why he had threatened Bartholomew as he was leaving Godwinsson, and why he had instructed Cecily not to contradict anything that was said. And it was also clear that Lydgate's aversion to Bartholomew inspecting Werbergh's body was not because he was trying to conceal his murder, but because he was keen to keep his imagined blackmailer away from events connected to his hostel.

'Not so fast,' said Michael, his eyes narrowing thoughtfully. 'We must consider this more carefully before jumping to conclusions. We found copies of Norbert's letters in a book. That tells us that he probably kept them to remind himself of the lies he had written, so he would not contradict himself in future letters. Perhaps he always intended to return to Cambridge to blackmail the man who almost had him hanged for a crime he did not commit.'

'Were these blackmail messages signed?' asked Bartholomew of Lydgate.

Lydgate shook his head. 'There have been three of them, all claiming I set the barn alight, and that payment would be required for silence.'

'What about Cecily?' asked Bartholomew. 'Could she have sent the notes? After all, you are hardly affectionate with each other.'

'She did not know it was me who set the barn on fire!' said Lydgate with frustration. 'No one does, except the three of us.'

'But why has Norbert not contacted me?' mused Bartholomew looking puzzled. 'I would have thought he might, given what I risked to save him.'

'Perhaps he is afraid you will not support him,' said Michael. 'How does he know you can still be trusted after twenty-five years?' He rubbed at the bristles on his chin. 'But it does seem that you were right and that Norbert has returned to Cambridge. We find his letters to you and Master Lydgate receives blackmail notes. It is all too much of a coincidence to be chance.'

'So it was Norbert and his associates who attacked us a week ago, looking for the book that contained that vital piece of evidence?' said Bartholomew, standing and beginning to pace, as he did when he lectured to his students and needed to think. He had sometimes carried the Galen in his medicine bag and it had probably been there when his room had been searched. But the night he was attacked, he had left the book behind because it was going to rain and he did not want it to get wet. Norbert and his associates had been unfortunate in their timing.

'And Norbert killed Werbergh?' asked Lydgate. He rubbed at his eyes tiredly. 'Even with my story and your information, it is still a fearful mess. I can make no sense of it. It was all clear to me when I thought Bartholomew was the blackmailer.' He watched Bartholomew pace back and forth, and then cleared his throat. 'One of the notes said Dominica would die as a warning,' he said huskily.

'What is this?' said Michael, aghast again. 'A warning for what?'

'This is painful for me,' said Lydgate. He leaned forward, resting his elbows on his knees, large hands dangling, and his head bowed. 'One note said that if I did not comply and leave money as instructed, my daughter would die. I sent her immediately to Chesterton for safety. During the riot, Edred came back to say she was in Cambridge again. I went out to see if I could find her but it was too late. She already lay dead, her face smeared in blood and her long golden hair soaked in gore and dirt. Ned from Valence Marie lay by the side of her, a dagger in his stomach. I pulled it out. I suppose it might be possible she was just a random victim of the riots, but I am sceptical so soon after I had the letter threatening her life.'

Bartholomew thought of Lydgate's story in the light of what he had been told by Cecily and Edred. They claimed they had seen Lydgate standing over the dead Dominica and Ned, holding a dripping knife. If everyone was telling the truth, then Cecily and Edred had indeed seen Lydgate standing over two bodies with a dagger, but had misinterpreted what they had seen. On the strength of these erroneous assumptions, Mistress Cecily had left her husband, and Edred had applied what he had known of the other deaths to reason that Lydgate had not only killed Dominica and Ned, but Werbergh and Kenzie, too.

Bartholomew rubbed the back of his head. Cecily, Lydgate and Edred all said it was Dominica they had seen lying dead near Ned from Valence Marie. In which case, where was Joanna? Bartholomew was certain she was dead, or the Tyler family would not have gone to such lengths to prevent him from looking too closely into her disappearance. But the more he thought about it, the more convinced he became that the woman with the unrecognisably battered face and long, golden hair was Joanna and not Dominica at all. It had been dark, both during the riot and in the Castle mortuary and that, coupled with the fact that the face had been battered, would have made definite identification difficult, if not impossible. And finally, there was the ominous patch of blood in the Tylers' house.

He glanced at Michael, wondering whether to share his thoughts with Lydgate. The monk had been watching him intently and gave a barely perceptible shake of his head. Michael had apparently guessed what Bartholomew had been reasoning, but thought the evidence too slim to give Lydgate hopes that he might have been mistaken and that Dominica might yet be alive.

'Dominica's name was not among the dead,' said Michael when he saw Bartholomew was not going to speak. 'Why did you not claim her body?'

Lydgate put his head in his hands. 'I did not know what to do,' he said. 'Cecily was gone, and there was no one with whom to discuss it. I decided to let Dominica's death remain anonymous until I had had time to think. You see, the soldiers at the Castle were saying that the woman who had died had been a whore. I did not want to risk Dominica's reputation by claiming that this whore was her. Half the town knew that she had a lover and she would always be remembered as the whore who died in the riots. I had to think before I acted, so I said nothing.'

'You went to her grave, though,' said Bartholomew.

Lydgate fixed his small eyes on Bartholomew. 'Yes. And you found me there. I thought you had come to gloat. You were lucky I did not run you through.'

'Does your wife know about the blackmail notes?' asked Michael.

'I told her I was being blackmailed, but I did not tell her why. She was concerned only for Dominica, and cared not a fig for me or my reputation should all this come out. She ran away from me the night Dominica died and lurks in her underground chamber at Chesterton.'

'You know where she is?' asked Bartholomew, startled.

'Of course!' said Lydgate dismissively. 'My wife is not a woman richly endowed with imagination, Bartholomew. I knew immediately that she would flee to the same place where we had hidden Dominica. And even if I had not guessed, my friend Thomas Bigod would have told me. Bigod has been a good ally to me. He gave me an alibi the night Dominica died and is keeping Cecily safe until such time as we can settle our differences – if we ever bother.'

'Cecily believed you killed Dominica,' said Michael baldly.

Lydgate gave a faint smile. 'So Thomas Bigod tells me. Silly woman! She can stay away as long as she likes. The house is more pleasant without her whining tongue.'

Bartholomew let all this sink in. Cecily was hiding away, and Lydgate had not been fooled for an instant about her whereabouts. Lydgate had told Cecily that Bartholomew had been blackmailing him, but she had shown no compunction about helping the man she thought was her husband's enemy. To Cecily, Bartholomew had been an instrument to use against her husband. That must have been at least partly why she had helped him to escape from the manor at Chesterton: she believed she was releasing her husband's blackmailer to continue his war of attrition!

Lydgate sighed. 'I knew Dominica was seeing a scholar. The day after I sent her away, I heard him throwing stones at her window. When he saw he would get no response, he left and I followed him. But I am too big and clumsy for such work and I lost him before we reached the High Street.'

Unfortunately for Kenzie, thought Bartholomew. He might still be alive had his killer seen the hulking figure of Lydgate pursuing him.

'All I saw was a man in a scholar's tabard,' continued Lydgate wearily. 'I could not see him well enough to identify him again.'

'It was James Kenzie, the David's student who was murdered,' said Michael.

Lydgate gazed at the Benedictine in mute disbelief, and then slammed one thick fist into the palm of his other hand. 'Of course!' he exclaimed. 'That student was killed the same night I followed Dominica's visitor. No wonder you paid me so much attention!'

Bartholomew and Michael exchanged a look of bemusement,

wondering how Lydgate had never put the two together in his mind before. Lydgate did not notice and continued. 'So, Dominica chose a Scot! She knew how to be hurtful. What more inappropriate lover could the daughter of a hostel principal chose than an impoverished Scot?'

'But if you did not kill him, who did? And why?' asked Bartholomew, wanting to get back to the business of solving the murders, away from Lydgate's domestic traumas.

Lydgate looked at him as though he were mad. 'Why, Norbert, of course,' he said.

Bartholomew paced up and down and shook his head impatiently. Lydgate followed him with his eyes. 'But why? Norbert has no reason to kill Kenzie.'

'What about the ring?' asked Michael. 'The lover's ring that Kenzie had lost to Edred that day?'

'Why?' said Bartholomew. 'Why should Norbert want the ring? And if you recall, Kenzie wore no ring when he died. Edred had stolen it earlier – or at least, had stolen the fake.'

Lydgate nodded. 'Edred tried to claim a reward by offering a cheap imitation of Dominica's ring. I grew angry with him and since then he has been sulky with me. That is why he accused me of those murders – as I said, it is the only thing I truly understand in all this muddle.'

'Ah!' said Michael. 'So, the slippery friar changed his allegiance. This begins to make sense. Repulsed by you in his attempts at winning favour, he was recruited by, or turned to, Norbert. It was Norbert who told him to make sure you were blamed for all those deaths by coming to us, and it was for Norbert that Edred searched Matt's room looking for the Galen. I think Edred believed what he told us was true and I think he was afraid of you. But he was working for Norbert all the time!'

It was dark in the church now and the only light came from the candles. There seemed to be little more to be said and Michael and Lydgate stood. As Lydgate stepped forward, he stumbled against Michael's bench. Bartholomew caught him by the arm and prevented him from falling. Lydgate peered down at the bench and grimaced.

'How long have your eyes been failing?' asked Bartholomew gently.

Lydgate glared at him and pulled his arm away sharply. 'That is none of your business,' he snapped, but then relented. 'My eyesight has never been good, but these last three years have seen a marked degeneration. Father Philius says there is nothing I can do. I have told no one except Dominica. It is worse at night, though. Everything fades into shadow.'

As they opened the door of the church, they saw an orange glow in the sky and, very distantly, they could hear shouting and screams carried on the slightest of breezes.

'Oh, Lord, no!' whispered Michael, gazing at the eerie lights. 'The riot has started!'

'My hostel!' exclaimed Lydgate and hurried away into the night without so much as a backward glance. Michael watched him go.

'How did you guess about his sight?' he asked.

Bartholomew shrugged. 'The signs are clear enough. He rubs his eyes constantly and he squints and peers around. When I paced, he spoke to me in the wrong direction. And he failed to see the bench he fell over. He lost Kenzie when he followed him and he, unlike Edred, did not see his bright yellow hose. But even more importantly, he probably did not see Dominica. It was Joanna he saw dead.'

'So, your theory was be wrong after all,' said Michael. 'Dominica and Joanna are different.'

'It would seem so,' said Bartholomew. 'The woman's face was bloody, and the street where he found her and the Castle mortuary were dark, where Lydgate admits he cannot see well. The dead woman was probably Joanna after all. But I am not the only one who was mistaken. Lydgate, Cecily and Edred all think Dominica died on the night of the riot. Edred and Cecily only saw a fair-haired corpse from a distance; Lydgate saw her close but has poor vision.'

'So Lydgate went to look at her body at the Castle,' said Michael, 'because he had not trusted his failing eyesight on the night of the riot.'

Bartholomew ran a hand through his hair and then scrubbed hard at his face. Although things were clearer – Joanna and Dominica were not one and the same; he now understood the reason behind Lydgate's hostility towards him; and they finally knew more about the treacherous Edred's actions – there were still many questions that remained unanswered. Where was Dominica? Where was Norbert? Why had Bigod and his cronies elected to organise a riot that night? And why had someone been to such trouble to ensure that Joanna's body had been mistaken for Dominica's? He and Michael sank into the shadows of the church as shouting and running feet began to echo along the High Street. It grew closer, many feet pounding the dust of the road.

'It sounds like an army,' whispered Michael, edging further back.

Torches threw bouncing shadows in all directions as the mob surged past, yelling and calling to each other. Bartholomew recognised some of them as tradesmen from the Market Square. They all carried weapons of one kind or another – staves, knives, scythes, sticks, even cooking pots. Where the torch-light caught the occasional face, Bartholomew saw that they appeared mesmerised. They chanted together, nonsense words, but ones that created a rhythm of unity. Bartholomew had heard that clever commanders were able to create such a feeling of oneness before battles and that the soldiers, whipped up into a frenzy, fought like wild animals until they either died or dropped from sheer weariness. The crowd that surged past Bartholomew and Michael ran as one, chanting and crashing their weapons together. Bartholomew knew that if he and Michael were spotted now in their scholars' garb, they would be killed for certain. No amount of reasoning could possibly work against this enraged mob.

As the last torch jiggled past and the footsteps and chanting faded, Michael crossed himself vigorously, and Bartholomew crept cautiously to the fringe of trees in the graveyard to check that the rioters did not double back.

'That was an evil-intentioned crowd,' he whispered, as Michael joined him. 'There will be murder and mayhem again tonight, Brother. Just as Bigod promised there would be.'

Michael regarded him sombrely. 'That was no random group of trouble-makers,' he muttered. 'That was a rabble, carefully brought to fever-pitch, and held there until it is time to release it.'

'We had better return to Michaelhouse,' said Bartholomew, his voice loud in the sudden silence. The fat monk tried to muffle Bartholomew's voice with a hand over his mouth.

'Hush! Or they will release it on you and me!' he hissed fiercely.

Bartholomew had never seen Michael so afraid before and it did little to ease his troubled mind.

Michael's beadles seemed pathetic compared to the confident

mob that Bartholomew had seen thunder past. They looked terrified, too. Each time an especially loud yell occurred, they glanced nervously over their shoulders, and at least two of them were so white that Bartholomew thought they might faint. One took several steps backwards and then turned and fled. Bartholomew did not blame him: the group that had been hurriedly assembled in St Mary's churchyard was pitifully small, and would be more likely to attract the violent attentions of the crowd than to prevent trouble. To one side, Guy Heppel stood in the shadows and trembled with fear. His hands rubbed constantly at the sides of his tabard in agitation.

The Chancellor stalked up and down in front of his frightened army, twisting a ring around on his finger with such force that he risked breaking it.

A sudden shout made several of the beadles shy away in alarm, and all of them jumped. It was Tulyet, his face streaked with dirt, and his horse skittering and prancing in terror. Only Tulyet's superior horsemanship prevented him from being hurled from the saddle.

'At last!' breathed de Wetherset, and smiles of relief broke out on the faces of one or two of the beadles. 'What is the news? Is the mob dispersing?'

Tulyet leaned towards him so that the fearful beadles would not overhear.

'One hostel has been fired, but it seems that most, if not all, of the scholars escaped. St Paul's Hostel is under siege but is holding out. Townsfolk are gathering near St Michael's Church and it looks as though there will be an attack on Michaelhouse soon. And at least three other hostels have been sacked.'

'Are the scholars retaliating?' asked Bartholomew, trying to stay clear of the horse's flailing hooves.

'Not yet,' said Tulyet. He flashed Michael a grin of thanks as the fat monk took a firm hold of his mount's reins, preventing it from cavorting by sheer strength of arm. 'But I have had reports that they are massing. Valence Marie are out and so are King's Hall.'

'What of Godwinsson?' asked Michael, stroking the horse's velvet nose, oblivious to the white froth that oozed from its mouth as it chewed wildly on the bit.

'That is the one that has been fired,' said Tulyet. 'The students are out somewhere.'

'What do you plan to do?' asked the Chancellor. There was

a loud crash from the direction of the Market Square, and he winced. It was only a short distance from the Market Square to St Mary's Church, the centre of all University business, and the place where all its records were stored. It would take very little for the townspeople to transfer their aggressions from the market stalls to the obvious presence of the University in Cambridge's biggest and finest church.

Tulyet scrubbed at his face with his free hand. 'I scarcely know where to begin,' he said. 'It is all so scattered. The best plan I can come up with is to remove temptation from the mob's path. I want all scholars off the streets, and I want no action taken to curb the looting of the hostels that have already fallen – if there are no bands of scholars with which to fight, the fury of the mob will fizzle out.'

'It is not the University that precipitated all this,' said de Wetherset angrily. 'The townspeople started it.'

'That is irrelevant!' snapped Tulyet impatiently. 'And believe me, Master de Wetherset, the University will lose a good deal less of its property if you comply with my orders, than if you try to meet the rabble with violence.'

'You are quite right, Dick,' said Michael quickly, seeing de Wetherset prepared to argue the point, his heavy face suffused with a deep resentment. 'The most useful thing we can do now is to urge all the scholars indoors, or divert them from the mob. Heppel – take a dozen beadles and patrol Milne Street; I will take the rest along the High Street.'

Heppel looked at him aghast. 'Me?'

'Yes,' said Michael. 'You are the Junior Proctor and therefore paid to protect the University and its scholars.'

'God help us!' muttered de Wetherset under his breath, regarding the trembling Heppel in disdain. Bartholomew could see the Chancellor's point.

'But do you not think it would be better to lock ourselves in the church?' Heppel whispered, casting fearful eyes from Michael to the Chancellor. 'You said it would be best if all scholars were off the streets.'

'I was not referring to the Proctors and the beadles,' said Michael, placing his hands on his hips. 'It is our job to prevent lawlessness, not flee from it.'

'I did not anticipate such violence when I took this post!' protested Heppel. 'I knew Cambridge was an uneasy town, but I did not expect great crowds of townsfolk lusting for scholars' blood! I was not told there would be murder, or that the students would be quite so volatile!'

De Wetherset swallowed hard, and glanced around him uneasily, as if he imagined such a mob might suddenly converge on the churchyard. Meanwhile, Heppel's fear had communicated itself to the beadles and there were two fewer than when Bartholomew had last looked. Michael raised his eyes heavenward, while Tulyet pursed his lips, not pleased that the University was producing such a feeble response to its dangerous situation.

'The students are always volatile,' said Bartholomew who, like Tulyet and Michael, was unimpressed at Heppel's faintheartedness. 'Just not usually all at once. And not usually in conjunction with the entire town. However, like the last riot, this is no random occurrence. It was started quite deliberately. And this time, I know at least one of the ringleaders.'

'Who?' demanded Tulyet, fixing Bartholomew with an intent stare. His horse skittered nervously as another volley of excited shouts came from the direction of the Market Square.

'Ivo, the noisy scullion from David's Hostel,' said Bartholomew, thinking about what had clicked into place when the stone had been hurled at him as he and Michael had gone to meet Lydgate. 'He was the man whose cart was stuck on the High Street earlier today. A fight broke out when it blocked the road for others. He threw a stone at us as we passed – it hit a wall, but he was probably hoping to start a brawl between scholars and townsfolk there and then. And then I saw him quite clearly leading the mob past St Botolph's, calling to them, and keeping their mood ugly. He was also one of the seven that attacked Michael and me last week, looking for the book and its hidden documents.'

'Are you certain?' asked Michael, cautiously. 'It was very dark and you have not mentioned Ivo before.'

'Something jarred in my mind when I saw him with his cart,' said Bartholomew. 'He was out of his usual context – the only other times I have seen him have been when he was crashing about in the kitchens at David's, and suddenly, he was in the High Street with a cart, purporting to be an apple-seller. As I thought about it, and listened to his voice, I realised exactly where I had seen and heard him before. It struck me as odd.'

'But this means that David's is involved,' said Michael in

disgust. 'And I thought we had settled on Valence Marie, Godwinsson and Maud's.'

'Only one of their servants,' said Tulyet. 'But this makes sense. I saw that fight on the High Street tonight, and I had a bad feeling that my men had not broken it up sufficiently for it not to begin afresh.'

'Enough chattering,' said de Wetherset, his agitation making him uncharacteristically rude. 'Brother, take the beadles and clear the students off the streets. Bartholomew, go to Michaelhouse, and warn them that they may be about to be under siege. Master Tulyet,' he added, peering up at the Sheriff, 'could you try to prevent the looting of at least some the hostels near the Market Square? It is too late for Godwinsson, but perhaps we might save others. Heppel – perhaps you had better wait with me in the church.'

Bartholomew grabbed Michael's arm, and gave him a brief smile before they parted to go in different directions. Michael traced a benediction in the air at Bartholomew as he sped up the High Street and, after a moment's consideration, sketched one at himself. He gathered his beadles together, and set off towards the Trumpington Gate, intending to work his way along the High Street and then back along Milne Street. The Chancellor watched them go and then bundled his frightened clerks and Junior Proctor into St Mary's Church, taking care to bar the door.

Figures flitted back and forth at the junction between St Michael's Lane and the High Street, and there was a good deal of noise. Bartholomew edged closer. One man in particular, wearing a dark brown tunic, yelled threats and jeers towards little St Paul's Hostel that stood at the corner. Bartholomew, watching him, saw immediately what he was doing: St Paul's had only five students and was poor. The man was using it to work his crowd up to fever pitch, at which point they would march on nearby Michaelhouse, bigger, richer, and well worth looting.

Bartholomew ducked down one of the streets parallel to St Michael's Lane and then went along Milne Street, running as hard as he could. On reaching the opposite end of St Michael's Lane, he peered round the corner and began to head towards the sturdy gates of his College. At the same time, a great cheer went up from the crowd and Bartholomew saw them begin to march down the lane.

They saw him at the same time as he saw them – a lone scholar in the distinctive gown of a University doctor. A great howl of enraged delight went up and they began to trot towards him. Bartholomew was almost at Michaelhouse's gates when he faltered. Should he try to reach the College, or should he turn and run the other way? If he chose the latter, it would draw the mob away from Michaelhouse and they might not return. There was sufficient distance between him and the crowd so that he knew he could outrun them – and he could not imagine that such a large body of people would bother to chase him too far along the dark, slippery banks of the river. His mind made up, he did an about-face. A second yell froze his blood. The crowd had divided – perhaps so that one group could try to gain access through the orchard, while the others distracted attention by battering at the front gates. He was now trapped in the lane between two converging mobs.

Both began to surge towards him, their inhuman yells leaving him in no doubt that he was about to be ripped limb from limb. He ran the last few steps to Michaelhouse, and hammered desperately on the gates, painfully aware that his shouts for help were drowned by the howls of the rioters. A distant part of his mind recalled that the surly Walter was on night duty that week and Walter was never quick to answer the door. By the time he realised one of Michaelhouse's Fellows was locked outside, Bartholomew would be reduced to a pulp.

The crowd was almost on him and he turned to face them. The man in the brown tunic was in the lead, wielding a spitting torch. In the yellow light, his features were twisted into a mask of savage delight, revelling in his role as rabble-rouser. Around him, other faces glittered, unrecognisable – nothing but cogs in a violent machine. It was not a time for analysis but in the torch-light Bartholomew recognised the man in brown as Saul Potter, the scullion from Godwinsson.

Bartholomew screwed his eyes closed as tightly as he could, not wanting to see the violent hatred on the faces of the rioters. Some of them were probably his patients and he did not wish to know which ones would so casually turn against him. He cringed, waiting for the first blow to fall and felt the breath knocked out of him as he fell backwards. He struck out blindly, eyes still tightly closed. He felt himself hauled to his feet and given a rough shake.

'You are safe!'

Finally, Master Kenyngham's soothing voice penetrated Bartholomew's numb mind. The physician looked about him, feeling stupid and bewildered, like Lydgate had been in the church just a short time before. He was standing in Michaelhouse's courtyard, while behind him students and Fellows alike struggled to close the gate through which they had hauled him to safety.

'It was lucky you were leaning against the wicket gate,' said Gray, who was holding his arm. 'If you had been standing to one side of it, we would never have got you back.'

'It was me who heard your voice,' said Deynman, his eyes bright with pride. 'I opened the gate quickly before anyone could tell me not to and we pulled you inside.'

'No one would have told you not to open the gate, Robert,' said Master Kenyngham reproachfully. 'But your quick thinking doubtlessly saved Doctor Bartholomew's life.'

Deynman's face shone with pleasure, and Bartholomew, still fighting to calm his jangling nerves, gave him a wan smile. Despite Kenyngham's assertion, Bartholomew was far from certain the other scholars would have allowed the gates to be opened for him with a mob thundering down the lane from both directions at once, and even if they had, the merest delay would have cost him his life. Deynman's uncharacteristically decisive action had most certainly delivered Bartholomew from a most unpleasant fate. He made a mental note to try to be more patient with Deynman in the future – perhaps even to spend some time coaching him away from the others.

Bartholomew noticed one or two students rubbing bruises, and eyeing him resentfully. It had not been the mob at which he had lashed out so wildly, but his colleagues and students. He grinned at them sheepishly and most smiled back.

The scholars trying to close the wicket gate against the throng on the other side were finding it difficult. The door inched this way and that, groaning on its hinges against the pressure of dozens of sweating bodies on either side.

'The door!' shouted Master Kenyngham, and Deynman and Gray hurried to assist their friends. 'And ring the bell! Other scholars may come to our aid.'

'No!' cried Bartholomew. Kenyngham looked at him in astonishment, while Bartholomew tried to steady his voice. 'Brother Michael is trying to keep the scholars off the streets in the hope that, with no one to fight, the rioters will disperse.'

He glanced around him. There were perhaps thirty students and commoners at Michaelhouse, and seven Fellows including the Master, as well as six servants and Agatha the laundress. Although there were at least twice that number in the horde outside, Bartholomew thought that with the aid of Michaelhouse's sturdy walls and gates, they could hold out against the rioters. Kenyngham, however, appeared bewildered by the situation and his appalled passivity was doing nothing to improve their chances.

'May I make some suggestions, Master Kenyngham?' Bartholomew asked him urgently. The other Fellows clustered around anxiously.

Kenyngham fixed him with a troubled stare. 'No, Matthew. Michaelhouse has always had good relations with the town and I do not want to jeopardise that by meeting its inhabitants with violence. I will climb on to the gate and try to talk reason to these people. They will leave when I point out the folly of their ways.'

Bartholomew regarded him uncertainly, while the more pragmatic Father William let out a snort of derision and jabbed a meaty finger towards the gate behind which the crowd howled in fury.

'Listen to them, man! That is not a group of people prepared to listen to reason. That is a mob intent on blood and looting!'

'They will be more likely to shoot you down than to listen to you,' agreed Father Aidan, flinching as a stone hurled from the lane landed near him in a puff of dust.

'Perhaps we could toss some coins to them,' suggested Alcote hopefully. 'Then they would scramble for them and forget about looting us.'

William gave him a pained look. 'Foolish Carmelite,' he muttered under his breath, just loud enough for Alcote to hear. 'What an absurd suggestion! Typical of one of your Order!'

'I suspect that would only serve to convince them that we have wealth to spare,' said Bartholomew quickly, seeing a row about to erupt between William and Alcote.

'You are quite right, Matt,' said Aidan. 'But we must decide what we can do to prevent the mob entering the College. What do you have in mind, Master?'

All eyes turned to Kenyngham, who had been listening to

the exchange with growing despondency. 'Do none of you agree with me that we can avert such an incident by talking to these people?'

Alcote yelped as a pebble, thrown from the lane, struck him on the shoulder, and Bartholomew raised an arm to protect his head from a rain of small missiles that scattered around him.

'What do you think, man?' demanded William aggressively. 'Talking would be next to useless – if you could even make yourself heard over the row. For once, Master Kenyngham, all your Fellows are in agreement. We need to defend ourselves – by force if need be – or that rabble will break down our gates and that will be the end of us.'

Kenyngham took a deep breath. 'Very well. Tell me what you have in mind, Matthew. I am a scholar, not a soldier, and I freely admit to feeling unequal to dealing with the situation. But please try to avoid violence, if at all possible.'

Bartholomew quickly glanced around him again. The students had finally managed to close and bar the gate and were standing panting, congratulating each other, ignoring the enraged howls of the mob outside. But they would not be secure for long. Bartholomew began to bark orders.

'Agatha, take all the servants, and find as many water containers as possible. Fill them from the well and be ready to act if they try to set us on fire. Alcote and Aidan, take a dozen students and make sure the College is secure at the rear. Post guards there. If the crowd breaks through into the orchard, do not try to stop them, but retreat into the servants' quarters. Father William, take the Franciscans to the servants' quarters and gather as many throwable items together as you can: stones, sticks, apples – anything will do. We might have to defend the back if the mob gets into the orchard. The rest of you, collect stones that can be thrown from the wall at the front. Pull down the stable if you need to.'

All, unquestioning, sped off to do his bidding, while Bartholomew considered the front of Michaelhouse. The gates were sturdy enough, but they would be unable to withstand attack for long if the mob thought to use a battering ram of some kind. He sent Bulbeck and Gray in search of anything that might be used to barricade the door, while he clambered up the side of the gate and on to the wall to look down at the surging mob below.

Michaelhouse had been founded thirty years before by a chancellor of Edward II, who was well aware that his academic institution might come under threat by a resentful local population at some point in the future. Michaelhouse's walls were strong and tall, and there was something akin to a wall-walk around the front.

The mob was eerily quiet; Bartholomew saw Saul Potter in a small clearing in the middle of them giving orders. Despite straining, Bartholomew could not hear what was said, but a great cheer from the crowd as Potter finished speaking made his blood run cold.

'I think we are in for a long night,' he said unsteadily to Kenyngham as he scrambled down. 'They are planning to attack us somehow. We must be ready.'

While Bartholomew and the students hurried to find usable missiles, the mob went ominously silent. Then an ear-splitting roar accompanied a tremendous crash against the gates, which shuddered and groaned under the impact.

Horrified, Bartholomew climbed back up the gate to the top of the wall, where a dozen or so scholars crouched there, each one armed with handfuls of small stones gathered from the yard. Deynman was enthusiastically applying himself to demolishing the derelict stable, and some very large rocks were being ferried to augment the waiting scholars' arsenals. Below, the rioters had acquired a long, heavy pole, and willing hands grabbed at it as it was hauled backwards in readiness for a second strike.

'Aim for the men holding the battering ram,' Bartholomew called to the students, looking down at the seething mass of the mob beneath, searching for Saul Potter. The battering ram had a carved end; he realised with a shock that someone had taken the centre-post from one of the river people's homes. He hoped it had not been Dunstan and Aethelbald's house that had been destroyed in the mindless urge for blood and looting.

The gates juddered a second time as the post was smashed into them, accompanied by another mighty yell from the crowd. Bartholomew saw the head of the post shatter under the impact. One man fell away with a cry as one of the splinters was driven into his side. But the crowd was oblivious to his distress and the great post was hauled back for a third punch.

Bartholomew watched as the scholars pelted the rioters with

their stones. At first, their defence seemed to make little difference, but gradually individuals in the crowd began to look up as the shower of pebbles continued to hail down on them. When a hefty rock landed on one man, the crowd wavered uncertainly. Immediately, Saul Potter was among them again.

'Our lads have breached the rear!' he yelled. An uncertain cheer went up. 'Come on, lads!' Saul Potter continued. 'Think of what will soon be yours! Silver plate, jewellery, clothes and all the University's ill-gotten gains. You will not let these snivelling scholars defeat the honest men of Cambridge, will you?'

This time the clamour was stronger. Encouraged, Saul Potter went on. 'These wretched, black-robed scholars do nothing for this town but take our women and make us paupers. Will you let the likes of them get the better of us honest folk?'

There was no mistaking the enthusiasm this time, and rioters began to peel off from the group to head for the back gate. Ordering Gray to keep up the barrage of fire from the front, Bartholomew slithered down from the wall to race to the back of the College, gathering any idle hands as he ran.

Sure enough, the mob had broken through into the orchard and were besieging the servants' quarters. Father William and his Franciscans were doing an admirable job in repelling them with a variety of missiles hurled from the upper floor, but the windows were small and allowed the defending scholars little room for manoeuvre. The crowd's reinforcements were beginning to arrive. On the lower floor, the doors were thick, but nothing like the great gates at the front. They were already beginning to give way under the rioters' kicks, despite Bulbeck's desperate attempts to block them with chests and trestle tables.

'This brings back memories,' came a quiet, lilting voice from Bartholomew's elbow.

'Cynric!' Bartholomew's delight at seeing his book-bearer up again was tempered by the sight of his drawn face under the bandage that swathed his head. 'You should not be here.' He saw Cynric held a small bow and several arrows.

'Just let me fire a few of these, boy, and I promise you I will be away to lie down like the old man I am,' said Cynric.

Bartholomew knew from the determined glitter in the Welshman's eyes that he would be unable to stop him anyway. He moved aside.

'Saul Potter,' he said. 'He is wearing a brown tunic.'

'Oh, I know Saul Potter, lad,' said Cynric, approaching the window and selecting an arrow. 'Agatha told me he was boasting in the King's Head about how he had kicked you witless last week. I was going to pay him a visit anyway. Perhaps I can settle matters with him now.'

Cynric's arm muscles bulged as he eased back the taut bowstring. He closed one eye and searched out his quarry with the other. The Franciscans had ceased their stone-throwing and were watching Cynric intently. Father William moved towards another window and began chanting a prayer in his stentorian tones. The effect on the crowd was immediate. They became still, their voices gradually faltering into silence and all faces turned to the window from where Father William's voice emanated. There was not a man in the crowd who did not recognise the words William spoke: the words spoken by priests when someone was going to die.

Saul Potter began to shout back, but his voice was no match for William's, which had been honed and strengthened by long years of describing from the pulpit the fires and brimstone of hell and the dangers of heresy.

The sound of Cynric's arrow singing through the air silenced William. It also silenced Saul Potter, who died without a sound, the arrow embedded in his chest. Cynric slumped back against the window frame with a tired but triumphant grin. Bartholomew helped him to sit down.

'I have lost none of my skill by living with these learned types,' Cynric muttered proudly. He tried to dismiss the admiring praise of the students who clustered around him, but the physician could see he was relishing every moment. Bartholomew stood to look out of the window again. Deprived of their leader, the crowd was milling around in confusion. Bartholomew made a sign to William, whose teeth flashed in one of his rare smiles. The friar took a deep breath and began chanting a second time.

The meaning was clear. As one, the crowd edged back and then began to run, leaving the body of Saul Potter behind. After a few minutes, Bartholomew took a group of scholars and scoured the orchard for lingerers. But there were none: the mob, to its last man, had fled. He left Father Aidan to secure the back gate and walked back through the orchard with William.

'Is it over?' asked William, the strong voice that had boomed over the mob hoarse with tiredness.

'It is at Michaelhouse,' said Bartholomew. 'But I can still see the glow from the fires in the rest of the town. And Michael is still out there with his frightened beadles.'

William slapped a hand on Bartholomew's back. 'Do not fear for Michael,' he said. 'He is clever and resourceful but also sensible. He will not attempt more than he knows he can achieve.'

They walked in silence, watching torches bobbing here and there among the trees, as the students still searched for hidden rioters. The immediate danger over, Bartholomew felt his legs become wobbly, and he rested his hand on the friar's shoulder after stumbling in the wet grass for the second time.

'I recognised the man Cynric killed,' said William, taking a fistful of Bartholomew's tabard to steady him. 'He is a servant from Godwinsson.'

'Yes,' said Bartholomew. His mind began to drift. He tried to imagine what Norbert might look like now, so that he might find him. He caught the end of William's sentence, and turned to face him in shock.

'I am sorry, Father. Could you repeat that?'

William clicked his tongue irritably, never patient with wandering minds. 'I was telling you, Matthew, that the University seems to be inundated with people who are not all they seem. That Godwinsson scullion was clearly no ordinary servant – it takes skill and experience to manipulate a crowd as he did and anyone with such abilities would hardly be satisfied with a position as scullion. And then I told you about my encounter with Father Andrew of David's. I told you I believe he is no Franciscan. I went to a mass of his last week and he did not know one end of his missal from the other. His Latin was disgraceful. I checked up on him with my Father Prior and learned that the only Father Andrew from Stirling in our Order died two months ago.'

Bartholomew recalled that William had been with the Inquisition for a time, an occupation that must have suited his tenacious mind. If William's suspicions had been aroused, he would not rest until they had been sufficiently allayed.

'What are you saying?' asked Bartholomew, exhaustion making his thoughts sluggish.

William sighed in exasperation. 'I will put it simply, Matthew, since your mind seems to lack its normal incisive skills. Father Andrew, friar and master of theology at David's Hostel, is an impostor.'

chapter 11

Few Michaelhouse scholars felt like sleeping as the last of the mob disappeared up St Michael's Lane. Bartholomew worked hard to buttress the main gates further and ordered the stones and sticks that the scholars had hurled from the walls to be collected to use again if necessary. Once he was satisfied that as many precautions as possible had been taken against further attack, the scholars relaxed, sitting or standing in small groups to talk in low voices.

Saul Potter's body was brought from the orchard and laid out in the conclave, where Kenyngham insisted a vigil should be kept over it.

'At least he did not die unshriven,' said Alcote maliciously. 'Father William yelled an absolution from the window in the servants' quarters before he was killed.'

Kenyngham crossed himself, his eyes fixed on the body and the arrow that still protruded from its chest. 'I asked that there be no violence,' he admonished, tearing his gaze from the corpse to Bartholomew. 'And now a man lies dead.'

'And you, Master Kenyngham, might have been lying here instead of this lout had Cynric not acted promptly,' said Agatha hotly. 'You owe your life to Cynric, Father William and Matthew.'

'But surely it could have been managed without bloodshed?' insisted Kenyngham. 'Now we have this man's death on our hands.'

'Nonsense, Master,' said William irritably. 'He brought about his own demise by his rabble-rousing. That mob intended serious mischief and Matthew's organisation of our defences and Cynric's marksmanship saved all our lives – to say nothing of the survival of the College.'

Aidan agreed. 'The College would have been in flames by now and all of us slaughtered, had the rioters gained access,' he lisped, his pale blue eyes flicking restlessly between his colleagues' faces.

'But to shoot an unarmed man in our orchard . . .' began Alcote, enjoying the dissension between the Fellows and seeking to prolong it until he could turn it to his own advantage.

'He was not unarmed!' said William loudly. 'He had a sword and a large dagger that should, by rights, be slitting your scrawny throat at this very moment. After all, you are the only one among us to own anything worth stealing. You would have been their first victim.'

'Hear, hear. And good riddance, too,' put in Agatha, eyeing Alcote with dislike.

Alcote swallowed nervously, disconcerted by the frontal attack from a combination of the forceful personalities of William and Agatha. 'But—'

'No buts,' said William firmly. 'And the man was probably a heretic anyway. At least the last thing he heard were the sacred words uttered by me. Perhaps I was his salvation.'

He glared round at the others, daring them to contradict him and then strode away to organise the students to patrol the College grounds until morning. Alcote slunk back to his room and, through the open window shutters, Bartholomew saw him unlock a chest to begin checking that none of his valuables had gone missing during the affray. Aidan knelt next to Saul Potter's body and began the vigil, while Bartholomew prepared to follow Kenyngham through the hall and down the spiral stairs to the yard. Agatha stopped him.

She poked him in the chest with a thick forefinger. 'Do not allow the Master and that loathsome Alcote to bother you, Matthew, for I am telling you what you did was right,' she said grandly. 'You, Father William and Cynric saved the College tonight. Now, I have business to attend – the kitchens do not run themselves, you know.'

She marched away, large hips swaying importantly as scholars scattered in her path. Bartholomew smiled. Agatha was of the firm belief that she was one of God's chosen because she had not been struck by the plague, and had used that belief to add credence to all manner of wild claims ever since. He supposed he should be grateful that Agatha thought his actions defensible – no Michaelhouse scholar enjoyed being in opposition to the formidable laundress, unless he did not mind clothes damaged in the wash and the worst of the food.

Outside in the yard Kenyngham took a deep breath and gazed up at the stars. 'Tonight saw some foul deeds, Matthew,' he said. 'No matter how Father William and Agatha might seek to justify them, a member of Michaelhouse murdered a townsman. How do you think the citizens of Cambridge will react to that? I, and Master Babington before me, have worked hard to establish good relations between Michaelhouse and the town, and now all is lost.'

'All might have been lost anyway had the rioters gained access to the College,' said Bartholomew. 'I agree that the death of a man in such circumstances is a terrible thing, but better Saul Potter than some of our students, or even one of the rioters. They are probably as much victims of Saul Potter's rabble-rousing as we might have been.'

Kenyngham remained unconvinced. 'This will have repercussions for months to come,' he sighed. 'How can I allow you to continue your good work in the town now? You might be slain in retaliation. Any of us might.'

'I do not think so,' said Bartholomew, stretching limbs that ached from tension and tiredness. 'The riot tonight was no random act of violence but a carefully planned event with Saul Potter at its centre. I do not think the townspeople will mourn – or seek to avenge – him once his role in all this becomes clear.'

Kenyngham eyed him doubtfully. 'I hope you are right, Matthew,' he said. 'Meanwhile, I must now ensure that none of our students slips away to take their revenge for the attack. And you should determine that Cynric has suffered no harm from all this.'

Bartholomew walked briskly to the servants' quarters to where Cynric slept peacefully. The physician smiled when he saw the book-bearer still held his bow; he imagined that Cynric might expect considerable acclaim as a hero by the students who had witnessed his shot, regardless of Kenyngham's misgivings. Bartholomew sat for the rest of the night listening to the Welshman's easy breathing as he slept, thinking over the events of the past two weeks.

Dawn came, and Bartholomew slipped out of Cynric's room to assess the damage to the gates. With Walter, he ran his hands over the splintered wood, impressed at the quality of workmanship that had withstood the assaults of the battering ram. He walked to the wharves and saw that the mob had demolished the first of the rickety structures that served as homes to the river folk in their hunt for a sturdy post. He knew that the old lady that lived there was away, and was relieved that the rioters had limited their violence to the destruction of a house and not turned it towards the people who lived nearby.

Dunstan and Aethelbald were already up and greeted him with enthusiastic descriptions of the events of the night before. Bartholomew was so grateful to see that they had been left unmolested, he did not even notice Dunstan stooping to fill his drinking cup from the river shallows.

He fetched warmed ale and oat mash for Cynric, then began to pace the yard as he waited for Michael to return. When the scholars, led by Kenyngham, went to a mass of thanksgiving for their deliverance the night before, Bartholomew asked to be excused.

After an hour, the scholars began to trickle back from St Michael's Church and made their way to the hall for breakfast. Bartholomew followed, but had no appetite, and looked up expectantly for Michael each time the door opened. Traditionally, meals were taken in silence at Michaelhouse, or eaten while the Bible scholar read tracts from religious and philosophical texts. But Master Kenyngham was lenient and often allowed intellectual debate at mealtimes, although the language was restricted to Latin. That morning, however, Bartholomew heard English, French, and even Flemish but no Latin, and the subject chosen was far from academic. Kenyngham chose to ignore it, although the Franciscans complained bitterly about the breach in discipline.

Bartholomew picked at the watery oatmeal without enthusiasm, and relinquished his portion of sour, cloudy ale to Father Aidan, who was eyeing it with undisguised interest. Bartholomew had a sudden longing for some of Mistress Tyler's fine white bread and wondered where she was and whether her daughters were safe.

The bell rang for lectures to begin, and Bartholomew tried to concentrate on his teaching. Bulbeck offered to read aloud from Isaac Iudaeus's *Liber urinarum* for the rest of the morning, and with a grateful smile, Bartholomew escaped his duties. The master mason came to report on the progress on Wilson's tomb, and Bartholomew listened patiently but without full attention to the mason's litany of complaints about the stone: it was too hard; it contained crystals that made cutting difficult; and black was a wearisome colour with which to work and really should only be carved in high summer when the light was good.

Bartholomew asked whether the marble slab should be abandoned and a cheaper, but more easily workable, material purchased instead. The mason gazed at him indignantly and claimed loftily that no stone had ever bested a craftsman of his calibre. Perplexed, Bartholomew watched him strut across the yard and then tried to apply himself to his treatise on fevers. So far, he had written five words and crossed each one out, unable to concentrate without knowing the whereabouts of his portly friend.

He had just decided to go in search of Michael himself, when the monk stepped through the wicket gate, commenting cheerily on the damage to the door and humming his way across the yard.

'Where have you been?' demanded Bartholomew, looking him over to assess any possible damages. 'Are you harmed? What of the riot? Why are you so late? I have been worried!'

'Aha!' said Michael triumphantly, pulling his arm away. 'Now you know how I feel when you disappear without telling anyone where you are going. Well, like our friend Guy Heppel, I am not a man for foolhardy bravery. I took one look at those mobs last night and took refuge with my beadles in the first University building I came across. If there were scholars insane enough to be abroad last night, then it would have taken more than me and my men to persuade them back to safety. I spent the night at Peterhouse, safe in a fine feather bed with a bottle of excellent wine to help me sleep. The Master was most hospitable and insisted I stay for breakfast.'

He rubbed at his ample girth with a grin. Bartholomew groaned, feeling exhausted. While he had fretted all night, worrying that Michael might be in the thick of violent fighting, the Benedictine had secured himself some of the most comfortable lodgings in Cambridge.

'Do you have news of what happened?' he asked, thinking that a Peterhouse breakfast must be fine indeed if it could last until so late in the morning. He was sure it had not been watery oatmeal and sour beer.

'I saw the Chancellor on my way here. He and Heppel spent the night cowering in St Mary's Church,' Michael said with a chuckle. 'Courage is not a quality with which us University men are richly endowed, it seems. There was damage, but mostly not major. Only two University buildings came under serious attack: Michaelhouse and Godwinsson, and only Godwinsson sustained any real harm. The students fled to Maud's, so there were no casualties. David's Hostel were out and most of those fiery Scots are currently languishing in Tulyet's prison cells – they were rash enough to attempt a skirmish with his soldiers. Master Radbeche was away and Father Andrew was unable to keep them in when the excitement started, although two of them – John of Stirling and Ruthven – are still at large.'

He paused in his narrative to assure Father William, who was passing them on his way to terce, that he had survived the night intact.

'Several smaller hostels were set alight,' he continued when William had gone, 'but the fires were doused before they did any real harm. The rioters gained access to about five of them, but you know how poor most of these places are. The would-be looters looked around thinking to find riches galore and were lucky to leave with a couple of pewter plates. If hostels own anything of value at all, it is likely to be a book and the mob had no use for any of those.'

'Is the rioting over, then?'

'Oh yes. A rumour spread that Michaelhouse had shot one of the leaders and it fizzled out like a wet candle.'

'I have been thinking most of the night about the evidence we have gathered so far,' said Bartholomew, tugging at Michael's sleeve to make him walk towards the orchard. 'It is beginning to make sense but there is still much I do not understand.'

'Well, I have given it no thought at all,' said Michael airily, grabbing a handful of oatcakes from a platter in the kitchen as they walked through it. As Agatha turned and saw him, he gave her a leering wink that made her screech with laughter. On their way out, Michael looked at the neat lines of containers filled with water, sand and stones, and spare trestle tables stacked against one wall to be pushed against the back door if necessary.

'If you have been thinking as hard as you say, let us hope these precautions will no longer be necessary,' he said. He became sombre. 'We must put an end to this business, Matt.'

Bartholomew led the way to the fallen tree in the orchard and, as Michael sat on the trunk eating his oatcakes, Bartholomew paced in front of him telling him what he had reasoned.

'We need to consider two things,' he said, running a hand through his hair. 'First, we need to establish the significance of these blue-green rings. And second, we must discover the identity of Norbert.'

'What do you mean, discover his identity?' asked Michael through a mouthful of crumbs. He brushed some off his habit, where they had been sprayed as he spoke.

'He has assumed another identity,' said Bartholomew impatiently. 'Father William told me he became suspicious of Father Andrew's credentials after he had attended one of his masses. He investigated him as only an ex-member of the Inquisition knows how, and discovered that the only Father Andrew from Stirling in Franciscan records died two months ago. William believes Andrew is an impostor.'

'That gentle old man?' choked Michael. 'Never! Well, perhaps he might not be Father Andrew from Stirling but I find it hard to believe he is your Norbert.'

'There are, however, four things that suggest Andrew is not all he seems,' Bartholomew continued, ignoring Michael's reaction. He scrubbed at his face tiredly and tried to put his thoughts into a logical order. 'First, he said he comes from Stirling. Now, his students, Robert and John, are also from Stirling, claiming to be the sons of a local landlord. I do not want to go into details, but they are nothing of the kind. The towns and villages in Scotland are small and people know each other. I find it hard to believe that Andrew, if he really is from Stirling, would not know that John and Robert's family are not who they claim.'

'Perhaps he does, but is maintaining silence for the sake of these lads,' said Michael. 'It would be in keeping with his character.'

'It is possible, I suppose,' said Bartholomew, disconcerted that the first of his carefully reasoned arguments had been so easily confounded. He tried again. 'Second, when I last visited, Andrew had been writing in his room. His hands and face were covered in ink, like a child who first learns to write. No real scholar would ever make such a mess.'

'And so, because he does not know how to control his quill, you think he is not a scholar. That is weak, Matt,' warned Michael.

Bartholomew pressed on. 'Third, while all the students have alibis for Kenzie's death and Werbergh's, we did not think to ask the masters. Either Radbeche or Andrew are with the students almost every moment of the day, but where are Radbeche and Andrew when they are not acting nursemaid? We did not think to ask that.'

'That was because we had no cause to ask such a thing,' said Michael with a shrug.

'And fourth.' Bartholomew took a deep breath. 'He was the man at Chesterton tower-house who said there would be a riot last night.'

'What?' exclaimed Michael, leaping to his feet. 'You have not fully recovered your wits, my friend! That is one of the most outrageous claims I have ever heard you make! And believe me, you have made a fair few!'

'I told you the voice was familiar, but that there was something about it I could not quite place,' said Bartholomew defensively.

'And why is it that you have suddenly remembered this fact now?' asked Michael, not even trying to disguise the sarcasm in his voice.

'It is not a case of remembering,' said Bartholomew, controlling his own sudden flare of anger at Michael's casual dismissal of his revelation. 'It is a case of recognition. Andrew speaks with a Scottish accent. Well, when I overheard him in Chesterton making his proclamation about the riot, he did not. He spoke in the accent of an Englishman. It was his voice, I am certain, but I did not recognise it immediately because he usually disguises it.'

'Oh really, Matt!' said Michael, sitting back down again and stretching out his large legs in front of him. 'The late Master Wilson would be spinning in his grave to hear such wild leaps of logic!'

'Logic be damned!' said Bartholomew vehemently. 'It fits, Michael! If you put all we know together, it fits!' He sat next to the monk and gave the tree trunk a thump in exasperation. 'We know David's is involved in this business somehow. Ivo, who pre-empted yesterday's riot with his broken cart in the High Street, works at David's. Kenzie was killed, and he was at David's. And the Galen, containing the letters from Norbert to me, was from David's.'

Michael shook his head slowly. 'I accept your point that Andrew is not who he claims, but I cannot accept that he is Norbert. He is too old for a start.'

'Grey hair and whiskers always add years to a man,' said Bartholomew. 'It is probably a disguise to conceal his true age.'

'Maybe, maybe.' Michael picked up another oatcake and crammed it into his mouth so that his next words were muffled. 'But tell me about the rings. What have you reasoned there?'

'I have deduced nothing new,' admitted Bartholomew. 'But we should reconsider what we do know. There are three rings. Dominica took two of them – the lovers' rings – from Cecily, kept one for herself and gave the other to Kenzie. One of his friends is certain that the ring Kenzie had originally was of great value. But the ring that was stolen from him by Edred was the third ring and a cheap imitation of the others. At some point someone, perhaps Kenzie himself, exchanged them. Kenzie's original ring then appeared three days after his death on the relic at Valence Marie. Cecily took the other half of the pair back from Dominica when she was sent to Chesterton, and gave it to me.' He removed the ring from his sleeve and looked at it, glinting blue-green in the morning light.

Michael took it from him and twisted it around in his fingers. 'So, what you conclude from all this,' he said, 'is that the Principal of Godwinsson's ring has ended up on Valence Marie's relic via a student from David's. And that Father Andrew is at the heart of it all, on the basis of William's records and the fact that Andrew is at the same hostel that owns the Galen. Am I correct?'

Bartholomew leaned forward, resting his elbows on his knees, and closed his eyes. Now he had repeated his arguments to Michael, they sounded weak and unconvincing, whereas during the night they had seemed infallible.

'Dominica,' said Bartholomew suddenly, snapping upright. 'Where is she? If she is not dead, then where is she?'

'She was ruled by a rod of iron by two extremely unpleasant people,' said Michael. 'She saw her opportunity to escape and took it.'

'I do not think so,' said Bartholomew. 'She is still here. In fact, I am willing to wager you anything you please that we will find her at David's.'

'In a hostel?' cried Michael in disbelief. 'You are insane, my friend! Adam Radbeche would never stand for such a flouting of the University rules!'

'Well, in that case, you will have no objection to coming with me to see,' said Bartholomew, rising abruptly and striding off through the orchard. Michael followed, grumbling.

'But where is your evidence?' he panted, struggling to keep up with Bartholomew's healthy pace. 'Where is your proof?'

Bartholomew grinned mischievously. 'I suppose I have none at all, just a feeling, a hunch if you will.'

Michael made as if to demur, but could see the determination in his friend's face and knew there was little he could do to dissuade Bartholomew from visiting David's. All he could hope to do was to minimise any damage Bartholomew might cause by wild accusations.

The signs of the previous night's rioting were obvious as they hurried along the High Street to Shoemaker Lane, but the damage was mostly superficial and already much had been cleared away. None of the townspeople's houses or shops had been attacked. The rioters had concentrated on University property. Bartholomew was puzzled. If he were to attack the University he would not choose Michaelhouse, one of the largest and strongest of the University's properties or some small and impoverished institution like St Paul's Hostel. He would pick those places that were known to be wealthy and not particularly well fortified – like Maud's. He would also attack St Mary's Church, since it was perhaps the most prominent of the University's buildings, and look for the University chest where all the valuables were kept. But Michael said that St Mary's had not been touched.

He frowned. The only explanation he could find was that the leaders of the riot did not want to inflict serious damage on the University. In which case, what was their motive? Now the curfew on the townspeople would be imposed more harshly than ever, entry into the town would become more rigidly controlled, and legal trading times would be curtailed. Also, the Sheriff would have to hang some of the rioters he caught as a deterrent to others, and there would be taxes to pay for the damage. After the previous night's riot, the townspeople would suffer more than the University.

He tried to clear his thoughts as they approached David's. Its strong door had been torn from its hinges and there were scratches along the wall where something had been forced along it. There was no reply to Michael's knock, so they entered uninvited. Bartholomew called Radbeche's name, but his voice bounced back at him through the empty corridor.

He hammered on the door at the end of the passageway that led to the large chamber where lessons took place, and shouted again. There was no reply, so he opened it, stepped inside and looked around.

The cosy room at David's, with its ancient, patterned window-shutters and warm smell of cooking food, was deserted. Bartholomew walked slowly to look over the other side of the table. Master Radbeche lay there, his throat cut so deeply that Bartholomew thought he could see bone beneath the glistening blood.

'Is Dominica there?' came Michael's voice from behind him.

'No,' said Bartholomew shortly. Michael elbowed him out of the way impatiently, but let out a gasp of shock when he saw Radbeche's body.

'Oh, Lord!' he exclaimed in a whisper. 'What happened to him?'

'It seems as though someone cut his throat,' replied Bartholomew dryly. 'With considerable vigour, by the look of it.'

'My question was rhetorical, Matt,' said the monk testily. 'As well you know.' He gazed down at the red-headed philosopher. 'Poor Radbeche! What could he ever have done to warrant such violence? The University will be a poorer place without his sharp intelligence.'

He shuddered as Bartholomew began to examine Radbeche's body. The Principal of David's had been dead for several hours – perhaps even before the riot had started, when Bartholomew had been talking with Lydgate and Michael in the church. Bartholomew sat back on his heels and looked around the room. He saw that the small door that led to the kitchen and storerooms was ajar, and picked his way across the floor towards it. The doorknob was sticky and Bartholomew's hand came away stained red with blood. He gritted his teeth against his rising revulsion, took a hold of it again, turning it slowly and pushing open the door. In the kitchen, pans had been knocked from their hooks on the wall and someone had kicked charred logs from the fire across the room. Bartholomew walked to the small storeroom beyond, shoving aside a strip of hanging leather that served as a door.

Alistair Ruthven sat on the floor cradling John of Stirling in his arms. At first, Bartholomew thought they were both

dead, since their faces were so white and their clothes so
bloodstained. But, slowly, Ruthven turned a stricken face
towards Bartholomew and tried to stand.

Bartholomew lifted John off Ruthven and set him gently on
the floor.

'Are you injured?' asked Bartholomew, looking to where
Ruthven hovered nervously.

Ruthven shook his head. 'I was not here when this happened.
John is dead,' he added, looking at his friend on the floor.
He suddenly looked about him wildly. 'Who could have done
this?' he wailed. 'Master Radbeche and John are dead and I
only escaped because I pretended to be dead, too.' His eyes
glazed, he stumbled into the hall.

'Stop him!' said Bartholomew urgently to Michael. With a
blood-curdling howl, Ruthven dropped to his knees and brought
clenched fists up to his head. 'He will become hysterical,' said
Bartholomew warningly. 'Take him outside, quickly. And send
word for the Austin Canons to come for John.'

With Michael's large arms wrapped around him, Ruthven
staggered along the corridor to the street. Bartholomew bent
back to John who, despite Ruthven's claim, was certainly not
dead. He suspected that a good deal of the blood had probably
come from Radbeche, for when he pulled away the lad's shirt
to inspect the wound, it was superficial.

John's eyes flickered open as Bartholomew slid a rug under
his head, rummaged in his bag for clean linen and set about
binding the gash.

'Am I going to die?' he whispered. 'Or am I dead already?'

'Neither,' said Bartholomew, smiling reassuringly. 'This is
little more than a scratch. You will be perfectly all right in a
day or two.'

'But all that blood!' He swallowed hard and looked at the
physician with a desperate expression.

'Lie still,' said Bartholomew gently. 'I think you must have
fainted.'

John smiled wanly, his eyes fixed on Bartholomew's face.
'The sight of blood makes me dizzy. It was bad enough seeing
Master Radbeche's, but someone came at me in the dark, and
then I saw some of my own.'

'So, what happened?' asked Bartholomew, cradling the student's head so that he could sip some water. 'Did you see who
attacked you?'

John shook his head, his face suddenly fearful. 'But I think it was Father Andrew. I think he killed Master Radbeche!'

'Start at the beginning,' said Bartholomew, not wanting his jumble of facts to become more confused by John's wild speculations. 'Tell me exactly what happened.'

'I went out at sunset with Father Andrew to buy bread, although Master Radbeche had gone away for the night, and I was surprised that Father Andrew would leave the others unsupervised. Anyway, Father Andrew met Father William from Michaelhouse, and they started to argue, so he told me to buy the bread on my own.'

If Radbeche was supposed to be away, thought Bartholomew, what was he doing lying dead in the kitchen?

John sipped some more water before resuming. 'It was the first time I had been allowed out alone for so long and so I determined to make the most of it. I met some friends and it was dark by the time I returned. There was a crowd of people outside the hostel, throwing stones and insults up at the windows and two people were stealing the door. I knew the others must have gone out, because they would never have allowed the hostel to come under attack like that without retaliating had they been in. I hid in the shadows of the runnel opposite, and watched.'

He paused again. 'After a while, Father Andrew approached. He addressed the people confidently as though he had done so many times before. The leader of the mob just led them away, like children. I was about to run into the hostel after Father Andrew, when I thought about what he had done: he had given the rioters orders and they had obeyed without question. His voice was different. I am not sure . . .'

'He no longer sounded Scottish?' asked Bartholomew.

'Yes!' exclaimed John. 'That was what was different! His voice was his own, but he sounded like a someone from here. I always thought his accent was not from Stirling.'

'Then what?' asked Bartholomew gently, helping the student to sit up.

John took a shuddering breath. 'After talking to the mob, Father Andrew went inside David's, but left again moments later. I came in and found . . . Master Radbeche . . . dead with . . . As I stood looking at him I felt a pain in my chest and I looked down and saw . . .' He shuddered and Bartholomew was afraid he might faint again. He eased the student back against the wall and gave him more water.

After a few moments, John began to speak again. 'I fainted and when I came round Alistair Ruthven was with me. He had been with me all night – he could not get out because of the rioters, although I tried to persuade him to leave in case Father Andrew came back. He had escaped by hiding upstairs.'

'But you did not see Father Andrew kill Radbeche,' said Bartholomew, 'or who attacked you.'

'No, but Father Andrew went into the hostel and then came out again. It must have been him!'

Bartholomew shook his head. 'That cannot be possible. You said Father Andrew came from elsewhere when he addressed the mob, and you had noticed that the hostel seemed abandoned. Radbeche must already have been dead when Father Andrew entered.'

'Then why did he not cry for help when he found Master Radbeche dead?' asked John, regarding Bartholomew with his dark, solemn eyes.

'I did not say that he is not involved, only that he probably did not kill Radbeche while you watched from outside,' said Bartholomew. He sat back and thought.

Andrew had met Father William at sunset. William could well have confronted him about the fact that he knew Andrew was not whom he claimed to be, and so Andrew must have realised that he had to complete whatever business he was involved in quickly. Meanwhile, the Scottish students had probably escaped the hostel as soon as Andrew had left them unchaperoned, taking quick advantage of their sudden chance of freedom, and Radbeche had arrived back to find the hostel deserted. So, either Andrew had killed Radbeche, left and come back again to be seen by John, or another person had done the slaying.

'Perhaps it was Norbert.' Bartholomew spoke aloud without intending to.

'Norbert?' said John, looking at him in confusion. 'You think Norbert might have killed him?'

'Do you know Norbert?' asked Bartholomew in astonishment.

'Well, yes,' said John. 'Not well, of course, him being a servant and newly arrived. But I know him. I cannot say I like him, though – he is surly and rude. And he smells.'

'What does he look like?' asked Bartholomew, wondering whether he would be able to recognise Norbert from a description twenty-five years after their last meeting.

'He is always dirty,' said John, 'and he wears a piece of cloth swathed around his head. We always say he looks like a Saracen, especially because his face is nearly always black with dirt. He usually wears lots of clothes, even in the heat, bundled round him in the way that beggars do in winter. Father Andrew brought him here about a week ago to work in the kitchens. He told us he was a mute and that we should leave him be.'

'How old?' said Bartholomew, feeling excitement rising.

'Perhaps sixteen or seventeen,' came the disappointing answer. 'It was hard to tell with all that dirt. Master Radbeche said if he were to stay, he had to wash, but Father Andrew begged for him to be left alone.'

'I bet he did,' said Bartholomew, a sudden flash of inspiration coming to him. 'Tell me, John, did you ever see James Kenzie's lover, Dominica?'

'No,' said John, his face clouding. 'But he talked about her: fair hair, blue-green eyes.'

'And what were Norbert's eyes like?' asked Bartholomew.

John looked at him with a slack mouth. 'Blue-green,' he said. 'Startling – the only nice thing about him. But surely you cannot believe . . .' He was silent for a moment, plucking at the edges of his bandage. 'There is probably something you should know.'

'What?' asked Bartholomew warily, sensing he was about to be told something of which he would not approve.

John shot him a guilty glance. 'I did not consider it important before, and anyway, Father Andrew ordered me not to tell.'

'Tell what?' said Bartholomew, spirits sinking.

'A couple of weeks ago, Father Andrew told me that if I were to borrow Jamie's ring, which he said was one of a pair of lovers' rings, he would pray over it that the relationship between Jamie and Dominica would finish. I liked Jamie, and agreed with Father Andrew that he would be better not seeing Dominica any more.'

'And he said that praying over the ring would cause this relationship to end?' asked Bartholomew, surprised. 'How peculiar! It is almost as bad as consulting the stars!'

John looked at him oddly before continuing. 'I borrowed Jamie's ring when he took it off to clean out some drains. Father Andrew kept it for several days and poor Jamie nearly went mad searching for it. When he eventually returned it, I lied and told Jamie I had found it between the floorboards because Father Andrew had made me promise not to tell him what we had done. He said it was for Jamie's own good that he should not know.'

Bartholomew groaned. 'I wish you had told us this a week ago, John,' he said. 'It would have helped us more than you can possibly imagine.'

John's face crumpled with remorse. 'I am sorry! I did not see how it could be important, and I had promised Father Andrew that I would not tell. It is only now, when Father Andrew seems to have been pretending to be something he is not, that I feel free to break my promise.'

'When I last visited David's, Father Andrew said that he did not know Jamie had a lover, and that he certainly did not know it was Dominica.'

'Then he was not telling you the truth. He knew all about Dominica, although I do not know who told him – it was not me.'

'Why did you not tell me that Father Andrew was lying at the time?'

'I did not hear him make any such claim to you. I was cleaning the yard on Monday and only heard the last part of your conversation, while the first time you came, I was with my sick brother upstairs. Believe me, I would have exposed him as a liar had I heard him say he knew nothing about Jamie's romance!'

'Did you tell anyone else about this peculiar plan to pray over the ring?'

'No. Father Andrew ordered me not to. I did not even tell Robert, my brother. He would not have approved of my stealing from Jamie anyway, even if it was for his own good.'

As Bartholomew helped him to sit, the colour drained from his face as he glimpsed the blood on the front of his shirt. Bartholomew had encountered people who were overly sensitive before, but none of them had been as feeble as poor John of Stirling. No wonder the lad had been insensible half the night! He made the Scot lie down again, his mind whirling with questions and fragmented pieces of information. What confused Bartholomew most was the relationship between Norbert and the disguised Dominica. It was too much of a coincidence that Bartholomew should have found copies of letters written years before, and Dominica just happened to be in the hostel where they had been concealed using the alias of Norbert. He racked his brain for answers, but every solution he could produce seemed flawed in some way.

He thought about Radbeche, who was supposed to have been away, but had returned only to die. Was he involved in the riot somehow? And perhaps most importantly of all, where was Father Andrew now that his hostel was abandoned and his Principal murdered?

It was not long before the Austin Canons from St John's Hospital came to help John away. Michael was waiting for Bartholomew outside and told him that Ruthven had been dispatched to inform the Chancellor that Radbeche had been murdered. Bartholomew was concerned.

'Was it wise to let the lad go on his own? He was deeply shocked by what had happened.'

'I released him into the care of one of Tulyet's sergeants,' said Michael. 'The one whose son you cured of an arrow wound last year. He will look after him, and I thought it best to get him as far away from David's as possible.'

'So, what did he tell you?' asked Bartholomew, still doubtful as to the wisdom of Michael's decision.

'Nothing much,' said Michael. 'As soon as Father Andrew took John off to buy bread, thus leaving the students without a nursemaid for the first time in days, they took advantage of it. All were out of the hostel before Father Andrew had scarce turned the corner, although Ruthven remained behind to study.'

'Ruthven and Davy Grahame are the two who seem most interested in learning,' said Bartholomew. 'The others would rather be away cattle-rustling.'

'You have been reading too much of the rantings of this English astrologer who casts national horoscopes,' said Michael admonishingly. 'Such a bigoted comment is unworthy of you. As I was saying, Father Andrew was barely out of Shoemaker Row when the David's lads were away, looking to enjoy themselves for a night on the town. Shortly afterwards, the riot broke out. Ruthven heard a mob gathering and objects were hurled at the windows. Terrified, he fled upstairs and hid under the pile of mattresses. He is not sure how long he remained there, but he only emerged when all was quiet. He found Radbeche dead and John mortally wounded. He sat with John until he died, and was too frightened to move until we arrived.'

'We should tell him John is not dead,' said Bartholomew.

'He just fainted at the sight of his own blood. Many people are affected in that way, although John's aversion is unusually powerful.'

'Did John tell you anything we did not already know?'

Bartholomew summarised what John had said as they waited for Guy Heppel to arrive and take charge of Radbeche's body. Heppel was, as usual, white-faced and wheezing.

'This is a dreadful business,' he gasped. 'Murders and mayhem. No wonder God sent the plague to punish us if the rest of England is like Cambridge!'

'Are you ill?' asked Bartholomew, concerned by the man's pallor.

'I feel quite dreadful,' replied Heppel, raising a hand to his head. 'I must have that consultation with you as soon as possible. I should not have gone to that Founder's Feast of yours without it, because I have not been myself ever since.'

'Did you eat any fish giblets at Michaelhouse?' asked Bartholomew suspiciously.

Heppel gripped his stomach and flashed him a guilty glance. 'I have always been rather partial to fish livers and you did not tell me why I should avoid them, specifically. You said Saturn was ascendant and that I should take more of the medicine you gave me, but that had nothing to do with fish livers.'

'I told you to avoid them because I knew they were bad.'

'Not because of Saturn?' asked Heppel. 'And not because Jupiter will be dominant later in the week?'

'Jupiter will not be dominant this week,' said Bartholomew, thinking to comfort him. 'Mars will.'

'Mars!' breathed Heppel, sagging against a wall weakly. 'Worse still! Once I see this corpse to the church, I shall return to my room and lie down before I take a serious sickness.'

'See?' demanded Bartholomew of Michael as they set off back towards the High Street, leaving Heppel and two beadles to take Radbeche's corpse to nearby Holy Trinity Church. 'Astrology is nothing but hocus pocus! Heppel imagined himself to be far worse when he thought Mars was dominant. And the truth of the matter is that Mars will be nothing of the sort. I made it up thinking it would make him feel better.'

'You should know better than to mess with Heppel's stars,' said Michael. 'And you don't lie! What has got into you? Have you been taking lessons from Gray?'

'Heppel is an odd fellow,' said Bartholomew, glancing back to where the Junior Proctor had his mouth covered with his pomander as he supervised the removal of Radbeche's body. 'Sometimes I wonder whether he is all he seems.'

'Who is in this town? We have old men pretending to be friars, rabble-rousers pretending to be scullions, and Principal's daughters pretending to be boys – not to mention the extremes to which prostitutes will go to slip into colleges.' He cast a sidelong glance at Bartholomew. 'The only people I am sure about are you and me. And even you have been revealing a different aspect of your character over these last few days with your indecent obsessions with all these harlots. You have become like a Mohammedan with his harem.'

Bartholomew sighed heavily. 'I have decided to have done with all that. One, or possibly two, members of my harem, as you put it, tried to kill me, while the other can only talk to me without causing a scandal if she dresses as an old lady.'

'Yes, you have shown an appalling lack of judgement in your choices,' said Michael bluntly. 'But you should not despair. Perhaps I can arrange one or two ladies . . .'

'Here comes Heppel again,' said Bartholomew. 'Now what? I wonder what caused him to leave Radbeche.'

'He has probably found out you have lied to him about Mars, and is coming to accuse you of heresy.'

Heppel's pale face was glistening under its habitual sheen of sweat. 'Master Lydgate is dying,' he gasped. 'A soldier has just informed me that he is at Godwinsson and recommends that you go there immediately before it is too late.'

'Oh, Lord, Matt!' groaned Michael, turning away from the Junior Proctor to hurry towards Godwinsson. 'It is all beginning to come together. Someone's master plan has been set in motion, and it is playing itself out.'

'But we still do not know what this master plan is,' Bartholomew pointed out, keeping pace with the monk. 'And, as has been true all along with this wretched affair, the more information we gather, the less clear matters become. How did Lydgate allow himself to be drawn into it after our discussion last night? It was obvious there was some kind of danger.'

Michael raised his eyebrows. 'As we know, Master Lydgate is not overly endowed with powers of reasoning. Come on. We should not dally if the man is dying.'

Bartholomew glanced behind him to where Heppel was

almost bent double, trying to catch his breath, fanning himself
with his hand. All Bartholomew's doubts about him bubbled
to the forefront of his mind yet again.

'That man is far too unhealthy for proctorial duties,' he com-
mented. 'I still cannot imagine what possessed the Chancellor
to make such a choice.'

'Since you ask, Matt, I made inquiries about Guy Heppel
while I was at Peterhouse last night. He is one of the King's
spies, planted here to see whether anything subversive is
underway.'

'Really?' asked Bartholomew, not surprised to learn that
Heppel had another role, but astonished that it was one of
such importance.

'After everyone else had gone to bed, I seized the opportunity to glance at one or two documents in the Peterhouse
muniments chest – the Chancellor often stores some of his
sensitive papers there in order to keep them from certain
members of his staff.'

'Such as you?' asked Bartholomew.

'Of course not such as me!' said Michael, offended. 'I am
one of his most trusted advisers.'

'Then why did he not tell you about Heppel?'

'I imagine he knew I would find out anyway,' said Michael
airily. 'Perhaps he thought it might provide me with an intellectual challenge.'

Bartholomew gave him a sidelong glance, wondering whether
he would ever understand the peculiarities of the University
administration.

Michael continued. 'It was all there in black and white.
Heppel is here as an agent of the King and his mission is
to detect why the town is so uneasy this year.'

'I would have credited the King with more common sense
than to plant a spy who stands out like a diseased limb,' said
Bartholomew. 'Heppel wears his cowardice like a banner –
hardly a trait to make him a suitable Junior Proctor.'

'It is not your place to question the King, Matthew,' said
Michael firmly. 'Again, I tell you, watch your words or you will
be accused of treason as well as heresy. Ah! Here we are.'

Godwinsson's once-fine building had been reduced to little
more than a shell. Its strong timbers were blackened and
charred and fire had blown the expensive glass out of the
windows. It littered the street below, causing considerable risk

to those who walked barefoot. One of Tulyet's sergeants waited for them and directed them to the solar.

Inside the hostel the fine tapestries had gone – those not burned had been ripped from the walls by looters. Chests lay overturned, and anything not considered worth taking had been left strewn across the floor. Even the woollen rugs had been stolen so that Bartholomew's footsteps echoed eerily in the room where sound had once been muffled by the richness of its furnishings.

Lydgate was sprawled on the floor. One arm was draped across his stomach and a thin trickle of blood oozed from the corner of his mouth. Bartholomew grabbed a partly burned rug and eased it under the man's head, trying to straighten his limbs to make him more comfortable. Michael began to drone prayers for the dying, his alert eyes darting around the room suggesting that he was more concerned with clues to find Lydgate's killer than with his eternal rest.

Lydgate started to speak, and Michael leaned towards him, expecting a confession. Bartholomew, respecting his privacy, moved away and went to fetch a jug of water with which he might moisten the man's parched lips.

When he returned, Michael was kneeling on the floor. 'Master Lydgate maintains he has been poisoned,' he said.

Bartholomew stared at him. 'How? By whom?'

Michael flapped a hand towards a cup that lay on the floor. Bartholomew picked it up and inspected it carefully. It had held wine, but there was a bitter smell to it and a grittiness in the dregs. He would need to test it, but Bartholomew thought it was probably henbane. The cup was sticky, which meant that there had been enough time since Lydgate had drunk the wine for it to dry, leaving the tacky residue. Therefore, it was not the same powerful poison that had killed Edred, or Lydgate would never have finished his wine without beginning to feel ill.

'I have things I must say,' Lydgate whispered hoarsely. 'Before I die. I must reveal my killer, bitter though that might be, and I must set certain things straight.'

'Can you give him an antidote?' asked Michael, sensing that Lydgate had a good deal to say, and afraid the man might die before he finished.

Bartholomew shook his head. 'There is nothing I can do. It is too late and there is no antidote that I know.'

'Poisons aren't your strong point, are they?' said Michael, somewhat maliciously.

Bartholomew winced, thinking of Edred. 'Do you know who did this to you?' he asked Lydgate, slipping off his tabard to cover the dying man. 'Was it Norbert?'

'I wish it had been,' breathed Lydgate. 'I wish to God it had been. But, for my sins, it was Dominica.'

'Dominica?' exclaimed Michael. 'I thought she was supposed to be the decent member of the family! Now we find out that she is a poisoner?'

Bartholomew thought quickly. Dominica was certainly alive – John's story proved that – and, if she had been driven to living in the hostel of her dead lover disguised as a servant, then she may very well feel bitter towards the father whose domineering nature had forced her there in the first place. But was she bitter enough to kill him?

'Dominica,' said Lydgate softly. He waved away the potion Bartholomew had made for him to ease his discomfort. 'I feel no pain, only a coldness and a tingling in my limbs. I must make my confession now, before this poison takes my voice. Stay, Bartholomew. You might as well listen, too. My only problem is that I do not know where to start.'

'Try the beginning,' said Michael. He sensed he was in for a lengthy session with the dying Principal, and glanced anxiously out of the window at the sky. He had a great deal to do and knew he should not spend too much time listening to the ramblings of the mortally ill – especially since Lydgate had already named his killer. Bartholomew also had patients waiting who had been injured during the night's upheavals, and he needed to be with people he could help, not those with one foot and four toes already in the grave.

'Shall I start at the very beginning?' asked Lydgate huskily.

'Well, start at the onset of events that led to your . . .' Michael paused, uncertain which word to use.

'Then I must take you back twenty-five years,' said Lydgate. Michael stifled a sigh, reluctant to sit through another tedious dive into local history, but obliged to do so since the man was making his final confession. Oblivious or uncaring, Lydgate continued. 'I was not entirely honest with you last night. You see, I did not burn the tithe barn, Simon d'Ambrey did.'

Bartholomew had thought he was beyond being surprised by Lydgate, but this latest statement truly confounded him. He wondered whether Lydgate was still in command of all his faculties, that perhaps the henbane had affected his mind.

'But half the town witnessed Simon d'Ambrey's death the day before the barn burned,' he protested. 'Myself included.'

'Then half the town, yourself included, was mistaken,' said Lydgate, a waspish edge to his voice. 'I also witnessed what I thought to be d'Ambrey's death, but we were all wrong. It was not Simon d'Ambrey who died that night at the hands of the King's soldiers, but his brother – the cause of d'Ambrey's downfall. D'Ambrey dedicated his life to preventing injustice, but his brother proved to be dishonest and stole the money intended for the poor. D'Ambrey himself was accused of the thefts and the townspeople were quick to believe the accusations. But it was d'Ambrey's brother who died in the King's Ditch.'

'This news will put a different slant on Thorpe's relic business,' said Michael, inappropriately gleeful given he was hearing a death-bed confession. 'He has the thieving hand of d'Ambrey's brother, a pretty criminal!'

'D'Ambrey went from being adored by the townspeople, to being despised as a thief within a few hours,' Lydgate continued softly. 'But he was clever. He led the soldiers to his house and told his brother – the root of all his problems – that the soldiers were coming not for him, but for his brother, and that he should run. He lent him his own cloak as a disguise and then sent him off. Everyone knew d'Ambrey's green and gold cloak and the soldiers spotted it in an instant. They chased after his brother like a pack of dogs. You know the rest of the story. He reached the Ditch, an arrow took him in the throat and he drowned. His body was never found.'

He stopped speaking, and Michael began to fidget restlessly, casting anxious glances at the sun and keen to be about his business.

'But what of Simon?' asked Bartholomew. He wondered how much of Lydgate's story could be true. He, with so many others, had seen Simon d'Ambrey on the bank of the King's Ditch, his cloak billowing around him. He recalled vividly the copper hair whipping around his face as he looked back at his pursuers. Bartholomew thought again. The copper hair was what he remembered, along with the green cloak with its crusader's cross on the back. He had not actually seen the man's face, and he had been a fair distance away watching in poor light, even with a child's sharp eyes. If Simon and his brother looked anything alike, it would have been possible to mistake one for the other in the fading daylight.

Lydgate coughed, and Bartholomew helped him sip some water. After a moment, the Principal of Godwinsson nodded that he was able to continue.

'Simon took the opportunity to escape. He was expecting his brother to be recognised, and a search sent out for him, but that did not happen – his ruse had worked more perfectly than he could have dared hope. Rather than set out immediately in pursuit of his fleeing household, and run the risk of meeting the three burgesses who were charged with hunting them down, d'Ambrey hid for a night or two in Trumpington.'

He paused, and Michael cleared his throat noisily. 'An interesting conjecture, Master Lydgate, but we must think about your absolution. Time is short. Do you repent of your sins?'

Lydgate looked at him, some of his old belligerence returning. 'You will allow a dying man the courtesy of completing his tale in his own time, Brother,' he whispered harshly. He coughed again, then continued, his voice growing weaker, so that Bartholomew and Michael had to strain to hear.

'At the time, I was betrothed to Cecily. It was not my choice, and hers neither. But the contract was sealed and we were bound by it. The day after d'Ambrey's supposed death, I saw Cecily enter the tithe barn and leave some time later. I went into the barn myself, hoping she might have a lover there. If that were the case, I might yet escape the marriage contract that I did not want. D'Ambrey was there, leaning back in the straw like a contented cat. It was quite clear what they had been doing and, even though it was in my interests to be glad he was Cecily's lover, I was moved to anger by his gloating. He told me how he had escaped, and I knew he would not allow me to leave the barn alive. We fought, but a lamp was knocked over and the barn began to burn. Then he hit his head against a post and I could not rouse him. I panicked and fled.'

Raised voices from outside distracted him momentarily, but they died away, and the house was silent once more. Lydgate continued with his tale, sweat beading on his face. Bartholomew wiped it away.

'I told my father everything. He said the marriage contract would stand anyway, and that I should conceal Cecily's indiscretions unless I wanted to be branded a cuckold. He suggested we accuse Norbert of starting the fire, since using him as a scapegoat, rather than someone else, would precipitate no feuds or ill-feelings among the villagers.'

'Most noble,' retorted Bartholomew, unable to stop himself. 'So Norbert was blamed so that you would not be seen to have an unfaithful wife, and Cecily would not be labelled a whore?' He stood abruptly and paced. 'He was a child, Lydgate! They were going to hang him!'

Lydgate shrugged painfully. 'You saved him.'

'What a dire tale,' said Michael unsympathetically. 'No wonder Norbert has returned to wreak havoc on the town.'

'But no body was found in the barn,' said Bartholomew, trying to rationalise Lydgate's story. The whole event, now he knew the truth of it, had an unsavoury feel, and he did not like the notion that he had protected the identity of a murderer for the last twenty-five years.

'The fire caused such an inferno that metal nails and bolts melted in the heat,' breathed Lydgate, swallowing hard. 'A body would never have been identified from that mess.'

'So, you were responsible for the death of Simon d'Ambrey?' asked Michael. 'Is that the essence of this lengthy tale? I take it you confessed to burning the tithe barn yesterday because you knew that was the crime of which Matt believed you were guilty?'

Lydgate nodded, and then shook his head. 'I became confused. The blackmail notes mentioned the burning of the tithe barn, and hinted at the murder of d'Ambrey while he was trapped in it. I was going to confess to both of them to you last night. Then I realised that you did not know about the murder, only about the fire. I did not see why I should have to confess to that sort of thing when I did not have to, so I just allowed myself to be guided by you, and told you only about the fire.'

'What a mess!' said Michael. 'These notes must have been very carefully worded if you were not certain whether they threatened to expose you for murder or arson.'

Out of the corner of his eye, Bartholomew saw something move. It was a shadow in the interconnecting passage between the two Godwinsson houses. Bartholomew, who had been taken unawares by it once before, was not fooled a second time, and darted forward to seize the person who hid there. Cecily gave a cry as she was unceremoniously hauled into the solar. She stared down at her prostrate husband, several blackened pieces of jewellery dangling from her fingers.

Lydgate saw her and gave a ghastly smile. 'My loving wife! It is not my impending death that brings you home, but your treasure.'

'I thought I should see what I could salvage,' she said coldly. 'Fortunately, I hid most of my belongings well.'

So much for her 'meagre inheritance', her 'paltry jewels', thought Bartholomew, eyeing the fistfuls of treasure in some disgust. No wonder she had been so concerned in Chesterton when she heard her room had been ransacked.

'Do you have everything?' asked Lydgate with heavy irony. 'Or shall I help you look?'

'You might tell me where you kept that silver chain,' said Cecily, before she realised he was not sincere. 'Have you seen that little gold crucifix of my father's? I cannot find it.'

'The last time I saw that, it was being fingered by Brother Edred,' said Lydgate maliciously. 'I imagine he stole it after you ran away. He was always covetous of that cross.'

'Why did you not demand it back?' cried Cecily, appalled.

Lydgate shifted weakly in what might have been a shrug. 'These things are no longer important to me, Cecily. I let him keep it, hoping it might throttle him in his sleep.' His words were becoming indistinct, and speaking was clearly an effort now.

'Your husband has only a short time left,' said Bartholomew, thinking it said very little for the sacred institution of marriage that the Lydgates so hated each other that they were prepared to squander his final moments on Earth arguing about jewellery. 'You might wish to be alone with him.'

'I have been alone with him for twenty-five miserable years. Why should I wish for more? I have things to do, and I have no time to wait around here.' She stuffed her jewels down the front of her dress for safekeeping.

'Then a few moments longer cannot make a difference,' said Bartholomew, gesturing for her to kneel next to him.

'Why should I?' she demanded with sudden anger. 'I have just heard him confess that he murdered the man I loved. All these years, and I knew nothing of this! I lived with a killer! I am glad Dominica poisoned him.'

'I thought you believed Dominica was dead,' said Bartholomew. 'You gave me that ring to help me find her killer.'

'I was mistaken. Poor Dominica was forced to feign her death in order to escape from her brute of a father. I discovered she was alive when she came to see me yesterday morning. My husband discovered she was alive when she and I came to see him together last night – when she gave him wine to help him recover from the shock.'

'And this medicinal wine contained henbane?' asked Bartholomew.

Cecily nodded. 'Justice has been done. She has killed the monster who murdered the man I love.'

'You still love Simon d'Ambrey, even though you believed he died all those years ago?' asked Michael, clearly unconvinced. Lydgate made a sound, that had he been strong enough, would probably have been a snort of derision.

Cecily smiled, caught in an untruth. 'Perhaps not, but I grieved deeply for him for several weeks. And I always knew this pathetic creature was not the father of my Dominica.'

'So, Dominica is the daughter of Simon d'Ambrey,' said Bartholomew in sudden realisation. On the floor, Lydgate gave an agonised gurgle. Although he could still hear, the poison had deprived him of coherent speech.

'That cannot be so,' objected Michael. 'Dominica is too young. Kenzie, her lover, was only eighteen or twenty.'

'Dominica was born the same year that Lydgate married Cecily – about six months after d'Ambrey died,' said Bartholomew, his mind working fast. 'Her early birth was the subject of speculation among the villagers for weeks. Dominica is about twenty-four.'

'But she cannot be that old,' said Michael. 'She would have been married off by now.'

'Master Lydgate is wealthy, and so it is unlikely that there will be a shortage of suitors for her hand – regardless of her age,' said Bartholomew. 'John of Stirling said Norbert was sixteen or seventeen. I imagine a young woman covered in dirt to disguise the lack of whiskers, might pass for a lad.'

'How could this oaf ever imagine he was the father of my Dominica?' asked Cecily spitefully. 'Dominica is clever – she fooled us over the matter of her death, and she helped Ivo and Saul Potter plan this riot so that we could be avenged on the man who destroyed our lives.'

'Destroyed your lives?' asked Michael. 'But you have just admitted that you grieved for d'Ambrey for a few weeks only and Dominica, with her secret lovers, has scarcely led a hard life.'

'It was a shame about poor Master Radbeche, though,' said Cecily, ignoring him. 'He was a kindly man.'

'What do you mean?' asked Michael suspiciously. 'You did not kill him, surely? What would you have been doing in David's Hostel in the middle of the riot?'

'Not Cecily,' said Bartholomew wearily. 'Dominica. Poor Radbeche must have caught her without her disguise at David's and so she killed him to ensure his silence.'

'That was my husband's fault, too,' said Cecily, her eyes narrowed spitefully. 'If he had not forced Dominica to take refuge at David's in order to escape from him, then Dominica would not have been forced to kill Radbeche to make certain he did not tell anyone who she really was.'

'I see,' said Michael. 'John told us that poor Radbeche was supposed to have taken a trip last night, but I suppose he heard rumours that there might be rioting and he, like a responsible Principal, returned to take care of his hostel. Of course, by this time, Father Andrew had gone for bread, the students had sneaked out and the hostel was bare – except, unfortunately for Radbeche, for Dominica.'

'And then,' said Bartholomew, easing Lydgate's head to one side as his breathing became more laboured. 'Dominica attacked John of Stirling because he almost caught her in the act of killing Radbeche.'

He saw that Lydgate's last reservoirs of strength were failing fast. Two tears slid from under the dying man's eyelids, and coursed down his cheeks. Michael pressed his hands together and began the words of the final absolution. Outside in the street, there were howls of merriment and smashing sounds, as children realised that throwing the shards of glass against the wall could be fun. The sergeant's voice cut over their laughter, but his tone was friendly, and he obviously thought they were doing no harm. While Michael prayed and Bartholomew bent to tend Lydgate, Cecily slipped away down the stairs and was gone. Michael looked up briefly, but let her go. Bartholomew was grateful, revolted by the malice and bitterness that seemed to taint all members of the Lydgate household.

When Michael had finished his prayers and Lydgate lay dead, Bartholomew followed the monk down the stairs. Instead of turning right to return to the street, they turned left to the kitchens in an unspoken agreement to take some time to think. All was deserted. Bartholomew opened a shutter and surveyed the yard. Against the wall lay a pile of wood – the remains of the shed that had been made to look as though Werbergh had died under it. And it had been Huw and Saul Potter – proven rioters and attackers of Bartholomew in the High Street – who had insisted that they had seen him enter it.

'Why did you let Cecily go?' asked Bartholomew. 'She might have been able to tell us where Dominica is.'

'I do not think so,' said Michael. 'It seems to me that while Dominica is central to this grand plan, Cecily is wholly unimportant. I think she knows nothing that she has not already told us, and I am not inclined to want to speak any further to someone who is so twisted with bitterness and hatred; such people see the truth through warped eyes. Anyway, Matt, the woman is not quick-witted like your Tyler daughters – she will probably head straight back for her bottle-dungeon at Chesterton, imagining that we will not guess where she is hiding.'

He looked around for a place to sit, but every stool and bench that could be carried away had gone. All that remained was a large table littered with broken pots and jars. He settled for elbowing Bartholomew to one side and perching on the window-sill. Bartholomew opened another shutter and followed suit, gazing gloomily at the looted kitchen.

'You know, we have allowed Lydgate's suspicions to mislead us, Matt,' said Michael, after a moment. 'It is not Norbert we are seeking, but Simon d'Ambrey himself.'

'And how have you reasoned that out?' asked Bartholomew, startled.

'I think he did not die in the barn, as Lydgate said, and that he escaped. He has bided his time, and he has returned to Cambridge to wreak revenge on the town that was so quick to believe ill of him after all his charity. It is he who is behind the riots; it is he who has brought about the death of Lydgate and the destruction of Godwinsson Hostel; and it is he who put the ring – Cecily's ring – on the hand of the skeleton that the town believes is his! That explains why the attacks against the University resulted in little destruction, except at David's and Godwinsson. The attacks appear to be aimed at the University, but they will ultimately damage the town far more.'

'That cannot be right,' said Bartholomew, wearily. 'We have one too many corpses belonging to the d'Ambreys as it is. We have the man who was shot with an arrow on the King's Ditch, the corpse in the burning barn, and the body brought back with the rest of d'Ambrey's household from Dover that I saw displayed in the Market Square years ago. Three corpses for two d'Ambreys – Simon and his brother.'

'No one ever saw this corpse reputedly burned in the barn,' persisted Michael. 'And regardless of what Lydgate said, I am sure he searched for it in the wreckage. I certainly would have done. And Lydgate's suspicions and unfounded conclusions are not the only ones to have misled us. Yours have, too.'

'Mine?' asked Bartholomew cautiously.

'Yes, yours!' said Michael, pursing his lips. 'Tell me again what you saw the day the tithe barn burned all those years ago.'

Bartholomew sighed. 'I saw Lydgate enter the barn while Norbert and I were swimming nearby. A brief while later, I saw smoke issuing from the barn, and Lydgate came tearing out. We followed him through the trees and saw him watch the barn burn for a few moments before he left to raise the alarm.'

'But that is not what you told me a few days ago,' said Michael. 'You said you saw someone run from the barn, you followed him, and then you saw Lydgate. What if the person you saw running from the barn was not Lydgate at all? Just because you came upon Lydgate moments later does not mean that he was the man you saw running. You have made the same assumption that misled Lydgate, Cecily and Edred over Dominica – you saw what you expected to see and not what was actually there.'

Bartholomew stared at him. 'But Lydgate's clothes were singed and he had been running hard.'

'Of course,' said Michael. 'He had just fled a fire. What would you expect? But Lydgate told us he left almost as soon as the lamp was knocked over and the straw caught fire. You saw a man running away after smoke had started seeping from the building. It would have been a couple of minutes at least before the fire had caught hold sufficiently for smoke to start pouring out. And by then, Lydgate was well away. The man you saw was Simon d'Ambrey.'

'But surely Lydgate would have seen him, too,' said Bartholomew, bewildered by the sudden turn in Michael's deductions.

'Not necessarily, not if he were concentrating on his own escape and was in a state of shock over what he had done. And we know Lydgate has never had good eyesight – he told us that himself in St Andrew's Church.'

'And Father Andrew, of course, is about the same age as Simon d'Ambrey would be,' said Bartholomew, rubbing his temples tiredly. 'There is our killer.'

ChAPTER 12

ICHAEL CLAIMED THE STENCH OF BURNING IN THE hostel had made him thirsty and, reluctantly, Bartholomew went with him to the secluded garden at the Brazen George. The landlord obligingly told three indignant bakers that they had to leave so that Michael and Bartholomew could talk in private, then brought them a large platter of roast lamb smothered in a greenish, oily gravy. Michael scraped the sauce away with Bartholomew's surgical knife, muttering in disgust when he discovered a piece of cabbage lurking in it.

'People who eat things that grow in the dirt will die young, Matt,' he pronounced firmly. 'And there is always the danger that there might be a worm or a slug served up with them.'

'Time is running short. We need to try to sort out some of this mess before it is too late.'

'Very well,' said Michael, his mouth full. 'We had just deduced that the kindly Father Andrew is none other than the villainous martyr Simon d'Ambrey himself. Sit down and eat something, Matt. You will wear yourself out with all that pacing.'

Bartholomew sat next to him and toyed with his food, trying to make some sense out of the mass of fact and theories. Michael carefully trimmed the fat from a piece of meat and ate it, pushing the lean part to one side.

'All right, then. Let me start. Father Andrew is too old to be your Norbert, but Father William has exposed him as a fraud, and there is clearly something untoward about the man: John of Stirling told us that Father Andrew had some kind of hold over the rioters last night, and there were all your suspicions that he was not all he seemed – the way he splattered ink when he wrote, the fact that you think you heard him while you were sneaking around the Chesterton tower-house, and so on. He is clearly up to no good. Meanwhile, we learn from Lydgate that he once roasted a martyr in the barn but, conveniently, no body is ever recovered. With one of those leaps of logic of which you are so fond, it is clear that Simon d'Ambrey escaped the fire in Trumpington, was never shot at the King's Ditch, and now he has returned to take his revenge on the town that so wronged him.'

He leaned back against the wall, pleased with what he had reasoned. Bartholomew rubbed a hand through his hair as his mind still grappled with the complexities of the evidence they had acquired.

'Who can blame him?' Michael added, gnawing on a bone. 'You all behaved abominably. I told you days ago that I thought the town had abused him.'

Bartholomew watched him. 'If all this is true, then d'Ambrey has succeeded in his revenge. The King, whose spy Heppel is probably here because of the growing unrest, will see the town as a hotbed of insurrection and he will clamp down on it hard. He will raise taxes, send more soldiers and shorten trading hours, so that Cambridge will be unable to compete with other market towns. Gradually, her wealth and influence will decline. Perhaps the University might even flounder, and take away another source of income, resented by the town though it may be. And as Cambridge sinks further into poverty – the poverty that d'Ambrey once fought so hard to reduce – he will have had his vengeance on the town.'

'Now this is beginning to come together,' said Michael with satisfaction, scrubbing the grease from his face with the sleeve of his habit. 'Although I cannot yet see where Norbert fits into all this – unless he and d'Ambrey are in it together.'

'They may be,' said Bartholomew thoughtfully. 'But something else became clear to me when the charming Lydgates were baring their souls. I think I now know what the two acts were that Matilde's client told her about.'

'From something the Lydgates said?' asked Michael, frowning. 'I cannot see what.'

'The riots were instigated to mask two acts,' said Bartholomew slowly. 'We thought at first that these acts might be burglaries, such as the one at the house next to Oswald, or perhaps the destruction of the Market Square. But now I think these were just coincidental. The two acts were matters much closer to d'Ambrey's heart: the first was his daughter Dominica's supposed death, and the second involved Will finding a suitable hand to use as a relic.'

'You reasoned this from something the Lydgates said?' asked Michael, unconvinced.

'Only the first one – Dominica's supposed death,' Bartholomew admitted. 'We need to review what we know and it involves Joanna.' Michael raised his eyes heavenwards. 'No, listen to me, Michael! It will make sense if you listen! A short while ago, Joanna, a prostitute from Ely and Agnes Tyler's niece, came to Cambridge. Mistress Tyler was not happy with her guest, because Joanna started some unofficial business from her home, putting her good name at risk – we had that from Jonas the Poisoner's wife and from the old river men. Obviously, Mistress Tyler would not want Joanna's clients calling at her house with three daughters to protect. Meanwhile, Dominica wanted to escape from the Lydgates, and what better way than to pretend she was dead? And Joanna had long, fair hair, like Dominica.'

'Now, just a moment,' said Michael, sufficiently startled to pause in his repast. 'Are you saying that Mistress Tyler plotted to have Joanna's body mistaken for Dominica's?'

'Yes,' said Bartholomew earnestly. 'Either she plotted with Dominica herself, or with d'Ambrey, who might well want his daughter back from the man who almost killed him in the tithe barn fire.'

'Why?' demanded Michael. 'Why should a perfectly law-abiding, honest woman like Mistress Tyler plot with a fallen martyr and his murderous daughter to have her niece killed and her body given the identity of another?'

'I have no idea what her motive might be,' said Bartholomew. 'But we know that the Tyler family are involved in something sufficiently sinister to force Eleanor to try to stop me from asking too many questions – and I am sure that something involves Joanna. Eleanor has virtually ordered me to stop investigating Joanna's death twice – once in the High Street and once at the Feast – and even the apothecary's wife suspects their sudden flight had something to do with Joanna.'

'All right,' said Michael grudgingly. 'We will ignore the motive for now – for your convenience – and concentrate on what we know. Continue.' He picked up Bartholomew's knife and began to prod the bones to see if there was any more meat to be salvaged.

'This plan would allow Dominica to be free of the Lydgates and her life at Godwinsson. She could help d'Ambrey in the last stages of his revenge against the town, along with his other faithful friends – Master Bigod, Saul Potter, Huw, Ivo, and so on, the ones whose names were recorded in the hidden documents in the Galen. And afterwards, she could go wherever d'Ambrey might take her.'

'I see,' said Michael. 'So, the plan was to kill Joanna and leave her for Lydgate to find. You told me that her face was battered, which would make her difficult to recognise. Dominica knew her father's eyesight was failing and he would be easy to fool. He was not a man given to reason anyway, particularly when enraged. He would storm off into the night searching for Dominica, see a blur of golden hair and assume his daughter was dead.' He shook his head. 'Unpleasant though it may seem, I suppose it is a just revenge on a man who had tried to kill d'Ambrey twenty-five years ago, and deprived him of seeing his daughter grow up.'

Bartholomew took up the tale. 'Edred must have been in on the deception – he tried to steal the Galen with Norbert's documents in it, so we can assume he was in their pay. Edred was the one who told Lydgate that he had seen Dominica in the streets of Cambridge. Naturally, Lydgate raced out to bring her back, while Edred and Cecily followed. Dominica knew the places Lydgate was most likely to look, so Joanna was killed at one of them by Godwinsson's Frenchmen, who first raped her.'

'No,' said Michael, stopping him. 'She was killed in Mistress Tyler's house – we saw the bloodstains – and then dumped at a place Lydgate would be likely to look. That was why Mistress Tyler would not allow you to try to oust the looters from her house, and why she – a woman who knows how to look after herself and her property – chose to abandon her house and spend the night with Jonas and his wife.'

Bartholomew nodded. It was beginning to make sense. 'Meanwhile, Cecily took the opportunity to run away from her husband, while Edred, after he had helped her, sneaked back and ransacked her room. Lydgate told us he had stolen a crucifix.'

'So, we have reasoned out Matilde's "first act",' said Michael. 'Ah, here comes the landlord with a pie. Apple! Excellent! Carry on, Matt. What of the second act – this relic business?'

'The answers to that have been staring us in the face all the time. Think about where the first riot started – at Master Burney's tannery. Everyone knows that the Austin Canons own the room underneath, and that they use it as a mortuary, thinking the smell of the tannery will eliminate any dangerous miasmas that might come from the corpses.'

'Mistress Starre's son!' exclaimed Michael in sudden realisation, his pie forgotten. 'That feeble-minded boy who was a giant and whom you put into the Canons' care when he was implicated in all that business with the saffron trade a while ago. We saw his body in the wreckage of Master Burney's tannery!'

Bartholomew recalled the tangle of limbs in the rubble after the tannery had collapsed, and remembered that he had even told Michael that Starre was one of the dead. 'There was too much else to be done with caring for the injured for the Canons to have been concerned with a missing hand, although I am sure d'Ambrey and his accomplices ensured that the body was carefully arranged so that the damage looked accidental.'

Michael shook his head in grudging admiration. 'These people are clever. They selected Starre's hand so that there would be no question that it belonged to a man because he was so big.'

'And, of course, there were signs that the hand had been boiled and there was a pin to hold two of the bones together. The hand had not simply been discovered in the King's Ditch – it had been carefully prepared. On top of all this, there was the ring it wore. John of Stirling took the ring Dominica gave to Kenzie at Father Andrew's – d'Ambrey's – request. D'Ambrey must have had an imitation made, which John then gave back to Kenzie, later to be stolen by Edred, thrown into the shed, and found by me. The real ring d'Ambrey must have given to Will of Valence Marie, with which to adorn the skeleton's hand. Cecily said the pair of lovers' rings were hers – perhaps they were a gift from d'Ambrey if he were her paramour.'

'And d'Ambrey could not simply use the one Cecily still had because it was too small to fit over the big hand they had prepared – she had the woman's ring, and they needed the man's. Dominica's generosity to James Kenzie brought about his death.'

'But it could not have done, Michael. Kenzie had the false ring, remember? And he clearly was unable to tell the difference and did not know the rings had been exchanged, or he would not have gone to Werbergh and Edred in his desperation to have it back.'

Michael sighed. 'Regardless, we had better apprehend this Simon d'Ambrey before he does any more damage. But what about Werbergh's murder? How does that fit into this foul web of retaliation?'

'We will have to work that out as we go,' said Bartholomew, reaching out a hand and hauling Michael to his feet. 'We have wasted enough time already. If we are correct in our deductions, then d'Ambrey's work is almost done here and he will soon be gone.'

'Where are we going?'

'To Valence Marie. That is where this relic purporting to be d'Ambrey's hand is, and that, I am certain, is where d'Ambrey will go sooner or later.'

They left a message with the sergeant to tell Tulyet of their suspicions – neither Bartholomew nor Michael felt there was much point in entrusting the information to the feeble Guy Heppel. Tulyet, Bartholomew knew, would not stop to question their message; he would hasten to Valence Marie and leave explanations until later.

The sun was high as they hurried along the High Street, but it was already beginning to cloud over with the promise of rain. As Michael raised his hand to knock on the great gate, Bartholomew pushed it away. The memory of Radbeche's murder at David's was clear in his mind. He and Michael had been incautious to walk so blithely into David's – Radbeche's killer could easily have been lurking still at the scene of his crime. He wished Cynric were with them, since he would know exactly how to proceed.

Bartholomew pushed open the door and peered round it. There was no porter at the lodge. He drew a surgical knife from his bag, while Michael found a sturdy piece of wood he could use as a cudgel. Bartholomew pushed the door open a little further, and stepped inside. Like the last time they had visited Valence Marie, it was eerily quiet. Bartholomew took a deep breath and began to make his way around the edge of the yard, Michael following.

The hall door was ajar. Standing well back, Bartholomew pushed it open with the tip of his knife and looked inside. It was deserted. Puzzled, he lowered the knife and walked in. It looked as though it had been the scene of a violent struggle. Cups and plates lay scattered on the floor and two of the long tables that ran down the sides of the hall had been overturned. Several tapestries hung askew, wine had pooled on the polished floor. Michael pushed past him, whistling at the mess.

Without warning, something heavy fell on Bartholomew from above. With a cry, he dropped to his hands and knees, the knife sent skittering across the stone floor. The minstrels' gallery! Valence Marie had a small gallery for musicians that was just above the main door; it was from here that someone had dropped down on to him.

Michael spun round with his cudgel, but was knocked backwards by a tremendous punch swung by Master Thorpe himself. Valence Marie scholars poured down the stairs where they had been hiding with howls of fury. Bartholomew attempted to regain his feet but someone leapt on to his back, forcing him to the ground. He tried to scramble forwards to reach his knife but one of the Fellows saw what he was doing, and kicked the blade away so hard that it disappeared under a bench on the opposite side of the hall.

Michael lay on his back, his stomach protruding into the air like an enormous fish, while Thorpe stood over him wringing his fist. Bartholomew began to squirm and struggle with all his might. He felt the man clinging to his back begin to lose his grip. Others came to help but Bartholomew had managed to rise to his knees. As one scholar raced towards him, Bartholomew lowered his head and caught him hard in the middle. He heard a groan as the student dropped to the floor clutching his stomach.

But it was an unequal contest and, despite valiant efforts, Bartholomew found himself in the firm grip of several of Valence Marie's strongest students. Realising that further struggling would merely serve to sap his strength, Bartholomew relented. He glanced nervously at Michael, still lying on the floor.

'What do you mean by entering my hall armed with a knife?' asked Thorpe coldly. 'We saw you sneak into our yard like a thief, without knocking or calling out to announce yourself.' He gave a superior smile. 'So the scholars of Valence Marie decided to give you a welcome you did not anticipate.'

As several students jeered triumphantly, Bartholomew wondered how to explain. He tried to see the faces of the men who held him, to see if Father Andrew were there but he could not move. He tried to think of an answer that Thorpe would accept, but the Master of Valence Marie did not give him the chance to reply before firing another question at him.

'What have you done with our relic?'

'Your relic?' repeated Bartholomew stupidly. 'The skeleton's hand? Has it gone?'

Thorpe looked hard at a small upended box that lay on the floor next to a piece of fine white satin and then back at Bartholomew, pursing his lips. 'I have no doubt that you have taken it. The Chancellor has already instructed me to get rid of it, but who am I to deny the people of Cambridge their heritage? I refused. One of the students thought he might have found more sacred bones, but while we were out to investigate his discovery, our hand was stolen. Then, even as we searched for it, you enter my College, without permission and armed.'

Bartholomew could see why Thorpe was suspicious of him. 'But if we had taken your relic, Master Thorpe, we would not still be here. We would go to hide it.'

Thorpe gestured to his scholars and Bartholomew and Michael were thoroughly searched. Bartholomew's bag was torn from his shoulder and emptied unceremoniously on the floor. Phials and bandages rolled everywhere, and the damaged copy of Galen shaken vigorously, as if it might produce a stolen hand. Bartholomew looked around him quickly. One of the men who held him was the burly Henry, who had been present when the hand was found in the Ditch. Standing to one side was another servant, his arm in an untidy splint. Next to him, not taking a part in restraining Bartholomew, but favouring him with a gaze that was far more frightening than the scholars' rough hands, was Will.

As Bartholomew looked into Will's glittering eyes, cold and unblinking, he knew he was in trouble indeed. Seeing Bartholomew was observing him, the diminutive servant moved his tunic slightly to reveal the long, wicked-looking dagger in his belt. The hand that rested on its hilt had a semicircular mark that Bartholomew immediately recognised as a bite. Michael had bitten one of the men who had attacked them on the High Street the previous week, while Bartholomew knew he had broken the arm of another: Will and the servant who stood next to him.

'Well, you might not have our relic with you,' said Thorpe,

oblivious to Will's implicit threat, 'but I know that you, or another of the Chancellor's men, have taken it away. We found this precious thing. It came to us in the knowledge that it would be revered and honoured at Valence Marie.'

To say nothing of its use to amass wealth, thought Bartholomew. 'I really have no idea where it is,' he said. 'And I cannot imagine that the Chancellor would arrange to have it taken by stealth. You do Master de Wetherset an injustice, sir.'

Thorpe clenched his fist again, and Bartholomew thought he was going to strike him. But Thorpe's hand had already been bruised by punching Michael, and he was loath to risk harming himself a second time.

'We will see,' he said. He turned to Will. 'Make sure they cannot escape. Lock them in, and we will go to discuss this with the Chancellor.'

He turned on his heel and stalked out. Bartholomew's arms were pulled behind him and tied securely. Will still regarded him with his curious glittering eyes.

'You go with the Master,' he said to the students, nodding at Thorpe's retreating back. 'Henry, Jacob and I will remain here and guard these two.'

Bartholomew struggled to stand. He thought quickly, knowing that if he were left alone with Will and his cronies, he and Michael would not live to tell how they knew that the hand of Valence Marie did not belong to Simon d'Ambrey.

'Can your Master not manage his affairs without the entire College at his heels?' he shouted, trying to shame some of the retreating scholars into staying behind. 'Do you find it necessary to follow him around like faithful dogs?'

Father Eligius, one of Bartholomew's patients, hesitated. 'This is an important matter, Matthew. If all Valence Marie's Fellows are present and in complete agreement, it will add weight to our case that this sacred relic belongs here.'

'But there is no sacred relic,' said Bartholomew desperately. 'It is the hand of a recently dead corpse planted in the Ditch by Will and his associates. It belonged to Mistress Starre's son.'

Eligius looked startled, while the other Fellows laughed in derision.

'Will has been a faithful servant since the College was founded,' said Eligius reproachfully. 'Such an accusation does you discredit, Matthew.'

'But it is true!' pressed Bartholomew. 'Think about it! Why

should a sacred relic have a pin to hold the bones together? Because it was carefully prepared by Will! And why was it wearing a ring recently stolen from the David's student murdered just outside your walls? And why did Will just happen to have a fine casket lined with satin to use as a reliquary for it?'

'This is nonsense,' said a burly, angry-looking man, whom Bartholomew recognised as Master Dittone, as he ushered the students from the hall. 'I am surprised at you, Bartholomew. I always thought you were a man of integrity. Now I learn that you steal, prowl around other colleges with weapons and make vile accusations against lowly servants who are not in a position to answer back.'

'Do not be too harsh on him,' said Eligius kindly. 'Doctor Bartholomew suffered a grievous wound to the head recently, and his stars are poorly aligned.'

Bartholomew's spirits sank. Would there be no end to the repercussions of Gray's impetuous diagnosis?

'The relic is a fake!' he insisted to the last of the retreating scholars. Dittone shot him a vicious look and, for a moment, appeared as though he would like to silence Bartholomew permanently, there and then. He was edged firmly to the door by Eligius, who then paused.

'Take good care of them, Will,' he said. 'Remember the doctor is unwell and needs to be treated with sympathy. It is not his fault that he was driven to steal the relic but the fault of the devils that possess him.'

'Eligius!' cried Bartholomew as the Dominican friar closed the door behind him. 'Stay with us!'

The door shut with a clank and Bartholomew's words echoed around the silent hall. Will exchanged glances with his friends. Bartholomew began to back away down the hall, while Will, ensuring that the door was locked, drew his dagger and followed.

Bartholomew saw Henry draw his own dagger and lean over Michael, who still lay flat on his back. The students had not tied the monk's hands, but he was insensible. Bartholomew looked around him desperately for some kind of weapon but realised that even a broadsword would be useless to him with his hands bound. He saw Henry hold Michael's head back as he prepared to cut his throat. Henry then watched Will, waiting for an order.

'That hand, Will,' said Bartholomew, hoping to distract them long enough to give him a chance to think of some way to escape. 'It was Starre's, was it not? You took it the night of the first riot.'

Will grinned, but did not stop his relentless advance. 'The first riot gave us plenty of time to acquire the limb of a recently dead pauper, and we did the body no harm. We could not risk you claiming the hand belonged to a woman because it was overly small.'

'But it broke as you boiled it. You had to mend it with a pin.'

Will pulled an unpleasant face. 'I might have known it was you who told the Chancellor that. Fortunately, Master Thorpe was not deterred by so minor a point and it did nothing to diminish his belief in the relic's sanctity.'

'And then, a couple of days later, with the hand suitably prepared, you pretended to find it in the Ditch. By then, it was wearing the ring that Father Andrew – Simon d'Ambrey, should I say – had given to you.'

Will began to gain on Bartholomew, who continued to speak as he backed down the hall.

'You had even made a fine box for it in advance, lined with satin for it to lie on.'

'What if I did?' asked Will with a shrug. 'But there is nothing you can do about it now and we cannot have you running all over the town claiming that our saintly relic is a fake.'

'But it *is* a fake,' Bartholomew pointed out.

'Did you take it?' asked Will, still advancing. He fingered his dagger. Jacob, the man with the broken arm, picked up a piece of broken pot in his good hand, and prepared to follow.

'I do not think he did, Will,' he said, 'or he would not have come back.'

'True, I suppose,' said Will grudgingly. 'But he has the book by Galen that Master d'Ambrey so badly wanted back. He will be pleased when I give it to him.'

'We know it was you who attacked us that night,' said Bartholomew. 'You three, with Master Bigod, Huw, Saul Potter, and Ivo from David's Hostel. Jacob's arm was broken then, and you were bitten. And it was probably you who searched my room the first two times.'

'We should have finished you then, in the street, along with that meddlesome monk. But Master Bigod was too squeamish, damn him, especially when he saw I was about to kill a man of God. Everything was going to plan until you two started to poke about.'

Jacob hurled his piece of broken pot. Bartholomew ducked as it sailed over his head to crash against the wall in a shower of shards. Undeterred, the servant looked about for something else to throw.

'And it was you who burgled those houses,' said Bartholomew, ducking a second time as a pewter jug narrowly missed him. 'Because you knew exactly where and when the riots would break out, you were able to use the opportunity to select the houses of certain rich merchants and steal from them.'

'So what?' said Jacob, leaning down to grab another jug to throw. 'Is it fair that fat merchants should have more wealth than they know what to do with, while the rest of us are starving?'

'You are not starving,' Bartholomew pointed out.

Will gave an unpleasant smile. 'Not now, perhaps, but we have to think of the future, and a man like Simon d'Ambrey always needs funds.'

'I bet he does,' said Bartholomew. 'Funds for paying people to incite riots, funds to have corpses desecrated, funds to assassinate people he does not like.'

Will came nearer, flanked by Jacob. 'I have had enough of this!'

He turned to nod to Henry to dispatch Michael. Seeing him momentarily distracted, Bartholomew propelled himself forward with an almighty yell, crashing into him and knocking him off balance. Will fell into Jacob, who dropped to his knees with a shriek as he cradled his injured arm. Michael's hands suddenly shot out, one grasping Henry's throat, the other the arm that held the dagger. As Henry began to choke with a series of unpleasant gurgles, Bartholomew turned his attention back to Will. Will lunged with his knife and Bartholomew jumped away.

'What is in all this for you, Will?' asked Bartholomew, flinching backwards as Will lunged a second time. 'Why should you risk your livelihood for d'Ambrey?'

'He once paid a surgeon to set my broken leg,' said Will, circling Bartholomew like a dog. 'I have always deeply regretted that I did nothing to help him when he was accused all those years ago. It is a second chance, and I will go with him when he leaves tonight. I will no longer be a mere servant, taken for granted and given the most menial of tasks to perform, but a member of a respectable household, the head of which will be the saintly Master d'Ambrey.'

'But the man has changed!' said Bartholomew, his feet crunching on broken pottery as he ducked away from Will's dagger. 'Saints do not kill and order the desecration of the dead!'

'Shut up!' hissed Will. He darted forward and caught hold of Bartholomew's tabard to hold him still.

'D'Ambrey must be held to blame for all the deaths that occurred in the riots he inspired,' persisted Bartholomew breathlessly, tearing away from Will's grip as a swipe of the dagger ripped his shirt. 'Including that of your brother. He died in the first riot, I understand.'

He jerked backwards to avoid another furious hacking blow and stumbled over a broken chair. Will was now incensed and his eyes flashed with loathing. Instead of distracting the man, Bartholomew had succeeded in enraging him to the point where any chance of escape seemed hopeless. Off-balance, Bartholomew crashed to the floor, while Will's arm flicked down and under in a swift, efficient movement aimed at the physician's unprotected stomach.

Even as the knife flashed towards him, there was a loud thump, and Will's head jolted forward. Will looked as surprised as Bartholomew, before crumpling into a heap on the floor. Jacob still sat hunched over his injured arm while Henry lay massaging his bruised neck.

Across the hall, Michael sank down on to a bench and closed his eyes. Shakily, Bartholomew climbed to his feet and joined him.

'Thank the Lord you like reading heavy books,' said Michael, pointing to where the Galen lay next to Will. Michael had hurled it in the nick of time.

As Bartholomew approached the door to leave Valence Marie's hall, he froze, and edged back into the shadows. There were voices – Thorpe's and d'Ambrey's, complete with the lilting Scottish accent of Father Andrew. Bartholomew opened the door slightly so he could hear what was being said.

'I am most distressed that the relic has disappeared,' d'Ambrey was saying, wringing his hands and appearing every inch the benevolent old friar. 'Most distressed indeed. I wanted to see it again before I left.'

'You are leaving Cambridge, Father?' asked Thorpe politely, but without interest. He had other things to worry about than an elderly friar who had missed his opportunity to view the relic. But the friar's concern was insistent – as well it might be.

'Do you have an idea of where it might be?' he said. 'Can I help you look for it?'

'You are most kind, Father,' said Thorpe. 'But we will manage. We have already turned the College upside-down in our quest to locate it – you should see the state of our poor hall! I am now on my way to discuss the matter with the Chancellor.'

'I know you will guard that relic and see that it is awarded the honour it deserves,' continued d'Ambrey. Thorpe looked at him sharply. D'Ambrey was overplaying his role, enjoying too much the opportunity to promote himself as the object of reverence.

He realised the danger, and bowed to Thorpe before taking his leave. He was shown out of the main gate by one of the students and Bartholomew saw him glancing this way and that as he walked, as though the hand might appear suddenly in the mud and refuse that lay ankle-deep in the yard. Thorpe dallied, his students milling about him restlessly.

'Has de Wetherset stolen the hand?' whispered Bartholomew to Michael as he watched them. 'Or Heppel?'

Michael shrugged. 'Possibly. What is Thorpe doing? Why does he not leave? We should follow d'Ambrey before he escapes us completely, but we cannot do so with Thorpe prowling around outside. His students are vengeful – they would hang us in an instant if Thorpe gave them his blessing, and even Father Eligius's claims that you are mentally deficient will not save us.'

Bartholomew regarded him sharply. 'Exactly when was it that you recovered your senses from Thorpe's blow?' he asked.

Michael looked uncomfortable. 'I am not sure. But I had to wait for the right moment before I acted.'

'You cut it very fine, Brother,' said Bartholomew, regarding the monk uneasily.

'The truth was that you were doing such a fine job of wringing a confession from Will that I decided to wait a while. He would never have been so verbose had I leapt to my feet and overpowered Henry. He was bragging to you simply because he thought he was going to kill you, and that you would never be in a position to reveal anything he had said.'

'He almost killed me several times during his confession!' said Bartholomew, aghast. 'How could you put Will's paltry revelations over my life?'

'Come now, Matt!' said Michael impatiently. 'Do not be so melodramatic! I knew what I was doing. I saved your life, did I not? And together we overwhelmed that unwholesome trio there.'

He glanced over his shoulder to where Will, Henry and Jacob sat with their backs to the serving screen, secured there with ropes that had been used to suspend the tapestries from the walls. Henry and Jacob were subdued, but Will was livid. He struggled and heaved against his bonds, making guttural sounds through the bandages with which Bartholomew had gagged him.

Bartholomew turned his attention back to the yard, and gave a start of horror as he saw Thorpe begin to walk towards the hall. His heart lurched in anticipation of being discovered free, and he was momentarily frozen with fear. Sensing his alarm, Will's struggles increased, and Michael grabbed Will's abandoned dagger, racing across to the serving screen to wave it menacingly at the gagged servant before Thorpe heard the noise.

Thorpe drew closer, and Bartholomew looked around in panic, wondering how they might escape. There was no other way out. Bartholomew knew instinctively that if Thorpe discovered they had overpowered his servants, he would give them into the custody of his vengeful students, and that would be their death warrant. As Thorpe's hand reached out to push open the hall door, a scholar emerged from the Master's quarters, carrying a bundle of cloth. Thorpe's hand dropped from the door and he began to walk away. Bartholomew was so relieved, his legs turned to jelly, and he had to lean against the wall for support. Next to Will, Michael dropped the dagger in revulsion.

Bartholomew gave the monk a weak smile. 'Master Thorpe does not want to confront the Chancellor improperly attired,' he explained shakily. 'He was waiting for a student to fetch him his best robe.'

Michael gnawed at his finger-nails. 'We will lose d'Ambrey if Thorpe does not leave soon!'

While they waited for Thorpe to be satisfied with the way his gown fell, Bartholomew crammed bandages and salves back in his medical bag and tucked the Galen into one of the side pockets. Michael fretted at the door. By the time Bartholomew had finished, Thorpe and his entourage had gone and Michael was already across the courtyard and out of the main gates. As they emerged into the High Street, they caught a glimpse of d'Ambrey's grey habit disappearing up the Trumpington Road.

They set off after him, pausing briefly to tell the guards on the gate that there were three felons secured in Valence Marie, and that Tulyet should follow as soon as possible. After a moment's hesitation, Michael tossed a small child a penny and sent her with a message to the Chancellor and Heppel.

'Wicked waste of a penny,' muttered Michael. 'De Wetherset will be in a business meeting and his clerks will be too frightened to disturb him on our behalf, while Heppel's presence while we apprehend a killer will be more hindrance than help.'

While they had been in Valence Marie the clouds had thickened, and a light, misty rain was falling. It should have been a welcome relief after the heat of the morning, but it served only to increase the humidity. Michael complained that he could not catch his breath; even Bartholomew began to feel uncomfortable. But the rain afforded some advantage, for it provided a haziness in the air that meant that Bartholomew and Michael were able to follow d'Ambrey with less chance of being seen.

They walked quickly and without speaking, alert for any sound that would warn them that d'Ambrey had stopped. One or twice they glimpsed him ahead and, as they went further from the town, Bartholomew began to wonder how far d'Ambrey was going to go. They reached the small manor owned by Sir Robert de Panton, where the land had been cleared for farming, affording uninterrupted views down the road for some distance. D'Ambrey was nowhere to be seen. Michael sagged in defeat.

As they dithered, wondering where d'Ambrey might have turned, they met Sir Robert himself, who told them that he had seen an elderly friar pass along the Trumpington Road just a few moments before. Encouraged, Bartholomew and Michael hurried on.

They continued in silence, the only sounds being Michael's heavy breathing, and their feet on the muddy road. As they began to despair that they might have lost him a second time, a thought occurred to Bartholomew. They were near Trumpington village, where d'Ambrey had almost been incinerated in the tithe barn fire. The new barn had been built closer to the village, so it could be better protected, and the charred timbers of the old one had been allowed to decay. Now, nothing remained, apart from one or two ivy-covered stumps and a clearing in the trees where it had once stood.

Wordlessly, Bartholomew led Michael off the main path to the site of the old barn. He was beginning to think he must have miscalculated, when he heard voices. One was d'Ambrey, speaking with no hint of a Scottish accent. Peering through the trees, Bartholomew saw an unwholesome creature wrapped in filthy rags, but standing straight and tall and speaking in a firm, clear voice. The murderous Dominica.

D'Ambrey said something, and there were growls of agreement from others: Huw from Godwinsson, Ivo from David's, and Cecily, who looked sullen. As Bartholomew turned to indicate to Michael that they should withdraw and wait for Tulyet, he heard the unmistakeable click of a crossbow bolt being loaded. He spun round.

'Ruthven!'

Ruthven smiled, and indicated with a small flick of his crossbow that they should precede him into the midst of Simon d'Ambrey's meeting.

D'Ambrey scowled when he saw Ruthven's captives. 'Where did you find these gentlemen?'

'Listening to you from the bushes over there,' said Ruthven with a toss of his head. He poked at Bartholomew with his weapon and indicated that he and Michael should sit on the grass.

'Well, we can do nothing until nightfall, anyway,' said d'Ambrey with a shrug. 'I would like Huw to return to Valence Marie and find out from Will what is happening about my hand.' He turned to Bartholomew and Michael, and smiled. 'Given long enough, I might be made a saint, do you think? Perhaps a fine abbey built around my shrine?'

'I doubt it,' said Michael. 'Although people do seem to worship the oddest things.' He smiled guilelessly back at d'Ambrey, ignoring Bartholomew's warning kick.

D'Ambrey saw Bartholomew's reaction, however. 'I see you seek to caution your friend, lest he moves me to anger, Doctor,' he said. 'You have doubtless seen many forms of madness since you have become a physician. Well, you have no need to look for any such signs in me. I am as sane as you. Angry, perhaps. Betrayed, certainly. And vengeful. But most assuredly not mad.'

He smiled in a way that made Bartholomew seriously doubt it. The only hope for him and Michael, he realised, was that one of the messages that they had left for Tulyet would reach him, especially the one with the guards at the gate. He prayed that the Sheriff would not be waylaid into helping Thorpe search for the missing relic.

D'Ambrey sat on a tree stump and smiled beatifically. Even with his accent and friar-like demeanour gone, Bartholomew felt the man still had a peculiarly saintly air about him.

'You are wondering what made me change,' he said, looking from one to the other of his captives. 'I was loved by the people. My brother and sister adored me. And then my brother betrayed me. He stole the treasure I had collected for the poor and flaunted it by wearing it around the town. People thought I had given it to him and turned against me. I ran to the woman I had always liked best for sanctuary. But she betrayed me too. She told her betrothed where I was and he came to kill me.'

'No!' Cecily rose from where she had been sitting, uncomfortable and bedraggled, on the grass. 'You know I did not betray you! I saw smoke coming from the barn and ran back to warn you, but it was already too late. I thought it was a terrible accident, not murder!'

'But you did not try to look for me after the blaze,' said d'Ambrey, with quiet reason. 'You were quick to assume I was dead.'

'But the barn was an inferno!' wailed Cecily desperately, moving towards him, arms outstretched. 'No one could have survived! Even the nails melted from the heat!'

'And then you married the man who brought about my death,' continued d'Ambrey relentlessly. 'And you allowed him to bring up my daughter as his own child. You did not even keep the rings I gave you. Somehow one of them ended up on a shabby little student at my own hostel and I had to go to all manner of contortions to get it back to adorn my relic at Valence Marie.'

'Dominica gave it to him,' protested Cecily. 'I kept both rings close to my heart for twenty-five years. I only gave one to Bartholomew recently because I thought he might be able to use it to catch Dominica's killer.'

'I did no such thing, father,' said Dominica disdainfully. 'She and Thomas Lydgate were far too mean to give me jewellery to dispense with as I pleased. She is lying!'

'I think you *did* give it to Jamie, Dominica,' said Ruthven uncertainly. 'He said you did.'

'My Dominica has no cause to lie,' said d'Ambrey, somewhat rashly, since it was clear to everyone in the clearing that she had every reason to stretch the truth. Cecily gazed at her daughter in mute appeal, and Bartholomew found he could not watch.

'Those rings belonged to my parents,' said d'Ambrey sternly. 'My father had them made to match my mother's blue-green eyes. They are not baubles to be dispensed to any snotty-nosed scholar who wanted one, especially a lad like James Kenzie, who was so careless. First he let John steal it and then he lost the false one I replaced it with while he was brawling on the High Street.'

'But I kept them safe!' shrieked Cecily. 'I did! Dominica stole them from me to give to her paramour!'

D'Ambrey turned from her and made a quick gesture to Ruthven. There was a swish and a thump. Ruthven was reloading his crossbow with a new quarrel before the shocked Bartholomew could act. Cecily looked at d'Ambrey in horror, her hands clawing at the bolt that protruded from her chest. Her bulbous eyes popped out even further as she sank on to the grass.

Bartholomew made to go towards her.

'Leave her!' d'Ambrey snapped, his gentle tones vanished. 'She deserves to die.'

Bartholomew looked at him in revulsion. 'Why?'

'She has served her purpose,' said d'Ambrey with a shrug. 'I only brought her into the plot at the last minute because she had hidden away her family jewels so well that neither Edred nor Dominica could find them. She kindly brought them – Dominica's inheritance – a few moments ago, although they are a little fire-damaged. But I do not want her slowing us down when we leave tonight. We will need to move fast if we want to escape.'

'I can give her something to ease the pain,' said Bartholomew, reaching for his bag and flipping it open.

'You will leave her alone,' d'Ambrey repeated, looking inside the bag with interest. 'You have my Galen, I see. A little late, perhaps, but I am pleased to have it back.'

Before Bartholomew could reply, d'Ambrey had plucked the tome from the bag, and was sitting with it on his knees. He saw immediately where Gray had torn the covers away and shook his head slowly, fingering the damage with sadness in his face.

'Is this the way scholars treat their books? Would you do this, eh, Ruthven?'

Ruthven came to peer over d'Ambrey's shoulder, looking at the torn cover. 'Was this where the documents were hidden?' he asked.

D'Ambrey nodded. 'I tried several times to get this back,' he said to Bartholomew. 'But if I sent someone to search your room, you would have it in your bag, and when I waylaid you on the High Street, you had left it in your room. And then, when I simply asked you for it, you offered to return it immediately!'

'My father wrote that book,' said Ruthven with pride.

'What was his name?' asked Michael.

'No one you would know, Brother,' said d'Ambrey. 'Just a scholar I helped many years ago. You should empathise, Doctor, for he was a man whose revolutionary medical ideas gave rise to an accusation of heresy. I gave him money to flee to Scotland to safety. He remembered me, unlike so many, and told his son, already a student here, to help me in my revenge against the town.'

'It seems you have engineered quite a plot against the town, Master d'Ambrey,' said Michael, knowing that as soon as d'Ambrey grew tired of them, he and Bartholomew would go the same way as Cecily. They had to try to keep him talking until Tulyet arrived. 'Perhaps you would care to entertain us with the details.'

D'Ambrey looked pleased. 'Shall I start at the beginning, then?' he asked sweetly. At Michael's nod, he settled himself comfortably and beamed around at his audience. 'Well, to take you back twenty-five years, I fled the burning barn and sought safety near the river. I was not the only abandoned soul that night. A lad named Norbert was also fleeing that horrible little village. We joined forces and lived rough for several days. He told me what you had done for him and it did much to cheer

me, Bartholomew. We exchanged our plans of revenge – me
on the town, him on the village – and he confided his plans
to become an archer at Dover Castle.'

'Oh, no!' said Bartholomew suddenly, an uneasy feeling
uncoiling in his stomach. 'It was you! You killed Norbert! It
was his skeleton we found in the Ditch after all!'

He gazed, horrified, at d'Ambrey, who smiled back at him,
unperturbed by his distress. 'I am afraid you are right. But
it was all a dreadful mistake. You see, one night, Norbert
disappeared, and I assumed that he had gone to fetch soldiers.
I was desperate to stop him and caught him near the Ditch
where my brother had died. I slipped up behind him and stoved
in his skull with a stone. He had just enough breath, before he
died, to tell me that he was going to burgle a house to steal
me a new cloak for our journey south together. I have been
sorry about Norbert ever since,' he finished, looking wistfully
at the crushed grass at his feet.

Bartholomew felt sick. The messages he had received had
been forged by d'Ambrey, and the copies in the back of the
book kept so he would not forget the lies told. Bartholomew
had released Norbert from Trumpington, only for him to fall
into the hands of a murderer.

D'Ambrey's eyes were guilelessly wide. 'I sent Bartholomew
letters – signed with the name of Norbert's sister so as not to
get him into trouble with his family – so that he would not
fret about the welfare of his young friend. It was a simple act
of kindness.'

Bartholomew gazed at him with renewed awe. Such dishon-
esty surely could not be considered kindness? He wondered
afresh at d'Ambrey's sanity. The man sat, still dressed in his
friar's habit, smiling benevolently down at them like a beloved
old grandfather. Yet he had ordered Cecily's brutal murder
without a moment's hesitation.

'And you needed somewhere to hide these letters,' said
Michael. 'Where better than the Galen? The book was never
used by David's students because none of them were studying
medicine. It would have been difficult to hide them otherwise
– hostels are notorious for their lack of privacy.'

D'Ambrey nodded. 'You have it, Brother. Scholars are naturally curious and I did not want them poking about in my
belongings and finding the letters. The Galen was a perfect
hiding place until Radbeche lent it to you! But we digress.'

He gave a huge sigh, and continued. 'It was my intention that Norbert's skeleton should be dredged from the Ditch and revered as mine at Valence Marie, assuming it had not washed away. But, ironically, it was you who prevented that, Doctor, by saying it was too small.'

'How could you know your brother's skeleton would not be dredged up?' asked Michael. 'Or his and Norbert's?'

'The Ditch was in flood the night my brother died,' said d'Ambrey. 'His body was washed a long way downstream. When I killed Norbert, the Ditch was low. The water did not cover him, and so I buried him in the mud at the bottom.'

'And then you went to Dover,' said Bartholomew, unsteadily.

'I did indeed,' said d'Ambrey, 'I went in pursuit of my fleeing household – as did the three burgesses from the town. It was easy to follow them, and I disguised myself as a travelling priest.'

Bartholomew closed his eyes in despair. 'And I suppose it was you who started the fire in which all those people died, your household included.'

D'Ambrey smiled. 'It was nothing,' he said modestly. 'An oven left burning in a baker's shop when it should have been doused for the night; a specially prepared pie that would ensure my household slept through any alarms that might have been raised before the fire was underway.'

'Dozens of innocent people died in that blaze,' said Bartholomew, appalled, 'not just members of your household.'

'It could not be helped,' said d'Ambrey. 'And I am sure you will understand my need for revenge after what had happened to me.'

'But how did you manage to make the burgesses believe that your brother was among the casualties?' asked Michael. 'His body was never recovered.'

'Never recovered?' queried d'Ambrey. 'On what grounds do you base such an assumption? Believe me, my brother's body lies in the grave that is marked with his name. I could not allow it to be found when all believed it was *me* who had died in the Ditch that day. Norbert helped me search for it and, when I assumed my disguise as a priest, I hid it in the portable altar I carried on my cart.'

'And then you left his body for the burgesses to find after the fire,' said Bartholomew.

'Exactly. I had to disguise the wound in his throat, but that was easy enough with all that falling timber. The whole affair was expertly brought to a satisfactory conclusion. I even heard later that the worthy burgesses were suspected of starting the fire themselves,' he added with a chuckle.

'But how could you know that the Ditch would be dredged at such an opportune time?' asked Michael, shifting uncomfortably on the sodden ground.

'Think!' said d'Ambrey with chiding patience. 'It was mainly Thorpe who set the scheme in motion in the first place: Will mentioned the money that might be made if the relics of Simon d'Ambrey were to be found by Valence Marie. Thorpe needed little encouragement once that seed was sown. I wonder what happened to that hand . . .'

He thought for a moment before resuming. 'I returned here two months ago and secured myself a place at David's. Ruthven's father sent a letter of recommendation, along with the name of a friar – recently deceased – whose identity I could assume. It was an excellent idea. After all, who would suspect an elderly Scottish friar? Any lapses in my theological knowledge would merely be put down to my nationality.'

Ruthven looked at him sharply and fingered his crossbow. But d'Ambrey was oblivious to Ruthven's patriotic ire and continued with his tale.

'I had settled in nicely by the time term had started; I had secured the help of people who owed me favours – Will, Henry and Jacob, who now work at Valence Marie; Huw and Saul Potter of Godwinsson; even Master Bigod of Maud's owes me a small favour – you see, I once loaned him the money to pay a hag to rid one of his mistresses of an unwanted child. Bigod was always one for the women, as Cecily will attest.'

He flung a disparaging glance at the writhing woman on the ground.

'You were right, Matt!' whispered Michael, as d'Ambrey stood to peer through the trees for signs of Huw returning with news of the lost relic. 'Cecily and Bigod were lovers! I do not know which one I feel more sorry for!'

So Bigod, like Lydgate, was being blackmailed, thought Bartholomew, watching d'Ambrey resettle himself on the tree stump with his Galen. That Bigod spoke of Dominica's death in the Chesterton basement, however, suggested that he was not party to that part of the plot.

'I sent Master Lydgate little notes,' continued d'Ambrey,

'reminding him that he had fired the tithe barn and hinting about my death. He was meant to be terrified that I had returned from the dead to haunt him. But he, foolish man, did not have sufficient imagination, and settled for a more practical explanation. He thought you were sending them, Doctor. How he justified belief in such a sudden and uncharacteristic move on your part, I cannot imagine. But Lydgate was not a man to allow reason to interfere with his prejudices.'

He fell silent, and the only sounds were the slight swish of wind in the trees, the drip of rain on leaves. Ruthven cocked his crossbow at Michael who was trying to make himself comfortable on the ground, while Dominica, bored by the narration, moved away to talk to Ivo. Horribly aware that as soon as they failed to keep d'Ambrey amused, Ruthven would be ordered to kill them, Bartholomew desperately searched for something to say.

'We know about your two acts,' he said. 'Faking the death of Dominica and producing a hand for the relic.'

'So, Matilde *did* betray me,' he said sadly. 'That cannot go unpunished.'

Bartholomew's stomach churned and he was furious at himself. Putting Matilde in danger was not what he had intended! 'She told us nothing! We reasoned it all out for ourselves!'

'I do not think so, Doctor. You simply do not have the cunning and clarity of mind to best me. No one does.' He frowned down at the soggy Galen. 'So, Eleanor Tyler was right after all about that harlot. She told me she was not to be trusted.'

'Where is Eleanor?' asked Bartholomew.

'Far away by now, I should think. Dominica needed to escape and what better way than by using Mistress Tyler's harlot niece?'

'Why did Mistress Tyler allow herself to become involved in this mess of lies and spite?' asked Bartholomew, not sure that he really wanted to know the answer.

'I was told you had a liking for her daughters, although you would have been kinder to have concentrated your efforts on just one of them rather than two. But Mistress Tyler helped me because she has a dark secret that I concealed for her many years ago.'

'What dark secret?' asked Michael, interested.

'Mistress Tyler killed her first husband,' said d'Ambrey casually. 'It was an accident, you understand. The cooking pot simply fell from her hand on to his head. But it was after months of abuse, and the man was a brute. I hired a physician to say that he died of a fever. So she is indebted to me. Her second husband was a good man and the father of her three girls. He died quite naturally during the plague I understand – no cooking pots involved there.'

'Did you help Mistress Tyler because you felt her crime had a just cause, or so that you could blackmail her later?' asked Bartholomew coldly.

D'Ambrey's smile faded and his eyes became hard. 'You are arrogant, Doctor, just as Lydgate said you were. For your information, I knew Mistress Tyler and her first husband and I judged for myself which was the victim.'

'*That* is arrogant!' exclaimed Bartholomew. 'On what authority do you presume to act as judge over your fellow men?'

There was a tense silence, and even Cecily desisted with her soft moans. Bartholomew thought he had gone too far and had tipped this unstable man across the thin boundary from sanity. He caught Michael's agonised look from the corner of his eye.

D'Ambrey's smile returned, and there was an almost audible sigh of relief from all in the clearing. From the tension of d'Ambrey's associates, Bartholomew judged that displays of temper were probably not unknown from this seemingly gentle man.

'I instructed Mistress Tyler to ensure Joanna remained indoors after the riot had started. She was simply to take her daughters and spend the night with her relatives. It was foolish of those French boys to have attacked Eleanor first, but it was even more foolish of the Tylers to have embarked on a friendship with you, given that you were obsessed with Joanna's death.'

'Did they know what you planned to do to Joanna?' asked Michael.

D'Ambrey shook his head. 'I simply told them to slip Joanna a little something from Uncle Jonas's store to make her sleep, and that she would be removed from their house never to bother them again. Of course, they were unsettled by the idea, but they soon saw sense when I pointed out that the alternative would be Mistress Tyler hanged for her husband's murder, and her daughters left unprotected.'

'Did you tell them to leave the town?' asked Bartholomew shakily.

'I did not, although what else could they have done, especially after foolish Eleanor sought to solve matters by trying to poison you? Silly child! Had she succeeded, Brother Michael would never have let the matter rest until he had discovered the truth and that, of course, would have been dangerous to me. I was relieved when they fled.'

Bartholomew took a deep breath, feeling the sweat prick at his back despite the chill of the rain. 'The second riot was different from the first,' he said, changing the subject with some relief. Despite the fact that he had already guessed that Eleanor had sent him the poison, he did not want to dwell on the matter.

'Godwinsson was to be destroyed,' said Michael, seizing on the opportunity to launch d'Ambrey into explaining another part of his plan, and thus buy them more time. 'And Michaelhouse attacked so that the Sheriff will be forced to take serious measures against the town. You incited both riots. You started rumours in the Market Square, Valence Marie and Godwinsson and they spread like wildfire. Experienced rabble-rousers, like Saul Potter, fanned them to see that they did not die out.'

'Right,' said d'Ambrey, nodding appreciatively. 'You have reasoned all this out very well. The complaints of the University that it has been attacked will be sure to evoke a response from the King. Extra troops will be called in and crippling taxes imposed. That was my plan all along. After last night's riots the Sheriff will be ordered to clamp down so hard on the townspeople – the townspeople that were so quick to believe ill of me after I had dedicated my life to helping them – that the town will be unable to function as a viable trading centre. Gradually, it will decline and the people will sink deeper and deeper into poverty.'

Bartholomew wondered whether d'Ambrey really believed that the people he was so keen to punish were the same ones that had failed to rally to his defence twenty-five years before. Few, if any, of the scholars were the same, since the University was a transient place, and so many of the townspeople had died of the plague that d'Ambrey was lucky to be remembered by anyone at all. Seeing d'Ambrey begin to fidget, Bartholomew continued quickly before he lost interest altogether and ordered them shot.

'Cecily told us that Dominica killed Radbeche. Is that true?'

Dominica smiled at him, distracted from her conversation with Ivo by the mention of her name.

'Yes,' said d'Ambrey. 'I had arranged for Radbeche to be away for the night, but he heard rumours that there might be a riot, abandoned his trip, and hurried home. Meanwhile, those silly Scots escaped as soon as I left the hostel – as I knew they would.' He paused and looked down at the book on his knees. The rain was making the ink run but he seemed oblivious to the damage.

'Unfortunately, when Radbeche came bursting into the hostel crying out that there would be murder and mayhem that night, he saw Dominica – not as Norbert the scullion, but as a woman with long, fair hair. She could not have him telling everyone about that, so she ensured his silence. Scarcely had she wiped the blood from her blade when John walked in.'

'Dominica ran him through, too,' said Ruthven, eager to tell his part in the story. 'But her aim was false in the dark, and I could not bring myself to finish him off, so I stayed with him until he died. My part was finished anyway. All I had to do was to explain to the proctors that the mob had killed Radbeche and John and then ask the Chancellor's permission to return to Scotland to recover from my terrible experience. I was convincing, was I not?'

Bartholomew hoped Michael would not reveal that John was still alive, or d'Ambrey was certain to order his death. But the monk was far too self-composed to make such an error. He assessed d'Ambrey coldly.

'Yesterday afternoon, when you went out with John, Father William left you in no doubt that he would uncover you as a fraud. Your work, therefore, had to be finished today, or you would risk being reviled by the townspeople a second time.'

'People are fickle,' mused d'Ambrey sadly. 'The scholars at David's were fond of me but I do not doubt for an instant that they would denounce me had Father William uncovered my disguise. You are right. I had to finish all my business today.'

Bartholomew wondered how he could have been so misled. The people at Godwinsson – Lydgate, Cecily, Edred and Werbergh – were an unsavoury crowd, but Bartholomew found them easier to understand than the smiling villains at David's. He glanced behind him into the trees, wondering how much longer they would be able to keep d'Ambrey entertained.

'But who killed Kenzie and Werbergh?' asked Michael. His thin hair was plastered to his head, giving it a pointed appearance, and he, like Bartholomew, was shivering – partly from sitting still in the rain, but mostly from the almost unbearable tension of wondering whether Tulyet would arrive in time to save them.

'I imagine Ruthven killed Kenzie,' said Bartholomew, looking hard at the Scot. 'Kenzie had lost his ring – or the fake – and was broken-hearted. Master d'Ambrey decided it was time to rid himself once and for all of the youngster who was not only careless with his belongings, but who had the audacity to fall in love with his daughter Dominica. So, Ruthven went with Kenzie to help him look for his ring, then hit him on the head when he, trustingly, went first along the top of the Ditch in the dark. Correct?'

Ruthven's eyes were fixed guiltily on Dominica.

'James Kenzie was entirely the wrong choice for my Dominica,' said d'Ambrey before the Scot could reply. 'Ruthven agreed to solve the problem before it became overly serious.'

Dominica did not appear to be impressed at this example of paternal care. 'You introduced me to him,' she said accusingly. 'Anyway, I was not planning to marry him. He was just fun to be with and he was imaginative in fooling my parents.'

'Well, Ruthven hit him on the head with the pommel of his dagger,' said d'Ambrey unremorsefully. 'And then poor Radbeche and I had to keep all our students in so that the University would think we were serious about discipline. It worked brilliantly. You never suspected any of us.'

'Actually, we did,' said Michael.

Dominica shook her head slowly at Ruthven, ignoring d'Ambrey's mild outrage at Michael's claim. 'But Jamie was your friend!'

Ruthven declined to answer and stared at the wet grass, fiddling dangerously with the winding mechanism on the crossbow.

'Very clever,' said Michael, turning back to d'Ambrey. 'Ruthven's alibi for the time of the murder was the man who ordered the murder in the first place.'

Bartholomew wondered whether Dominica might launch herself at Ruthven in her fury, and tensed himself to take advantage of the situation while Ruthven battled with her. He was unprepared for her sudden, dazzling smile. His spirits sank.

'Such loving care! My parents never managed to prevent me from seeing the men of my choice but you two have!'

'Men?' asked d'Ambrey suspiciously. 'There were others?'

'And what of Werbergh?' asked Michael, uninterested in Dominica's romantic entanglements. 'Why was he killed and his death made to look like an accident?'

'Ah yes, Werbergh,' said d'Ambrey, still looking uncertainly at Dominica. 'Werbergh was employed by me as a spy to keep an eye on Lydgate's movements, but he was next to worthless. He was so nervous that it must have been obvious to a child what he was doing. I began to distrust his discretion, so I had Ruthven slip out and kill him as he came back drunk from the celebrations at Valence Marie. Will hid the body near the Ditch, until Saul Potter and Huw were able to make his death look like an accident.'

So that explained why the body had been wet and there were pieces of river weed on it, thought Bartholomew. It also explained why Werbergh had died so long before his accident in the shed, and why Saul Potter and Huw were the ones who said that he had been going to fetch some wood.

'But I do not know what happened to Edred,' said d'Ambrey. 'I sent him to spin a few tales to confuse you and to have a good look for my book, but he never returned. He was playing a double game, passing information to Lydgate as well as to me. He could not be trusted either.'

Bartholomew understood why Edred's fear had been genuine: it was a dangerous game indeed that he had been playing.

D'Ambrey stood. He held the book, now beginning to warp from the rain. 'It is unfortunate you took my letters, but there are few who will understand their importance should they fall into the wrong hands. Now. It is getting dark, and it is time to leave.'

He gave Ruthven a cursory nod, and began to gather his belongings together. Ruthven swung his crossbow up and pointed it at Bartholomew.

'But why wait twenty-five years?' asked Michael, his voice sounding panicky to Bartholomew's ears. 'Why not strike sooner, when those that wronged you were still alive?'

'Oh, I had other things to do,' said d'Ambrey carelessly. 'I travelled a good deal and used my considerable talent for fund-raising to my own advantage. And anyway, I wanted to wait until the time was right. People would have recognised me had I returned too soon, and Dominica would not have been old enough. But that is none of your concern. Ruthven, make an end to this infernal questioning.'

Bartholomew forced himself to meet Ruthven's eyes as the student checked the winding mechanism on his crossbow, and pointed it at him.

The little clearing was totally silent. Even the birds seemed dispirited by the rain, while the group of horses tethered to one side hung their heads miserably.

'Hurry it up,' ordered d'Ambrey. 'We have a long way to go tonight.'

Ruthven took aim.

'Drop it, Ruthven!' came Tulyet's voice, loud and strong from one side of the clearing. Bartholomew's relief was short lived, as Ruthven, after lowering the weapon for an instant, brought it back up again to aim at Bartholomew's chest. There was a whirring sound, and Ruthven keeled over, his loosed crossbow quarrel zinging harmlessly into the ground at Bartholomew's feet. Bartholomew forced his cold legs to move and scrambled upright. Tulyet's men were suddenly everywhere, advancing on the clearing with their clanking weapons. Huw was with them, held between two men-at-arms, and gagged securely. Hovering at the rear, away from any potential danger, was Heppel, swathed in a huge cloak against the rain.

D'Ambrey looked at them in disbelief. 'What is this?' he cried. 'Where have you come from? You should not be here!'

'So it would seem,' said Tulyet dryly, helping the stiff Michael to his feet. 'I have been listening to you for quite some time now, Father Andrew. Or do you prefer Master d'Ambrey? What you have said, in front of my men, will be more than enough to interest the King.'

'Are you accusing me of treason?' asked d'Ambrey, his voice high with indignation.

'I would consider inciting riots and killing His Majesty's loyal subjects a treasonable offence, yes,' said Tulyet. He motioned to his men and they began to round up d'Ambrey's band of followers. D'Ambrey watched aghast.

'Not again!' he said. 'I have been betrayed again!'

'This time,' said Tulyet, 'you have betrayed yourself.'

D'Ambrey bent slowly to retrieve something from the ground. His action was so careful and deliberate that it seemed innocent. But then he straightened with frightening speed, a knife

glinting in his hand. He tore towards Tulyet who had turned
to supervise his men. Bartholomew hurled himself forward. He
crashed into d'Ambrey, his weight bearing them both to the
ground. D'Ambrey began to fight like a madman and, despite
his superior size and strength, Bartholomew felt himself loosing
ground.

Tulyet and his men rushed to help, but it took several of
them to drag the spitting, struggling man away, and to secure
him in a cart.

'He would have killed me!' exclaimed Tulyet in horror. 'The
man is possessed! Is he mad, do you think?'

Bartholomew shivered and not only from the cold. 'It would
be convenient to think so,' he said ambiguously.

Tulyet looked uneasily at where d'Ambrey glowered at him.
'Well, I will only be happy when we have him well secured in
the Castle prison.'

'Me too!' said Heppel with feeling. 'That man is extremely
dangerous and so are his associates!'

'Be careful,' Bartholomew warned Tulyet. 'There are people
who consider d'Ambrey a martyr. If it becomes known that
you have him in your prison cart, you might well have a riot
to free him.'

'Heaven forbid,' said Tulyet with a shudder. 'I hope we have
rounded up all the ringleaders of these riots now. With them
gone the people will grow peaceful again in time. I plan to
send the prisoners to London for trial. We need no more local
martyrs here.'

He turned his attention back to his captives, while Bartholomew
went to Cecily. She was past anything he could do, and her
breath was little more than a thready whisper. Thinking to
make her more comfortable, Bartholomew loosened the tight
bodice of her dress, recoiling in shock at what tumbled out
into his hands.

There, still with the blue-green ring on its little finger was the
hand from Valence Marie. It was warm from being in Cecily's
gown and sticky with blood. Bartholomew flung it from him
in disgust.

'So, it was you who took it from Valence Marie,' he said
softly. 'You slipped into the College when that greedy Thorpe
and his scholars were off hoping to find more relics.'

But she was past confirming or denying him. He stared up
at the leafy branches of trees that swayed and dripped above

his head. When he looked again she was dead, a grimace fixed on her face and her eyes turning glassy.

Tulyet's men came to take her away, while Michael retrieved the hand from the grass. 'I expect the Chancellor would like this,' he said, turning it over in his hand.

'Each to his own,' said Bartholomew, climbing to his feet. He handed Michael the rings from his sleeve. 'Give him these, too. I imagine he will destroy them all together.'

'I cannot think why he would keep them,' said Michael. 'Simon d'Ambrey returning from the dead twenty-five years after half the town saw him die is enough to make him a martyr all over again. The Chancellor will not want bits of him around the town acting as a focus for gatherings.'

'Make sure Thorpe understands that,' said Bartholomew.

'I had news from the King this morning,' said Heppel, pulling his cloak more closely around his neck. 'Thorpe, although he does not know it yet, is going to be offered a position as master of a grammar school in York.'

'A grammar school?' echoed Bartholomew. 'That is something of a step down from Master of Valance Marie. Will he accept?'

'Oh, he will accept,' said Heppel. 'One does not decline an offer from the King, you know. Thorpe is too unsubtle to be Master of a College.' He exchanged a knowing glance with Michael, and moved away to talk to Tulyet.

'Is he saying that if Thorpe had managed the matter of the hand with more tact and less zeal, he might still be in office?' asked Bartholomew.

Michael laughed at his shocked expression. 'Undoubtedly,' he said airily. 'And do not look surprised, my friend. You have listened to a most appalling tale over the last hour. You cannot raise your eyebrows at the King – or the Chancellor for that matter – when you have just heard the confessions of the Devil Incarnate.' He began to laugh, and draped an arm over Bartholomew's shoulders. Bartholomew shrugged it off quickly when he saw that it was the one that held the hand.

'What a revolting affair,' he said, moving away from the monk. 'D'Ambrey was supposed to have been saintly, and look how many people have died because of him – Kenzie, Werbergh, Edred, Lydgate, Cecily, Radbeche, Joanna, the riot-dead, not to mention his entire household and a good part of the population of Dover twenty-five years ago.'

'I always said Cambridge used d'Ambrey badly,' said Michael.
'It is a shame he decided to use violence to avenge himself. Had
he elected to resume his charitable acts, I think many people
might have flocked to him, perhaps even me. He could have
been a saint had he chosen to be.'

'I do not think so, Brother,' said Bartholomew. 'Saints do
not harbour murderous intentions for twenty-five years, help
wives conceal the killings of their husbands, or assist scholars
to rid themselves of unwanted pregnancies.'

Michael yawned. 'So you have solved the mystery surrounding
Joanna – she was killed to allow Dominica to be free of her
parents. But it seems your Tyler women did not know what
d'Ambrey intended – at least, not before it happened. They
guessed afterwards because they must have found all that blood
in their house.'

'I hope they are well away by now,' said Bartholomew.

'But by killing her first husband, Mistress Tyler is as much
a murderer as is d'Ambrey!'

'I know, but Mistress Tyler is a good woman. She could have
left me to the Frenchmen on the night of the riot, but she
chose to stay and help, risking her life and the lives of her
daughters. She also invited us in when we were attacked on
the High Street without even knowing who we were. It was
an act of selfless charity. I hope she reaches London safely
and starts a new life.'

But what of Eleanor? he thought. Would her escape from
justice encourage her to use murderous means the next time
someone did something of which she did not approve? That
she had gone so abruptly from being friendly to attempting to
kill him left him oddly disoriented. The more he thought about
it, the more he hoped their paths would never cross again, and
realised that Matilde had definitely been correct when she had
accused him of knowing nothing of women. He decided that
he would most definitely not embark on any more friendships
with them until he had devoted more time to understanding
them. Had he done as much years ago, he would not have
been jilted by Philippa, and would not have allowed himself
to become embroiled in the uncomfortable business at the
Feast. Michael's vast yawn interrupted his morose thoughts.

'We were right about the riots,' said Michael, yawning again.
'We thought there was more to them than random violence
and we were correct.'

'All the clues that we uncovered piecemeal now fit together,' said Bartholomew, smothering a yawn of his own, brought on by watching Michael. 'I did not think they would ever match up.'

'If you are honest, some do not,' said Michael. 'It was pure chance that Norbert and Kenzie were both killed by wounds to the back of the head, and we saw a connection where there was none. Well, not a direct one anyway. We also thought Bigod was at the centre of the whole business, since you heard him when we were attacked on the High Street. And you heard him discussing the second riot at Chesterton. But he was just following orders.'

They began to walk back through the dripping trees towards Cambridge. Ahead of them was Tulyet's convoy with its prisoners, the wheels of the carts groaning and creaking and the low voices of Tulyet's men drifting on the breeze as they talked among themselves.

'What will happen to d'Ambrey and his associates?' asked Bartholomew.

'Tulyet will send them to London for trial,' said Michael with a shrug, 'but no one will be in any hurry for the facts to emerge. Years will pass, people will die, and one day there will be no records that any such prisoners ever arrived.'

'And the legends of d'Ambrey?'

'Oh, they will fade away in time,' said Michael. 'Have you considered that it may have been people like Will, Dominica and Huw that kept them alive all these years? Now they have gone the stories, too, will melt away to nothing. This incident will not be recorded in the University history and in fifty years or so no one will know the name of Simon d'Ambrey.'

'Talking to you is sometimes most disheartening,' said Bartholomew. 'Everything is to be forgotten, buried in the mists of time, covered up. Unwanted people are sent to places where they will never be heard of again. Events of which the University does not approve do not get written in the University history. What will people think of us in the future when they come to read this great history? That there was no crime, no underhand dealings, no deceits?'

'Not unless human nature undergoes a radical change,' said Michael blithely. 'They will have their own crimes, underhand dealings and deceits, and they will understand that the silence and blanks in our history say as much as the words.'

'That is not particularly encouraging,' said Bartholomew. He remembered Wilson's tomb and compared it to the vanishing pile of earth that marked Norbert's small grave. 'What will people think when they see Wilson's black monstrosity? Will they think that here lies a man that Michaelhouse loved and revered? Or will they know he paid for his own memorial? That vile man will be remembered long after poor Norbert is forgotten. It does not seem fair.'

Michael did not reply, and screwed up his eyes as the wind blew needles of rain into his face. 'Summer is on its way out,' he said. 'I complained about the heat and now I can complain about the cold.'

Bartholomew smiled reluctantly, but then froze as he heard shouting from ahead. A figure darted from one of the carts and disappeared into the thick undergrowth at the side of the road.

'That was d'Ambrey,' he said in a whisper. 'Escaped!'

Tulyet's men tore after him but Bartholomew knew that their chances of finding him were slim. There were so many ditches and dense bushes in which to hide, that all d'Ambrey needed to do was to wait until dark and slip away. Even dogs could not follow a scent through the myriad of waterways at the edge of the Fens.

A ragged cheer rose from d'Ambrey's supporters and Dominica made as if to follow while the soldiers' attention was engaged. She slithered out of the cart and began to run after him. She slumped suddenly and the howls of encouragement from her friends petered away.

'Good shot,' said Michael admiringly to Heppel. The Junior Proctor looked at the small pebbles in his hands in astonishment. Luck, not skill, had guided the missile that had felled Simon d'Ambrey's daughter.

Heppel grasped at Michael for support. 'Oh, Lord! I have just damaged my shoulder with that throw! I should not have tried to embark on heroics.'

'It is a pity you could not have struck d'Ambrey down too,' said Michael, unsympathetic. 'Now this business might end very messily.'

'Especially for Dominica and her associates,' said Bartholomew, looking to where she was being helped back into the cart. She saw Heppel and her eyes glittered with hatred.

'I grabbed these pebbles to hurl at d'Ambrey if he tried to

harm me,' said Heppel shakily. 'I can assure you, I had no intention of trying to do the Sheriff's job for him. I was just carried away with the excitement of the moment when I aimed them at Dominica. It most certainly will not happen again. I shall suffer agonies from this shoulder injury for weeks and all because the Sheriff hires poorly trained guards! The King shall hear of this!'

Tulyet had ordered half his men to escort the remaining prisoners to the castle and the other half to search for d'Ambrey. His face was dark with anger and his temper was not improved by Heppel's accusations of incompetence.

'That gentle nature of d'Ambrey's beguiled my men,' he said in a voice that was tight with fury. 'He looks and acts like a friar and he made them feel as though they were escorting their grandfather! He fooled them into relaxing their guard and was gone in an instant!'

'I doubt that you will get him back,' said Bartholomew. 'It is not the first time he has escaped from the jaws of death in this area. History repeats itself.'

'He will be old indeed if he tries again in another twenty-five years,' said Michael.

'But, if there is a next time, he will not fail,' said Bartholomew.

epilogue

ROWN LEAVES RUSTLED ON THE GROUND OF THE churchyard as they were stirred by the breeze. It was already dusk, even though the day's teaching was barely done, and there was an unmistakeable chill of winter in the air. St Michael's Church afforded some protection from the wind, but was damp and cold, and Bartholomew stamped his feet to try to keep them warm.

The mason added a few final taps and stood back to admire his work. The black tomb was in its place in the choir, stark and dismal against the painted wall. In place of the effigy stipulated by Master Wilson was a neat cross, carved into the polished marble with simple but elegant swirls and knots. Bartholomew nodded his satisfaction and the mason left, warning him not to touch the mortar, which was not yet set.

From the vestry, Michael's rich baritone rose as he sang while preparing for compline. Bartholomew went to find him.

'Is it done? Have you atoned for being sick on his grave?' Michael asked, raising a humorous eyebrow. He began thumbing his way through the gospels to find the correct reading for the day.

Bartholomew winced. 'It is done,' he said, sitting on one of the wall benches in the cramped room.

'You have done Michaelhouse a great service – dallying so that Master Wilson's smug face will not sneer for eternity on our scholars from his effigy,' said Michael, peering at the open text in front of him.

Bartholomew was inclined to agree. 'Norbert's will, though.' Michael regarded him uncertainly.

'I sold d'Ambrey's Galen to Father Philius, the physician at Gonville Hall. Then I gave the money to that mason, so he will carve Norbert's likeness on one of the sculpted heads that will be in St Mary's new chancel. He says he remembers Norbert from the tithe barn incident.'

'You do have a strange sense of justice,' said Michael, amused. 'Still, I suppose Norbert has as much right to his immortality as Wilson.'

He sniffed suddenly. 'I can smell perfume, Matt. Is it you? I thought you had given up on women after your deplorable lack of success with them.'

'Master Kenyngham told me I would find you here.'

Bartholomew and Michael started violently at the sound of Guy Heppel's breathy voice at the door of the vestry. As Heppel moved towards them, the fragrant smell grew stronger and Michael sneezed.

'Are you still in Cambridge?' said the monk, not entirely amiably. 'I thought you had returned to Westminster.'

Heppel smiled, his white face appearing even more unhealthy than usual in the gloom of the late-autumn dusk. He rubbed the palms of his hands on his gown, as if there was something on them he found distasteful. 'I had one or two loose ends to tie up first and I thought I would come to bid you farewell before I left.'

Michael nodded, but Bartholomew eyed him suspiciously. Once d'Ambrey's followers had been dispatched to London, Heppel had dropped all pretence at being the Junior Proctor and had announced himself to be one of the King's most trusted agents. Since then, he had been negotiating with the Sheriff as to how the King's peace might be maintained, trying to balance the King's opportunistic demand for extra taxes to pay for his continuing wars with the French, with the welfare of the people. A compromise had finally been struck, which left the people poorer than before, but less so than they would have been had d'Ambrey's plans come to fruition.

'Farewell, then,' said Michael, turning his attention back to his work. 'You should not tarry too long in this cold church, Master Heppel, or your cough will become worse.'

'My cough?' asked Heppel. He smiled suddenly. 'Oh, that does not bother me any more. Since you have been so busy, Matthew, I availed myself of the services of Father Philius. Once my stars had been consulted, my cough healed most miraculously. I cannot tell you how relieved I am to know my stars are favourable.'

'You mean Father Philius cured you?' asked Bartholomew incredulously.

'Totally,' Heppel said, and beamed. 'You should forget all

those heretic notions of hand-washing and herbs, Matthew. Astrology is where the real power of healing lies.'

Michael roared with laughter, his voice echoing through the church. 'Take note, Matt! Astrology is the way forward for modern medicine! Perhaps you are a heretic after all!'

'You may like to know that Master Bigod met with a hunting accident,' Heppel said, changing the subject abruptly.

Bartholomew raised his eyebrows. 'A fatal one, I am sure,' he said.

Heppel regarded him askance. 'Well, naturally! Father Aidan of your own College has been appointed his successor at Maud's Hostel, while Master Thorpe will be settled in his grammar school by now. His successor at Valence Marie will be you, Brother Michael, should you decide to accept such an office.'

Michael inclined his head, his face expressionless. Heppel, disappointed at not getting an answer, continued.

'Given your interest in the business of the prostitute Joanna,' he said, turning to Bartholomew, 'you may also wish to know that the two surviving French students from Godwinsson were apprehended in Paris by the King's agents. They confessed to the girl's murder and are doubtless at the bottom of the River Seine by now. Joanna is avenged, Matthew.'

Bartholomew studied the floor. It gave him no pleasure to learn that yet more people had died in this miserable affair, but at least Joanna could rest easy now her killers had been punished. Heppel was right: loose ends were being tied indeed. Joanna's killers were dead, Thorpe was dispatched to the north, Bigod was dead. The only person to have escaped all this tying up was d'Ambrey himself.

It seemed that Heppel could read his mind. 'You are thinking that d'Ambrey, the cause of all this mayhem, has escaped unharmed. He has not. He lies in his grave as securely as all the rest.'

Bartholomew and Michael stared at him in astonishment.

'That cannot be,' said Michael. 'We saw him escape ourselves. Despite valiant efforts, Tulyet could not find him.'

'That was because Tulyet did not look in David's,' said Heppel, his pinched features lighting into a faint smile as he witnessed their growing incredulity.

'Do not play games with us, Heppel,' said Michael impatiently. 'D'Ambrey would not have returned to David's.'

'But he did,' said Heppel. 'He was found there this morning.'

'This is not possible,' said Bartholomew. 'He has been missing for three weeks now.'

'And that is probably as long as he has been dead,' said Heppel. As Bartholomew stood in what Heppel judged to be a threatening manner, the ex-Junior Proctor moved backwards and continued hastily. 'Late the night that d'Ambrey escaped, as the soldiers scoured the dark countryside, two hostels were boarded up – Godwinsson, irreparably damaged; and David's, which was shabby and unsafe anyway. You yourself, Brother, had seen to it that the surviving David's students were dispersed to other hostels so that they should not be together to inflame each other to riotous behaviour.'

Michael made an impatient gesture with his hand and Heppel hurried on.

'Carpenters were ordered to seal David's that night, so that it would not become a centre for gatherings of d'Ambrey devotees. It was late, they were tired, and perhaps they were a little fearful. The building was not properly searched before they started their work. Yesterday morning, David's Hostel was due to be demolished. As work began, Meadowman, the steward, was instructed to salvage anything that he thought might be reusable or saleable. Inside, he found d'Ambrey. He went straight to the Chancellor and the Chancellor informed me. Sure enough, the body in David's was d'Ambrey's.'

'But why did he return to David's?' asked Michael, not at all convinced. 'He could have been out of the country once he had escaped into the Fens.'

Heppel shrugged. 'I can only surmise that he considered it the safest location for him the night he escaped – it would certainly be the last place I would have considered looking for him. The carpenters did a good job of boarding up the hostel but d'Ambrey could have got out had he really wanted. He was found sitting in a chair at the kitchen table surrounded by quills and parchment. There was ink everywhere.'

'Was he planning to write his own version of the events of the last few weeks, do you think?' asked Bartholomew.

Heppel nodded. 'It would seem so, although the parchment in front of him was blank.'

Michael gave a snort of disbelief. 'Was it, now? That I find hard to believe.'

Heppel gave him a cold look. 'The parchment was blank.

Anyway, the body was very decayed, and I think he must have died within a day or two of his escape: he had no time to embark on a lengthy treatise before he died. Perhaps the shock of seeing his plans fail so completely made him lose the will to live. Perhaps the stress of that day gave him a fatal seizure. We will never know.'

'Where is he now?' asked Bartholomew.

Heppel smiled pleasantly. 'I thought you might ask that. Come.'

They followed him through the dark church and into the graveyard. Heppel picked his way around the mounds to where Wilson's grave had been, before he had been installed in his permanent tomb in the church. Next to the yawning hole, shivering in the cold, knelt Meadowman, guarding something wrapped in a winding sheet.

Bartholomew crouched next to him and pulled the sheet away to reveal the face. D'Ambrey's beatific features loomed out at him, and Bartholomew judged that Heppel's estimation of the time of his death was probably right – two or three weeks. He covered the face again and looked up at Heppel.

'So now all the loose ends are tied, and you can return to your King with a complete story,' he said.

Heppel nodded. 'The excavation of Master Wilson's grave was most timely. Now, only the four of us will know it did not remain empty.'

He gestured to Meadowman, who rolled d'Ambrey's body into the yawning hole, where it landed with a soft thump. The steward shovelled the earth back into place, until only a dark mound remained.

'There. It is done,' said Heppel, rubbing his hands on his robe, even though it was Meadowman who had done the shovelling. 'And now I should go. Father Philius tells me my stars are favourable for travelling tonight, so I should take advantage of them.'

'I hope we will not have mysterious accidents,' said Michael, eyeing Heppel distrustfully, 'to ensure our silence on these matters.'

Heppel gave his sickly smile. 'Do not be ridiculous, Brother. You are the Master of a respected College.'

He shook hands with them and melted away into the darkness, Meadowman following.

Bartholomew watched them go. 'So were Thorpe and Bigod,' he said softly.

As Heppel slipped out through the trees of the churchyard on to the High Street, they saw him wiping his hands on the sides of his robe, as if trying to clean them.

ḥISTORICAL NOTE

I N THE FOURTEENTH CENTURY, THE UNIVERSITY AT
Cambridge was an uneasy institution. The townspeople's
attitude towards it was ambivalent: it provided employ-
ment, spiritual support and a demand for rented accommo-
dation, allowing Cambridge to became an important, prosperous town in the region; on the other hand, it clearly
caused resentment among the locals, who objected to the
scholars' assumed superiority. Scholars took minor orders in
the Church and so offences were dealt with under lenient
canon law, rather than the much harsher secular law that
applied to the townspeople.

Riots in Cambridge were commonplace. One of the worst
occurred in 1381, during which the University was targeted for
a vicious attack by the town. Ten years previously, scholars had
been indicted for breaking into town houses, assaulting their
owners, and stealing fowling nets. Beside the town–gown
strife, the University was a battleground within itself. Scholars
from East Anglia fought those from the north, and 'foreigners'
such as Scots, Welsh, Irish or French, were always considered
fair game for attack. A good proportion of the University
comprised scholars from the religious Orders, and disputes
were common between the mendicant friars (the Franciscans
and Dominicans) and monks (like the Benedictines). The friars
made themselves especially unpopular with the general body
of students by applying to the Pope to grant them exemption
from various parts of the curriculum.

The plague of 1348–1349 evinced many changes in England.
It is thought that in its wake many people turned to sources of
miraculous intervention to plead for deliverance from its return.
Relic selling was a profitable business in the Middle Ages, and
there were many shrines that were the centres of pilgrimages.
Among these were the tomb of Thomas à Becket in Canterbury

Cathedral, the shrine of Our Lady of Walsingham in Norfolk and the shrine of St Swithin in Winchester Cathedral, to name but a few. Traditionally, great abbeys and churches grew up around the shrines, built from the benefactions of grateful pilgrims. For an institution to be in the possession of a relic, therefore, would have been lucrative indeed.

Throughout the Middle Ages, the King's Ditch was a stagnant ribbon of foul water that surrounded the settlement, and was used by town and University alike for waste disposal. Parliament met in Cambridge in 1388, and legislation was passed making illegal the use of public waterways as sewers. It was doubtless the state of the notoriously filthy King's Ditch that prompted such legislation. There was no such person as Simon d'Ambrey, and the King's Ditch was never dredged for relics, although it was doubtless cleaned from time to time. The Master of Michaelhouse in the summer of 1352 was Thomas Kenyngham, and the Master of the Hall of Valence Marie (now called Pembroke College) was Robert de Thorpe.